Perry and Koepp craft a sweeping tale of valor, adventure, and dragons. A must read!
The Bond of the Sword is a sober, riveting, coming of age tale filled with large scale battles with a unique look at both warfare and dragons.

Parker J. Cole
USA Today Bestselling Author

Published by
Bear Publications, LLC.
Wichita Falls, TX
76302

Cover design by Jenneth Dyck

First edition
ISBN:978-1-964769-02-8

THE BOND OF THE SWORD

TRAVIS PERRY

WITH CINDY KOEPP

BEAR PUBLICATIONS

Table of Contents

Table of Contents

Dedication

For those **who served** in warfare, who did their duty and made it back alive, even if not all the way as they would have wanted.

Special Thanks

I'd like to offer thanks to my friend and collaborator Cindy Koepp. While this story mostly came out of the mind of Travis Perry (me), I got stuck in a number of places and turned to my friend Cindy to help me out. She wrote about a third of this book, yes, using characters and situations I established, but still, this story probably would never have been finished without her help. Her work ethic, reliability, and humble dedication to carrying out my story earns a level of gratitude that I can't easily put into words.

Even so, thank you for everything, Cindy.

Coauthor Information

Originally from Michigan, Cindy Koepp combined a love of pedagogy and ecology into a 14-year career as an elementary science specialist. After teaching kiddos, she pursued a Master's in Adult Learning with a specialization in Performance Improvement. Her published works include science fiction, fantasy, and GameLit novels, a passel of short stories, and a few educator resources. Many of her stories take advantage of her studies in Spanish and Italian Renaissance rapier dueling, pike corps, and Wu style Tai Chi Chuan. When she isn't reading or writing, Cindy is currently working as a business execution consultant, hat collector, quilter, crafter, and strange joke teller.

Part One

The Tournament of Swords

⫻ Chapter 1 ⫸

My son, I sit here at our mealtable, trying to find a way to answer in writing the questions you had for me tonight about what it was like for me to fight in the Second Dragon War. Writing is easier that speaking sometimes, at least for me. At least about this.

Yes, I was in the war, but you already knew that. Yes, I was injured, but to fully explain how requires me to explain the circumstances I was in and what happened. I could, I suppose, tell you I was lashed to a dragon, but you'd want to know why I was lashed to it. I could tell you it had to do with digging a well, but that would make no sense either. Not unless I went back further and explained more.

In fact, I realize I must begin long before the war itself. You see, it's not only true what almost everyone knows, that every war is different—so my uncle's experiences in the First Dragon War were different from mine in the Second. It's also true, and much less well-known, that every soldier has his own personal experience of battle. To know how the war was for me, you have to know things about me that you don't know now and may not understand even after I tell you. But still, I feel I owe it to you to try to tell you, just as my uncle *tried to tell me. I'm not going to follow the rules of our heroic songs as I write this. You may not realize there are rules to such things, but there are. In the songs, heroes are always greater than any real man can be; something I really want you to understand is not true. Still, I'll do my best to make this interesting and worthwhile for you, writing with the best style that I know. That includes sometimes making my best guess at details of my story that I don't really remember with crystal clarity anymore—other times it means leaving out details I remember all too well.*

My story actually begins with the Tournament of Swords when I was fourteen years old:

I gripped a sword made of iron mined in our province, forged into steel in our furnaces. My opponent, a Southlander my age but a whole head taller, slashed his opening blow at my chest in a wild arc that flew fast and hard. I blocked it with my shield, but the blow staggered me with its force. The Southlanders watching roared a cheer while our Mountaineer team barked encouragement and warnings at me.

My opponent's sword was identical to my own. I silently cursed my uncle for that.

I came back at the Southlander in an overhead chop, dripping with sweat more from nervous fear than heat or exhaustion. He leapt to the right, easily dodging my blow, which pulled left, bobbing his head, moving like a dancer instead of a soldier. I'd never seen such grace before.

Right away I followed with a backhand swoop which he ducked under, while jabbing the point of his sword into the chainmail covering my chest, not as hard as he probably could, but hard enough for the deliberately dulled tip to separate links and pierce my under-armor padding, the blade slicing a tiny cut in the skin directly over my heart.

"Point!" shouted the green-eyed Andrean line judge.

Southlanders are richer in bravery than material things. My opponent wore only thick cloth armor, with no helmet of any kind over the tight black curls over his head. His woolly locks twisted in tighter curls than any sheep I've ever seen. His left hand gripped a wicker shield, which I knew could not hold up to a hard steel blow, so I swung the edge of my shield at him in a broad circle, followed fast by a low slash of my sword at his near leg, bringing my body weight down over my forward leg as I moved, imitating my uncle's favorite battle maneuver. My opponent jumped back from my shield swing and his mouth flashed a grin of ivory white teeth, which against his dark brown face gleamed almost like snow on a sunny day. But as he leapt, his legs spread legs wide apart and landed that way. His near shin was close enough—I steered the tip of my blade so it impacted his cloth-padded bone with a hard thunk.

"Point for the Mountaineer!" barked the other line judge, who was a Midlander, over the roars of my teammates. My uncle shouted, "Good move, Therin! Recover fast, keep your eyes open."

The Southlander should have felt some pain at the impact to his shin. But he never showed any sign of it. He did change his tactic after that, keeping clear of my shield, circling round me in quick dashes, bobbing his head to trick me into thinking he was going left, then dashing right. Or he'd feint right then duck in quick to the left with a slash of his Iron Mountain Province-forged blade and leap back away again, quicker than I could counter-attack. I barely managed to meet his blows with my shield. The sweat poured down my back like a horse on a long gallop as I struggled to keep up with him.

He continued like that, circling and ducking in. I plowed straight towards him, my broad shoulders and chest, not to mention my armor, making me far heavier than my taller opponent. I kept trying to trap him in the corner of the sword ring, trying to force his back to the short wooden fence that boxed in the square of clay where we fought our tournament bout.

Matches were in three rounds of five minutes each. At the call of the match judge, I returned to my corner, huffing and blowing, sweat running down my face, burning my eyes with its salt. My opponent was barely winded, only a trace of dampness on the cloth over his chest suggesting he'd been working at all. The five minutes of fighting in the first round tired me far more than I ever expected, not just from exertion, but from the fear of failure working against me. However, my uncle had trained me hard, so I knew I could continue on. "You're doing good," he told me as he gave me water to drink from a tin cup. "Keep it up. Don't forget the crouching move I showed you—remember that gave you your only point so far."

"Yes, Uncle," I panted.

At the north end of the square stood the table for the match judge and his recorder, on the east and west side of the ring the line judges looked for scored points and rule violations. Beyond the fence, staked ropes traced out areas where spectators were allowed to watch the match. The entire team of Mountaineers, all fifteen of us—sixteen including my uncle, the head of our team—were present. But we were very much outnumbered and out-voiced by what must have been fifty or more Southlanders.

There were nineteen other rings like the one I stood in, in two rows of ten, and a twenty-first further off surrounded by a rising circle of seating set aside for the championship matches. All this lay in the festival outskirts of the great capital of Andrea, between the summer palisade closest to us on the south and the great white stone outer wall of the city towering behind the match judge's table to the north.

On the table, the small hourglass marking the time between matches emptied down. The match judge called, "Time!" and I stepped forward as he tipped over the larger match hourglass. I didn't know how I could keep going through that second round, but I did, just as I'd been trained. I learned the lesson my uncle had taught me, the lesson that you can do more than you think you can. Learning that was probably the best thing to come from the tournament. This isn't the same as the sayings you've heard: "Wanting to, is to be able to" or "You can do whatever you put your mind to." Those bits of wisdom have a point to them, but in the end they are untrue. Every man can do more than he first thinks, but every man also has a limit, a point beyond which he can do no more, no matter how much he may desire otherwise.

My third round defending the honor of Iron Mountains Province brought a new sort of tiredness. Not only was it hard to move my body, my sword arm began to get heavy, the sword feeling like some giant beam of wood in my hand, hard for me to swing. I think my opponent also found his blade growing leaden. His blows came slower, even though his feet moved as swift as ever.

About halfway through the round, I thought I had him trapped at last. I pushed forward in a burst of energy, backing him towards the northeast corner of the ring—he hadn't managed to dash away as he'd done every other time. I pressed my advantage, steel shield held up on the left, my right arm pulled back to deliver a storm of hard blows.

The Southlander ducked low and swung into the shin of my left leg like I'd done to him earlier and dashed away before my own downward slash had a chance. "Point!" shouted the Midlander judge.

Aware the score was now two points to one and the time was running down, a new frenzy of desperation hit me, and I charged after my enemy, growling in rage. He danced to the right and let me pass. In combat, he could have killed me by stabbing me in the back, but in the tournament back blows didn't count for points. Instead of attacking, he sprang away and let me hit the fence. I rolled on it and swung around toward him, my shield arm wide. His arm snapped out and the point of his blade poked my belly.

"Point!" called out the Andrean.

Flustered, I charged again and missed again. I thrashed around in a frenzied pivot in the center of the ring. The Southlander whacked my right shoulder with a backhand blow before I realized I was facing him.

"Point!"

Now discouragement gave new life to my exhaustion. The remaining moments of the match I trudged after him as he danced away. I swung a few half-hearted blows that had no chance to hit home. My opponent flew out of my range with ease, no longer attacking, the ivory brightness of his teeth shining with his already-won victory.

"Time!" shouted the match judge. The Southlanders cheered and began to chant a victory song, their deep voices adding to my sense of shame and failure. My eyes blurred as tears streaked down my sweaty cheeks.

My uncle placed a foot on the lowest pole of the fence and flipped his other leg over, crossing into the ring, not without wincing in pain from his war-wounded leg.

"Therin," he said in a stern tone, "You didn't follow my instructions. I told you to duck down and attack and you only did it once in the match. And it turns out the Southlander used the move on you! If you're gonna keep going in this tournament, you need to start listening—"

"Maybe you shoulda listened to me! When I said we shouldn't give *our* extra swords to the Southland team—he used one of our swords to beat me!" I wiped tears from my eyes as I spoke, my shame instantly flashed into anger.

He squeezed both eyes shut, opened them, and answered, "Nephew, that makes no sense at all. First of all, as I already explained to you, the Southlanders are brave men, some of the best I ever fought alongside in the Dragon War. You don't forget your friends—"

"What about me, Uncle? You forgot me! When you gave a sword to my enemy—you gave him the chance to win!"

His face flushed red and he took hold of my shoulders and squeezed hard. "Pull yourself together, nephew," his voice rasped in anger. "You're embarrassing yourself and this team." He turned away and took two steps, then turned back to face me again, his voice newly calm and quiet. "First, you woulda lost on points even if the Southlander had a wooden sword. What I did made no difference in that. Second, there is a difference between an enemy and an opponent. The Southlanders are not our enemies. Never treat an ally like an enemy. Learn to tell the difference between the two." He moved away again, crossed to the other side of the fence, and kept walking all the way out of the tournament area. I didn't see him for several hours after that.

"Tough break, huh?" said Lankin from behind me, right after my uncle had crossed the fence. Lankin's father held the profession of ironwork merchant, trading our swords and

8

armor for the foodstuffs and other goods that provide the needs of our Mountaineer people. By the way, "Ironwork" is what people still call it everywhere in the Bond, even though we've been making steel for generations. In his trade, Lankin's father made voyages each year to the Bond capital, Andrea.

This is how he had known about the Tournament of Swords, which is how his son Lankin knew. Lankin got it in his head what a terrible shame it was that the greatest sword-making province didn't compete in the greatest sword-fighting competition in the Bond. Lankin overflowed with natural leadership ability, the sort of person who easily inspired confidence in others. In our mining town of Rogin, he searched for anyone who'd entered the tournament before and learned from me that my uncle had competed in it once. Lankin and I knew one another from school. Only a few years before I was born our Council of Elders decreed that no Mountaineer would be allowed to become an Elder of the province if he were unable to read the Table of Laws out loud and recite the words to the Five Greatest Songs of Heroes and the main hymns to the Sky Father. So, because of that, the council started to provide common funds for all available boys to attend school, to provide for the future needs of the Council. In my day, not all boys attended, but both Lankin and I did.

"Your uncle fought in the Tournament?" asked Lankin breathlessly during one of our breaks from class. "Are you sure?"

Our school building was not inside the mountain like yours, son. When I was a boy, only some sections of the province had mastered the skill of underground ventilation, so many people in my village considered it healthier for a child to be outside as much as possible. So, my school stood on the surface of Headstone Mountain, near the ridge entrance to the mines and the underground sword factory.

I formed a ball of the mountainside snow and threw it as hard as I could at a Lankin. "Of course I'm sure!"

He ducked below my toss and scooped up a handful of snow. He threw it back in a straight fast line, hitting me hard in the arm. "Ow!"

"So how did he do?"

"I don't know. One time I asked him what made our swords the greatest in the entire Bond. He told me there were great swords from other provinces and kingdoms, some of which might be considered greater than ours. So I asked him how he knew that, and he told me he'd been in the Tournament as a boy and had seen them. And had seen some in the Dragon War, too." As I talked, I scooped up snow. I removed my knit mittens (just like the ones your grandmother makes for you) and began to squeeze the snow into an ice ball, using the heat of my hands to form and melt the snow as boys have been doing in snowy places for as long as there have been both boys and snow. The melting white mass trickled water off my hands and turned them numb, while my breath poured out in clouds of steam that bright, cold winter afternoon. I intended to get my revenge on Lankin for the way he'd pegged me just moments ago.

"Could your uncle lead a team, you think? Could he train us?"

"Of course he could train us. My uncle knows swords better than 'most anyone!"

Lankin and I were off to the right side of our school. I remember the roof having icicles all around its edge, some long enough to reach down to the ground. Most of the boys were on the left, playing a bit of rock ball on a snowy bit of flat ground as Lankin and I talked.

"Of course he knows swords better—he's an inspector at the factory!" Lankin tossed another fast snowball at me, hitting me hard in the chest this time. "That's not the same as knowing how to use them."

"My uncle is a hero of the Dragon War! He and his brothers, including my *father*, fought against *dragons* with swords."

"So did my grandfather. He's been teaching me."

"Where was your father, though, huh? What was he doing back then?"

"Selling ironwork to bring home food for our mothers. You're not gonna tell me there's anything wrong with that!" He threw another snowball and this time I managed to duck low and fast enough for it to deflect off my back.

"No," I said. At that moment a flash of insight swept over me, inspiring my next words far beyond the way I normally used to think. "No, not anything wrong. But not really all that right, either. *Your* father took care of your family. *My* father died for the whole country."

Lankin flushed red, and I saw my chance. I hurled the ice ball at him as hard as I could. Sad for me, I was never very good at ball throwing. Nor all that good at the bow, nor at anything else that requires my eyes to work with my hands into the distance—the one thing I liked during my school years, no surprise I suppose, was to write poems, songs, and little stories. It might have been poetic justice (considering my choice to attack him when he felt down) if I had missed Lankin altogether with my ice ball, but I didn't. I hit him at the side of his hip—hit him, but with a glancing impact with not enough force to hurt him at all, in spite of having hurled hard ice with as much power as I could manage.

Even though I failed, he didn't care much for me ambushing him: "You're about to die for your country, too!" he bellowed and charged after me. He wrestled me down in spite of my bigger body size and pushed my head

11

into a snow bank. Maybe that sounds like a serious fight, but it wasn't really.

We soon were laughing and joking again. Lankin started telling me again and again how much we needed to enter the tournament, how much fun sword fighting can be, what a great chance it would be for us to learn something, and how we'd show everyone else in the Bond how great we were, imagining between us that the courageous boys of the great Iron Mountain Province would defeat all comers. We had the whole tournament planned our in our shared imagination. The only part we didn't agree on was which one of us would take first place.

In the aftermath of my first match, still standing in the ring, that beautiful dream had begun to shatter for me. But not yet for Lankin. He'd somehow entered into the ring behind me without me noticing. I started walking toward the ring fence and crossed over it, not answering his call to me, wiping tears and sweat from my face. My other teammates, young men from our province aged thirteen to seventeen, avoided my eyes as I left the ring, looking down, as if I'd embarrassed them. Just as my uncle had said.

Lankin continued, "But it was fun to watch. You should have seen yourself, Therin. Nice shield work—until the very end, anyway."

I gave him an angry glare. Lankin, in the middle of crossing under the top rail of the fence I had just passed over, lifted his head up and grinned at me. "Seriously! You can really swing a shield."

"Thanks," I answered, my head hanging down, thinking of how much I wanted to get my revenge on that South-lander who'd humiliated me. And how hurt I felt that my uncle had let me down.

⊣⊢ Chapter 2 ⊢

he day after the first match, I fought again, this time against a Shos Hillcountry boy. His shield and sword were the same make as mine, though his armor was of rawhide leather plates, since the Shos Hills produce no metal at all. But they're famous for their cheese, cows, and goats which they sell to our province in exchange for our metalwork.

The boy I faced, like the Southlander from the first match, stood a whole head taller than me. But this one had a barrel chest even bigger than my own, with very long arms and relatively short legs. In the first round I plowed into him with my shield low and made a low slash at his legs. "Point!" called out the line judge.

He pushed back into me, his round iron shield screeching across mine as he forced his weight down and over me. He stabbed down over the shield and hit me on the armor over my left collar bone. "Point!" shouted the other judge.

I backed up and hit him again. I slashed low, and he stabbed from high. He had weight on me, but I had a lower center of gravity, so we slammed into each other and pushed one another around in between exchanging blows. My uncle was shouting instructions for me to back away, but I decided not to pay attention.

By the end of round one, the score was 10 to 9 in my favor, but I was already exhausted. Uncle Haelin leaned closer to me across the rail of the ring. "Therin, I can tell you're mad at me. You really shouldn't be, 'cause I'm just trying to help you. But listen to this, listen," he said again louder, until my eyes met his. "For this match, what you're doing is more or less working. But if you ever fight in a war, don't ever trade blows with a massive enemy like that. Hit him, low like you're doing is good. Then back away if you can. There is no courage it taking a blow you don't have to take."

The second round went about the same as the first, except slower, since both of us were tired. My uncle shouted, "Don't trade blows with him!" but I didn't listen, so things continued the same as before. At the end of the round, we were tied at 16 to 16. My uncle only said to me, "I'm gonna go to Lankin's first match now. It's about to start."

I won the match, only by one point, 21 to 20, but that was enough to keep me going in the competition. Anyone who lost twice was eliminated from the tournament.

After the match, still sweating and tired, I lumbered over to the third ring to see Lankin's first bout. Lankin had been the only member of the team who'd had any prior sword training. So Uncle Haelin entered Lankin in the second tier of the competition, based on his training, which didn't begin until after the first eliminations for the first tier. Entering him in second group hadn't been easy for my uncle to do because by tournament rules he did not qualify as a sword-master, having never been certified. In fact, the whole matter of Uncle Haelin not being a swordmaster had been a big problem on our arrival. It had nearly kept our province out of the tournament.

On arrival in Andrea, after a twenty-nine day trip that proved to be eventful in itself, Uncle Haelin eventually got around the problem that only a certified swordmaster could enter a team by persuading the Southlander swordmaster to enter our team into the tournament and to appoint him as our "team leader." By the rules a team leader could do a lot of things a swordmaster could do, but didn't require the formal school which issued a certificate. Which is what the Tournament of Swords officials had demanded from my uncle when he'd attempted to enroll the team on his own.

"You must *obey* the law of this tournament," Guffey, the master official had said, one of the legal Heads of Swords. He spoke this in a slow Midlander drawl, a voice I hear in my dreams sometimes. "We will not tolerate disorder around here."

"I'm not trying to disobey," answered my uncle, his face flushing red. "Just trying to solve a problem. Please let me know what I can do fix it. There's almost always some way to make an arrangement."

"Are you trying to bribe me?" asked the official coldly.

"No, sir." My uncle's eyes were wide with surprise.

"Because if you were trying to bribe me, I'd have you thrown in our public prison—I have the authority to enforce this punishment for any tournament attendee who would violate our rules. And if no one can pay the fee for your release, I assure you, sir, you will rot in there."

Uncle Haelin didn't care much for rules that didn't make any sense, so he kept working on the issue until he found the way around it. Or so he thought by getting Southlander help. Their swordmaster also formally entered Lankin into the second tier, though there was a long debate among the tournament officials over whether or not the rules allowed a swordmaster from another team to do so. Guffey championed the position that the rules did not allow any such thing and did not seem at all pleased to have another official show him chapter and line in the rulebook to be wrong.

So I said all of that to explain how Lankin made it into the second tier. And his first match in that tier had already started by the time I finished my match and heavily trudged over to the third ring. "How far along is he?" I asked my uncle, wiping sweat from my forehead, gladly having removed my steel helmet, my hair completely matted wet. I didn't say so, but I felt resentment that my uncle had left my match before it had ended to catch the beginning of Lankin's bout.

"First round still," he said, his voice tense.

The tension surprised me. Uncle Haelin might get angry or show other unexpected emotion, but I hadn't known him to show fear. But that's what I heard in his voice.

Before that moment there had been another time on our way down to Andrea, at the end of a long day in the carts, the sun just beginning to set after we made camp along the roadside. A bird appeared, iridescent green, red, and yellow, with a mouth and teeth like a lizard instead of a bird's beak, flying with two sets of wings, one high on its back and one low toward its long bright-feathered lizard-long tail, a creature which suddenly flapped into our camp. It made my uncle jump and his face turn white.

It was the first time I'd seen a dragonbird. I thought the bird, barely the length of my forearm, was the most amazing and beautiful thing I'd ever laid eyes on. But my uncle jumped up in a startle; his face as pale as ash. "What's wrong, Uncle?" I'd asked.

"Nothin'," he answered. "I just hate those damn things—excuse my swearin'." Then he threw a rock at it.

As I began to watch Lankin's match, I wondered what could have frightened my uncle this time. Then I saw it.

Lankin's opponent, who I later learned was the son of a lesser noble of Andrea, had a long dark streak of blood smeared across his sword blade. Lankin's blood.

⊹ Chapter 3 ⊱

"Stop the match, Uncle!"

Blood flew in small droplets from the blade as Lankin's opponent swung. The boy wore a full-body suit of chainmail which I recognized as having been made in our province, some of the lightest and most costly work our factories do, but then clearly fitted to this swordsman about my age by a master armorer, hugging him like a second skin. Other than his armor and a steel shield also from our province, he wore high boots over his mail of the softest but most durable mountain nete leather. His sword clearly had not been forged in the Iron Mountains—instead of being black, straight, and simple, it was a much thinner blade, a handbreadth longer than one of our swords, with a silver engraved handguard and an ivory-white handle, inscribed and inlaid in delicate silverwork.

"I can't stop the match," he answered me. "Only a swordmaster is authorized to pull a contestant from the middle of one. Besides, I've seen worse—this isn't as bad as it looks." The worry in his tone of voice flew contrary to the confidence of his words.

"It's a lot of blood," I said, stunned to find my uncle doing nothing.

"It's nothing compared to what a man can bleed, believe me," he snapped. "That's not what bothers me."

Lankin's opponent unleashed a hailstorm of quick blows that plinked his armor and shield when Lankin couldn't dodge them, blows without enough force to knock him over or even off-balance. This was not how my uncle had trained us to fight, when he'd given us wooden swords and had us hack at wooden poles with them. When he'd lined us up against each other, shield to shield, and taught us to keep our bodies crouched low and drive our shields upward into our opposites, then drop back down and slash at legs of unbalanced opponents, or to divert high blows with the shield and then make a sudden low slash at a single leg. The legs were the target of most attacks the way my uncle taught us. Even blows to the head or body were intended to open up an attack on the legs—once wounded in the leg, the man would fall. Once fallen, you could finish him from above. This combat method he modified somewhat for the tournament. Our swords were dulled at the tip but still had a bit of a cutting edge, as per the protocol of the tournament, but not as sharp along the edge as they could be. He trained us to knock into our opponents, but not with all our force. This was, after all, a tournament—not real war.

The Andrean noble's son, intently and silently watched by men who by their clothing clearly also came from the capital and who also clearly possessed far more wealth than we'd ever seen, used his shield almost as an afterthought and then only to block aside hard blows from Lankin. The rest of his attack was pure swordplay, slashes and quick flicks, most aimed at the unarmored bits of the head or neck or the backs of

Lankin's hands, where if he hit home, the line judge would call out a point. He never aimed for the legs and never tried to knock Lankin off balance.

Lankin had quick hands but had been taught by his grandfather and my uncle a method that used more body motion than hand movement. As a result his attacks were incomparably more powerful but always slower than his opponent. The noble's son proved skilled at dodging, evading, and deflecting Lankin's blows. And he attacked with fast slices far more frequent than my friend could counter. It's strange to realize how clearly I understand all of this now, even though I barely understood any of what was going on back then.

After what seemed a very long time, the hourglass emptied down and the first break between rounds began. Uncle Haelin rushed into the ring to help my friend. I trotted around to the backside of his corner. He had numerous small cuts on exposed skin from hands to head. One wound on his temple bled more than all the rest, blood having poured down his face on onto his armor. "You all right?" panted Uncle Haelin.

"That bastard! Did you see what he did to me? Nothing but little bitty cuts. All designed to make me bleed!"

"Watch your language," answered my uncle calmly as he sopped blood from the head wounds with a wet lake sponge. "I do understand cursing; I do it myself sometimes. But it becomes a habit real easy—don't let it be a habit. What you say matters to both the Father God and man. You can never take any of it back."

"I'm holding back what I want to say! And is that all you've got for me? A lecture on bad language? How 'bout telling me how to win this fight!"

Uncle Haelin paused and then looked down at the ground. "He's already got ten points. Lankin. I don't see you winning this."

"Great! Thanks for nothing!"

Blood still spurted from the wound in his temple in angry little gushes, in spite of my uncle's efforts to stop it. He took Lankin's face in his hands, looked him in eye and said, "I'm worried he might bleed you worse than this. I'm worried your life is in danger. What I'm telling you to do is avoid him. Stay away from him. Let him win."

I saw Lankin staring back at him as I stood behind and a bit to the right. His eyes scrunched together while his mouth pulled down into a determined frown.

"Time!" shouted the match judge and Lankin lunged forward into round two. His opponent in contrast calmly advanced. The way they carried themselves showed much of the difference between them. Lankin squared up with his opponent, knees bent, ready to power upward with a hard drive of the shield he held out forward, as my uncle and his grandfather had trained him. On the other side the dark-haired, green-eyed swordsman with a trace of black whiskers on chin and under his nose stood with his body turned to the side, feet shoulder width apart, his shield tucked in close, his sword held forward from an arm straight out at the shoulder level.

Within a few heartbeats after the opening of the round the Andrean made three quick slashes at Lankin's head and neck. The first my friend met with his shield—but then he lunged forward, swinging a hard sideways blow with his sword. His opponent hopped a quick sidestep in the direction of the swing, so the blade still impacted his shield, but not with the full arc of its power. Then the nobleman's son snapped out the other two sword flicks, one clearly aimed at the external jugular vein under Lankin's left ear (even back then I knew about the jugular vein), diving under a fold in the chainmail caused by the motion of Lankin's head.

My uncle drew in a sharp breath. "Get back from him! Stay clear!" Some of my fellow teammates watching with me muttered shocked grumbles about what they saw, but most held a sort of bewildered silence, not really understanding what was going on, just as I didn't really understand.

This time Lankin listened, his eyes wide with realization. Near the jugular under his loose-fitting chainmail the skin was cut, but not the vein itself. For which I silently prayed and thanked the Sky Father. Lankin leapt back from his opponent, shield up, and focused on defense. But that didn't keep his opponent from pressing the attack. Lankin ran, dodged, and covered himself, but this boy chased after him in fast, precise steps, still flicking his very sharp blade at sensitive areas of Lankin's head and neck.

Lankin managed to stay safe until the match judge called the end of the round. But there was a low chorus of grumbles from the other side as the boys returned their corners. A voice shouted from the other side, "This is a mockery! I protest!"

A tall man with dark hair and a trimmed beard streaked with gray, with a strong resemblance to the boy in the ring, wearing a cape lined with what looked like fox fur strode over to the match judge's table. "This is a mockery! I demand you end this so called 'match' now and take the full action against those individuals perpetuating this sham."

"What!" growled my uncle as he crossed out from the inside of the ring toward the match judge table (he'd already stepped inside to attend to Lankin). "Sham! The rules of this tournament don't make us win this or any match. And this boy," he pointed his whole hand at the nobleman's son, "Is clearly trying to kill our contestant. Death blows have never been legal in this tournament!"

The match judge, a Midlander whose large brown eyes showed a tender kindness, drawled, "The rules do forbid blows designed to kill. But they also state that no punitive action will be taken against non-penetrating slicing cuts smaller than the width of three fingers, for these 'may be accidental.' Therefore, cuts shorter than the length of three fingers, no matter where they are, have always been treated as legal in this tournament. Some recently—the first time about five years ago now—have taken to exploit the wording of this rule. In effect overriding the death blow rule by a technique that keeps deadly cuts under three fingers long. Efforts on the part of others, including myself, to modify this rule for the betterment of the safety of contestants have had no effect." The judge lowered his eyes.

The mid-aged Andrean noble, I think the father of the boy in the ring, added in an angry, haughty tone, "Not only is this mountain hermit wrong in his understanding of death blows, the rules also require that contestants 'demonstrate a vigorous defense' and it is forbidden that any contestant shall 'deliberately fail a match, as if bribed to do so.' 'Contestants who do not obey these rules may be punished in full accordance with the laws and customs of Andrea,' which includes fines and imprisonment."

My uncle violated his own rule about cursing. Face flushed bright red, his hands squeezed tight into knuckle-white fists, he stopped himself with a visible effort and stammered in rage, "You…you mean b-boys are killing each other in this tournament, and that's *legal*. Yet—yet stopping it by not fighting and saving a life is *illegal?*" Uncle Haelin cursed again, then added, "The God forgive my mouth."

"The rules are what they are," answered the judge, eyes lowered to the table, face flushing a bit pink. "They also allow you to seek an exception to policy with the tournament head. But this year that head would be Guffey of Hasterry district."

My uncle suddenly took a deep breath and his fists unballed. "Guffey. I've met him…I don't believe that man will make any kind of exception, certainly not for us…so…it may be necessary…" Uncle Haelin swept his hands back through his mane of hair, mostly gray but still somewhat reddish brown, thinning in front and back, "For me at this time to deliberately violate the rules of this tournament and accept any fines or imprisonment that may come as a result —if that's what it takes to get my boy out of this match."

The judge stroked the graying black whiskers of his chin as his eyes met my uncle's again. His plain leather jerkin pointed to a background that probably had not included a lot of wealth. I've at times wondered, looking back, how that judge advanced to be in the position he was in and I sometimes have tried to guess what happened to him afterward. For I never heard nor saw anything of him after that day. "You may accept fines or imprisonment, but be warned, Guffey has the legal right to punish the entire team for any violation. That would be an extreme application of the rules, but as you said, you know Guffey…" his voiced dropped off as his eyes lowered again to the table.

"Imprison him now!" snapped the Andrean nobleman. "He and his team are making a mockery of the dignity of this event."

"Perhaps prison would be better," said my uncle, now very calm, but with hands trembling. "At least all of us would leave the tournament with our lives intact."

"I'm afraid you can't say that," answered the judge quickly, "I don't know if you're aware of this, but Andrean custom considers it wrong to provide for the sustenance of a prisoner at public expense. Friends and family are expected to provide food for you. If no one can do so, you will starve to death in the public dungeons."

My uncle's face drained of its red. Clearly thinking over his words before answering this time, he said, "The dear God...so it's not enough to kill one of us—the tournament rules will kill us all? Is there no one at all who would show us mercy?" My uncle's blue eyes stared into the judge's soft browns.

The brown eyes answered back with compassion. "I would feed you at my own expense, as best as I am able, even though my means are limited," he paused, "I so swear it. But even so, you must understand, Andrean jails are full of foul disease and violent law offenders—who are not separated from other prisoners. Andrean laws do not do much to stop violence among prisoners—or violations of younger ones by their elders. It happens often and usually just as the new young ones pass inside. Please understand."

My uncle stood silently for a time, hands still trembling. His face had now turned completely white and sweat beaded on his forehead. "So the public dungeons would not be a good choice." His voice rang calm, but held a tremor.

"That is very true."

Uncle Haelin put the palms of his hands to his forehead for a moment, then dropped them. "We should get back to the match."

"No we should not!" protested a man standing next to the Andrean noble, who I learned later to be one of the swordmasters for the Andrean team. "This man, who was already in violation of tournament rules, has also just interrupted the match past the time allotted for the next round to begin, a clear infraction of the non-interference rule. Have him arrested, now."

"No. I will not," replied the match judge, in his clear calm drawl. "This contestant has asked for an explanation of the rules, and I have given it to him. It is my right to render explanation of any rule or rules without restriction. In fact, I will restart the timer for the break and allow this team leader to minister to his fellow contestant."

The Andrean noble protested in a loud voice, but Uncle Haelin softly said, "Thank you," to the judge and then strode back to Lankin. He reached his hands to my friend's face and examined his temple, "The bleeding has stopped here. That's good. How are you feeling?"

"What just happened?" Lankin pointed back toward the judge's table.

"What just happened is my lack of prior preparation showed itself. I should have found out how the tournament had changed before I got here, instead of assuming things were the same as when I'd been a contestant thirty years ago. It's always good to be prepared, whenever you can be." He said this in a low gravelly voice, with his eyes lowered, ashamed.

Lankin stared at him blankly as if he did not understand. In a louder voice, looking him directly in the eye, he added,

"Lankin, you need to fight. Or at least look like you're fighting. You need to keep your enemy away from you for just another five minutes, all right? Only five minutes.

28

Stay away for five minutes, but don't look like you're staying away. You have to make look like you're fighting back or they can throw the whole team in the dungeon, which could be the death of all of us. Use your shield. Block aggressive, make him eat the shield edge. Understand?"

Lankin stared into his eyes for a moment without saying anything. Then he nodded his head.

"Time," announced the judge.

My friend stepped forward, toward the center of the ring. The nobleman's son smiled at him. There was nothing warm or friendly about that smile.

Lankin held his shield out from his body as far as he could. It must have killed his arm to hold it out like that, as tired as he must have been already. The opponent held his sword far from his body, wrist ready to snap out quick blows with his thin blade.

For a few moments, they circled, glaring into one another's eyes. I remember Lankin's ragged breathing and the sweat and blood mingled together flowing down the side of his neck and from his face. The nobleman's son looked poised, excited, only a trace of sweat visible on his upper lip.

The blade flicked forward and Lankin met it with the shield. He aggressively followed up, chasing the sword with the shield, trying to smack the sword before it could come back after him. He impacted it with a clatter, knocking the sword arm aside and lunged forward, swinging a low swipe at his opponent's forward leg. The Andrean leapt backward, barely managing to retain his grip on his sword, but not fast enough. The tip of Lankin's blade chinked into the chainmail covering his enemy's shin.

"Point!" shouted the left side line judge.

Lankin leapt forward in a long bound and drove the edge of his shield upward toward the other boy's head. The opponent sidestepped quickly and made a quick thrust under Lankin's extended arm, jabbing into the armpit.

"Point," noted the other line judge.

My friend grunted in pain and instinctively pulled the shield in closer to his chest. The Andrean flicked his blade toward Lankin's face.

Lankin ducked, dodging the blow and thrust his shield upward at the sword. He fought that way for a while, shield chasing sword. But each time he did so, the Andrean punished him with a jab to his shield shoulder or the arm or under the arm.

"That's it! Keep doing it! You can do that all day!"

Of course, I know why my uncle cheered for him and told him what he did, but Lankin actually could not keep up the attack with the shield. It weighed too heavy for his tired bleeding body and the jabs to the arm kept weakening him. Soon, not more than halfway into the round, Lankin's shield arm began to droop, in spite of all of his efforts.

The nobleman's son smiled again. "I've got you now."

Lankin, huffing and blowing, suddenly switched to the sword, not seeking his enemy's body, but trying to knock aside his opponent's blade, his dark mountain-forged blade hunting after the silvery whiteness of the Andrean sword. With speed of hand his opponent answered, dodging around Lankin's blade, making quick flicks at his face or neck, then dodging again. Small new cuts opened in my friend's face, small streams of blood flowing down.

I cannot fully explain to you, my son, the terror I felt at this moment, the terror that my friend would be killed right in front of me. I have in fact since that time seen more terrible sights, but then I was older and more ready to face them. At fourteen, the approaching death of a single friend went far beyond anything my heart could contain.

Lankin continued to fight back, of course, but as blood from fresh slices to his forehead flowed into his eyes (head wounds bleed more than wounds elsewhere in the body), his ability to see, to move, to resist, visibly grew less over the few minutes remaining in the round.

Perhaps, I thought back then, even if his jugular was cut and he made it to the end of the round, a healer would be able to save him. Son, I was wrong about that. If your jugular is cut, you are pretty much finished. It's only a matter of time and not much time at that. Though this is also true of many of the wounds warriors die from in battle.

You hear in the heroic songs that a warrior was "struck and died," but unless he had his head cut off, he was in fact "struck and dying." Sometimes it takes hours for death to arrive, but at fastest wounds still take at least a few minutes to kill, even after the most mortal of blows. Yes, there are healers from places in the Bond that could save you with a magic spell from the sort of grievous wound like a cut jugular, but there are not very many of them and certainly none were on hand at Lankin's match. I told myself a hopeful little lie that Lankin could be healed, hopeful in that I desperately wished it to be true, though I was unable to escape a sense of dread that it was not.

His shield arm drooping, his sword held forward in an unsteady right hand, my friend drew back from his opponent.

"Now you die," said the nobleman's son.

The dark-haired boyish killer lunged forward in a fast step, his sword expertly seeking precisely the right spot on

Lankin's neck, guided with precision as if it were aimed by magic. The moment was right to commit himself, a moment when my friend seemed already finished.

In a last burst of power Lankin slashed his sword, swatting away his opponent's thin blade, fast followed by a counter swing of his shield. By sheer luck, or perhaps a twist of providence, the hard steel edge of the shield caught his opponent in the chin, right at the point of it, his jaw loudly clacking. I remember the whites from the Andrean boy's eyes rolling up into his head as he plummeted backward onto the hard clay of the match ring. He twitched once on the ground. There was silence, everyone watching drawing in a shocked breath.

"10 . . . 9 . . . 8 . . . 7 . . . " counted backward the nearest line judge, the one on the left. When he got down to one, the judge shouted, "Victory by incapacitation!" And the match was over.

The Andrean swordmaster crossed into the ring, rushing towards the dark boy. Likewise Uncle Haelin jumped over the match fence with an agility I didn't know he still had in him and rushed over to Lankin, who had fallen to his knees. My uncle had cloth in his hands to press on my friend's facial wounds. I did not know if I should laugh or cry as I realized Lankin won the match.

Which meant he would have to fight again.

⊹ Chapter 4 ⊨

As the sun lowered itself behind the western end of the summer palisade, our team reached our patch of Andrean soil for our camp. A common latrine ditch with a steep incline flowed some one hundred yards behind our site, under the wooden wall of the palisade and out to where I did not know. The odor wasn't too bad, but the flies sometimes were. But that evening, as we circled around our campfire, there were not that many of them.

Each team from outside the city was assigned a piece of ground inside the palisade for the tournament. Hundreds of teams were in residence from every region of the Western Bond. There were far more people at that camp than I'd ever seen anywhere before. Their skin, eye, and hair colors were from as dark as the Southlanders to as pale as snow. I even saw a few boys with snow white hair and skin and pink eyes, though that might sound hard to believe.

Tents had been erected, in the differing shapes and sizes and colors of all the nations of the Bond. At night, the lights of cooking fires would shine in the darkness and smells of strange foods of many nations floated in the air.

Iron Mountain Province is your home, son, and I've seen you have the same blind pride in it I had at your age. By "blind pride" I mean I imagine that you think that our province is the biggest, the best, with the most people, the greatest army, the most beautiful women, the best poets, the best war songs—the best of anything there is to have that we have. I imagine you think that because I used to think that way. But loving your home, son, doesn't mean it has to be the greatest in every way. It's like me loving your mother—love doesn't mean I can't think other women could perhaps be more beautiful than her, but it does mean that no other beauty matters to me except hers alone.

I say what I do about pride in our place because it may surprise you to hear that our province has few people compared to many other places. And while our mountains are vast and high to the sky, the Western Mountains are higher and their range is much longer, and the Heavensfoot peaks are higher and broader still. Our province is in truth far removed from the center of power of the Bond of the Western Kings and most of us don't really know very much about the Andreans or the king who sits on their throne, the guardian and Lord of the Western Bond, to whom our Council of Elders long ago swore the Oath of Trust and Protection.

I don't think about it much anymore in light of what happened afterward, but one of the most exciting things about being at the tournament was the chance to taste and smell and experience so many strange and unusual things and to learn about so many other lands. I remember in particular along the way, the especially rare sight of real wizards performing magic tricks for crowds who paid them. Doing things like levitating stones and lighting fires from a distance.

I don't know how many people were there for the sword matches—I heard at the time twenty thousand, but I wonder now if that was correct, because while our team was one of the smallest at fifteen, no team was larger than one hundred. But it was true that most teams came with a full set of admirers from back home who followed their own with enthusiasm. In the camp, sounds of voices, thousands of voices, drifted in the air, especially during the early evening. Our Mountaineer team had no tents. Just our two wagons were parked in our spot, maybe twenty yards by twenty, and the four oxen. Hay had to be paid for along with the wood and water and all our food. Lankin's father and his merchant friend had provided funds for all these things, though they barely had enough to pay for it all. The merchants also provided rough wool blankets for us boys to keep us warm as we stretched out under the wagons each night, seeking what warmth and cover we could as we slept. It wasn't so bad when it didn't rain. It never rained during the tournament but had several times on the way down. There are few things more miserable than trying to sleep on soaking wet ground during a rainstorm, with only a single blanket to keep you warm.

I remember the night after Lankin's match the sky was clear, though the stars were not easy to see due to so many lights and fires and so much smoke rising into the air. My uncle sat by the fire in our little camp, staring into the orange dance of mysterious flame. A wagonmaster, who might have been Malinkin (I remember his face very clearly, but I'm not sure I remember his name right), announced to the assembled boys, "I've got a special treat for you tonight. I managed to get some tender goat meat, good for searing and fresh from the seller, for the same price I've been getting you the tough mutton we've been boiling into stew." Malinkin had been out on numerous merchant journeys and had a skill I've always admired but never possessed. He could barter for a diamond and pay in dust —people used to whisper that he was the key to Lankin's father's success.

We boys were delighted to eat the meat that we skewered on short spikes of softwood and roasted over the fire, with hunks of vegetables between the meat, the way the Andreans commonly sear their food. Of course, you know we eat seared meat outdoors every Spring Celebration in our province. I loved fresh meat roasted over a fire; it was probably my favorite food. But Uncle Haelin smiled when Malinkin offered it to him, his face a bit pale. "Push mine into the stew pot for me, will you?"

"But it's so good, Uncle," I told him, pushing my stick in his face.

"Therin, take that away from me, please," he said, holding his hand up, his face serious. I realized at that moment I'd never seen him eat any of the seared meat at Spring festival. He always insisted on having stew. He made stew for himself that night, too, and was the only one to eat it.

Afterward he said, "Gather around, boys." None of us had been too far away to start with, but we crouched down as a group, forming a close semi-circle, like when we always did when he called us close when he wanted to instruct the entire team on some point having to do with sword fighting. Actually, the fire blocked part of the left side of the semi-circle, so a few of us kneeled a bit behind Uncle Haelin.

He looked up at us and turned his head to see our entire group, the flame illuminating his face more on the right and from underneath, making him appear to be a man from another world. "Boys, I'm sorry to have to tell you this, but this tournament has changed since I came here myself as a lad. You probably have already heard how—I've overheard some of you talking about it."

"I'm telling you up front that because this is a very dangerous thing now, this tournament—though at the same time, it's chilling, but it's more popular than ever, So I mean to withdraw each and every one of you from your matches as soon as I can figure a means that won't land us in jail…so I just wanted to tell you boys to put aside any dreams you might have had of winning this tournament. They weren't very realistic dreams to start with, as you know, because I've told you. But I let you dream a little by saying things like, 'You'll probably lose quick, but you never know what will happen in a tournament like this.'" He grunted something that sounded almost a laugh, "In fact, that's proven truer than even I thought, hasn't it? Though not at all in a good way. It actually kinda reminds me of war. War is like that…" His voice trailed off.

I was near the center of our group. I glanced back and forth at the faces near me. Foreheads scrunched and eyes were wide with puzzlement, mouths held firm with questions unasked. It looked to me that everyone else wanted to know as much as I did, so I said, "War is like what, Uncle? I don't understand."

"Really? I thought I was being clear…um, war is unexpectedly bad. You think it might be bad, but it's worse than you think."

"I don't think it's bad," I said, genuinely puzzled at my Uncle's attitude. "War is glorious…isn't it? The War Songs make it sound that way."

He laughed, not without a certain bitterness. "Yes, they make war sound pretty good at times, don't they? Loss of friends and all that, but our glorious army marches on to victory."

"Are you saying war is not glorious?"

He thought for a moment, "Actually, there is a glory in facing danger with courage, so war has a glory to it, or can have it, but the price, the price of that glory is so high, it's not worth it. Not for glory. If you want to face danger, it's better to save someone's life. Or fight a mine fire or something. Anything like that is better than going to war, because it has the heroism of trying to save lives, without deliberately trying to take them."

"But...Uncle, didn't you kill a dragon?"

"You mean all by myself? Therin, I'm just a man."

"No, I mean your unit. You and your unit killed a dragon. That's...amazing."

His eyes filled with tears. "I suppose it was...but we didn't do it for glory, even then. It was...to save each other's lives we fought, ...and we didn't do a very good job of that." A single tear streaked down his cheek into his mostly-gray beard, but at the same time he chuckled.

"But you didn't run," said Elin, the youngest boy with us— a kid with a bright grin, who always seemed happy. "You stood like men. And you did kill a dragon—that was glorious."

My uncle wiped his eyes. "We were too stupid to run." He laughed again, harder this time, almost as if crazed. None of us laughed with him. As a group, our faces showed confusion. And a terrible fear hit me at that moment, son, a fear that Uncle Haelin had actually been a coward...that everything I had heard about his heroism had been a lie.

"Besides," he finally said. "It isn't as if Kung Tzu didn't just breed more dragons to replace the one he lost. I would say, in fact, it's better—more important—to save someone's life than it is to kill a dragon."

"I want to see war," Elin said. "And stop a dragon attack. I want to fight and be a hero."

Among us, I think he was the only one completely unfazed by what my uncle had already said.

"Oh, I understand you think you want to see war. I used to be the same way. But believe me—you do not want to see war. You think you do, I know, but you do not want to see it for real. You just–just don't know you don't want to. I very much hope you don't ever learn why not." My uncle spoke these words with great force and tears brimmed in his eyes. He prodded the fire with a stick and continued in a softer voice, "You want to prove yourself? Be a good man, tell the truth, love your family, teach your children. Those things are a lot harder than you think. If that's not enough, invent something, climb a mountain, save a life, do something, anything good. You don't need war."

I asked, a lump in my throat, "Are you saying we should run away from fighting? That we should hide when enemies attack us—that when the Kings of the East invaded we shouldn't have sent soldiers to fight with our friends in the Western Bond?"

His eyes sought mine. With kindness, he said, "No, I'm not saying there is no such thing as a necessary war. There is —and even…even just war. But if any of you find yourselves on the Council of Elders someday and you have the chance to vote for war or against it, don't be eager for war. Find another way, if you can. But…there's a limit to what men can do. The truth is we each come to times when things happen we didn't choose. And all we can do—and we can barely do that, sometimes—is face what comes our way with courage. And with goodness. Boys, there is something you really need to know about war, in case you ever find yourself in one."

He paused and all of us stared at him with expectation. "In war, it becomes very easy to become cruel. You'd be astounded at the things you find easy to do in a war. Don't give in to that. And it's also easy for soldiers to misspend money and chase women. And get drunk. Don't do those things either. Remember what you've been taught—the God is watching you. Avoid, as much as you can, needless killing and doing stupid things. Protect, as much as you can, women and children and the innocent. Support your allies."

Elin said, "What do you mean 'as much as you can'? A hero always protects women and children and does good. That's what I would do."

Uncle Haelin looked at him and smiled, "I believe you would, Elin. As much as you can, anyway—that's the part you don't understand. We are just men, not heroes from the songs. We all have limits…we all have only so much that we can give…though, truthfully, that limit usually goes far beyond what we think it is—and sometimes it proves to be enough. Sometimes." His eyes fell back down to stare into the fire with a kind of grim fascination.

He said nothing else that night. Not long afterward, the silence stretching long, we took our blankets and crawled under the wagons to sleep. I dreamt of war, of lopping off a dragon's head with a single blow. We came back through my village and everyone cheered for me, the hero—except for my uncle, who wept.

⊶⊦ Chapter 5 ⊨⊷

At ringside the next day, the prince circled, his long loose blond hair tumbling down his back. Other than the prince, I'd never seen an Andrean with blond hair. He held his thin-bladed, ivory-handled sword in a style very much like the Andrean who had fought Lankin.

His opponent was the Southlander who had so easily beaten me. The prince had already cut two quick flicks across the Southlander's forehead. Blood poured down into his eyes. My former opponent danced backward, without even cloth armor this time, with just his wicker shield for defense—and an Iron Mountains-forged sword for attack.

This match, though only in round four of the tournament, took place in the twenty-first match ring, the one surrounded by the raised seating which allowed for many hundreds of spectators. For this match was the first for the prince, Rory-Galstaff, heir to the throne of Andrea and presumed future federal head of the entire Western Bond.

The Southlanders, who had very much outnumbered our team during my first match, were now in turn very much outnumbered by the stands full of Andreans cheering for their prince. "Kill him! Kill him!" some were chanting. I remember the look on my uncle's face as he heard that. His brows pressed down and his face flushed red in indignant fury.

He stood next to the swordmaster heading up the Southlander team, whose name I have forgotten, but might have been Mwezi. Mwezi barked instructions to his fighter in the deep tones of the Southlander language, clearly ignoring the crowd. He had already waived silent the cheering of the other young men of the South, so his voice could be heard more clearly.

At that moment, I stood on my uncle's left, looking across at the faces of the two men on my right. The clang of metal on metal drew my eyes forward.

The Southlander's blade twisted downward, the prince parrying a blow that must have flown just beforehand. The Andrean followed up with a quick flick aimed for the jugular under the left ear of my former foe, who flinched in time to take the cut in his cheek instead. He danced back from the prince and wiped his eyes, unfazed by the pain, blood flowing down from his newest cut, down his jaw, his eyes surrounded by a mask of red, those same dark eyes searching for weakness in his blond opponent. All my former desire for revenge against my opponent faded at that moment. And I began to hate Andreans.

The prince stepped forward, his movements nimble and swift. Wearing the best and lightest armor from our province, custom-fit to his body, his feet strode with a speed that rivaled that of his Southland adversary—and with its long, light blade, his sword proved much quicker.

Three fast flicks, the Southlander parried one and danced out of the range of the two others. The prince lunged forward in a flash and his foe swung a slashing blow in return at his chest. The prince didn't even bother to parry, dodge, or raise his shield.

His armor stopped the blow, "point!" shouted the line judge and at the same moment the prince darted a backhand slash at a particular spot of unarmored skin over the jugular vein under the Southlander's right ear. The tall youth from the southern continent flinched his shoulder upward, but the tip of the blade nicked its mark nonetheless. Dark blood spurted from the wound and the crowd roared a cheer.

Some part of my mind noted that no point had been called for the prince's blow—cutting blows were not penalized, but not rewarded either. On points alone the Southlander could still win the match. If he survived to see its end.

The Southlander swordmaster thundered instructions in their language. Afterward my uncle, who had familiarity with their tongue, told me he thought he might have said, "You are dead already—*so attack.*" At the time, even though I didn't understand the words, the intensity of the swordmaster's voice called my attention. My eyes turned right.

The swordmaster of the South watched the match with a blazing intensity, the veins in his neck distended, the whites of his wide-open eyes shining forth from his dark face, his teeth likewise shining as he shouted loud. Uncle Haelin turned to the man. "For the God's sake, end the match. There might be a healer here who can save him!"

"No," said the Southlander in the Western language, his voice low and quiet, not even glancing in my uncle's direction. "This is war!"

A loud shout and a flurry of motion in the ring turned my attention that way. My old opponent, the one who was

THE BOND OF THE SWORD

not my enemy, was shouting and charging at the prince, holding his neck with his left hand has blood poured between his fingers, swinging the sword in a rage with more precision than I'd shown in my own enraged thrashings days before. Rory-Galstaff proved a skilled defender, his footwork continually retreating without backing into a corner or against a rail, his sword parrying, his shield blocking. I will not describe to you in detail, son, how much blood had already flown from the Southlander youth's partially severed external jugular vein. As the match went on far longer than I would have believed it did if I had only heard the story, blood spattered the arena with droplets of red, given flight by the frantic attacking movements of the futilely brave young man from a land far to the south of Iron Mountains province. The prince didn't even bother to attack anymore, not at all.

He defended, defended, and waited.

The Southlander had slowed down by the end of the first round but amazingly was still standing, still moving, smeared in his own blood, his skin a peculiar shade of gray. "Time!" shouted the match judge as the hourglass ran down. The contenders returned to their corners with thunderous applause from the crowd in the stands.

The Southlander swordmaster leapt over the rail and my uncle was not far behind. My uncle offered a cloth and the swordmaster pressed it to the neck of his teenage contestant. But it was far too late for that. By the time the last grain of sand fell in the glass marking the minute break between rounds, my former opponent and ally had stopped breathing. When the match judge perceived this, he shouted, "Victory by incapacitation, Prince Rory-Galstaff!" The crowd roared again and the prince stepped into the center of the ring and raised his hands in ritual triumph. Though I remember he wasn't smiling. The cheers grew louder.

The Southlanders pulled their contestant out from the ring, between the rails, and four of them hoisted his dead body onto their shoulders, carrying him like carpenters moving a house beam. They began to chant a mournful low song as they carried him out of the arena, back toward their camp. I stood watching this, both the cheers that had begun to fade from the Andrean crowd and the Southlanders bearing away their dead, as if I did not in any way matter, as if I were not even there, as if all my life consisted of witnessing that moment.

"Therin!" shouted back my uncle to me. He had crossed the ring fence and was following after the Southland sword-master. And then I remembered why he and I had come to the match—to persuade that same swordmaster who had allowed our team entry into the tournament to now do us the favor of releasing us.

For some reason in that moment of a death that had come too suddenly to seem real, my mind drifted back to how I'd persuaded my uncle to take part in this tournament in the first place:

After school, the day of the snowball fight with Lankin, I had charged into a downward-spiraling mountain tunnel, branching off to the right toward the factory. The air smelled of coal smoke from the furnaces and the more pungent smell of burnt wood from household fires. I passed through the oil lamp-lit entry of the factory and waved at Lanka, the pretty older woman who collected receipts for payment and arranged for shipment of finished swords. She'd seen me enter the factory so many times to see my uncle that I barely caught her notice. Her eyes peering close into a ledger book, she waved at me with a single drop of her left hand.

Past her I entered my uncle's inspection shop. Numerous overhead oil lamps clearly lit the large square steel table in the center of the room. The table held some five or six swords, while an open iron case of ten swords sat at my side of the table. On the other side I saw two closed cases, and near the doorway from the inspection office to the sharpening room floor, I saw my uncle talking with an old woman with a hunched back, the sharpening supervisor. In the background, dozens of hammers peppered the air with pings, the sound audible but faint because the shaping chamber lay a number of rooms distant.

"Lemna, I appreciate what you're tellin' me," said my uncle, a sword in his hand. "The kid works hard and finishes a lotta swords. But what good is that if he doesn't do 'em *right*? These grooves at the edge of the blade are completely unacceptable. Tell Marin to fix this or he's gonna have to join the coal shoveling gang." He showed her, holding the blade near her face.

She squinted, then moved her head back as if doing so could somehow magically improve her vision. "I see what you mean," she answered slowly. "I'll talk to him about it. My, my." She reached out for the blade's handle, "Let me show him."

My uncle, a tall man with a barrel chest, powerful in spite of his war injuries, looked down on Lemna with a smile. "Sure you wouldn't like me to carry that for you? You're looking a bit frail."

She smacked him on the thigh of his bad leg with a grandmotherly chuckle. "So are you, you big cripple. But both of us keep doing what we must do since your little war."

She took the sword from his hands, still joking, but turned serious when she glanced up at his face.

My uncle turned back my way, tears brimming in his eyes. Lemna left the room.

"Are you all right?" I'd asked.

"Fine, Therin. It's nothing unusual anymore. Sometimes my eyes just get watery. Or sometimes I get angry for not much reason. It's been like that since the war." He wiped his eyes and seemed to immediately come back to himself.

"Because your leg hurts?"

"No," he chuckled and shook his head. "That's not why."

"Why then?" Other than pain, I couldn't see what crying had to do with war—war was glorious, just like the songs said.

"I don't know. I didn't used to be like this, but it doesn't matter. What can I do for you *this* time, Therin?" The word "this" carried a bit of a growl to it, as if doing for me as much as he always did was getting to be a burden. I realize now that this reaction may have been the aftermath of embarrassment from talking about his feelings. Funny that I remember this with understanding so clearly after all these years, yet at the time I did not understand at all.

"Can you train us for the Tournament of Swords?" I blurted out in excitement. "Lankin and I've been talkin', and he says his dad will help fund a team to the capital and that maybe some other families can help with the money. I told him already that you fought in the tournament once and know all about it!"

"Therin, that's been over thirty years ago now. And I only went once—I hardly know all about it. Why are you making a promise that I can help when you didn't know all the facts? Making promises you can't keep is never a good thing, nephew."

"I'm sure you can, though! You can train us, right?"

My uncle smacked the palms of his hands over his eyes and drew his hands down his face until his nine uninjured fingers rested on the beard of his chin. He'd lost half of the tenth finger, his right hand pointer, in the war. Sometimes he'd joke with me and push his stub up his nose and say he was picking his brain, but at that moment he shook his head in disbelief, dropped his strong hands to his sides and told me, "Yes, I can train you—I can show you what I know—but that doesn't mean I know the tournament well. I think it would be better off to have our own tournament, our local boys facing off against each other. If we did that for a few years, then perhaps we'd build up some skills worth taking to the main Tournament of Swords for the whole Bond."

"Uncle, please! Lankin's father will help pay our way down to Andrea—"

"And it's only four months from now. That gives us hardly any time. I don't know who'd go with you, but I don't think any of you know *anything*."

"Lankin does. His grandfather's been teaching him."

"Has he? I remember the old man from the war. He was in a different unit, so I didn't see him much, but I heard he was one of the best fighters among the old-style officers. If Lankin can fight, that's good, but he will have to prove what he knows—"

"He can."

He sighed. "Well, then. Maybe he should go by himself. The rest of you boys could learn something in a local tournament, while he went off to Andrea to compete for real. Would save his father a lotta money, too."

"Please, Uncle," I begged.

And I kept on begging over the next several days.

My uncle was an old soldier and pretty gruff, but I knew he had a lot of kindness in him. I also knew he cared about me personally. My father and he had been two of five sons from the same family. All five of whom had gone off to fight in the First Dragon War, among whom only my uncle had returned home alive. Among the brothers, only my father, the eldest, had married before the war. I'd been his only child, born nine days before he'd gone off to fight. And so, I was my uncle's nearest kinsman. I know you've already heard some of these things, son, but I'm repeating it to make it clear that I knew if I kept asking, he'd give in.

So in the end, he agreed, and we gathered up a whole team, at first mostly boys from the village, whose parents worked in the sword factory, though Lankin's father knew two sons of other merchants who joined us, too. While my uncle trained us over the few months he had to work with, the upcoming tournament became a matter of local pride as boys told their parents and their parents talked. My uncle had wanted to keep what we were doing quiet, but soon everybody knew about it. That's in part because Lankin's father told someone who told someone who told a close friend who sat on the Elder Council. Once the council knew, the word got around even outside the village and some other boys joined the team.

When spring snowmelt came and the roads were dry enough for wagons to pass, around a month before the tournament was due to begin, the Elders arranged for us to have a big send off, with all the parents of us boys and some of the elders, the students who didn't go with us and their parents, from both my school and the merchant sons' schools, along with girls from the factory schools, and everyone in our village, plus all the sword factory workers

who'd donated weapons and armor, everyone standing outside on the cool mountainside, just beginning to turn green
with spring as we rumbled off in our ox-drawn wagons.
These were two bare metal platforms with rails mounted on
wheels. Designed to carry ironwork, not boys.

I call us boys now because that's what we really were, but
I can tell you when that crowd was cheering, I felt like I'd
achieved manhood. At fourteen, I was in my last year of
school, about to start my vocation in the mountain factories,
which probably would have been working with my uncle, my
nearest relative. Most of the other boys were like me, on the
verge of finishing school or not long since finished with
school and beginning adult work, excited to be going off on
this one adventurous journey to represent the province,
villages, and families we loved and were so proud of. Most
of us had never been outside of our own villages, let alone
Iron Mountain Province.

The crowd cheered, while my uncle, who hadn't been shy
in telling people not to expect too much—he explained to me
it was better to tell a hard truth up front that deliver a bitter
disappointment later on—muttered grumpily under his
breath. Lankin's father and another merchant, Alkin (yes, the
one you're thinking of), provided the carts at no small cost to
themselves. Because as long as we were at tournament, those
carts lost money, not hauling steel goods from our province
factories off to trading stations or to other provinces. As a
result, none of the merchant fathers could afford to come to
the tournament themselves—they had to do extra work to
keep the businesses going. Nor could any other parents afford
to come. Only a pair of wagon drivers went along with us. So
Uncle Haelin was the only grown man in charge of fifteen boys
eager to prove themselves men. He was a brave man, my uncle.

"Therin!" my uncle shouted back at me a second time, as I stood by the twenty-first match ring in Andrea, breaking my chain of thought. "Hurry up!"

I revived from my puzzled trip into memory-land and ran after him. By the time I'd caught up, the Southlanders were outside the arena and my uncle had caught up to swordmaster Mwezi. As I trotted up, puffing a bit, I heard Uncle Haelin say:

"I need you to withdraw our team from the tournament." At first the Southlander didn't answer.

"Please, Mwezi, we want to leave the tournament."

Mwezi stopped and gave my uncle and angry stare. "And why would that be, mountain man?"

"No boy should have to die here as yours did, my friend."

"He was not a boy," growled Mwezi. "He was a man, and he died like one. And even so—boys die in war too sometimes, as do even girls and women at times. But it is mostly men who die in war. You know this. Do you think this is a game, this tournament? This is training for war, where men die." The Southlander's voice had grown quieter and quieter as he'd delivered his response.

"But men don't die in training for war—" my uncle began to reply.

The swordmaster cut him off, "In our training, yes, sometimes men die."

"Well not in ours, or they're not supposed to, anyway. So please, my friend, release us from this tournament."

"What are you, a coward?" The Southlander puckered his lips in disgust. Some part of me noted that the rest of their team had not waited for their leader, but had kept carrying away the body of someone whose name I have never even known.

Uncle Haelin's face flushed a bit red and his eyes hardened for a moment. But then he said, "If you want to call me a coward, call me a coward. Just let our team go."

The Southlander, taller even than my uncle, looked down on him with disgust. "I will not."

"Please, Mwezi, please," begged Uncle Haelin. And then he actually dropped down to his knees, shocking me—and by the sudden roundness of his eyes, the Southlander too. "My boys are not ready for this. They aren't properly trained for it. Please, please release us so I can give them proper training, to–to make them into the men that those with you are."

"They are not ready?" The Southlanders voice had softened just a little.

"No sir, they've only had a few months training."

"And whose fault is that?" said Mwezi sharply, who without another word pivoted on his heel and followed after the body of his slain warrior.

I stood behind my uncle, not fully understanding, but afraid nonetheless that he would blame me. After all, it had been me that had persuaded him to lead us. But in fact, he didn't say a word to me about that, not then and not at any time afterward.

But it did take some time before he got up from his knees.

⚔ Chapter 6 ⚔

The morning of the next day my uncle shook me as I lay under the sword wagon. "Therin, wake up!"

I sat up in a heartbeat. The sky remained completely black, moonless, lit only by the stars and eight of the wanderers.

"Where's Lankin?"

"Uh," I muttered, my head far from clear. "To my left… over there." I waived my hand vaguely, like a pine bough in a breeze.

Clearly my uncle felt more alert than I did, because he quickly found my friend. "Lankin," he said. "Get up."

"Whatever you say, Uncle Haelin." Which I think was the only time I ever heard him call him "uncle."

"Help me wake up the rest of the boys, quietly." So we did. I felt surprised to learn the oxen teams for the wagons were on hand, the wagon masters in the process of hooking them up. "Load up, boys," whispered Uncle Haelin.

"Where are we going?" asked Elin in a voice too loud. Four or five of us tried to "Shhhh" him, making our-selves louder still.

My uncle calmed and quieted all of us with a low soothing voice, "Quiet now, boys. I know all of you trust me, so trust me a bit more. Get in the wagons. Feel free to fall back asleep if you like." So we, a set of sleepy-eyed boys on the verge of manhood, piled into these two wagons, which soon began to roll. The morning was unexpectedly warm and the motion of the cart lulled my still heavy eyes back into a sleep as the oxen slowly plodded forward, the drivers handling them in low voices. Next to me sat Elin. Even though I dozed in and out, I was aware in my awake times of his posture—he sat upright, wide awake, excited, and alert.

Eventually the rolling carts no longer rolled forward with a sudden stop that jerked me awake. I remember noticing most of the boys being groggy, having dozed off as the cart rolled, or fast asleep like I had been. But Elin still sat upright, looking around with bright eyes. I'm sure he hadn't slept at all.

"Where are we?" I whispered.

"We're at the gate leaving the tournament palisade for the main road," answered Elin, not loudly, but not whispering either.

"Oh," I said. "What's going on?"

"Let's go find out," said Elin. So he jumped off the wagon and I followed him, stumbling a bit. We were the only two boys I saw doing so. I didn't even know where Lankin was, so he must have been in the other wagon.

We walked up behind Uncle Haelin and overheard him speaking with the gatekeeper, who resided in a shack of palisade wood, the upright cured logs of the palisade, their ends sharpened into spikes, mirrored in the gateshack, except its logs running vertically in a square shape, were not as wide or long. The roof of the shack appeared to be covered with a kind of rough cloth. The gatekeeper himself, standing in front of this log gate with massive black cast iron gate hinges, held a spear as his armament, four men with him, likewise equipped with spears and leather jerkins.

"No, sir," said the guard at the moment Elin and I walked up.

"So you're telling me that without a pass there is no way I can exit this palisade? Even if everyone on the team has been eliminated in the tournament and there's no reason to linger around?"

"Not until the tournament has ended, sir. No team may leave without a written pass, though you should be able to get one easy enough if everyone is finished in the tournament. Leaving without one would be cheating."

"Cheating? That makes no sense to me at all. Who in their right mind would think that leaving a game is cheating? Why is this such a problem?"

"Well, in times past, people would gamble on the games, placing bets, ya know . . . peoples still do that from time to time, meself included, though I'll deny it if ya tell any'un," added the gatekeeper with a snaggle-toothed grin. "But then there were a whole racket of folks who figured how to make money off by where they's deliberately throwing games they placed bets on, cheating the results of the tournament to win the bet. That's the why withdrawing from the games without permission or refusin' to fight is very stric'ly forbidden now, that's why you can't leave early unless ya got a pass issued by the head of the tournament. This year that's—"

My uncle interrupted, "Guffey of the Midland district of Hasterry. Yeah, I know him. Thanks."

"I'm sorry, sir."

"Me, too. But let me be sure I'm clear about this—once the entire tournament is finished, everyone is free to go, no pass required."

"Of course, sir."

He turned around and saw Elin and I standing there. "Come on, boys, get back in the wagons." So we did. I heard him speaking to the wagon masters in a low voice, but I didn't quite hear what he said. The wagons rolled back in the direction of our designated campsite, but this time I wasn't so drowsy. I looked over at Elin, his face still bright and excited, as if this had been nothing more than some sort of late night adventure for him. I wanted to ask him what he thought about what had just happened. But I didn't.

After the wagon wheels had rumbled over the hard dirt road inside the palisade for a while, when we were maybe only one hundred yards from our camp, I heard Uncle Haelin's voice calling softly, "Lankin, Therin. I need you to get up." The oxen carts stopped rolling and my uncle gestured to us to come to him. We both did, though I never saw where Lankin came from until he stood beside me. Then my uncle turned to one of the drivers, "Finish taking the wagons back. Let the boys continue to sleep."

"You, two come with me," he said to Lankin and me, "If we can't do this one way, we'll do it another. It's always a good idea to have a backup plan." I didn't understand at all what he meant by that, but I remember the east glowing pale, brighter than before, showing the first sign of morning approaching. But most of the sky remained black, now lit only by the brighter stars and the brightest six wanderers.

Two still-drowsy boys followed an alert man, who limped badly with morning aches but moved with determination, past camps of darkened tents and campfires mostly died down. We headed toward the central stadium, which held the twenty-first match ring.

The sun had just crested over the sharpened log palisade to the east by the time we reached the outside wall of the stadium. One wall of the octagonal brick structure was dominated by the match board. "Match" because it held a diagram that showed the position of each boy in the tournament—"board" because as incredibly large as it was, from its wood grain this board some five paces wide and more than fifty long seemed to have been cut from a single board, from a single impossibly massive tree, sawn, planed, and sanded.

The board held tiny little nails that supported wooden square chits maybe twice as wide as my thumb with numbers painted on them in fairly small print. Each chit had a single hole in the top center, so the chits could be placed on the small nails and moved about as a contestant moved up in the tournament. Dark painted lines on the board marked with match numbers (which could be checked on another board to find match times) made a pattern in which a massive set of team members on either side of the board became fewer and fewer as each round of the tournament progressed, ending in a final match in which two contestants faced off against one another, like deep branching roots ending in twin trees on either side— which decided the winner, the victor of the whole spectacle, which I still saw as nothing but glorious.

Colors marked the various teams but so many teams competed in the tournament that certain colors got used over and over again. The faded red that marked the color of our mountaineer team chips was shared by four other teams. My personal number was 787, while Lankin's was 772. Perhaps three or four swordmasters and as many Team Leaders subordinate to them milled around the board that morning, looking for their candidates. I knew by then from experience that in perhaps a half hour, the board would be swarmed by dozens, maybe hundreds, of officials and leaders of teams as the first match of the day began.

A few eyes glimpsed our way as Uncle Haelin searched the board for our chits. Contestants did not normally come to the board, though I never heard any specific rule stating that it wasn't allowed.

"Therin, do you see yourself, way up there?"

I nodded. "Against bright yellow 342—that's the best of the Tsillis team, right, Uncle? Their camp is two down from ours. I talked to that guy the day before yesterday—he looks impressive. It'll be a tough fight for me."

"I'm pulling you out of that match. I'm gonna put Elin in your place."

"Uncle, he's brave but he'll lose! He's way too small to face the Tsillian."

"Exactly. He'll lose, but to the Tsillians, who aren't killing anyone—and that will be his second elimination. You'll face his opponent, a match you should win without much risk, leaving just you and Lankin as contestants."

"Oh," I said, not really understanding.

"So then after that I'm gonna put you in Lankin's bout. You see who he's up against?"

While my eye searched for his chit, Lankin answered for me, "That's the Southlander blue, isn't it? 704? Who is that?"

"His name's Koto. He's a great athlete. He'll have no trouble beating Therin."

"Uncle!" I protested.

He turned to look at me. "And that will be your second defeat…saving your life, perhaps, dear Nephew." His gaze met mine as he managed to combine a comforting smile with a stern warning in his eyes.

"But Uncle…" I said, still not quite understanding.

"So, what happens to me?" asked Lankin, "Do I do Therin's match?" A linen bandage that had been white in the evening wrapped around his forehead and covered him from crown to halfway down his ears. It had been white, but now bits of dirt from the ground Lankin had slept on soiled it… and in the front, several blotchy yellowish stains marked where he had wounds that still seeped.

"Well…that part's the reason I brought you boys over here. Those two matches are happening at the same time— look—here and here. I plan for Therin to fight his, but I need you boys to help me keep it quiet that I'm gonna try and see what happens if I don't substitute Lankin for any other match at all. What I mean is, I won't put anyone into the bout Therin is scheduled for. Then once they substitute someone else in the match, we all just wait around for the tournament to end before we all roll out of here with everyone else, everyone alive and healthy."

"You want us to lie about the match?" I asked, my mouth open in shock.

"No, don't lie. Lying is bad. The God doesn't approve. But don't volunteer the information. Keep it quiet. If someone asks you about the substitution, tell 'em to talk to me, your Team Leader."

"It won't work," Lankin said dryly. "Substitutions are on a one-per-one basis. They'll realize that you're not switching the same players for the same matches."

"Hmmm. Well, I'm praying to the God you're wrong, Lankin. I've seen the officials get real busy right around noontime, just before they stop everything for the lunch hour. I've got a hunch I might be able to cause a little mistake to be made…give 'em the impression without saying so that our swordmaster has withdrawn you from the tournament, so they automatically bring in someone to replace you. Once they do that, we're in the clear. And it so happens the matches in question come just after lunch, so *if* they notice, it'll probably be after your match is fought, which would be too late to put you back where you belong. If we're lucky, they'll disqualify you for it—hey, it would be great if they disqualified the whole team?—as long as they don't throw us in the dungeon.

The higher you go in this tournament, the more Andreans there are—and more of other teams that use their same tactics. It concerns me that you haven't lost a single match yet."

An objection began to rise in my throat but died away as understanding dawned on me. It was stupid of me as I look back on it, but not until then did I fully understand what my uncle was doing and why. He loved us and wanted to be sure there would be no chance that any of us would lose our lives —so he was using what limited power he had as a Team Leader in our best interests. I actually understood when he asked what he did next: "Any questions, boys? Can you keep this quiet?" I said:

"No questions, Uncle. And I won't tell anyone."

Chapter 7

"Damn that thickheaded kid!" growled Uncle Haelin Elin, just a bit over half the size of the Tsillian champion, struck another blow to the much larger, stronger, and more skilled boy's shin. "Point!" shouted the line judge.

"Time!" shouted the match judge, marking the break between rounds two and three.

"There's more where that came from!" shouted Elin at the Tsillian as he walked back to his corner.

"Elin! ELIN!" shouted my uncle, "Come here! COME HERE!"

Elin trotted back to our corner, grinning and sweating, pasted with ring dust. I glanced at Uncle Haelin and watched him breathe deep, visibly trying to calm himself down.

"Hey, did you see that, sir?" asked Elin, his voice trembling with excitement. "I'm winning by two points now!"

"Elin," my uncle's teeth sat on edge.

"Yes, sir?" said Elin as he waived to some of our Mountaineer teammates at the side of the ring.

"Elin! Are you listening?"

"Yes, sir."

"Remember when I said I wanted to get you boys out of this tournament?"

"Yes, sir."

"Do you remember when I said at the beginning of this match there is no shame in you losing?"

"Yes, sir."

"I said that . . . because I want you to lose."

"But, sir, I'm winning," said Elin with a grin.

"Yes, yes, I know." Uncle Haelin put his hands on the top of his head and sighed. "Therin, give him some water."

I handed our youngest teammate the tin cup full of clear liquid. His hair shone that light blond color of young children in our land, freckles marked his nose and cheekbones, and his flushed red lips still pulled upward as he gulped down his drink.

"Elin, losing is good. I wanna make sure you leave this tournament alive."

"Oh, I will, don't worry, sir," Elin said as he lay a comforting hand on my uncle's arm.

"Time!" shouted the match judge. And Elin entered back into round three.

I talked with the Tsillian afterward (his name was Arvad) and he told me he felt handicapped by the situation. He easily could have knocked Elin over and maybe would have won a "victory by incapacitation," but it didn't seem right to him. Not honorable.

And being how all my uncle's training taught leg attacks, coupled with Elin being so short, our little guy kept making points of the Tsillian's legs. Over and over again.

Of course the Tsillian countered again and again with skilled blows all over Elin's body, but none of them discouraged him. Like a little dog fiercely going after an ankle bone, he attacked, attacked, attacked, and never gave up. "Time!" shouted the match judge eventually.

Elin jumped up on the bottom rail of the ring fence nearest him, raising his arms and the sword over his head. "WOO! I won by three points! Woo hoo!"

"Great," grumbled my uncle from our ring corner. "The plan is unraveling already." And I had already won against Elin's scheduled opponent.

From there we walked back to our campsite, Elin grinning and shouting. A couple of the boys, including Lankin, tried to explain to him he shouldn't be so happy. He brushed aside their comments, grinning from ear to ear.

"Therin, you're with me. The rest of you boys, stay here."

"Me too?" asked Lankin.

"Especially you."

After walking a few paces I asked, "You aren't even going to take Lankin to the site of his original match?"

"No. I'm not even sure why I was thinkin' I'd have to." He looked across at me, bit his lower lip, then said, "Follow me to the match office by the outer stadium. I'll make the arrangement to substitute you in Lankin's match, then find out if we can get him replaced for not showing up for his new match, if the God lets me get away with that. I'll do it by trying to simply not mention who the replacement is, and hope in the bustle they don't notice I that I didn't...then, when the time for your former match comes just after lunch, hopefully they'll realize the contestant is absent and find another player to put in your place. Or disqualify you. But you'll actually be in Lankin's bout later this afternoon, so hopefully he'll be disqualified."

"Ah that sounds a little complicated. Don't you know what will happen, Uncle? I thought you'd done this before."

"Yeah. Once. Thirty years ago and rules have changed since then. I tried readin' the official rulebook once I got here, but they only will hand out copies to swordmasters, which I am not. I barely know more than you."

"Really? But you always seem to know what to do."

"Do I now?" he grunted before adding, "That's a leadership thing, actually. When you are charge it's important to act confident, even if you're uncertain."

"Is that something you learned in the war?"

"Yeah," he said, then spat on the ground, the pained look on his face closing off any further commentary.

He didn't say anything else until we reached the offices. He didn't tell me where to wait, he just pointed at tree beside the roadway and I stood at that spot and waited.

I watched the crowd go by, my eye picking out certain individuals as they passed me. I found myself watching a young Andrean woman with black glossy hair all the way down her back blocking much of her long white sleeveless dress. The hair swayed back and forth as she walked away from me and I found myself admiring the way she moved. I hadn't had much interest in girls when I was a boy, but that had begun to change for me not long before the tournament.

A voice to my side blurted out, "Are you on the Mountaineer team!"

I turned right, toward the voice, and saw a girl with curly red hair and bright blue eyes, in a dark brown Mountaineer-style dress with leggings, staring at me.

"Uh, yes."

"Oh yay!" she jumped up and down as she exclaimed it, reminding me of Elin. She was about his height, too.

"Er, how do you know me?"

"Oh. Hello." She held out her hand for me to shake, "I'm Arta, Alkin's daughter."

"Therin," I mumbled as I reached my hand out.

"You know Alkin? I'm his daughter."

Son, you may have heard that shaking a woman's hand used to be uncommon, but that would have been back when my uncle was a boy. By my time, the lack of men after the First Dragon War had pushed women in all kinds of jobs men had always done, so they'd picked up the man's custom of handshaking. I'd shook hands with quite a number of women at this point in my life, but for some reason felt embarrassed to take the grip of this girl—maybe because of the Andrean young woman I'd just been staring at. But I did it anyway, while I felt my face flushing red, "Uh, sure, he's one of the ironworks merchants who lent us a cart. Along with Lankin's father."

"Right!" she said. "Well—I talked mother into sending me down here. So I'll get to watch all of you in the tournament and cheer you on!"

"Oh," I said, thinking of Lankin in his match, blood pouring down his face. "Oh!"

"What's wrong?" she asked, perceptively studying me. "Ah…" At that moment I was at a complete loss for words.

I just stared into her blue eyes for what seemed an hour, not wanting to crush her excited enthusiasm, definitely not wanting her to watch any of the matches.

My uncle appeared from nowhere, saving me. "It's done then, Nephew. Say, who's this?"

"Arta, Alvin's daughter," she replied, shaking his hand.

"A pleasure to meet you," replied my gruff uncle with a charm I didn't know he had. The two of them chatted for several minutes, me standing there, still not knowing what to say.

Then Uncle Haelin began walking, Arta strode beside him, still chatting. He said, "Coming along, Therin? We're going to your match."

"Uh...yes," I said, trotting to catch up.

"Arta dear," he smiled as he unslung the water skin from his shoulder. "Could you fill this for me? You can see one of the public wells just over there, to the left." He pointed.

"Certainly!" she exclaimed with bright enthusiasm, taking the half-filled skin and skipping away toward the well.

"Uh...so what are you going to do about her, Uncle? She can't watch the matches."

"We'll let her watch this one, with you and Koto. Seeing you completely outmatched and eliminated from the tournament should dampen her enthusiasm."

"Uncle!"

"What?" he asked, grinning at me. "You like her, do you? Don't want to be embarrassed in front of her?"

"I don't like her—she's loud and annoying. It's just that... just that..."

"Hmmmp," grunted my uncle in a near-laugh as he limped along, the corners of his mouth turned up ever so slightly.

Quicker than I would have thought possible, Arta was back, the water skin full. She kept chatting away with my uncle, even though now he barely answered. In minutes we were at the fourteenth match ring, the fifty or so South-landers, minus at least one, standing at one side of the ring.

Koto waited inside the fight enclosure on the hard-packed clay, a wicker shield on his arm and an Iron Mountains- forged sword in his hand. The whites of his eyes flashed as he grinned at me fiercely. I felt distinctly sick that this would not go well.

What can I tell you, son? I'd like to tell you a tale of how, even though I lost, I managed to impress the redhead girl with my courage and stamina. It would be a nice story, but I'm committed to telling you the truth. She cheered loud for me at first, loudest when I scored my one point in round one, but by the time I'd lost the match nineteen to one, by the time I stumbled back to my uncle's corner, sweaty and defeated, when I glanced over at her now-silent face, I saw an expression there built of an odd mixture of feeling sorry for me and being ashamed of me.

Uncle Haelin turned to her. "Sorry you had to see that, lass. I'm afraid the tournament has mostly been like that for us. In fact, virtually the entire team has already been eliminated."

"Oh—well, I remember you telling everyone that could happen. That no one had enough training."

"I certainly did. And of course, it's always a mistake to go out without enough training."

"Yeah–um–I think I'll be going now." She looked at me as if she were about to apologize. After staring at me for a moment or two, she said, "Goodbye, Therin."

"Goodbye, Arta," I mumbled, thinking to myself, *That's probably the last I'll ever see of her.*

Chapter 8

My Uncle's plan to wait until the entire tournament ended seemed to go well at first.

"So when is my next match?" Elin would ask, aware of the fact that he should be still fighting his next bout sometime, somehow unaware of the fact that my uncle planned to avoid that very thing.

"I'm not quite sure," my uncle would answer. "But it's not today." Or he would say, "Hmmm. Let me go check on that when I get the chance. But I'm busy right now." And Uncle Haelin would stay right where he was, not leaving our camp at all.

The wagon masters left to buy food, but no one else departed for even a moment. Uncle Haelin had us wait as if we didn't have much money left, which was certainly true, and we'd all already been eliminated, which was very nearly true. Most teams in our position were watching whatever matches they could, but some few remained at the campsite, doing nothing much, including the Tsillians down the way. We weren't the only ones.

Five days passed—it was late evening when I heard the jingling of metal and clapping of hooves on the dirt road leading to our campsite. I'd been getting ready to settle down for bed, trying to arrange what little straw that remained in my spot inside the wheel into something approaching comfortable. When I heard the noise I arose and found Andrean cavalry, two squads, lined up in neat rows at the edge of our camp. As if waiting to begin a parade. My uncle stepped away from the fire that had almost completely died down and hobbled toward their commander, who wore a long, feathered plume of white that swept down from the spike at the top of his helmet. "Who are you looking for?" asked my Uncle.

"Team Leader Haelin of the Iron Mountains Province Team."

"I'm him. Why?"

Four men dismounted from their horses at that moment. They drew long curved cavalry sabers and strode up to my uncle. "You, sir," said the still-mounted leader in a matter-of-fact tone, "Have violated the laws of this tournament. You have deliberately allowed matches for your team to go unchallenged—as if you had been bribed to throw this event in order to sway the outcome of gambling pools. This is a criminal offense, sir—aiding and abetting bribery and illegal gambling, possible grand larceny—punishable by fines and imprisonment."

I stood watching this happen, still by the wagon, some twenty yards behind my uncle, my mouth open in shock.

"Get the swords," Lankin whispered loudly (like an actor onstage in a Spring Festival play), astonishing me more by his presence of mind than by what he'd said. When I stared at him blankly, he repeated, no longer whispering, "Get the swords! Come on everybody, we need to help Haelin!"

And so not-yet-asleep boys were grabbing blades from out of their storage racks on top of the wagons as I opened the locks (my uncle had entrusted me with one of three keys).

Elin was the second to receive his blade and began to run toward my uncle. "Wait!" shouted Lankin, grabbing him by the shoulder.

In the dim light Elin's eyebrows scrunched down in a scowl, but he waited, stomping his foot as he did—not every one of us took a blade, but in less than two minutes ten or eleven of us charged toward the horsemen, me vaulting down the top of the wagon, my work as the supplier of weapons finished. As we ran toward these tall dark horses, I realized Uncle Haelin had already mounted on one of them, behind a rider. His arms were folded behind his back, as if they'd bound his wrists together. Some part of me wondered how he'd gotten up on the horse.

Since I'd jumped off the wagon instead of running around it, I was one of the first to arrive, Elin and another boy (whose name I've forgotten but whose face I remember very well) right with me. As we charged, we began to yell. As we began to yell, the rest of the horsemen drew their dangerous, gleaming sabers, not making a sound other than the scraping of metal out of scabbards. Me and the other contestant about my height, but of a much more slender build, came to a sudden halt about five paces away from the horses. It became instantly very clear to me that a man on horseback can easily chop off the head of someone who is dismounted, who in turn would be struggling to reach the leg of his opponent.

But Elin didn't slow down. The horseman he charged made a movement in the saddle and his horse pivoted in place, swinging away its hindquarters—Elin charged at the right rear flank of the horse. In almost casual move, at the same time as the horse pivoted, the horseman swung a looping blow with the flat of his blade, hitting Elin in the back of the head and knocking him hard to the ground, face first.

72

Instantly on his feet again, Elin shook his head and growled. He charged the horse again, but before he'd gotten even a single pace, my uncle shouted, "ELIN! Stop that!"

The boy pivoted around, looking up at the horse Uncle Haelin had mounted, not far behind him. "Put the swords away! You try to fight these men with swords, they'll *kill* you with *their* swords. Drop it, Elin, now! All of you boys, drop your weapons, right where you are—right now! You can pick 'em up in the morning."

And all of us, in shock, did what we were told, our blades impacting earth in irregular thuds. Even Elin.

"Stay here, boys! Maybe I'll be back soon. If not, the wagon drivers will get you out of here."

The two of them, the wagon drivers, stood there in shock—one had taken hold of a few of the boys before they could run around the wagon. That was one of the surprising things about that night for me. As a boy, grown men had always seemed to know and understand more of what to do than I had. But Lankin had come up with a plan quicker than anyone and Elin had moved quicker than anyone, while the wagonmasters hadn't known what to do. I wouldn't have expected that. That moment helped plant a seed of doubt in my mind that I didn't even know was there until later— perhaps, I began to think, perhaps what grown men and women had told me, including my Uncle Haelin, wasn't really right after all.

As the horses trotted off, taking Uncle Haelin away, Lankin said to me, "C'mon, let's follow him!"

He began to run. So I followed him.

One of the wagonmasters, perhaps Malinkin, shouted back at us, "Boys! You come back here!" I glanced over my shoulder and very nearly obeyed. I saw the man had Elin in his grip and that he and his companion were blocking a number of boys. I'd always been taught to obey and I very nearly did—but I saw the wagonmasters were too busy to come after me and Lankin kept running. So I did, too.

Following the horses proved easy. The darkness of the evening showed the lateness of the hour—most of the teams had bedded down, just as we had been about to do. A couple of bends of the hard packed road took the cavalry squads out of our sight, but we could still hear their hooves clattering on stony ground, so we knew which way they'd gone. And they ran a trot instead of a gallop, not an impossible pace for someone in good shape to run, though I remember Lankin having an easier time of it than I did.

The horsemen rode up to an open covered area not far from the match board, actually across from the place where I had met Arta. Hands behind his back still, my uncle managed to swing his good leg over the horse, then slide off on his chest, stumbling as he fell, but still upright. At this point, Lankin and I had stopped running. The covered area was well-lit with many lamps and as we walked forward, still in the darkness outside of the circle of lamplight, trying to control our heavy breathing without even thinking about why, the steam from out breath unnoticeable because of the horses in the area, making their horse snorts and loudly shifting their hooves on the cobblestones of this part of the street.

A plain rectangular table of heavy wood and four plain legs stood under the covering. Uncle Haelin, hands shackled behind his back, a cavalryman flanking him on either side, walked up to perhaps three paces in front of a large wooden table. A man sat there, on the opposite side from my uncle and the horsemen, facing them. The man was Guffey—two other game officials stood next to him. Papers of some kind lay on top of the table, with an inkwell and a goose quill.

"So nice of you to join us," said Guffey with unsmiling sarcasm, his voice carrying quite well in the night.

My uncle chuckled in a deep voice. "With the gentle invitation you sent, how could I refuse?"

"Are you mocking the dignity of this event?" snapped the tall thin man with white hair and a white goatee standing on Guffey's right. He wore the black, tight-fitting clothing I'd come to recognize as that of Andrean nobility.

"Totally inappropriate," tsked the man standing on the left. He was short and round, with a bowl haircut and very thick droopy lips, wearing a long white robe I later learned was common among dwellers in the Great Desert. "Totally inappropriate to laugh, given the dignity of this event and the seriousness of the charges."

My uncle's back was to me, so I don't know what his face indicated at that moment. If he said anything, it was too low for me to hear.

"Well, I can see you're not laughing now, sir," drawled Guffey in his slow Midland accent (he pronounced "sir" like "suh").

Lankin tapped my arm and waived his hand for me to follow him. So he and I worked our way to the left of the horsemen, seeing some shrubbery at the edge of the lit area that would give us cover from the official's eyes. After we got there, we'd be able to see faces and hear the conversation better.

"Are you taking bribes?" The thick-lipped official's lips smacked as he talked.

"Why are you making a mockery of our traditions?" snapped the Andrean.

"You are guilty, sir," said Guffey, "Of violating numerous rules. You are worthy of punishment."

By now I could see my uncle's face. He studied each of the men facing him. He turned over his shoulder and looked back at the cavalrymen still on the street and the two dismounted horsemen on either side of him, nude sabers still in their hands. He turned back to Guffey, clearly considering his words before he spoke.

"Gentlemen, I requested a formal copy of the rules of this event when I first arrived. I spoke to the head of this tournament personally about this matter." He nodded his head at Guffey. "I was denied a copy of the rules on the grounds that I am not a swordmaster. So I must tell you in all honesty, I don't really know what the rules here are and are not." He turned his face to the tall man in black. "I am not Andrean—please forgive my ignorance of your customs." Facing the thick-lipped man, he said, "And I have never taken a bribe. Not for anything. Not at any time. Not ever—nor would I. Nor have I gambled on any of these matches. Not now and not when I was a contestant here thirty years ago."

"Thirty years and you never graduated from contestant to swordmaster." Guffey chucked in a way that made the hairs on the back of my neck stand up. "Well, gentlemen, what you see here then *must be* the case of a simple mistake." Guffey gestured with both hands wide apart, as if appealing to the two men beside him. "Isn't that right, sir?" Guffey now moved both hands together, pointing them at my uncle.

Uncle Haelin's brow pressed down in suspicion. But his mouth remained closed.

"A simple mistake. You first are noted for loudly complaining how our legally accepted practices could kill your precious boys, though I admit I don't know what you see in them…and then afterwards, but sheer *oversight* you make an improper substitution to eliminate one of your own team-mates from the tournament, your own *nephew* no less… and then you have two others that should still be in the tournament, but well, you simply forgot to take them to their matches. My, my, what an error! But don't you fret, we can fix that." Guffey smiled in a way that seemed almost friendly. And I'd never see him smile at all before that moment. "Step hither, sir." Guffey rolled his hand with a flip of the wrist his own direction, summoning the Mountaineer forward.

Uncle Haelin stepped forward two paces. The cavalrymen stepped with him.

"You see this diagram?" asked Guffey, shoving a leaf of parchment his way. Not waiting for an answer, he continued. "It shows a proposal for the quarterfinal matches of this tournament." Haelin looked down at the paper. His eyes widened in shock and his mouth dropped open.

"You're gonna put my boys in the finals!"

"Well, just the three," said Guffey. "The two who hadn't been eliminated already and your nephew, because what you did was an illegal substitution."

Uncle Haelin violated his rule about swearing, then added, "Against three of the best in the tournament?"

"All Andreans in the finals, except your boys. And just one other exception—one Southlander whom you might know by the name of 'Koto'," added the tall man in black, his hair and goatee pure white.

My uncle stood there staring at the man. His face flushed a deep red. The chains binding his hands strained and for a moment I thought he was going to rip them apart. But then he stopped and breathed deeply and looked at the three men facing him, each in turn. All of them stared back at him, their eyes wide and expectant.

"Surely there must be some way out of this. Why else would you be discussing this with me, as if makin' me an offer?"

"Why would you want a way out? I thought you made a simple mistake. I'm correcting the mistake. Doesn't that make you happy?"

"My boys—you yourself said you know I'm trying to keep them alive. And you're putting them in a situation where they could die."

"Oh, that bothers you, does it?" asked the Andrean.

"This tournament is preparation for war," snapped the thick-lipped man.

"Hells it is!" but then Uncle Haelin breathed deeply twice. He stared into Guffey's eyes. "What do you want?"

"A full confession."

"Of what?"

"Conspiracy to throw matches. Gambling."

My uncle stared at them, breathing hard. "Will it get my boys out of these matches?"

"Why, yes, it will," said Guffey.

"But then what happens to the team? Will they be imprisoned?"

"For misconduct of their team leader? Certainly not! We're not barbarians! Just you will be punished...in fact, with their Team Leader eliminated from the tournament, they will not even be allowed to compete, since a team at a minimum must have a Team Leader. They will be sent home at once."

Uncle Haelin pondered this for several deep breaths. "So how do I make this happen—I don't believe in telling a lie, but if it saves lives—I'll take this punishment."

"Sign the confession here. Unshackle him." Guffey produced another paper. "Can you write your own name?"

"Yes, I'm literate," growled my uncle as the cavalrymen released the chain binding his hands. "Why would I have asked to read the rules if I can't read?"

The Andrean handed him the quill pen and pushed the inkwell his way. "Just one more thing," added the man in the white robe of the Great Desert, his lips smacking, "You must name your accomplices."

"Accomplices?"

"Yes, we've investigated the major gambling pools. We know you've laid no money anywhere. So you must have had accomplices who did so. Perhaps the Southlander who helped you, Swordmaster Mwezi? Perhaps he should be eliminated?"

"*What the…*" roared my uncle, and I saw him bite his lower lip. Literally. And then he threw the quill at the man in the white robe, marking it with a blob of black. The piggish man snorted in disgust and wiped at the inkblot angrily.

"I don't know what you–you *think* you are doing here, but I won't partake" My uncle's hands shook in rage. "I will not name an innocent man as an accomplice! An ally no less!"

"Hmmm. I heard a rumor he refused to remove your team from the tournament. Isn't that true?" asked Guffey mildly.

"Go pound sand!"

An exaggerated sigh slipped from Guffey's lips. "Well, I'm sorry it's come to this. I suppose your boys simply have to compete. The rules require it. If they refuse, we will imprison the whole team. Sign, or your precious boys will suffer."

"The God help me!" cried out my uncle. And tears began to flow down his face. He made no effort to wipe them away, as I had always done when I cried, ashamed of myself.

"Your emotions are really quite extreme, sir. You need to get better control of yourself. This isn't difficult at all—I'm offering you a very simple choice here," Guffey seemed almost sad. "You should take the deal."

"Wait a moment, wait a moment—I know what this is about! This is to eliminate Koto, isn't it? Isn't it?" he glared at each of the three men. "If his swordmaster is eliminated, he will be, too. What, you can't take the chance a Southlander could win your tournament? Does that violate your so-called 'tradition'?"

None of them answered. They simply stared at him, grim-faced during a long silence until Guffey said, "Is his chance of victory worth the lives of your boys? Because it's either his elimination or their likely, ah, defeat."

"There must be something I can do, Sky Father," moaned my uncle, turning his eyes upward. "An honorable way out of this. Something without injustice. Something…"

"Yes," cooed Guffey. "You can sign the confession. And name your accomplice."

Uncle Haelin hunched down over the table, his hands on its edge, breathing hard, sweat pouring from his brow, dripping on the wood.

Suddenly, he snapped upright, his face calm. "Wait a minute. What was it that one official said?"

"What one official?" Guffey's voice showed annoyance.

"He said something…about me being a fellow contestant —he said I could minister to my fellow contestant, when Lankin was hurt."

"I don't see why this is important—"

My uncle cut him off, "And you said, earlier tonight, that I eliminated one of my own 'teammates'—that was the word you used. 'Teammate'."

"Sir, I am frankly losing patience with this—"

"And you also said, making fun of me, that I had never gradu-ated from being a contestant. That means I'm still one, doesn't it?"

Guffey didn't respond.

My uncle continued, "So it must be that a team leader is legally defined as a member of the team? Isn't that so?"

Guffey glared back without a word.

"And that would mean I can fight in the tournament, doesn't it?" My uncle looked into the eyes of all three men.

None of them answered. Uncle Haelin chuckled, wiping away his tears and sweat. "So that's it then, this is easy—I will substitute myself for my boys. I will take their places in the finals."

"For all three? You may not do so."

"In series, I believe I can. Not so? I can substitute for one and then the other then the other? If I am actually a member of the team."

"That isn't legal," snapped the thick-lipped man.

But both Guffey and the Andrean glared at him icily. Apparently there were limits to what they were willing to do. Anything was fair for them as long as the rules allowed it—but they would not deliberately lie about the contents of the rules.

"On the contrary…that would be…within the accepted interpretation of the rules." Guffey's voice started from very low, but raised louder as he continued. "But I doubt you will succeed at all three. Or any. Your opponents will be among the best this tournament has ever seen—they will destroy you in the ring. Do you want that? If you cannot physically compete past the first round, you will not be able to substitute yourself for anyone in subsequent rounds."

My uncle grinned triumphantly. "But if I can't compete anymore, in absolute terms, then there will be no team leader for my team. The boys not only will not be required to fight —they will not be allowed to fight. Isn't that true?"

Guffey looked down at his papers and shuffled them, not saying another word that night. After a few moments he indicated with a wave that my uncle should be released.

⊶ Chapter 9 ⊷

The next day, Uncle Haelin surprised me with his silence. He had walked back to our camp directly after his face-to-face encounter with Guffey. Lankin and I, who had found it easy enough to sneak into the bushes nearby, found it hard to get out of there right away. Too many people were milling around. Eventually we left, of course, after the group cleared. But Uncle Haelin, even though limping as he always did, had moved far in front of us down the road by the time we began to move back. We followed him from a distance.

The next day, just after breakfast, he laid out a full set of mail—mine actually, because I was closest to his size—a shield, and selected a sword. He adjusted the links, loosening them mostly, obviously working to make the mail suit fit him tightly, especially around the neck and face. He also fitted a hood for himself of thick leather that went over his head and neck, under the chainmail. I'm not sure where he got the leather, but he knew exactly how to shape it. Then I didn't understand why he did that, but now I know that chainmail does a poor job protecting against stabbing blows—leather is much better in that regard. Malinkin helped him a bit with that part, but he did most of the work himself. He also put a leather sword strap around his right wrist.

After our noon porridge, he began to sharpen the edge of the sword (but not the tip, because sharpening that was illegal) with a whetstone and oil. He did all of this without telling anyone what he was preparing for. Elin asked him and he simply said, "It is not yet time for me to tell you. Later." Though, of course, Lankin and I already knew. We also knew that the first match of the quarterfinals was to take place at the third hour of the afternoon, just a bit more than two hours away.

The other camps nearby us were empty. Even the Tsillians, who like us, hadn't been watching the matches, were gone. We'd seen all of them streaming down the road from the contestant campsites in the direction of the twenty-first ring, the one surrounded by stands large enough for thousands to watch.

Elin said to my uncle, "I heard from one of the boys passing by that everyone is going to watch the quarterfinal matches. That this is a big event here. That they have clowns and acrobats first. And jugglers. I'd like to see jugglers."

In fact, we could hear the noise of the crowd from our campsite, something like a mile away—faint roars of laughter and shouts of applause.

"Hm. Now's not a good time for that, Elin." Uncle Haelin glared at him in a way that seemed to say, "Don't ask me again," and even Elin, who was nothing if not persistent, said nothing more.

After a bit more than an hour of sword sharpening and putting on his gear, Uncle Haelin walked up to the second wagon and turned his back toward it. "Take a knee, boys.

And come closer." We formed a half-circle, facing him, on our knees, literally looking up to him. The two wagonmasters stood behind us.

"Boys, I've told all of you that …the rules of this tournament have changed. How they've become unfair, how they risk your lives for no good reason. But I want you to understand that I don't believe in breaking rules, not even if they are unfair, not as a general rule anyway." He chuckled, perhaps because he realized he'd just used the word "rule" twice in a row, in two different senses.

He looked down at his hands after his brief laughter, paused, and then looked up at us again. "I don't want to give you an example of being a lawbreaker, someone who goes against the rules at a whim. I want you to know there was no whim in what I did, boys. What I have done and what I'm doing is for you. Maybe there was another way to get you out of this tournament without breaking the rules. But couldn't think of it. I'm just a man and I don't always know what the right answer is." He cleared his throat before he continued.

"So, anyway, I broke the rules of the tournament. And it so happens there's only one way to make that right, and at the same time save you boys—only one way that falls within the rules. Which means I have to do the fighting now in your place."

His eyes met mine, then Elin's. "I understand some of you boys would probably want to watch me fight. But I don't think that's good. I may lose. It may get bloody, which I don't think you boys really need to see. It's just as well you stay here—this isn't a game anymore."

I thought of the links he'd fitted tightly with experience of a veteran preparing his gear. And the sharpened sword.

And that my uncle had fought dragons. In an awed and shocked voice I said, "You're gonna kill the Andreans, aren't you, Uncle?"

He chuckled. "You mean all of 'em? That's quite a lot."

"No—I meant just the three in the quarterfinals."

He blinked at me in surprise. "How would you know about that, that I've got three matches? I didn't tell you yet." I felt my face flushing. I glanced sideways at Lankin, who gave me the "you're an idiot" eye roll.

Uncle Haelin glanced between the two of us. "Well, it doesn't matter how you know. So let's just say this is serious. I'm not going to be playing any games with them, that's for sure."

He opened his mouth to say more, but one of the boys behind me, I don't know who, cheered. "Woo hoo!" and a bunch of the others joined in, clapping. I found myself joining them, thinking something like, *Finally, someone was going to show those Andreans what we Iron Mountains men are made of.*

Uncle Haelin stood a moment or two in shock before recovering. "Boys! BOYS!" he shouted, chopping his hand to his neck to tell us to cut it off. A few moments passed before the applause died all the way down.

"Boys…I appreciate your enthusiasm. But…I just told you how serious this situation is. Which probably isn't the best of times for cheering. Maybe you don't understand—maybe you never will. In fact, I hope to the God you never do. Uh, well, I'd like to say more, but I've gotta go real soon. I've got two matches today and then, the God willing, one tomorrow. If I'm not back by sunset, I'm not leaving you alone, the wagonmasters know what to do. Obey what they tell you and they'll get you home if that time comes."

"Excuse me," he said as he walked through the group of us, his voice then softer and meeker than I would have expected. He moved past the wagon, picking up a water skin as he passed by it. And then he turned and walked down the road toward the twenty-first ring without ever looking back at us. Some part of me wondered, *Is that it? Isn't he going to say anything else?* Clearly, he was not.

After he'd gotten past a bowshot down the road, just before he was about to move around the bend that would hide him from our sight, Lankin said, "Elin, Therin, you're with me. Let's go."

"What are you doing?" asked Elin. "He just told us to stay."

"Did you ever wonder why you never fought your last match? It's because he's covering it for you now. He's covering for Therin and me, too. We, the three of us, owe him, to at least go see how he does."

The wagonmaster, not Malinkin, said, "You boys better stay right here. It's clear that's what he wanted."

Lankin met the adult's gaze with a boldness I never had back then. "If he gets eliminated from the matches, they're gonna come looking for the three of us to fight anyway. We might as well be on-hand. The rest of the boys can stay."

It wasn't quite that easy. The discussion went back and forth for a bit. Lankin and I wound up telling the wagonmasters and the rest of our team most of what we knew from the night before. But after all was said, we three took off after my uncle, our fighting gear loaded in sacks that we slung over our shoulders in case we would need them. The chainmail got heavy for Elin and Lankin to carry it (because it's easier to wear the weight of armor on your body than port it as a load), but I was able to help them as we moved to the finals ring, taking each sack for them several times along the way. I could do that easy enough because my chainmail wasn't with me—my load was much lighter than theirs, because my burden had been taken away on my uncle's body, carried down the same road we walked.

The sounds of cheering and applause from the tall stands grew louder as we approached. I'd never witnessed so many people in the same place at the same time and I found the sheer noise of the numbers intimidating. Of course, combat itself is like that in the middle of action, thunderously loud, louder than the loudest sound you've ever heard, but going on and on and on seemingly without end when it's at its full. Deafening.

I began to slow down as we drew close, dragging my feet as I looked upward and listened. Lankin grabbed me by the arm and pulled me forward, scowling at me. Elin walked to my right with a light, quick step and a grin on his face as if thrilled by the chance to see some jugglers.

Large gray Andrean square-cut stone formed the bottom level of the stands. Above that the outside wall was still made of stone, but the floors of the four levels above the ground were made of wood and the benches spectators hunched over were also wooden—but on the ground floor, they were stone, like the floor and walls. A number of tunnels with arched roofs were on the ground level between seating sections, but only one went all the way through to the inside of the ring, where the elevated platform for the match stood. I'd already been there with my uncle, while watching a Southlander whose name I never knew die. So we knew where to go.

Lankin, Elin, and I headed for that tunnel. On either side of the entrance stood an Andrean Royal Guard cavalryman, each in his distinctive steel plate armor, made exclusively for them in our province. "They're gonna stop us," I whispered toward Lankin from the corner of my mouth.

"Just act normal. Follow my example." Lankin strode forward with confidence. This tunnel was barely wide enough for us to walk side by side, more than half narrower than all the other tunnels. So it made sense in a natural sort of way that he'd pull forward in front of us, leaving Elin and I walking next to one another. He actually went between the guards and about half a pace past them without them saying a word to him. But the man on the left had been studying my face as I came up, some five paces or so behind my friend. It seemed to me at that moment that he knew every thought of my mind. But there was a long pause before he spoke:

"What are you boys doing?" He said this with his eyes still fixed on my own, while his right arm snapped back and he gripped Lankin by the shoulder.

"N-n-nothing," I stammered.

At the same moment, Lankin said, "Going to see the upcoming match, of course."

"This entrance is for contestants only," said the Cavalry-man on the left.

"We're contestants—or we're supposed to be," said Elin with a cheerful smile.

"If you're contestants, where's your swordmaster?" the man on the right said.

"Our team doesn't have a swordmaster. Just a team leader," Elin answered.

"Very well, where's your team leader?"

"Inside, getting ready to compete," said Lankin.

"Say, you boys are with the Mountaineer team, aren't you?" The soldier on the right was still staring at me as he spoke.

Lankin glanced at me and then at Elin, with a stern look, which maybe he meant to keep us quiet.

But I felt obliged to answer, "Y-yes."

"Stand over to the side here and wait," he ordered. It never occurred to me to disobey. I immediately walked to the spot he indicated and stood there. Elin followed me. To my surprise, when I glanced over at Lankin (who hadn't moved at all) his eyes got that same look he used to have when a hidden snowball was in his pocket and he was about to nail me with it—as if he were about to dash for the inside. But instead, he looked at me, sighed, and walked over to join the two of us.

The left guard trotted off toward the officials' hut faster than you'd think a dismounted Royal Guard Cavalry in armor would move. After what seemed very long minutes, Guffey himself came out to join us.

"What are your contestant numbers?" he drawled dryly. We told him. "So you're here to see your team leader fight, are you? Here to see him rectify your team's violation of the rules?" His lips very nearly smiled after his last question but his eyes seemed far from amused. Sinister even.

"Yes," said Elin, while Lankin and I both were still pondering how to best reply to the question.

He gave a short, single laugh, then said, "It so happens that your leader's got three matches in front of him and if he gets eliminated from the first two, one of you boys might have to enter the ring for the third—so I do believe it serves the purposes of this tournament to let you go ringside. The rules don't actually specify where team members should be when they watch a match, so I am *permitted* to allow you in, though for convenience sake we generally limit who is allowed ringside. The rules do say, however, that while you may speak to him, you are not allowed to assist him in any way, even to give him water, not until he leaves the ring. You are not swordmasters and not team leaders, so you have no rights to intervene at all. You are not even allowed to touch the ring platform, since you are not escorted by a swordmaster or team leader. Understand?"

"Yes." Again, Elin was the first to answer.

"Then you may enter, though I would ask you to talk some sense into your Team Leader when you get the chance. Remind him he can end this with a simple signature—it's not too late," he said, nodding at the two Cavalrymen. At that moment, I realized the guards had been plain Andrean infantry when I'd been to the ring the first time. I wondered why they'd changed.

But that thought left my mind as the three of us stepped forward through the low narrow archway into the ring. Through the tunnel, we saw the floor of the stands paced by healers, team members, and swordmasters who looked back at us suspiciously, and stands towering over us packed full of crowds thundering in a way I found utterly intimidating. And in the raised ring at the center of it all, just as Elin had anticipated, stood four jugglers in each corner of the ring, tossing Iron Mountain Province-forged swords at one another, catching them and twirling them upward and over in timed perfection as the crowds roared cheers and applause.

⊹ Chapter 10 ⊱

My uncle raised his sword blade. The time for entertainment had passed—the time for the first match had begun. This match was clearly different from all the previous ones. Uncle Haelin had entered the ring, after which a crier had announced him to the crowd, his deep booming voice supplemented by a large copper cone he held to his mouth:

"In an unusual substitution, the Mountaineer team has elected to replace a contestant with one more elderly than is customary for the tournament, which I remind the crowd has no fixed age by law—" at that point, the crowd began to boo, very loudly, cutting the man off. That's when Uncle Haelin lifted his weapon, accepting the jeers against him without shame, as if they had been applause. I remember that moment very clearly. I can close my eyes and see it.

Lankin and Elin and I had come up behind him, pushing our way through the people seated in benches to stand on the ground right next to the raised ring. At the moment people were booing, Elin shouted, quite loud for someone so small, "He fought in the Dragon War and killed a dragon! Show some respect!"

The ring was elevated just short of two yards off the ground that was surrounded by stands. A lip about a yard wide wrapped around the ring fence. That's where the crier stood, high but outside the ring, his feet near-level with my head. Everyone nearby turned and stared and some laughed, including the crier.

"All by himself?" asked the grinning man, not shouting, the cone away from his face. I remember him as very tall and thin, in green holiday clothing, with lips that stood out because they were painted bright red.

"Not just him, his unit," I found myself shouting. "Fourth Battalion Iron Mountain Volunteers!" When I said that, some heads nearby snapped my way, including my uncle's. Especially among men my uncle's age or older.

"Well, then, hear that, good people—we have a genuine dragon slayer here! Our contestant is a veteran of the Fourth Battalion Iron Mountain," thundered the crier through the cone, his deep voice mocking, though he became more serious with what he said next, "This might be an entertaining match after all."

I heard quite a lot of laughter at first, but some of the people in the stands were not laughing at all. Especially among men my uncle's age or older.

I glanced over at Uncle Haelin, meeting his narrowed eyes as he stared right into me. Which indicated his clear displeasure at the fact we'd come to the match. But he said nothing. The crowd noise would have made it hard to hear him, anyway, even if he had shouted. Most of the crowd was still booing.

Diagonally across from my uncle, a dark-haired Andrean entered the ring. "GENTLEMEN and ladies" thundered the announcer. The man had a voice of truly exceptional roaring volume. After the "gentle" of "gentlemen," the crowds at ringside and up in the stands mostly quieted down. I could see the anticipation in the faces of people nearby, as if they were eager to hear the name of the young Andrean, even if he would only be fighting my old uncle.

That was the first time I'd thought of him that way, "my old uncle." Like he was some old man in a place he didn't belong. Not a hero. Not someone I loved.

"From one of the great noble families of Andrea, a family of champions, who have won this tournament, one member or another, nine times in the past sixteen years," the crowd roared its approval at that statement, so that the announcer needed to pause for a moment. "We welcome this youngest Hidlestan-Galstaff," the crowd thundered, "… to his first quarterfinal in this tournament, future champion and High Duke, future hero—Tomas Hidlestan-Galstaff!" The crowd roared and stomped their feet and the young man raised his sword arm over his head, as my uncle had done, but to a totally different reaction.

He looked very much like the Andrean Lankin had beaten and he dressed the same way, in custom-fit Iron-Mountains- forged chainmail in black and tall soft leather boots, but with a very long thin sword, not from our province, with a silver engraved handguard and an ivory-white handle, inscribed and inlaid in delicate silverwork, and a shiny bright high-cost steel shield. In fact he looked so much like the other Andrean, he may well have been his brother. The same swordmaster who'd been present at that previous match stood outside his corner.

There also came the introduction of the line judges and match judges (Guffey himself sat as one of the match judges for this bout). But soon enough, one of them flipped over the five-minute hourglass for the first round. The match began. Uncle Haelin circled to his right, limping a bit as his knees were bent, his shield held high, his sword in close and upright.

The Andrean, circled too, watching my uncle with a smirk on his face, standing fully upright, moving with a quick light step, his shield pulled in tight, his long sword stretched out with his long arm, twitching this way and that with little feints. One feint transformed into an attack, a quick swipe at my uncle's face, who easily met the flick with his shield.

The circling continued for what must have been at least a minute and someone in the crowd booed. But then, when the Andrean backed a little closer to one of the corners than he had previously, my uncle leapt forward, faster than I thought he could move. He pulled the shield tight across his face and made a blind low sweep at his opponent's legs with his relatively stubby sword.

The Andrean leapt over the blade like a girl jumping rope at Spring Festival, but not straight up. He jumped up and sideways, to his left, and while in mid-air sliced downward so the edge of the blade just below the tip slashed under Uncle Haelin's right ear. Which might have severed the jugular vein and killed him, except for the tough leather he wore underneath his chainmail.

Immediately Uncle Haelin came back with a backhand swing, again at the Andrean's legs. His much younger opponent, sideways to him, stabbed behind the shield into the upper chest, above the heart, and bounced back out of my uncle's range. "Point!" barked one line judge and "Point!" added the other.

My uncle circled like before, but after a mere half-turn lunged forward, starting a low swing feint but thrusting his body upward into a leap instead, trying to power his weight into the Andrean's body. His opponent had already quick stepped to the side and he jabbed my uncle in his sword-arm shoulder joint. "Point!" announced the line judge on that side, barely audible over the roar of the crowd.

I remember feeling shocked. And disappointed. My uncle, the hero, wasn't doing any better than Lankin would have done.

Uncle Haelin had begun to puff with his efforts. He circled in the ring again with an Andrean who showed not the slightest sign of having worked hard. This time Uncle Haelin thrust forward and swung his sword at the Andrean's legs with this shield lowered enough that he could see well. The Andrean leapt back into the corner then thrust forward with a slash just over my uncle's shield at a high angle, slicing a gash between his upper lip and his nose. My uncle's face erupted in blood.

With the Andrean now in the corner, my uncle raised up fast and swiped downward at the shoulder of the younger man, who seemed trapped. The Andrean met this hard blow with a clang of the shield and twisted away, powering backward, moving himself out of Uncle Haelin's snare in a flash. On his way out the Andrean flicked a hard backhand slash behind the bended knee of my uncle's right leg. "Point!" moved the lips of a line judge, while the other waived his hands and mouthed "no point!" the sound of their voices hidden in the roar of the crowd. There was a brief moment of dispute among the judges, but Guffey waived his hand, indicating no point was counted for the last hit.

Uncle Haelin turned and circled again. Now with each outward huff of his heavy breath, blood ran down his sliced mustache and thick red droplets blew forward. And blood ran down around and into his mouth, down his chin, onto his chest and onto the floor of the ring.

"Dragon! Dragon!" started chanting someone in the crowd. Other voices picked up the taunt.

Uncle Haelin showed no sign of hearing them. He kept circling and attacking, spitting blood, circled and attacked, usually coming in for a low blow, but on occasion he swung high. In either case, the Andrean punished him, earned points, and moved away without harm.

Mercifully, the end of the first round came. Elin, Lankin, and I had backed away from the edge of the ring so we could see the whole area of combat better. But now we came as close to Uncle Haelin's corner as we could without touching the ring platform itself.

He grabbed the water skin he'd left on the lip, just outside his corner. He sprayed water and his face and some of the blood that had begun to dry grew wet again. His mustache and beard looked like one giant oozing scab. He drank water greedily, huffing and sweating, dripping red.

A pair of acrobats had appeared in the center of the ring while I wasn't looking, a man and a woman. They tried to avoid standing on spots of my uncle's blood as the two of them performed tricks, including the man tossing the woman in the air and catching her. I suppose their routine, though brief, made the time between rounds a bit longer than it otherwise would have been. Under other circumstances, I would have watched them very closely, especially the woman, who had that beautiful dark Andrean hair and wasn't wearing much clothing. But at the moment my mind was fixed on my uncle.

"You shouldn't be here," he said down to us.

"If you lose, we'll have to replace you," said Elin.

"Unless I'm dead," he answered, "Then, without a leader, the whole team will cease to exist."

"What are you saying, Uncle?" I blurted out in horror.

"Don't worry, I plan to win this match. Then no matter what, I'll only have to make it through the next two. Even if I get eliminated from both, none of you boys will have to fight."

"It doesn't look like you're trying to win," muttered Lankin. I don't think Uncle Haelin heard him over the final cheers for the entertainers. Finished, the acrobats gracefully leapt over the ring fence in a single bound, each of them in turn, spreading their arms and legs, fortunately caught by a crowd of their ringside admirers.

"Pray for me," said my uncle. Then the second round began.

This round Uncle Haelin made fewer attacks. He circled still, but when he did strike, did so with single lunges, thrusting his right arm forward very hard in a stabbing motion, aiming for the torso of the Andrean. The Andrean struck back with slashes or stabs of his own. But he did not try for Uncle Haelin's face or jugular at all in round two. He just accumulated points. He was up to fourteen by the end of the round, while Uncle Haelin had only two.

The next round break came to crowds that seemed bored. Their cheering picked up when a team of four came out; two were bowmen, each of whom fired at two other men who managed to catch the arrows. The end of the brief show featured one of the men catching an arrow in his teeth.

Uncle Haelin didn't say much during this break, which is partly why I remember that entertainment better than the acrobats. But he did drink water and I happened to notice him removing the leather sword strap from his wrist. He had taught us that attaching a sword strap to your wrist was very useful in combat, in case your sword should fall from your hand, it would still be attached to your wrist and you could grab it again. But I'd forgotten until then, until he took it off, that he'd been wearing one.

The third round began and it seemed it would be the same as the second. Uncle Haelin made thrusting attacks and circled. The Andrean attacked and circled, too, except his attacks were with a faster sword and hand, and were better aimed and made points more frequently.

But then, in a move that came so unexpectedly I almost missed it, Uncle Haelin thrust his sword arm forward hard towards the body of the Andrean, just like he'd been doing, but this time he let go of the sword. The blade flew at his opponent, who leapt sideways away from it, toward my uncle's shield side, because he was further away from the ring fence on that side than the other. After throwing his blade my uncle did not pause—he lunged the way he must have known his opponent would leap, swinging his shield.

The heavy iron edge caught the young man at the corner of his jaw, at the side of his face. He fell to the ground like a dropped sack of bulb roots.

The crowd erupted in a collective shocked "ah" which slowly transformed into booing.

Uncle Haelin respectfully stepped back as a line judge rushed into the ring to check on the future High Duke. The crowd was so loud, that if the nearest line judge was counting, I couldn't tell. But he was supposed to be counting from the moment the contestant fell.

My uncle's sword had sailed clean out of the ring, causing a brief moment of terror for a few privileged spectators sitting at the stone benches on the ground floor of the match ring, who either earned the right to such a close vantage point by paying for it or by inheriting it.

But no one got hurt.

Without a moment's hesitation, Elin ran after the sword. He told me later he pulled it from underneath a stone bench with a quick, "Excuse me" to the noble Lords and Ladies sitting there. He ran back and tossed it toward my uncle so that it slid across the floor of the ring.

My uncle retrieved it just as the crowd noise began to die down. After I don't know how much noise, I expected the count to be nearly finished when I heard it. But the line judge counting was only at "TWO."

He continued counting, very slowly compared to what I'd seen in other matches. I saw my uncle stride over toward the elevated judges table on the north end of the ring. I was curious about what they were going to say, but I hesitated to go over there to find out. Elin did not hesitate. He ran through and among people, shouting, "Excuse me," as he did. I could hear my uncle shout toward the table over the still-restless crowd, but I couldn't tell what he was saying. Guffey's voice gave some sort of an answer, but I couldn't tell what it was either.

But I could hear the count, which continued slowly, maybe three times slower than I'd heard before. If the count had reached "TEN" with the Andrean still down, they would have announced, "Victory by incapacitation!" and that would have been the end of the match. But at the count of "NINE," the Andrean managed to pull himself up. The crowd roared in approval.

With a look of plain disgust on his face, Uncle Haelin went on the attack for the rest of the round, this time swinging his shield edge at the Andrean's head and following with the flat of his sword. But the Andrean ran, demonstrating clearly that a forty-something man with a limp had no hope to catch a teen highly motivated to stay away from him. The crowds seemed bored but only a few people actually booed. No swordmaster on our side was able to formally object that the contestant didn't offer "a vigorous defense."

By then Elin had come back over to Lankin and me. "What did Uncle Haelin say to the judges?" I asked him.

"Oh. He demanded to know if the count was legal."

"And?"

"They said it was. No rules specify how long the ten count has to last."

"Of course," said Lankin with a frustrated sigh.

It wasn't long before the time ran out. I saw my huffing, sweating, and bloody uncle stand next to the nobleman's son, who still wobbled in the knees a bit. The announcer blared with his copper cone, "With a clean count of twenty-eight to five, your victor in this afternoon's match is the future High Duke Hiddlestan-Galstaff!" The majority in the stands cheered approval. But I did notice a few faces that did not seem entirely pleased. Especially among men my uncle's age or older.

⊶ Chapter 11 ⊸

After the match Uncle Haelin lumbered over to the edge of the ring, wincing as he limped. He reached the fence and pulled himself over it with an effort. He grabbed the waterskin and we helped him slide off the lip beyond the fence and onto the floor where we stood. He slid all the way down, until he was seated, his back leaning against the wall of the raised ring floor. Then Uncle Haelin finished the water in the skin and turned to me, "Remember where the public well is, where I sent Arta? Could you go out there and refill this for me?"

"Sure, Uncle." I turned but before I could move more than two paces, a young Andrean cavalry officer snapped at Uncle Haelin, "Quit bleeding on the floor, old timer! You're making a mess!"

An older nobleman who had been nearby glared at the cavalryman but said to us, "There are changing rooms that way that you may use to rest." He pointed out an arched stone doorway.

So first we moved Uncle Haelin down this hall to the first room on the right, which had a simple wooden bench and a large basin with rather dirty water in it. My uncle lay down on the bench before I trotted out, on the mission to get clean water.

With the match over some people remained inside for the next entertainment (which was singing clowns), but others streamed outside to take a break, to use the latrine stalls or get water. Fortunately, I arrived at the public well before too many others did, so I didn't have to wait very long.

When I came back through the tunnel, after dodging some people coming out, just as I arrived back at the threshold of the changing room, I saw locks of red hair leaning over my uncle in the dim light. Once I stepped in, I realized both Arta and her father were there, both redheads, actually, though Alkin's hair had a lot of white in it. Alkin was bandaging my uncle's wounds, which were mostly on his face. He worked with the skill of a man who'd done this sort of thing before. It wasn't until later that I learned he had served in the Dragon War, too—not as a soldier, but as a healer's assistant. He had a kit of various linens and some instruments of bronze, including scissors he used to cut the linen. Arta assisted him. Her face was even paler than her normal complexion, but she did not flinch away from my uncle's bloodiness.

I came close and reached out to hand the waterskin to my uncle, but Alkin took it, "Thank you, young man. I'll use this to clean up Haelin here." Sea sponges lay on the floor nearby and Alkin began rinse them with water from the skin.

"Excuse me, young man, what was your name?" asked Alkin without looking my way.

With my usual "quickness" of speech I began to answer, "Uh…well, I'm…"

"He's Therin," said Arta. "Haelin's nephew. Hi Therin," she added, not looking at me.

"Uh, well, hello, Arta. I guess you–um–must have been in the stands?"

"Yes. I can't believe that count! They totally cheated!"

"It is what it is," said Uncle Haelin.

"What do you mean? It was completely unfair," she sputtered, her face flushing red.

"I mean it cannot be undone. That happens—things happen that cannot be changed. All I can do is hit the next guy harder." My uncle's voice was low. He seemed very old to me at that moment. I'd seen him stagger into the room —three rounds of five minutes seemed to have almost finished him—and he bled, his voice low, the way he sweated, the way the Andrean had dominated him most of the time in the ring. He seemed not only old to me. He seemed broken.

"How long is it until the next match?" asked Lankin.

"One hour from the end of the last," Uncle Haelin said.

"Plenty of time," said Alkin.

My uncle grunted in reply.

"Pardon me," drawled a voice from behind me. My uncle's eyes rounded to the whites and he sat up on the bench. I glanced back. I'm sure my eyes widened too when I saw Guffey standing in the entrance to the room.

"Well, well," said Uncle Haelin, "What can I do for you, High Tournament Official Guffey? Or is that just Match Judge Guffey?"

"The two roles are not incompatible—"

"So you say."

"Well." Guffey spread his hand wide in a gesture that seemed intended to be conciliatory. "Call me what you like. I'm here to be reasonable."

"Reasonable. Very well."

Alkin said, "It's hard to get your face to stop bleeding while you're talking."

"Sorry. But I've got a feeling this won't last long."

"No. I do not believe it will, sir. I've come to make a direct offer. The answer should be a simple yes or no."

"Hmmm. Let me guess—you're here to see if I'm ready to name my accomplices yet?"

Alkin raised an eyebrow when he heard that.

"Well, it would ensure that no matter what happens in the next match, your team will be released. Your boys will be spared." Guffey raised his eyebrows as he made the suggestion.

"Hmmm. Tempting. But no."

"Don't be too hasty, sir. If you are physically unable to complete a second match, you shall not be allowed a third. One of these boys will enter the ring instead. And if I may say so, you don't seem to be in the best condition just now, sir."

"Hmmm. True. But no."

"But sir—"

"That was my final word." Uncle Haelin raised himself to his feet and pulled his sword from his sheath. "Don't make me come over there."

"Wait! Wait!" said Guffey as he retreated out of the room.

"That was easy," muttered my uncle as he plopped back down on the bench.

"Accomplices?" asked Alkin.

"It's a long story. And you want me to stop talking."

So Alkin continued to work on my uncle, prepping him for the next match.

Arta helped, and Elin approached her with his usual boldness. "Show me what you're doing. I'd like to be able to help heal someone." So he and Arta talked, not just about medical things. After a bit, Lankin joined in on their conversation.

I did not join it. I stood off to the side, worried and confused. Praying a little bit to the God under my breath for my uncle to win the next match, because that's what he wanted me to pray. And for some reason, I felt jealous of Elin and Lankin talking to Arta.

But then I noticed how she kept glancing up at me, in spite of talking with my friends. And some part of me felt a little bit happier.

⊣⊢ Chapter 12 ⊨

The crowds booed my uncle again. Again he raised his sword, as if it were a cheer.

In the ring, he looked different than he had in the changing room. He seemed ready to fight. It never occurred to me until years later that perhaps my uncle hid most of his pain from everyone most of the time. I had, unthinking, assumed that all he showed was all he felt.

It was the seventh hour after noon and the sky over the stands had begun to take on hints of the reds and oranges of approaching sunset. The crowds, drunk in a manner of speaking with entertainment (and some of them actually drunk with beer), started booing when the announcer had bellowed through his coppery cone, "And again, in another substitution of the same contestant, the Mountaineer team has elected to—." Some time passed before he was able to continue.

After he managed to finish my uncle's introduction, I saw another dark-haired Andrean enter the ring, this one also looking as if he may have also been a kinsman of Lankin's former opponent. Though perhaps not as close a relative.

A different swordmaster stood outside the ring fence and he gestured the announcer to come over to him. Once there, he cupped his hands over the ear of the tall announcer and spoke into it. I couldn't hear him but I doubt that was because he whispered—the crowd noise still rumbled too loud for that. The announcer turned back to the crowd, waiving his left hand downward with fingers spread, motioning them to quiet down as he thundered through the cone, "GENTLEmen and ladies, we have a special announcement. Evvan Javon-Galstaff will not compete in this match." A shocked hush fell over the crowd, like a collective gasp. Now that the announcer had their full attention, he stood in silence for a bit before continuing, the upturned corners of his mouth and his alert posture as if ready to spring, spoke of him relishing that moment, where everyone was eager to hear his next words.

The Andrean in the ring snapped his head back toward his own swordmaster, obviously shocked to hear this as much as the people in the stands. It seemed no one had consulted him.

"INstead, in a special substitution, the contestant for this match will be my crown prince and yours, Javon Rory-Galstaff!"

Son, I don't know to this day for certain why the Andreans chose to substitute the prince into this second match. Perhaps it was because my uncle's plan had come too close to working in the first. And perhaps they felt certain he would not be able to knock out the prince.

Whatever the reason, the crowds who had been booing in discontent roared their approval. Perhaps that was reason enough—to give the people a reason to celebrate.

Rory-Galstaff entered the ring, raised his hand and waived at his adoring public. He smiled but he seemed distracted somehow. Or some similar emotion, something less than genuinely pleased. I've never known why.

His clothing was the same as the other Andreans I'd seen, black, close-fitting chain; tall, soft boots; shiny, elite shield; long, silvery sword. But his shoulder-length locks of golden blond hair made him seem entirely different. Perhaps that's why he was such a favorite of the crowds. That, and his place in line for the Andrean throne, and thus, for the eventual, future leadership of the entire Western Bond.

My uncle looked over at the prince with his eyebrows scrunched together. I noticed the leather strap connecting his sword to his wrist was back in place. So clearly he wasn't planning to throw the sword again. Maybe that's something he believed would only work once.

Applause sounded from the other side of the raised fighting ring and we saw people who had been seated in that direction stand up, but the ring itself blocked us from seeing why. The crowd on that side of the ring broke out into spontaneous applause and the prince, turning that way, made a formal half bow. Four Andrean Cavalrymen wearing the purple band of the Elite Guard started coming around to our side of the ring, two on the left and two on the right. Lankin said to Elin, "Go over there and figure out what's going on." Elin had already moved two steps that direction before Lankin finished the sentence.

After the applause died down, the announcer blared through the cone, "Gentlemen and ladies, we welcome to the floor of the finals arena His Imperial Majesty, Agger Rory-Galstaff the Third!" Now the entire arena took their feet and applauded. I found even my hands clapping.

But soon enough the cheering died down and Guffey flipped the hourglass and the prince and my uncle came out of their corners. My uncle did not change his fighting stance in the slightest, even though it had been proved not to work well before. He also circled the prince as before, his eyes searching him for weakness in quick glances that covered the length and breadth of his body. The prince, on the other hand, looked my uncle directly in the eye and seemed to rely on peripheral vision for everything else. He looked supremely confident. And very deadly against my old, limping uncle.

"The king is watching the match from the other side of the ring!" announced Elin as he ran up to us.

"We heard, everyone did," remarked Lankin dryly.

And then Uncle Haelin suddenly lunged forward, his shield high, his sword swinging low. The prince sidestepped twice fast while seeming unhurried, my uncle's surge passing him. He pivoted awkwardly on his bad leg to face the prince. And in a single blur of movement, the tip of the prince's blade reached out and flicked away the end of my uncle's nose. Blood spurted and ran down my uncle's face, like before. But worse this time, because the soft part of my uncle's nose, the entire thing, dangled from a piece of skin.

Uncle Haelin, his eyes tearing so much water flowed down the sides of his face to mingle with his spurting blood, stepped backward and raised the shield, covering himself as he retreated. The prince did not pursue him or press the attack, though in terms of good tactics, from what I now know, he should have.

Uncle Haelin released his sword, letting it dangle by the strap and touched his face with his right hand. His probing fingers found the dangling end of his nose. Then he made a fist around it and yanked it the rest of the way off. And then threw it at the prince.

Rory-Galstaff flinched away from this bloody missile, even though he just as easily could have blocked it with his shield. Uncle Haelin thrust his body forward at the moment of the flinch, his shield close to his chest, clanging hard into the prince's shield, staggering him two paces backward. His sword still dangling, he followed up with a hard right cross punch over the prince's shield that connected on the point of the prince's cleft chin with a loud clack. The prince stumbled back until he impacted into the ring fence, the whites of his eyes showing in dazed shock.

The crowds roared loud boos corrupted with some cheering. My ear noted a girl's voice among the cheers, and I glanced into the stands and in the fourth row up saw a red-head girl on her feet, bellowing approval, both fists raised over her head. Arta.

More cheers roared now and I snapped back to see a prince off the fence, backing fast into the center of the ring, shaking his head to clear it. My uncle followed after him, his sword back in his hand, but now the prince used his longer weapon to keep my uncle at bay. He stabbed and retreated, stabbed and retreated, pivoting and shuffling fast to avoid being trapped in the corner. The prince no longer looked unhurried. His eyes wide, his face white, his steps a bit awkward as if still dazed, the prince nonetheless easily avoided my uncle's repeated attacks. And every one of his thrusts into Uncle Haelin's chest or shoulder or neck earned him a point. Uncle Haelin had earned no points at all—the punch did not count as a sword impact.

By the end of the round the prince regained most of his poise. And my uncle's limp had grown noticeably worse. He breathed hard and had slowed down. Splotches of his blood covered the ring floor and his face was forever marred at the nose. It was painful to watch how his power had been picked apart, how weak and old he seemed. The first round ended with a score of twenty-two to zero.

But other than the one attack on the nose, Prince Rory-Galstaff hadn't cut any part of my uncle's face. The stabs and quick slashes he'd made to the neck and chest and shoulder were all not only legal but ordinary blows, all blocked by Uncle Haelin's armor.

This time the quick between-round show featured a heat magician, burning up wooden arrows fired at him before they reached him, the entertainers ignoring blood on the floor that servants with towels came forward to mop up.

Uncle Haelin stood hunched over in his corner pouring water from the skin around the mess of blood around his mouth. Elin started to climb up to help him but one of the Elite Guardsmen, who had posted themselves all around the ring, pulled him down roughly.

"It's alright, son," said my uncle to calm Elin, whose face was red with an outrage that seemed about to launch him into a fight with a soldier of the one of the most famous units in the entire Western Bond—who also happened to be around twice Elin's size.

After a bit of self-cleanup and gulping down water, my uncle began to loosen the chainmail links around his neck. Then he pulled back the hood of chainmail and quickly undid the inner leather hood drawstring and loosened it. And then he pulled it off himself, removing the thick leather that protected him from the kinds of cuts to the head and neck I had learned to fear.

"What are you doing?" called out Lankin.

"It's chaffing me," answered my uncle. His mouth opened to say more but removing the leather inner hood had taken up most of the break between rounds. The performers finished their routine and whatever my uncle would have said got lost in waves of applause. Uncle Haelin turned back around toward the center of the ring, his neck and head now completely uncovered.

Round two began where it had left off. The crowds should have booed, I suppose; it wasn't thrilling to watch a middle-aged man limp forward in attacks that achieved nothing against a blond god of Andrean nobility who collected points each time. But they maintained a respectful hush, for the sake of the prince, I suppose.

"Come on, prince," huffed my uncle. "Is that all you're gonna do?" He swung his sword in yet another failed swipe at Rory-Galstaff's legs, who danced aside. "Where's the training for war in that? Where's the style?"

Two quick jabs, two more points, and the prince answered, "I'm winning."

"Are you? Say, did your father ever tell you about the Dragon War?"

The prince didn't answer.

"Did he ever mention the time his griffin's wings were broken? And he crashed into a sewage trench on the side of a road, covered in brown water?" Uncle Haelin swung his shield this time and followed with a slow swipe of the sword. The prince easily dodged the moves and in a backhand swipe to the mountaineer's shoulder earned another point.

"Did he tell you that Kung Tzu himself came after him? Him, and other dragons? Riding on the great gold dragon, the type that breathes fire forever?" Two pings of the sword tip on chainmail lodged two more points for the prince.

"Did he tell you Fourth Battalion Iron Mountain advanced to save him? When the Elite Guard ran for their lives?"

Uncle Haelin swung and missed with a grunt. "Your daddy in a sewage ditch. And men like me saved him. He was crying like a baby, did you know that?"

The prince slashed off the tip of my uncle's left ear. A few voices cheered but I still heard him reply, "Take it back!"

Blood flowed down the side of Uncle Haelin's head, but he ignored it. "I can't take it back. Your daddy, in terror, saved by men like me." The prince slashed off the top of his other ear.

"You knew already, didn't you? You knew your father is weak. And so are you." Uncle Haelin laughed in what was almost a bark, so unlike his normal laughter. The prince slashed twice across my uncle's forehead, once vertically, once horizontally, forming a bleeding +. My uncle didn't even flinch.

"Stop it! Or I don't care what the general says we owe your unit—I *will* kill you!"

"Am I supposed to be afraid of you, kid? I've stood in battle against a *dragon*." Then in a roar of effort my uncle threw his shield at him (when he'd loosened it from his arm, I didn't know). The black mountain-forged metal spun in the air, and a glimmer of my imagination dreamed of it catching the prince in the chin, knocking him out, my uncle victorious.

But my uncle hadn't even aimed for the head. He'd hurled the shield straight at the prince's shield. It clanged loudly and Rory-Galstaff flinched backwards. Uncle Haelin followed up with a sword swing that probably was as fast as he could manage. And the prince lashed out with his sword.

His first blow cut the left side of my uncle's mouth two inches wider than the God had meant it to be. The second flicked into his left eye and clear fluid gushed out of it.

His third hit Uncle Haelin below the right ear, at the external jugular vein. Not a complete severing, but a thick flow of blood surged out. The crowds roared their approval.

Uncle Haelin laughed now, his real, ordinary warm laugh, but with his left eye clamped shut, his mangled mouth wincing in pain in spite of the sound coming out of it. Dark blood flowed down his neck and from his face in an ominous stream.

The prince took off the rest of his left ear and then the rest of the right. He made quick little slashes more times across Uncle Haelin's face than I could count. Who didn't even try to block or dodge the strikes. My uncle fell to his right knee. Some people in the stands were cheering, but not many. Not even the Andreans wanted to watch this sort of butchery.

The Andrean swordmaster was shouting at the prince, who finally heard him and retreated. What he said at first I didn't hear, but I remember him yelling at that point, "One blow! One blow is all you have!"

Rory-Galstaff turned back, walking slowly. An ordinary walk, not the pacing of his ring fighting style. Uncle Haelin turned his head upward toward the sky, his one uninjured eye seeking One beyond the dark blue above the circle of the arena. Both hands held his sword, loosely now, but still upright.

The prince, breathing harder than he had before in the match, took his one blow on the left side of my uncle's neck, under the ear, at the other jugular vein. With this gush of blood, the vein completely severed, Uncle Haelin collapsed, face forward, onto the ring floor.

Elin leapt up onto the side of the ring. The Elite Guardsman did not try to stop him. Lankin followed and then I came afterward. With effort we rolled my uncle over.

He was still bloody and there was a lot of blood nearby. Puddles on either side of him, still dark and thick. But his bleeding had stopped. His jaw lay loose, opening his mouth into what almost seemed a grin. The skin of his neck was very pale, bluish even, though his marred face was much more red. His eyes, even the cut one, lay open, the muscles around them relaxed, as if at peace. And even the sliced eye still seemed to be staring upward.

Some part of me registered a voice shouting through a coppery cone, "Victory by incapacitation, your prince and mine, Prince Javon Rory-Galstaff!" And the crowds cheered, though not quite so loudly as when the prince was first introduced.

A moaning sob escaped my lips and tears flowed down Elin's face, though he made no noise. Lankin had tears in his eyes, but his face flushed red with anger at the same time.

For some reason, I looked up to a spot I knew in the stands, in the fourth row from the bottom. Arta had her head in her hands, weeping in full, so hard that water flowed from between her fingers as if poured, her father with an arm across her back, trying to comfort her. And I felt so much worse, seeing her weep like that. It was the worst moment I'd ever experienced.

Part Two

The Bond of the Oath

⚔ Chapter 1 ⚔

Alkin took my uncle's body. He paid for a marker and buried him in the graveyard reserved for Dragon War veterans in the city. He mentioned some trouble came from that, because it had been mainly filled with *Andrean* war veterans. But he made it work somehow. I don't know how exactly, because I only heard about the trouble he had years later.

Most of us boys wanted to take the body home with us. But that wasn't possible. It would have been worm-eaten long before we got home.

Early in the morning of the day after my uncle's death, the wagonmasters loaded us onto the vehicles that were their livelihood and rolled on out. Uncle Haelin's death had released us. The tournament wasn't over yet—Koto advanced to the final against the prince, since there was no longer any permissible "correction" in the rules that allowed him to be excluded. But seeing the end wasn't important to any of us anymore. Not even Elin.

The oxen pulled us along at a slow pace out of the city. It took us well into the afternoon before we'd cleared first the summer palisade, then the summer festival camps, then finally the villages and farm fields closest to the Andrean capital.

As the sun began to go down, the wagons finally on the open road, Lankin jumped off the end of the first rolling platform, a leather sack casually draped over his shoulder. Elin followed him and walked by his side. They strolled back to the second wagon, where I'd placed myself specifically because I didn't want to talk to them.

"Come on, Therin, walk with us," said Lankin.

Boys hopping out of the rigs and walking alongside was common enough, since we could outpace the oxen without much effort. (I don't believe you've ever ridden on an ox cart, but they really are that slow. If it hadn't been for the food and battle gear they pulled along, there wouldn't have been any advantage to using them at all.)

"Please," said Elin.

I sighed and hopped down to the ground. "What do you want?"

"Wait a bit." Lankin kept his pace slow, making sure we soon trailed the wagons and the other boys. After unwanted ears had slipped out of range, he spoke again, "We want to talk to you about your uncle."

"What about him?" As I asked as I wiped new spot of wetness from my eyes. Which surprised me, because I didn't know my body could shed any more tears.

"I've talked to Elin and we agree. We need to avenge him." I snorted in derision, surprised at myself how strong my reaction was. "And how are we supposed to do that? What are we going to do, sneak into the capital and assassinate the prince? The royal family *only* has hundreds of bodyguards. Not to mention the entire Andrean military."

"No, no," replied Elin. "We shall challenge him to honorable combat."

This time I actually laughed—an angry, mean laugh, unlike I'd ever laughed before. "Did you notice the little thing where he killed my uncle? And my uncle could outfight any of us? So how is getting ourselves killed going to avenge anyone?"

"We're not fools, Therin," said Lankin.

"You coulda fooled me!"

"Therin," Lankin said in a raspy half-whisper. "Not so loud. We don't want the wagonmasters to know what we're planning."

"And what is that exactly?" I replied. For the first time since hopping off the wagon I really *looked* at my companions, studying their faces, trying to anticipate whatever in the world they could be thinking.

"You're right, of course," said Elin. "We need more training. That's the plan."

Looking at my face, which must have shown bewilderment, Lankin quickly added. "In more detail, what we're planning to do is sneak away from the wagons and find someone at the tournament who will take us in as sword apprentices. We'll swear by an oath that we will study swordsmanship day and night until we're sure we've mastered it. And then, once we are swordmasters ourselves, only then we will return to the city and challenge the prince to honorable combat. If one of us should fall to him, the others will fight him in turn, until all of us have either fulfilled our oath or died trying."

"Become swordmasters? That will take years."

Elin nodded soberly. "Yes."

"We can't just…disappear for years on end. What will our families think?"

"Therin," said Lankin in a low stern voice, "your uncle died for *us*. We were the ones who were supposed to be in that ring. How can we live with ourselves if we don't do something about that? How can the death of the man who saved our lives go unpunished?"

I hesitated. Something seemed very wrong with what he was telling me, but I couldn't find the words to say why.

His eyes narrowed as he watched me think and his voice grew rougher. "Didn't you love your uncle at all, Therin? He was part of *your* family."

"Of course I loved him." I found myself both angry and blinking back tears. "But I love my mother, too, and I don't want her to worry about me."

"Well, you can't see her. You know why? Because you are dead."

"W-what?"

"You are dead, or at least you deserve to be. You are dead and the only way you can win back your life is to repay what was done to your uncle. Once you've done that, then you will have earned the right to return to your family. To see your mother. But not now."

"We will send them a message," said Elin. "Once we find a swordmaster to train us. So they don't worry so much."

I thought over the plan as we slowly walked side by side, trailing the other wagons, the sun setting at that moment. It was then, even though other reasons mattered to me as well, I decided I couldn't let it seem like I loved my uncle less than two other boys not even related to him.

"All right," I said in a low voice. "I'll do it."

Elin grinned and slapped me on the back. But Lankin frowned. "You have to swear it."

"I swear."

"No, the full oath."

"I swear…in the name of the God of our ancestors, the Sky Father, I swear to get sword training with Elin and Lankin. And…and to kill the prince," I stammered.

Lankin wasn't satisfied. "Say I swear to stay away from my home and family."

"I swear to stay away from my home and family."

"To do nothing else but train until my Uncle Haelin is avenged or I die trying to avenge him."

I repeated his words. "So help me the God."

"So help me the God." And I added on my own initiative, "So let it be."

⊷ Chapter 2 ⊷

The wagonmasters had already said they would not make camp the first night because there were too many robbers in close vicinity of the city. Before halting to rest, they had planned to go into the early hours of the morning that first day until they arrived at a free forage area by a lake that Malinkin knew well.

So as the sun went down, the three of us simply turned around and walked back towards the city. Of course we must have been missed after the wagons made camp in the morning, but it had been my uncle who had made sure where every boy was before, not the wagonmasters. If they called out for us or tried to find us, it was long after we left —we never heard or saw any sign of it.

As we began moving along the dark road back to the tournament grounds, Lankin opened the leather bag. It proved larger and contained more items than I had realized. He handed me and Elin unsharpened training swords from within. And he strapped onto his own body the belt of the same black, partially sharpened sword my uncle had carried into the ring.

"In case there really are robbers on the road."

"I don't suppose you packed any food, did you?" I asked.

"A little. What, are you hungry already?"

"I will be."

Andrea has warmer weather than our mountains, but the night began to get cold long before we were anywhere near the palisade. In the relative cold of the night, the stars there were nowhere near as clear as they are in our province, because hundreds of villages burned thousands of fires that raised up enough smoke to make a difference. The air smelled of wood smoke and burning dried cattle dung (which doesn't stink as bad as you might imagine).

The half-full moon lit the road well enough for us to follow it. As our eyes adjusted, it was bright enough for us to see moving shapes some distance away from us. But the smoke of the fires gave the moon a reddish hue.

From time to time I saw plenty of shapes moving across the road as we walked, about equally from the right to left as the left to right. I couldn't usually tell what the shapes were but sometimes they were close enough to reveal a farmer herding a cow or a mother holding the hands of children, or other familiar peasant figures walking across the road from one village or one part of a village to another. The Andrean peasants didn't carry the lamps our people would have carried to find their way in the darkness, at least not when the moon was out, and they didn't go to bed as early. Some of the village houses leaked a bit of light from the inside, especially at first, but less and less as the night went on.

Once, three horsemen in armor passed us from behind (we cleared off the road when we heard them coming), carrying bright lamps with them, but that was the only time we saw anyone traveling the road that night, other than us of course.

I clutched my fairly useless sword's handle as I walked along in the sheer darkness of the partly obscured moon, without any other significant light of any kind, with the strange moving shapes I've described, into the growing coldness filling me with a powerful sense of dread. For fear of seeming like a coward or a baby, I didn't express my anxiety to Elin or Lankin. Instead I clutched my sword handle and kept moving without saying a word. Elin and Lankin kept their silence as well. It's funny but we didn't even discuss stopping anywhere to rest.

After many hours of walking, a dark shape on the horizon began to draw closer. Its serrated edge took an odd irregular bite out of the star-lit sky. "See, it's the palisade," whispered Elin.

Before I could answer, a shape stepped onto the road that for the past several miles had become cobblestone instead of packed dirt. "Well, hello," said a man's voice. "What do we have here?"

"Don't answer," said Lankin at the same moment Elin said, "Travelers."

"Ah," said the man, "Don't answerlers. That explains a lot." Then he laughed. The stone wall of a house near the road blocked the light from the moon, now low on the horizon, from falling on the stranger. His shape blurred into the darkness, so it was evident something was there, but what exactly and even how big I could not see.

I could not see him, but I could smell the mead on his breath from more than ten feet away.

"Shoo off, you drunk," said Lankin.

"I will. Once you give me all of your gold."

"We aren't carrying any," I said, my teeth chattering with a mixture of cold and fear.

"Whatever you have that's valuable then."

"Let me warn you, sir! We are armed," said Elin.

"Very good. Give me your swords. They should be worth something."

Lankin and Elin pulled their blades free from their belts. Hastily I followed their example as Lankin said, "You'll have to take them from us, you old drunk."

The man laughed hard. "I'm not that old." He stepped into the moonlight and now I could see a bit of him, his hair black like the night, his limbs and chest covered in some form of leather armor. A sword on his belt he pulled with the unmistakable scraping of metal coming out a metal scabbard. The blade stretched long and thin, like an Andrean blade, and it glinted with reflections of dim moonbeams.

His silhouette outlined him as a medium height, very broad-shouldered fellow, but how much of that was actually him and how much was his armor and equipment, I couldn't have said. I had no armor other than my shirtsleeves and no sword other than a practice blade. Not much better than a stick–I had my doubts at the moment that it would cut through water.

The man struck an erect pose almost like the Andrean fighters.

Uncle Haelin's last bout washed through my mind. We were all going to end up just like him. I tried to put that out of my head, but the same few scenes replayed over and over. My hands shook, wobbling the sword's tip almost at hand length. I couldn't see Lankin or Elin clearly, and if their teeth were chattering, I couldn't hear them over my own.

"I'm warning you, we were taught by the best in our village, a veteran of the Dragon War." Lankin tried to sound threatening, but he only managed to sound slightly braver than me.

"Then you weren't listening." The moonlight on the blade shifted slightly.

I hopped backward and gripped my practice sword tight.

The man snickered. "He should have taught you the value of your lives." He turned toward Elin and Lankin.

I could have attacked him in that moment. With his attention diverted, I could have stepped in and struck his head with the unsharpened sword, but my feet must have grown roots into the cobblestone road. Bile rose in my throat. I swallowed hard.

"Nothing you're carrying is worth your life." The man darted forward faster and more steadily than the mead on his breath should have allowed.

His thin blade lashed out like a rock viper twice. Lankin cried out and stumbled backward a few steps. Elin's attempt at a parry came too late. He, too, gasped and stepped back. Not until later did I find out that both of them had shallow cuts on their cheeks. Painful, yes, but not threatening.

I clutched my useless sword with both hands and quivered.

Elin growled and rushed back into the fight. Metal struck metal and he cried out again.

"Humph. He also would have taught you to never attack in anger." The man's voice had a built-in sneer.

"We're done playing, old man." The growl in Lankin's voice told me he was about to do something we would all regret.

"A pity. I don't look forward to killing boys." All sense of amusement was gone from the man's voice. Even some of his drunken slur seemed to fade with that comment, though I might have imagined it.

One thing I knew for sure. I couldn't lose my best friend and my uncle in so short a time.

"Then teach us!" My exclamation surprised even me.

"Therin!" Lankin shrieked at the same time Elin yelled, "Are you crazy?"

"Teach us how to do better," I said, a little calmer than a few moments before.

"This drunk?" Lankin aimed his sword at the man.

I lowered my unsharpened sword. "Look, he's better than all of us even when he's drunk. We could learn from him. Then when we're that good, we can go find a real swordmaster."

The man laughed, and I heard more derision than amusement. "I am a real swordmaster, boy, but why would I want to teach you?"

"Because m—" I started.

Lankin shushed me. "We took an oath to become swordmasters."

"Why?" the man asked.

"That's our business, sir." Elin pressed his fingers to his face then tipped his hand toward the moon.

I can still feel the tears that burned in my eyes when I thought about "our business." Even now, so many years later. Never mind the ridiculous platitudes. There are some wounds even time won't completely heal. That's not weakness—that's reality. Anyone who says differently is hiding from himself or from you.

The man lowered his sword slightly and relaxed his guard without seeming any less dangerous for the effort. "You boys are from Iron Mountain Province." It wasn't a question. "I can hear that in your accent. I even think I know who you are, which gives me a good guess about your 'business.'" His voice dropped to a whisper, and the only part I could make out clearly was "…shame that was…" He sighed and filled the air with the odor of stale mead. "I don't teach for free."

"We'll do work for you," I blurted out, desperation replacing the fear of a few minutes ago. "Chores, anything."

Both of my companions hissed my name.

The man laughed. "Well, that might be worth a bit of something. You do what I say and when I say, got that?" he said. "Now put down your swords."

I put my unsharpened sword down and glared at Lankin and Elin. "Come on!"

"I don't know about this, Therin," Elin muttered, but a moment later, his sword was on the ground.

Lankin growled his disgust, but set his sword down, too. At the time, it seemed like a brilliant move to stay alive, but in hindsight, perhaps I should have been more careful. Maybe we could have just given up our swords and left.

⚔ Chapter 3 ⊨

We camped that night set a ways back from the road but close enough to hear carts rolling and men walking on the cobblestone path. Activity never seemed to end altogether, not even in the darkness. A stand of dense shrubs and scraggly trees blocked the light of the campfire we made. The modest fire only did a little to chase off the chill of the night and our exhaustion.

Ombree–for that was the name of the swordsman we encountered–came and went from the fire. Each time he stepped away, he told us to stay put. When he came back, he usually had a grin on his face. Once, he had food, and when he'd finished eating, he gave us the rest: half a loaf of not quite stale bread and a couple pieces of jerky. A couple other times, he had a bottle or skin of something that smelled of alcohol, which he promptly emptied into his own stomach. In the flickering light of the fire, I could see our new teacher more clearly. From his voice and the stench of old mead, I had expected a man whose girth matched his height, a balding ruffian with ragged teeth. To my surprise, Ombree had a fair face, dark eyes, and wavy, dark hair. He was a heavy, broad-shouldered man, somewhat like Uncle Haelin, but not nearly so tall. Ombree's ornate but practical leather armor was imprinted with swirls that mirror-imaged across the center. At the time, I had no idea how much a suit of such intricate leather armor would cost. I now know, and can tell you that Ombree made an impressive living as a highwayman.

As the fire dwindled and traffic on the cobblestone road faded, Ombree went into a small but well-constructed tent. We boys weren't invited, and there probably wouldn't have been space for us anyway, so we slept under the stars for the few remaining hours of the night, shivering in the chill as the fire waned. Shivering but not quite comfortable enough with each other to bundle together for warmth. Twice, Elin wandered off and came back with some sticks to toss onto the embers.

Morning came and was long gone before Ombree left his tent dressed in his armor and carrying a satchel with a long shoulder strap. He pointed at me first and then at Lankin and Elin. "Tend my horse. You two, strike the tent. Be quick about it. We have a long way to go." He sat near what was left of the fire and ate dry sausage, cheese, and hardtack.

I darted over to a palomino hobbled nearby. I'd never taken care of a horse before. They were even less common in our province during my boyhood than they are now, son. "Uh, excuse me, sir? What do I do?"

Ombree strode over, annoyance marking his face. But his voice came clear and calm, "Take that brush. Use it on the animal, across the back especially. Take the saddle you see there. Put it on the back. Apply the strap underneath and cinch it by looping it tight." He continued eating as I worked, seeming to pay no attention to anything I did. Until he interjected, "No, the cinch must be tighter. A horse will pooch out its belly to keep the saddle from fitting properly.

But the master must insist the beast serve him whether it likes it or not. No, tighter!"

And he showed me how to gain more leverage with my foot as I pulled the strap. Then he went back to his leisurely consumption of food. I had the horse brushed and saddled before Lankin and Elin had finished with the tent. Ombree inspected my work and made an unnecessary adjustment before he handed me a couple palm-sized pieces of hardtack and wedge of cheese. Lankin and Elin finished folding up the tent.

Ombree rolled his eyes. "Is there *anything* you Iron Mountain boys know how to do? Never dealt with a tent, have you."

"No, sir." Elin studied his boots.

"If you wanted it a certain way—" Lankin didn't get to finish.

Ombree grabbed Lankin by the shirt collar and lifted him up onto his toes. With a grin and a light-hearted tone that would have seemed friendly under other circumstances, he said, "Watch your mouth, boy." He shoved Lankin back.

He staggered back several steps before falling on his rear. I jumped up from my spot and rushed to Lankin's side. Elin got there first and helped Lankin back to his feet.

"Watch. I won't show you again." Ombree shook out the tent and folded it into a long strip before tightly rolling it and tying a leather strap around the middle.

That was the first time I'd seen a tent packed for travel, and it's the way I still do it. Funny what things stay with you through life.

Ombree gave Lankin and Elin each a piece of hardtack, but there was no cheese or sausage left, so I shared part of my cheese with them. We were on our way shortly after. Ombree rode his horse while the rest of us jogged. He kept the horse at a slow pace most of the way, but we still had to either jog or walk fast to keep up. Asking him to slow down earned a derisive laugh and–only sometimes–a short rest.

For the most part, the trip was uneventful. Each day played out just like the one before and the one after. We were on our fifth evening of travel when we rounded a bend and came across a large, leafy log blocking our way. Ombree slowed and chuckled.

"Well, boys, looks like an obstruction in the road. I guess we'll have to stop for a moment and clear it." He spoke too loudly for normal conversation and tried with only limited success to contain a smirk as he dismounted his horse and handed me the reigns. "Let's be quick. This sure is a lonely stretch of road."

We took two steps toward the branch when a cluster of five men in dark clothes stepped out. Black bandanas hid all but their eyes.

"Hand over your money!" the lead bandit demanded.

Ombree looked him over and snorted. "You really don't want to do this. It'd be the biggest mistake of your pitifully short lives."

The lead bandit drew an old, heavy, iron sword that looked remarkably well-kept in spite of its age. The others were armed with clubs and hammers. "I said hand it over!"

"This is your last warning. Quit this while you can still scamper back to the rock you crawled out from under." Ombree motioned for us to stay put and took a few steps closer.

I looked at Lankin's and Elin's still-healing faces and then back at the bandits. Ombree had been drunk when he'd so easily overpowered us. How much more deadly would he be when sober?

Lankin nudged me in the ribs with his elbow. His smile stretched from ear to ear. "This should be funny."

Funny wasn't a word I would have used. In a way, I looked forward to seeing a demonstration of Ombree's skills, but at the same time, I remembered Uncle Haelin's telling me over and over to take no joy in the misfortune of others. Judging from the ragged looks of these bandits, even I could tell that not a one of them was anywhere close Ombree's caliber.

The swordmaster drew his Andrean blade and patted the satchel hanging from his shoulder. The contents clinked and jingled. "If you want it, come get it."

The bandits came forward one step at a time, fanning out to hit our master from multiple sides. Ombree, looking bored, stood still and shifted his weight to one leg. My guts knotted. I knew the swordmaster was skilled, but he let the group of bandits come within range, making it seem like they'd overpower him with their numbers—at least from my angle it looked like they were in range—without doing anything.

The lead bandit drew back and swung like taking an axe to a tree. Three others swung at the same time with grunts and yells. Ombree deflected his opponent's attack with quick, precise snaps of the sword, leapt back, blows missing him as stabbed at hands and arms swinging weapons. Hammers and clubs dropped with cries of pain.

The lead bandit arced the sword up for Ombree's head, but the swordmaster had the parry in place in plenty of time. I expected him to strike the man dead, but Ombree let him recover.

The swordmaster smiled as if playing with children. "Care to try again?"

Eyes narrowed, the man reared back for an overhead chop, his companions lingering back this time. As the sword descended, Ombree brought his sword up parallel to the ground then pushed the iron sword aside. I expected him to stop with the parry this time, but the swordmaster continued his motion and brought the sword around in an elegant sweep that would have cleaved the bandit's head from his shoulders. Except he slapped the man in the neck with the flat of his sword.

The man hopped backward. Then he pressed Ombree's sword aside as he advanced. Ombree stepped back to free his sword then drove in his own cloud-to-ground chop, straight towards the man's shoulder, faster than he could block or parry.

Ombree pulled up more than a foot short. "I'll grow bored with this soon. You should leave before that happens." His eyes of his companions nervously shifted back and forth over their bandanas.

If I had been that bandit, I might have turned and fled, knowing I was outclassed. This man, however, stepped back, shook himself and waded back in. "Come on!" he shouted to his companions, who made no move to help him.

Ombree launched an attack of his own. The silvery Andrean blade flashed out and back like a bolt of lightning, leaving a narrow, short cut on the man's cheek. The parry arrived after Ombree had already backed away. My eyes were drawn to the same marks on Elin and Lankin.

Ombree sighed. "That's your last warning. Seek a less deadly target or end your fledgling career now." He drew his sword back, shook the blade, and screamed a battle cry.

The man turned and ran into the brush, his friends following him, one of them pausing long enough to pick up a small pouch.

As Ombree sheathed his sword, he laughed and turned to us. "Clear the road and let's be on our way."

We darted on ahead. I took hold of the heavier end of the log and waited for the other two to find somewhere to get a grip on the other side. In spite of its size, the felled tree weighed less than I thought, and we soon had it moved off the road. By the time the way was clear, Ombree was back on his horse, and we resumed our trip.

We passed through the broad open spaces and forests of the Midlands, on occasion meeting Midlanders with their distinctive drawl. Eventually we passed to the drylands just east of the Western Mountains, which towered higher, and yes, more rugged than the mountains I'd known from our province. We didn't know where we were going until we arrived in Tsillis, but the days were all the same. We traveled generally northwest past nightfall and set up camp back from the road a ways, but within hearing distance. We went around villages and towns instead of passing through them. We boys took care of camp chores—collecting firewood, tending the horse, raising the tent, and starting the fire—while Ombree disappeared and came back several times, usually bearing provisions or other things he tucked into his satchel without showing us. Sometimes, especially when we were near a town, he'd be gone all night and wouldn't return to us until late morning.

There wasn't any sword training, but that was just as well. The travel alone wore me out. I was often the first asleep and the last boy up.

Finally, we came into Tsillis, the city on the bay of the Western Ocean, filled with merchants and the bustle of more people than I'd ever seen before in my life. Other than in Andrea. I'd heard stories, rumors really, about the kinds of people in the region. There were dark-haired Andreans, dark-skinned Southlanders, and fair-complexioned people from the Midlands and northern reaches, even a few from the Iron Mountains. Passing through the city and seeing the variety of people reminded me of the tournament again, which did little more than firm up my resolve to avenge my uncle's death. In my mind I confirmed the oath that Prince Rory-Galstaff would die for what he'd done.

The buildings of the city were well-constructed from white stone and finely crafted timber. The city smelled of waste and the sea, and to this day, the smell of the saltwater conjures up images of Tsillis. It was late in the evening when we first entered the city, so all the shops we passed were closed except a tavern at the north edge. The shrill sound of a piper and the boisterous rumble of the tavern's patrons carried on the sea breeze. Ombree stopped, tied up the horse at a post and stepped inside. Lankin and Elin followed. I stepped inside and froze. There were dozens of people in the tavern, twice as many men as women. The air reeked of sweat, burnt meat and grain, and old ale.

Ombree swaggered up to the bar, dug into his satchel and produced a handful of coins. "Whatever you've got for dinner for me and the boys. And a round of mead on me!"

The tavern erupted in a cheer.

Lankin and Elin followed Ombree. Lankin turned and gestured for me to come along. With a deliberate effort, I pried first one foot then the other off the sawdust floor and joined them.

A woman in a short red dress with a tight bodice wrapped her arms around Ombree. "I missed you on your long trip, baby. Who are these poor boys? I haven't seen them before."

"Sword students." He reached into the satchel and took out a gold ring with a red stone. "Picked this up for you on the way, honey."

She slid it onto her finger and admired it before kissing Ombree while his hands wandered over her body. My cheeks grew warm, and I looked away before anyone else could notice.

Exactly what happened after that, I couldn't say. Food came, consisting of loose, burnt-tasting soup of mostly over-boiled grain. I ate slowly and watched my bowl more than the surroundings.

Many mugs of ale and mead later, Ombree pushed away from the bar and waved to everyone. "Pleasure for you to see me!"

Several of the patrons chuckled, and a black-haired Andrean, in the midst of his laughter shouted, "Get out of here, you old drunk."

"After you." Ombree gestured toward the door with a flourish.

The Andrean turned his attention back to a blond woman who smiled at Ombree when her man wasn't looking. Ombree smiled in return and winked, but instead of lingering to see what might come of that (as I eventually learned he normally would do), Ombree swaggered out the door. He took his horse by the reins and led us out of the town, past the hills that ringed the city. Thankfully, the wind was across our path, which helped with the stench of mead surrounding him. He turned up a path to a stone and timber house.

The house was dark, but Ombree left his horse at the door and entered. "Take care of my horse. Start a fire if you want one. Get some sleep. Your training starts tomorrow."

We divided up the chores. Elin got the fire going, and Lankin cleared space around the hearth for us to sleep while I found the stable around back and got the horse settled. A red and gray blanket that seemed too fine for a horse was draped over the low wall of the stall. I tossed it over the palomino's back and returned to the house. The other two were already asleep by the fire. I stretched out in the open space they left for me, but I don't think I slept much that night.

My thoughts whirled, recalling my uncle's laughter and the tournament battles he fought on our behalf. The oath I'd taken came to mind, and now I wondered if I'd been foolish to swear such a thing. But what did it matter now? I'd sworn an oath before the God.

Mixed with those thoughts came a giddy excitement. We would start our training tomorrow. I wanted to impress our new teacher with how well I could fight. At the same time, Uncle Haelin's opinion of how raw our fighting skills came to mind. Would Ombree laugh us off his property?

With those thoughts chasing each other through my mind and Ombree snoring loud enough to crumble the Iron Mountains, what sleep I got that night was fitful at best. Morning came, but I tried to ignore it.

Lankin grabbed my shoulder and whispered, "Come on. You know he'll want us to do the chores."

I groaned and shrugged away from him. The sound of his footsteps walked away on the wooden floor but then came nearer again. Cold water dripped on my face. I swiped it away and sat up, glaring at Lankin. Elin stood behind him stifling a giggle. My friends pulled me up and we went outside.

In the daylight, the little house looked shabbier than the night before. Weeds grew around the property. A chicken coop off to one side was built mostly from rotten wood. The stable around the back was missing some boards.

My jaw fell open, and I remember wondering how a man of Ombree's talents could possibly live in such a dilapidated wreck. Ombree, who could afford to buy the entire tavern a drink, who could give a tavern girl a gold ring, and who wore the finest of leather armor, and yet his house and the outbuildings that went with it would not survive a heavy frost.

We checked on the livestock—a couple of chickens, the horse, and a few sheep—and came up with some eggs that we tested in water and set aside for breakfast. The ones that failed the test became part of target practice against a distant tree. Then we got started tidying the place up. Repairing outbuildings would take materials and know-how we didn't have at the time, so we started clearing debris and weeds from the space in front of the house, the only place big enough and flat enough for our lessons.

At first, the sun's warmth felt welcome, but the heat drained us by the time midday came around. We took a break and went inside to cook our eggs in a little brass pot we found on a peg by the fire. My mouth watered for my share of those fried eggs, but Ombree chose that time to rouse himself from bed. Without any word of thanks, he helped himself to nearly all of the eggs and tossed us the last of the hardtack from the trip. We split the remaining two eggs among us and made hardtack egg sandwiches. The eggs kept squeezing out of the edges of the hardtack. I wound up eating most of mine off the wooden floor.

With breakfast over, Ombree led us outside. By this time, I knew better than to expect a word of gratitude for our efforts to straighten things up. Ombree looked around the lot and grinned before he disappeared into one of the outbuildings and came back with four wooden practice swords and round, wooden shields a couple feet across. He tossed each of us a sword and spun the shields into the dirt at our feet. Elin managed to catch his sword. Lankin swatted his to the ground and picked it up. Mine hit my wrist and clattered to the dirt.

"You and you." He pointed to Elin and Lankin. "You were so anxious to prove your skills to me. Show me what you *think* you know."

A light mocking tone in his voice raised up a defensive impulse about my uncle's lessons. He'd been in the Dragon War. He'd fought in the Fourth Battalion Iron Mountain volunteers. I remembered the men my uncle's age sitting in the stands for the bouts my uncle was in. They'd all gotten very serious, very solemn. That meant something. But I said nothing as I picked up a practice sword and shield and backed away.

Ombree perched in the shade of a tree. I found my own patch of shade near the house as Elin and Lankin squared off. They crouched down as Uncle Haelin taught them and went for leg shots. They traded blows, striking low and using shields and footwork to defend. I kept score in my head. Elin, smaller and faster than Lankin, took an early lead in the scoring, but as he wearied, Lankin's greater endurance evened the score.

Across the way, Ombree sat chewing on the stem of dry grass and smirking like the whole demonstration was strictly for his entertainment.

The amusement in his eyes gradually muted to boredom, and he stood. "All right, all right. That's enough. I've seen plenty. Get over here and sit down, all three of you."

Elin and Lankin, both puffing hard, made it to the shade of the tree before I did.

Ombree leaned against the trunk. "This Dragon War veteran of yours taught you to fight like that?"

I nodded. "My uncle."

"Huh." Ombree shook his head. "Well, such tactics are better than nothing if you're a militiaman whose main virtue is the ability to march into battle like a lamb to the slaughter. But if you want to be a real swordsman, instead of some poor slob who only knows how to die on command, all of that is a waste of time, poor technique. Horse manure, actually. We're going to have to start over from practically nothing if you want to get anywhere."

I clenched my jaw, and my stomach churned.

"We only studied a few months, sir." Elin glanced at me. "Maybe he didn't have time to teach us better ways."

"Well, perhaps," he said with a smile. With a wink, he added, "Though he didn't use any other style when Prince Rory-Galstaff outfought him and killed him, did he?"

"You saw that match?" I asked.

"I did indeed. What do you think I was doing in Andrea? Other than conducting a little business along the road?"

I felt a fuming rage about what he'd said about Uncle Haelin, but at the same time I realized he was right. The prince *had* outfought my uncle.

Ombree added, "Either way, get your things, and let's get started."

I expected him to teach us the Andrean style, or something like it, so I was surprised when he took a stance that was neither Uncle Haelin's crouch nor the Andrean's erect posture.

Holding my shield and sword higher and the sword closer took an effort. Blows chopped from above to hit the head

146

and upper body or swept below the shield to strike the belly—if the opponent was foolish enough to leave that line of attack open. Ombree spoke of sectors and distances and parries and choices to close or not close, things I did not understand at all at first and which he didn't explain in detail until later. What he did emphasize were the basics of his stance, unlike what I'd learned before. That difference was driven home with a blow to the gut or shoulder if we lapsed into Uncle Haelin's teaching.

That first week, all we did was practice holding the sword and shield and moving around. Forward, backward, sideways, circling the opponent. Lankin was bored with the drills by the third day, but Ombree insisted we would continue that way until he could see no more of my uncle's faulty instruction. Those insults aimed at my uncle, who had given his life to spare ours, stung more than the blows to the shoulder that Ombree delivered when I let my guard slip or started to crouch too low.

But then I remembered that my uncle had never claimed to be a great swordsman, while Ombree clearly knew a great deal about swordplay.

By the end of that week, all of us could maneuver around without any reminders from Ombree. Then we moved on to defending with the shield, spending a fortnight on that. At that rate, I was certain Prince Rory-Galstaff would be old and gray by the time I could fulfill my oath. Which didn't seem right.

⫶⊢ Chapter 4 ⊱

For six months, the pattern continued. We'd get up early and take care of chores while Ombree slept.

Then we'd train until nightfall, and Ombree would call an end to our studies for the day. He'd go inside while we put our equipment away, and he'd come back out dressed in finery most days of the week. Twice a week, he came out in his armor instead. Either way, with a wave and an admonition to stay at the house, he left. For that half of a year, if we went anywhere, it was to buy food with the few coins he gave us when we did good work on our chores. We never went without, but we did have to spend our coins carefully.

One day, after the trees had finished their change from green to yellow and all the leaves had fallen (but winter is nowhere near as cold in Tsillis as it is in our province, son), Ombree joined us for the midday meal of bread and the soup we'd made the night before.

He scooped some soup into a bowl and sat in the only chair, a sturdy but plain wooden one. "You boys are doing well with your training. A couple of you may even be swordmasters someday." Clearly he meant Lankin and Elin, because as much as I tried, I was the clumsiest of the three of us and without any doubt the worst swordsman. Though being the biggest and strongest did compensate for my lack of skill to a degree. "So I think we are ready for a new lesson. How to fight as a group under a specific combat scenario."

"We won't need to fight as a group to meet our oath, sir," said Elin. We had told Ombree all about the oath, of course.

"Perhaps not." Ombree flashed a smile. "But it could prove useful to you at some point in the future. Perhaps…the near future. Grab your practice gear and let's step outside."

He took us a couple dozen steps down to the rough road leading out of Tsillis up to his house, which was not one of the main communication routes that went north and south along the coast, where most of the people lived along the Western Ocean. Though in fact the road was in fact one of only three leading inland from the coastal city.

"Say you found a carriage moving down this road, and you needed to stop it." He physically moved me to the center of the road. "First, you want to have a roadblock, the bigger the better, because you want the driver to decide to stop rather than try to blow through. Therin here stands for the roadblock, which could be a log or a jack fence or something. But you have to be able to move it. You don't want a fence across a road when a military unit, say a troop of cavalry on route patrol, comes riding down the way. So you need a mobile barrier and you need to man the barrier. With your most impressive-looking guy, not necessarily the best swordsman." He smiled at me.

"Thank you. I guess," I muttered.

"I'll be up front, with the roadblock. Since I will speak, the driver will probably address me in return, tell me to stand aside or something. He may have a crossbow. He'll probably fire at me, but he may aim at one of you, especially Therin, because he's very visible up here. What do you do if fired upon?"

"Block with the shield, sir?" asked Elin.

"Of course. Simplicity itself, right? You good with that, Therin?" I nodded but his expression remained doubtful. "We'll do shield and bolt drills tomorrow, after we master the basics here."

"So where do you need us?" Lankin said this with a smile.

"Yes, glad you asked. Elin will take the left side of the coach. Someone could jump out of the coach from that side with a sword, though it's probably more likely someone would exit from the right. Which is where you need to be, Lankin. Both of you back, in the shadows a bit, so anyone jumping out will not know you are there, since they'll be looking forward at Therin and me. Deal with any such threat very quickly, before they realize you're there. Then the rest of the operation will go very smoothly."

Elin's eyebrows scrunched down and his face began to flush red. "What do you mean, 'deal with'?"

"Disarming is good," said Ombree with a smile. "Especially if the one jumping out appears to be a nobleman. Noblemen reward mercy handsomely. Though in an operation such as this, killing someone is sometimes necessary. However, a firm tone of voice can prevent that most of the time."

"An operation such as what?" demanded Elin, both his fists balled tight.

Nobody answered immediately. Lankin glanced my way and at Ombree and Elin. Elin's eyes remained fixed on our swordmaster. Ombree's perpetual smile broadened. "Surely you know what I do for a living?"

Elin paused before replying. "I try not to think about that... sir."

Ombree gestured toward us by pushing forward the pommel of his sword. "I told you boys your lessons wouldn't be free."

My blond younger friend's eyebrows scrunched together in a scowl. "I thought that's what our chores were for."

Ombree chuckled warmly, but his sharp eyes staring at Elin did not match that tone. "No, no. That helped with the cost of the beginning lessons, but my fee for training advanced swordsmanship is higher. I don't demand hard gold, feel lucky that I don't, because none of you could afford the fees a professional sword trainer charges. But I've got a business and you boys need to start supporting it. Tomorrow night, once we get our practice sessions down... we'll go out. And not only will doing so pay for your training, I'll give the three of you a one-fourth share to split among you. You should be pleased."

"You mean, a *robbery*?" Elin's voice rasped.

Ombree shrugged, his face not smiling quite so much now. "The technical term is doing the job of a 'highwayman,' but call it what you must. That is my business and you *will* partake if you wish to continue on with me."

The boy facing him stood straighter and his scowl cleared. "Then I do not wish to continue on with you. Sir."

"Fine." The man no longer smiled at all. "You may leave as soon as the balance of what you owe me for the beginning lessons is paid. Or else you can fight me for the right to leave."

Elin clutched the wooden sword in his hand with a look of determination on his face, while Ombree faced him with his right hand resting on the pommel on his fine Andrean hand-crafted sword, smiling again. Very coldly.

"For the love of the God!" I cried out. "Don't be a fool, Elin!" We all knew that whatever else Ombree may be, he was an extremely deadly swordsman.

Elin's hand shook as he lowered his wooden weapon. "How much do I owe you then? Sir." The last word came out in a growl.

Ombree's right hand moved from his sword to rub his chin. "Let's see, a gold piece a day for beginning lessons, you've been with me, um, six months, or about one hundred eighty days. But it's been a bit more than six months, so we'll call it an even two hundred days. Your little chores around my place I'll generously consider half of that. So. You owe me one hundred gold pieces."

Son, that was just as much money then as it is now. More than an ordinary worker in most jobs would earn in ten years. I drew in a shocked breath.

"Very well," said my friend, his eyes lowered.

Ombree stepped forward, smirking, and put a hand on Elin's shoulder. "Don't worry, my boy. Your share of the quarter I'll give you will bring in a lot more than you think, especially now that we can take on carriages. Before you know it, you'll be on your way."

Elin didn't reply.

"Shall we continue with the lesson?" asked our master.

I nodded and Lankin said soberly, "Sure."

Lankin caught on the fastest, which was typical. To him, this was all some grand game like playing griffins and dragons at home with the boys from school. By midafternoon, he looked and sounded as confident as Ombree did while demonstrating. Elin, however, tripped over his tongue and his feet as badly as I usually did. He improved by evening, but his frowns and scowls demonstrated over and over again what he really thought about the lesson. I, however, was mostly hopeless, even more than typical for me. I tripped over pebbles and fumbled with my practice sword. My voice stammered when I talked, and I sounded as threatening as woodpecker. Ombree's corrections, often disguised as jokes at my expense, made little improvement in my efforts.

As the sun set, Ombree heaved a terrific sigh. He went into the equipment shed and brought out our two unsharpened swords and the one sharpened one. He gave the sharp one to Lankin. Elin and I got the other two.

"You are not ready to take a coach yet. I believe perhaps you're just nervous about the act itself and need a little something to break the ice. So, tonight you'll rob someone without me on hand to help. Just the three of you. Look for a single individual traveling alone, in fine clothing. There aren't many potentials who do that after dark, but after we shift over to the coast road going south, you'll see that there are some. After we set up, I'll leave, and you boys will do the business on your own. Just to prove to you there is nothing to be so nervous about. Any questions?"

Each of us looked at one another, Elin and I clearly unhappy.

"All right. Lankin, it'll be up to you to do all the talking." He jabbed his finger at me and Elin. "You two will just have to stand there and look like you mean business." He smirked at me. "Or at least stay upright and hang onto your sword, so you look large and menacing. Which you can do as long as you keep your mouth shut. You can handle that, right?"

I stared at the dirt. "Yes, sir."

He went inside.

Elin waited until a few moments after the door closed. He leaned closer to us. "We should *not* do this!"

Lankin shrugged. "We're not going to hurt anyone."

"No, just take all their stuff," I mumbled, remembering how hard people I'd known all of my life back home had to work to get what few things they had.

Elin said, "How do you think Haelin would feel about all of this? Do you think he'd be proud that we've become highwaymen?"

"We'll only focus on those people who look like they can afford to have a temporarily lighter purse, okay?" Lankin rolled his eyes. "All you two have to do is stand there and look dangerous. I'll do the rest. Can you be fine with that? Besides, with Ombree not around, we'll each get a larger share. Which will get you closer to your one hundred gold pieces, Elin."

"I wouldn't count on that," I said.

Ombree, decked out in his ornate leather armor with his sword at his hip, came out at that moment. He had his satchel cross-belted from left shoulder to right hip and carried a somewhat smaller one that he tossed at me. "Make yourself useful and carry that to keep whatever you collect. Come on. Let's get you set up somewhere."

Instead of heading down the road to where it met the southern coast road, he turned toward the back of the house and took us overland, across a ridge and through some woods going generally south until we hit a trail heading west, downhill towards the coast. When it forked, he veered left. This one was a little more overgrown with plant life, and it disappeared in a couple places. I wasn't sure I could find my way in the dark, but I did the best I could to mentally mark out landmarks, and I broke a few twigs here and there to show the way.

The trees abruptly ended at the edge of a cobblestone road, not too unlike the one where we'd first encountered Ombree. The road curved in both directions. He stopped and turned toward us. "This is a good spot. Set up here and wait. Today was a major market day, so there should be plenty of people coming and going. Follow the instructions I gave you and you should be fine. Don't expect to see me at the house when you come back." He started back down the path then turned, walking backward a few steps. "Wait until well after nightfall and keep the moon behind you." Ombree soon disappeared back up the path.

"Where's he going?" Elin asked.

Lankin gestured us back into the trees. "There are two main roads out of this city you know. Maybe he's going to find a spot on the other side of town."

Night seemed to take forever to fall. The whole time, my hands shook, and I felt queasy. I must have stepped away to relieve myself a dozen times. While we waited, a few small groups and lone travelers passed by. Some wore clothes slightly better than rags and carried a few meager things in a small basket. A couple were on horseback. Purses jingled and jewelry glittered. Most of the travelers were between those extremes. On several occasions, a mounted patrol of armed cavalrymen trotted by, providing a show of protection against people engaged in what we were about to do.

Once the stars were out and the night was too dark to see much clearly beyond a dozen paces ahead, we listened for footsteps on the cobblestone. We let horses go past unchecked, and groups of people walked by safely. Ombree had said to focus someone walking alone. The footsteps of the first one who came by slapped the cobblestones hard.

Lankin waited until the tall heavy-set man passed us before he stepped out and drew his sword. "Stop where you are!"

Elin didn't move, but I followed a moment later. My sword got stuck in the sheath briefly but when I pulled harder, it jerked loose. I stepped forward to check my balance.

The man started to turn, but Lankin pressed the point of his sword into the man's back. "Don't turn around. Just drop your purse and head on your way."

"There are stiff penalties for thieves in this province," the man said as he loosened the string on his belt.

"My problem, not yours." Lankin prodded the man. "Drop the purse."

My heartbeat sounded hollow in my ears. At any moment now, someone else would come around that corner, and we'd be caught. Then what? Thrown into prison? Executed? I didn't know what the penalty for theft in this province was, but I knew I didn't want anything to do with it.

The purse hit the stones with a muffled clink of coins.

The man made a sudden move for something on his left hip. I wasn't sure what it was, but I leapt ahead, leading with the sword, but aiming for a space in front of my target.

He gasped and lifted up both hands. "Two of you, eh?"

"Even more, actually." Lankin moved in closer and gave the man a shove. "Get going and keep going."

He stumbled forward then hurried off.

Lankin scooped up the purse and shoved it into my chest. "Here. Put that in the bag."

I nodded and clutched the purse in one quivering hand while following Lankin back into the brush and trees at the side of the road. The shaking in my hands made the clasp of the satchel hard to open, but I managed it and slipped the bag inside.

Lankin cut loose with one of Ombree's favorite curses. "I forgot to see if he had other valuables." He turned to Elin and backhanded his shoulder. "You were useless."

"I'm not doing this." Elin huffed and stood. "I've reached my limit."

I got up and caught his arm. "Wait, where are you going?"

"Home." He jerked his arm away from me.

"You can't! What about our oath?"

"Do you remember what your Uncle taught us, Therin? About a man reaching his limit? Now I think I understand at least part of what he meant. I can't do this. I won't. I have reached my limit. The oath said nothing about becoming thieves. The God doesn't want us to break our oath—but he doesn't want us to rob people, either."

I stammered several useless syllables but couldn't come up with any clear words.

Lankin darted in front of Elin. "The oath was to learn from a swordmaster until we were good enough to take on Rory-Galstaff. Working with this swordmaster means doing this to pay our way."

"Ombree is not the only swordmaster in the world." Elin planted his hands on his hips. "I'll find another one. One who's honest. Once I earn the money to pay him with honest work back home."

I finally found my words, but they came out barely louder than a whisper. "The oath also said we couldn't see our families again."

"I will seek the God for His forgiveness. I don't believe in being an oath-breaker and I don't want to go back on the idea I would pay Ombree one hundred gold, even though I never directly said I would. But I cannot become an evil man for the purpose of avenging a good one. That is too much.

For me, too much. Maybe the God will forgive me. I have hope He will." He looked down for a moment before turning toward me. "I'm real sorry about your uncle, Therin. I loved him, but this isn't the way. You should come with me."

Lankin wrapped his arm around my shoulders. "No way. Therin's staying here with me and doing what we set out to do. Aren't you Therin? You wouldn't betray your oath to avenge your uncle, would you? You loved him, more than this traitor friend of yours, right?"

"Yes, yes, I did love him." Tears burned in my eyes as I remembered that last bout.

Elin sighed. "I'm no traitor." He gripped my shoulder as he walked past. "Goodbye. May the God protect you."

"Roads are dangerous for the lone traveler. You'll be killed along the way," Lankin said.

Elin kept walking away from us, but turned towards us to speak. "If it's the God's will for me to die, so be it. At least I'll be able to live with myself until then."

"You won't even be able to feed yourself—especially if you won't rob anybody! Elin, you need to stay with us. You'll die!"

Elin's only response to this was to keep walking north along the coast road, doing what I should have done, my child. On the other side of Tsillis, far north of it somewhere, a road went back eastward to Iron Mountains Province. Though it would take months for anyone to walk there. And he couldn't possibly have known the way.

I stood there watching, wondering if I should run ahead and catch up with Elin, long after he disappeared into the darkness of the night. Lankin shouted after him one last time, "Go ahead and die then, traitor!" His anger at Elin seemed genuine. His hold on me tightened for a moment.

"Ah, we don't need him. Come on, Therin. We can do this. Just long enough to pay for our lessons. Just you and me. Then we can kill that bastard of a prince when we're ready."

I followed him back into the trees as the sound of horse's hooves rounded the corner.

Chapter 5

The next morning, Lankin and I were up earlier than usual. We hastily ate our breakfast of porridge and went outside into the chilly morning air to do our chores. The sun stayed hidden behind a ceiling of gray clouds, but at least there was no wind. I took care of the livestock then joined Lankin, who was working on tearing out dead weeds. The weed pulling was somewhat easier now that most of the plants had withered or gone dormant for the winter. Some, especially where the ground was packed, had to be dug out. I stuffed all the weeds into a shallow pit surrounded by a knee-high ring of stones. My teeth chattered as I lit the fire. Lankin joined me and we warmed ourselves while the weeds and other trash burned down.

I rubbed my hands together and glanced at Lankin. "What are we going to tell Ombree?"

Lankin snorted. "What can we tell him? Elin left yesterday while we were practicing our new skill."

"He left after that, not during."

"When he didn't join us for the first one, he was already gone." He glanced both ways then leaned closer and whispered, "And we might get in less trouble with him if he thinks we didn't have a chance to stop Elin because we were busy."

First stealing, now lying. It might seem strange to you that lying would bother me after I'd spent the half the night stealing people's valuables, but I felt like I was piling crimes on top of each other. Someday, I knew I would have to account for all this before the God—and hope for his mercy. I clenched my jaw and sighed. Most likely, Lankin would do all the talking anyway, and I could just sit there and keep quiet.

Once the fire burned down, we returned to the chores and had the pit half-full again when it was time to go in. I added a log to the fire and put the porridge back on the heat. Lankin sliced up what remained of yesterday's bread and spread it among three shallow bowls. Ombree joined us at about the time the porridge started bubbling. I pulled it off the fire and ladled a share for everyone.

Ombree counted the plates then pierced Lankin and me with a hard stare. "Where's your friend with the overzealous conscience?"

"He left last night while Therin and I were dealing with a man on the road. There was no way we could stop him. He just up and run off." Lankin retrieved the satchel I had carried last night and handed it over. "But look what Therin and I did on our own."

Ombree dumped the money and jewelry on the table and sorted through it. "Just you two? Not bad." He divided the pile into four pieces then split one of the quarters into thirds, keeping one for himself and pushing the rest toward Lankin. "That's for you two to divvy up however you want." He pointed to the other third. "Until Elin's debt is paid, his portion is mine. Be satisfied with that." He grabbed a shallow bowl of porridge and bread and returned to his chair.

When I picked up my bowl and spoon, I looked at the portion Lankin and I would be splitting. My eyes widened and my jaw dropped open. Just our part was more than some people in our village would see in a month. Then I considered the property Ombree owned. If he did these highwayman attacks twice a week, where was all the money going? I had a guess, and not too long after that, I found out for sure. But I'm getting ahead of myself.

Once lunch was over, we went outside and picked up our gear.

"Now, when we take on carriages, keep watch on all the people. You never know who is or is not armed. Even the most beautiful flowers have thorns. You'll have to keep an eye out for a man with a crossbow." Ombree walked around the yard while he spoke. From time to time, he picked up a fist-sized rock and made a pile about twenty feet in front of us. "He'll often be with the driver, but sometimes, he'll be with the passengers or even on the back of the carriage. Wherever he is, you've got the perfect defense right there on your arm."

The round shield on my arm was a couple feet across. Mine was wooden with a metal rim. Lankin's had metal strips across the front, and Ombree's was iron. If you've heard of knights with fancy heraldry on their shields, you might be surprised to learn that ours had no decoration. Nothing about them stood out, which would make identifying us that much harder.

Ombree scooped up one of the rocks he'd been collecting and lobbed it at me.

162

I flinched and ducked behind my shield. The rock thudded off its middle and hit the ground a couple feet away.

He smiled. "Not bad."

I peeked over the top of my shield. Ombree had resumed his pacing so I stood and pivoted in place, keeping my shield between us. While he walked, he lectured us, telling us a tale of a successful robbery then telling us what he wanted us to learn from the story. Seemingly at random, he picked up one of the rocks and threw it at one of us. At first, the underhanded throws were slow and easy to see, but he gradually increased his speed until he was throwing rocks at a fantastic speed. And he kept doing it, way longer than seemed necessary. My arm wearied of holding the shield at the ready. Muscles burned and shook.

Still keeping an eye on Ombree, I lowered my shield to a more comfortable position. He scooped up a rock, turned, and hurled it at me in one move. I tried to raise my shield in time, and almost had it in place. The rock hit the metal edge of the shield and glanced off. I turned my face away as the rock struck my cheek. The blow stung and my teeth hurt.

Ombree wagged his finger at me. "Don't lower your defense."

I looked down at the dirt. "Yes, sir."

He darted to the shed and came back with a big crossbow and a handful of blunt-ended bolts. He drew the crossbow back and loaded it. "Now, as hard as those rocks were, a heavy crossbow will hit harder. You're going to have to brace yourself better or you'll get hurt."

After setting the now loaded crossbow down, he led us back toward the edge of the trees and brush.

"Now, when we stop a carriage, you two will have to be in your positions. Therin, you'll have to take over Elin's place.

I'll handle the front myself." He took about ten steps back from us. "You'll want to be about this far from the carriage.

Much closer, and you won't be able to keep an eye on your side well enough. Too far back, and you won't be able to stop people who try to exit. While you're standing there, stand with one leg forward and the other back and turned at an angle. Brace your back foot against a rock or tree just like bracing against another pikeman when setting for horse."

I had no idea how pikemen "set for horse," but I understood enough of his instructions to figure out what he meant without asking. Looking down at my feet, I found a good-sized tree trunk and pressed my back foot on the trunk.

Ombree rolled his eyes. "Not like that. You boys never seen a pike corps set for a cavalry charge?"

I shook my head at the same time Lankin said, "We don't have a pike corps in the Iron Mountains. Just spearmen."

"That's right, you're from one of the more backward provinces in the Western Bond, aren't you?" Ombree frowned and shook his head as he rejoined us and demonstrated. "Back foot flat on the ground, turned to the side, and against something that will support you if you're hit with a bolt. Front toes pointing toward your target. Knees bent. Sword in one hand. Shield in the other and held where it will actually do you some good. Got it?"

Before we could answer, he darted back to his crossbow. I checked my feet and brought my shield up. A moment later, the crossbow clacked. Lankin grunted and rocked back.

He rolled his shoulder and grimaced. "Be ready for that one."

Some part of me wondered if it really would be all that bad. After all, I'd had a sword hit my shield in the Tournament of Swords lots of times and I hadn't been braced.

Ombree reloaded and shot at me. The bolt hit the center of my shield. I leaned into it some, but the force drove the shield back toward my chest and reverberated all the way up through my arm. That crossbow hit hard!

"Good!" Ombree said.

I think that was the first time he'd actually complimented me and meant it.

We practiced blocking bolts for half the afternoon before changing back to sword skills. By that time, I was sure my left arm would fall off. Even as strong as I was, my arm was sore for days after that practice session—that's how powerful that particular crossbow was.

Nightfall came and Ombree went inside to get his armor. I sat where I was. After such a strenuous practice session, the cool air was a relief. With a break in activity, my mind wandered, remembering Elin's departure and wondering whether he might've been right to go.

Lankin sat next to me. "Stop thinking about him. We'll do what we have to do and be done."

I nodded, not entirely convinced, but there was no way I could find my way back to the Iron Mountains on my own even if I'd wanted to.

At nightfall, we headed overland to the main road along the coast. When we got there and found a suitable curve, we constructed a movable roadblock out of deadfall and branches we hacked off of trees, but we didn't block the road until well after nightfall. Even then, we waited until after the patrol passed before setting up our roadblock. Ombree crouched in the brush near the roadblock. Lankin was on one side, and I was on the other. The first few travelers through there were men traveling alone. If the traveler looked like he had some wealth, Ombree stepped out of the shadows and took the man's purse and whatever else there was of value. If we heard multiple horses coming but no carriage wheels, we quickly removed our barricade, just in case the patrol was on the way through. One time, we barely made it back under cover before the patrol rounded the corner.

While we waited, I shivered and tried to contain the sniffles. My muscles cramped and I walked back into the woods a few times, making sure to stay close enough to dart back into position if someone came along.

When we did hear carriage wheels and horse's hooves, I found a good position where I could brace against crossbow bolts. Across the way, Lankin, too, found his place. Ombree stood behind the roadblock with his shield and sword in hand. I rose in my place and checked my footing. My heart beat at a rapid pace. I scanned along the length of the carriage, watching for the crossbowman.

"That's far enough." Ombree began.

He continued to talk, but he could have been speaking gibberish. I was too focused on the carriage, waiting for that crossbow bolt, not a padded one like we'd practiced, but one with a point, one that was aimed to hit me, not my shield.

Ombree whistled. "BOY!"

I jumped and looked toward him.

"Get over here and move this thing so these nice people can be on their way." He beckoned me over with the wave of his sword.

I sheathed my blade and ran over. Lankin and I cleared the roadblock and the carriage moved on.

Ombree clapped my shoulder hard enough to knock me off balance. "You'll get over the nerves, boy."

He herded Lankin and me over to where the carriage had stopped. Rings, bracelets, coins, and other trinkets littered the ground. We collected all the loot and put it in Ombree's bag.

We'd finished just moments before we heard men's voices coming closer. No horses hooves, no carriage wheels, just men. I started for my hiding place but Ombree grabbed me by the collar.

"Stand your ground. If I think they're worth it, we'll take them. If not, we're just travelers on the road the same as them." He started toward them on the road.

Lankin and I followed a step behind.

A trio of men came around the corner clad in dark doublets and trousers that glittered in the moonlight. Two of them wore wide-brimmed hats with plumes but the other carried his hat in his hand.

Ombree drew his sword. "Good evening, gents. Let's have your valuables, eh?"

"What if we say no?" one of them asked.

All three drew long, thin, Andrean blades. The one carrying his hat tossed it away.

"Well, then we'll just have to ask a different way." Ombree closed with the one closest to him.

The one nearest Lankin charged at him. The third drew the sheath from its hanger and darted into range with me. He drew back for an overhand blow. Six months of training took over. I blocked his strike with my shield and swung my own sword at his arm. The sheath flicked out to block it. I hadn't expected that something so light could deflect my sword, but it's all in the leverage.

My opponent backed away. Instead of chasing him, I hung back waiting for his next move. This time, when he advanced, he drew back with his arm out to the side. I met his swing with my shield, stepped off to the right, and swung at a different angle, one that avoided his sheath. Getting past his defense surprised me so much I pulled the blow short. What should have been a killing blow only cut through his doublet and nicked his side.

The wound wouldn't amount to much. Even I could tell that, but my opponent gasped and staggered backward. He dropped his weapons and held up both hands shoulder high, palm out. "You can have it. You can have it. It's not worth dying for."

He loosed the string and tossed the purse to the ground at my feet.

That's when I realized how much I had actually learned from Ombree in six months. Far more than I'd learned from Uncle Haelin. Perhaps my uncle, a veteran of the Dragon War, a member of the Fourth Battalion Iron Mountain Volunteers, hadn't been as great a man as I'd thought.

PART TWO: THE BOND OF THE OATH

⫞ Chapter 6 ⫝

Son, the fact is that Ombree and Lankin and I spent three years working out of that house in the foothills on the western end of Tsillis. The actual sword lessons came with less regularity, since our *real* business was, in truth, highway robbery, but when they did come, they were increasingly advanced. Ombree also taught us other weapon disciplines at times, especially how to fight unarmed. Though at first those "lessons" amounted to him punching us, smiling the whole time, when he was in fact frustrated or angry with us. I did learn to take a hit, though. And eventually to hit back.

Please understand that as a grown man I don't believe the sword and other lessons for the supposed reason to avenge my uncle were at all worth becoming a criminal to gain that knowledge. But at the time, I believed it was worth it. Or better said, I wanted to believe so. I tried very hard to convince myself every day that all that was going on was actually a good thing.

About twice a week we went out to one major road or the other. Some were close to the house. Others took a

170

considerable hike, but they all had the same thing in common: a curve on a well-traveled road near trees. We never followed a pattern for where we'd set up, but we did return to the same places from time to time. Usually the three of us could stop and rob a carriage without bloodshed, but maybe one time in ten at least one of our victims had be wounded or killed before we got the goods. Usually, Ombree or Lankin was quicker to act than I was, but during the three year's time, I badly wounded two men myself. I don't know if they lived to see the next day or not. I'm not proud I did that, but at the time I told myself I had to do it to stay alive. Since we specialized in carriages of the rich, the haul was considerable. Even the third that Ombree allowed Lankin and me to split gained considerable heft. At first, I had an oil rag that I kept my share in, which I stuffed under the mattress of the bed that Lankin bought for the two of us to share. Eventually I needed a burlap sack to hold all my loot and the lump it formed under the bed would not let me sleep, so even though I felt uncomfortable about it, I simply stitched up the sack and left it on my side of the bed, the left side. I'd unstitch and re-stitch every time I got something new.

There was a good reason for me to feel uncomfortable. Once we began to successfully hit carriages, Ombree purchased an impressive array of silk clothing, imported at high price from the land of the Kings of the East. This was to impress the ladies, he said. He also brought pearls in necklaces and bracelets, gemstones in rings and amulets. For the ladies. He often went out to meet them but increasingly brought them to the house. When he began to do that, he started paying money for paintings and vases and new furniture to make the old place look somewhat better. He always enjoyed drink, but with more money the wines he drank became finer; he always enjoyed meat, but with money the cuts of meat became pricier. He rarely had any loot left over at all from week to week. When buying something particularly expensive, he did not hesitate to ask Lankin or me for extra money to make the purchase. He always promised to pay us back, but he may have actually done so only twice. Or maybe it was only once, because the other time he took something else at the exact same moment he repaid a previous debt.

I wanted to save my money, of course, for the trip that Lankin and I would eventually have to take to Andrea to face the prince. At first Lankin felt the same way and saved his money, too. But after a year or so he began to go out to taverns with Ombree. And after a year, he began to bring women back to the house for himself, just like our swordmaster did, and just like him, spent all of his money. I spent more nights than I can count out in the barn so my friend and one of his mistresses could make use of the mattress we supposedly shared. More times than I can count I had to air out that increasingly soiled hunk of fabric stuffed with goose down that we slept on. More than once I'd come back into the room to find my sack unsewn, items missing, Lankin or his latest girl helping themselves. I complained but Ombree and my once-upon-a-time friend always talked me down, always promised to repay.

I tried to tell Lankin that things he was doing were against what the God commanded, but when I did, he'd laugh at me or get angry, so it wasn't long before I quit trying.

"Look, Therin," he said more than once, "We aren't little boys anymore. We are men, like Ombree. We might as well enjoy the things men enjoy!"

I should have kept trying to convince him, I suppose. Either that or be like Elin and on my own set foot on the road back home. But I was afraid to do that—I knew something of the sort of people who lurked along the roadways. Some of the other highwaymen were much quicker to kill than Ombree. A strange reality of this time was that while what we were doing was supposed to be in order to gain the training we needed to avenge my uncle, Lankin and I talked about him less and less. Lankin did talk about Prince Rory-Galstaff, though. Nearly every day. How that arrogant bastard prince would rue the day he trifled with us Mountaineers, how much he would enjoy delivering the killing blow to that arrogant, rich waste of flesh. The crime the prince had done in Lankin's telling shifted into terms of what it had meant to the team, what an insult it had been to our province, to our pride. Only on occasion, when Lankin came back from the tavern still during the night instead of the next day, mead or wine on his breath, would he weep and hug me and talk about my uncle. So over time, I came to accept the things we did. Things I would never have dreamed of allowing when I was younger became ordinary, standard. Uninteresting even. Getting so accustomed to evil that you don't even notice it anymore takes a man most of the way down the road to becoming corrupt. Don't be like I was in any of these things, son.

At lunchtime on one particular day, Ombree snatched up his bowl of thick soup and bread and flopped on his chair. "Boys, I happened to overhear you talking yesterday. It's your birthday, isn't it, Therin? I say a celebration is in order! Starting with those work rags you're wearing, they're no good. You need to get some decent clothes for our celebration."

I looked down at the clothes I'd bought a few months ago after growing out of my old ones. They were utilitarian, but they were better than anything I'd ever owned before and heavy enough to keep me fairly warm when we went out on our nighttime raids. I'd resisted spending money on fancy silks and linens, and he hadn't said anything about it until now. What did he have in mind that would require fancier clothes?

Ombree finished the meal and set the bowl aside. As if he knew what I was thinking he remarked, "What you've got is good enough for our job, but not for our celebration. Besides, you're seventeen now. You should look like the man you are. Let's go."

I quickly slurped down the rest of my soup, scalding my tongue, and followed Ombree and Lankin into town. I don't know what I really expected, but Ombree brought us into a shop. I always thought fine clothes had to be tailored, but this place had shelves stacked with different kinds of clothing, both men's and ladies'. I hung back and let Ombree do the talking. Lankin confidently walked into the place and started picking a few things up for himself, unfolding them and comparing them to his own body, as if he'd been in this place before. He soon had a white shirt, gray doublet, and black trousers suitable for any Andrean nobleman.

Outfitting me took more effort. There weren't many options for a young man of my height, broad shoulders, and thick chest. Most of the clothes were much smaller than I was, and the ones of an appropriate size didn't meet Ombree's approval. He finally settled on something that was large enough but a little too long, but decided it was good enough and said I'd grow into it. He was right about that much. They eventually fit better.

To my surprise, Ombree paid for everything by bartering an exquisite silver platter for our outfits, but I should have known better. I later realized the platter had come from my loot bag.

Once we had our new clothes bundled in brown burlap and string, I followed Ombree and Lankin out.

"There now." Ombree grinned widely. "You'll look better in that than the original owners did, I'm sure."

My guts soured. So now we were buying *stolen* clothes? "What do you mean?"

Lankin rolled his eyes. "That store buys clothes from the estates of dead people. How else do you think we'd get ready-made clothes?"

"All properly laundered, Therin, so don't worry about that." Ombree clapped my shoulder.

Back home, we put our clothes inside and spent the afternoon practicing more sword skills. Ombree even made a few remarks about how I was finally beginning to look like a real swordsman. But Lankin was further advanced than I was, so after giving me a drill to do, Ombree spent most of the time with him. I made progress, but my natural clumsiness made all improvement slow and hard for me.

Evening came, and we lost the light.

"That's it for today. Let's get changed and go have our celebration." Ombree darted inside.

Lankin and I put our equipment away before we went in and changed into our new clothes. I fidgeted with the way the sleeves sat and profoundly wished I could just go do this "celebration" in my normal clothes.

Ombree came out shortly after I was dressed and grinned.

"Excellent. Now you look the part. I've got your money, so let's go."

I followed the others. Ombree jingled when he walked. "Where are we going?" Lankin asked.

"For a grand night in town." Ombree wrapped his arms around our shoulders. "You both have earned it. And it's time for you, Therin. Time you became a man." He said the last part with an enormous grin.

He took us to a tavern very unlike the one we stopped at our first night in Tsillis. Instead of the smell of stale ale, old wine, and bad mead, there was a heavy dose of overly sweet perfume, almost choking me at first. Numerous crystal chandeliers hung from the ceiling and the walls were covered with paintings in velvet. Men outnumbered the women two to one, but what women there were wore very little in the way of clothing and a lot of the face paint the Tsillians call "cosmetics." The noise rivaled the smell, not just the talking and loud shouting. There was a four string band with a drummer, musicians playing the beat of Tsillian popular dances. I stopped just inside the door, wondering if I could somehow sneak back out. Ombree had to pay before we could even enter the place.

Ombree swaggered across the room, the elegant sword with a gem-studded ivory handle on his hip swaying as he walked, slapping a dancing girl's rear on the way, and slammed a small bag of coins on the mahogany wood bar. "A round of whatever's good for everybody and some special attention for me and the boys." He waved us over with a wink.

"Relax, Therin." Lankin clapped my shoulder. "We're here for a good time." He headed across to the bar.

A fish might have felt more at home in the desert.

I threaded my way through the room, dodging patrons leering at and groping for girls attempting to dance to the music. Fortunately, after Lankin found his spot at the bar, the only bar stool left was the one nearest the wall.

A group of a half-dozen dark-haired Andrean men wearing fine swords occupied one corner, leaning close to tell stories, then laughing riotously. One of the girls was perched on the knee of one of the men but the rest seemed content to do without, at least for the moment. Nearer, a larger group of young men smoking westweed were challenging one another to down a large mug of ale without taking a breath. A pile of money in the center of the table waited for the man who could do it. The rest of the tables were occupied by men sitting alone or by small groups chatting or enjoying the entertainment.

Mugs painted with intertwining vines arrived at our spot on the bar, delivered by an older, larger woman with more ample silks and more face paint than the younger women. I looked into the mug and saw a red fluid. Ombree smiled at me, "Drink, Therin. It's your birthday!"

Lankin held up his mug at me and smiled. "Fortified wine!" He drank a deep draught. I drank, too. The taste was fruity and sweet but it burned going down my throat. After that round, Ombree insisted I drink two more.

He then grabbed a girl walking by and pulled her into his lap. "Where's our attention?" She tapped his nose with the tip of her finger. "I'll be right back, honey."

"You do that." He let her go and joined the group of young men at the center table.

A very tall and muscular brown-haired guy with his front teeth missing standing by the table pointed at Ombree. "If you're gonna play, ya gotta pay."

I didn't see what happened next. Slender arms wrapped around me from behind, and I nearly jumped the height of the Iron Mountains.

The young men began drumming on their table.

A girl's chin pressed on my shoulder. "Relax, baby. Let's have a good time." I looked behind me and realized another young woman had her arms wrapped around Lankin.

From the middle of the room, the collective groan from the group heralded Ombree's success.

The girl behind me came around and sat on my knee, looping her arm around my shoulders. She was about typical height for a woman and curvy, her silks showing more of her than I had any right to see. Her long, dark hair streamed down her back like a waterfall.

I leaned back, trying to get a little space. As easy as the girl was to look at, my thoughts darted back to a blue-eyed redhead I'd last seen at the tournament. I hadn't thought about Arta in months, maybe even years, but at that moment, her fair face and blue eyes came to mind. Along with what I'd always been taught about the God's command that a man should only be with his wife. Along with what Uncle Haelin said about the God watching.

But what did it matter? I wouldn't ever see Arta again. Even if I did, would she even want to have anything to do with a highwayman? Certainly not. The spiced wine burned in my belly, and I realized I wanted to have what was right in front of me. What looked and felt so good.

I slipped my arm around the girl's lower back, and she slowly leaned down toward my mouth, as if to kiss me.

Some part of me vaguely realized that at the same moment, Ombree had returned to the bar and had just offered his winnings to pay for drinks for everyone. The tavern's patrons cheered.

In a sudden burst of enthusiasm, watching the girl's mouth approach my own, I decided to return her kiss.

I thrust my head upward, fast. My teeth slammed into the girl's teeth, knocking her backwards with a loud *clack*.

She hopped off my lap, her lip bleeding. She slapped me very hard. Twice.

Ombree joined us again, his right arm around the waist of the girl who he'd pulled into his lap before. He laughed and shook his head. "Only Therin could fail to get lucky with a prostitute!"

Lankin laughed hard but eventually said, "Don't worry, Therin. We'll find you another one." But they both soon got preoccupied with what they were doing and they never did find me another one. Which I'm glad for. It was one of the moments of my life I'm most sure that the God was looking out for me.

After a long uncomfortable night of me sitting in a corner and feeling embarrassed, the other two not even with me most of the time, Ombree and Lankin and I eventually walked back toward Ombree's place in the pre-dawn cold of fall.

I smelled smoke long before I saw the flames, but as we walked up, I realized Ombree's house was on fire.

⟞ Chapter 7 ⟝

The fire had already collapsed the roof and most of two walls. There was no wind to speak of, which kept the fire contained. The God must have been guiding us boys over the previous years because if we hadn't worked so hard to clear all the weeds and brush from around the house, the fire would have easily spread to the barn, outbuildings, and even the surrounding forest.

I stood there and stared with my jaw hanging open. The heat radiating from the blaze obliterated the chill. Ombree stormed closer. For a moment, I thought he might be crazy enough to try searching for some of his things in that blaze, but he stopped halfway, knelt, and studied the dirt.

Curiosity overcame my shock, and I crept closer to see what had captured his attention. I was almost there when he growled a string of curses and swept his hand through the dirt.

"I was going to take care of you." He stood and shouted at the sky. "I just needed more time!"

After coming up behind me, Lankin flopped to his knees on the ground. I drifted back a couple steps and sat next to him. I expected the house to burn for hours, but the wood was so old and so dry, it went up like paper. When the whole structure had burnt down, we stretched out on the hay in the barn and slept for a while.

I woke up with a headache and a queasy stomach. My muscles ached, and I was thirsty enough to drink the ocean dry. I stumbled past Ombree and Lankin and out of the barn but froze at the door. A few short, skeletal timbers and a lot of black and gray ash was all that remained of Ombree's house. Smoke still rose in many places and a few spots still glowed.

On my way to the well, I paused where Ombree had studied the dirt. A few trails from his fingertips marred the words, but I could still piece them together. "Paid in full. Ride out before sunset, or else."

It wasn't until later, when Ombree was drunk, that he complained about the official who had crossed him. He'd made an arrangement with the local law to divert patrols around the locations where we set up, only Ombree had spent the bribery money on his evening entertainments. This didn't make his contact happy. And burning the house had been repayment for that.

While waiting for Ombree and Lankin to wake up, I took a long stick and went to the edge of the debris where my extra clothes and my bag of money had been. I didn't expect to find the clothes, of course, but the metal should have survived. I pushed the stick through the ash, overturning larger, charred pieces. Warped, discolored metal peeked through the rubble. A small handful of coins and a small silver bell were all I could find. The silver platter that had been used to pay for the clothes I was wearing had come from my own stash, it seems. I knew it hadn't simply vanished, and if anything, silver would've melted, not burned.

The heat radiating from ash was enough to make branding irons of the coins. I used the stick to scrape them into the dirt. Then I got some water from the well to douse them. Steam rose with a hiss. When the coins and the bell were cool enough to touch, I slid them into a pocket stitched to the inside of my doublet and fastened the little button there. The doublet fit loose enough that the coins and bell didn't make an unnatural-looking bulge.

Except for Ombree's palomino, which apparently had made a break for the forest but returned in the morning so we could find him, all the livestock were gone, whether they ran off or were part of the "payment" he'd owed. I collected chicken eggs, but only came up with a few. That wouldn't be enough for breakfast. My queasy stomach wasn't too interested in food at the moment, but once it settled, I knew I'd want more than a couple of eggs. Then there was that warning to leave the area before nightfall. Travel meant we'd need provisions.

Lankin and Ombree still slept in the barn. I headed for town and went to the market. I'd been there almost daily for the last few years, but something was very different this time. Many people grew quiet as I approached. Those further away whispered behind their hands. When I walked up to a booth where a baker had set up, he became busy with other customers and wouldn't even look at me.

I walked up to him and waited patiently, but when he finished with his current customer, he turned away from me, and addressed someone else.

"Excuse me, sir." I tapped his shoulder.

He shrugged me off and glared. "Move along, boy. Nothing here for you."

I fell back a pace. After doing business with this man for three years, he had nothing for me? I backed away and moved on.

Tsillis was large enough to support more than one baker in this neighborhood alone, so I went across the market to another booth. The proprietor smirked as I approached. I chose a couple loaves of bread, one for our breakfast and the other for the road. The baker's smirk grew into a chuckle as he quoted a price nearly double what I had paid for a much better loaf two days ago.

"Why so much?" I asked.

"You think there's one person in this quarter who don't know what happened last night at Ombree's place? There's only one reason folks get burned out of their houses around here. You'll find many who'll grudge you the sunlight, so you'll take my price and like it or go without."

What choice did I have? I paid for the bread and continued on my errand, collecting jerky, nuts, and dried fruits and vegetables. The effort took longer and cost more for less than I wanted, but in the end, I had at least enough to get us started. Perhaps friendlier merchants waited in other towns. By the time I got back to the ruins of the house, Lankin and Ombree were sifting through the ash. I went into the shed hoping to find a shield to use for a table, only to find that all our gear was gone with the livestock. Our old practice swords were there, but the better swords, shields, crossbows, and tools of all sorts had been taken.

At that point, nothing surprised me. I kicked a loose board off the barn and used that for my table. Lankin and Ombree said nothing while they searched for a spare trinket or two that might have survived the blaze. In the meantime, toasted some bread on the dying embers of the house and watched.

Ultimately, the paltry amount I had recovered exceeded what the others found combined. I was tempted to think that the God had shown favor because I hadn't sunk as low as Ombree or Lankin in the drunkenness and debauchery, but that was pure arrogance. The God plays no favorites, son, and to violate His law in any regard is to violate it in every regard. The truth was, I tended to hide my wealth, but Lankin and Ombree put it out for all to see. That alone was why I found more than they did.

We ate in a silence that was thick enough to walk across. I didn't dare mention the baker's comments nor the difficulty I'd had procuring our food. I ate my share of the breakfast, washed it down with a few swallows from the well, and then went to saddle the horse. By the time I'd finished that, Lankin had collected the remaining food and Ombree had gone into the shed. With what little we had in the saddlebags, strapped to the horse, or hanging from our belts, we set off, taking a southeasterly, overland route that avoided Tsillis.

The trees here were dense with plenty of low-hanging branches, so Ombree led the horse by the reins. After a couple hours of hiking, we turned back toward the southwest. I knew this area. Three years ago, this was the route we'd taken for that first robbery.

Ombree slowed and held up his hand to stop us. Hoofbeats were coming closer from the city. I strained trying to pick out the sound of carriage wheels on the cobblestone road. I heard none, but there was a lot of clanking and jingling of armor and weapons. That meant either a patrol or a well-armed escort for a nobleman. We stopped well inside the trees as a patrol rode past. Their decorated tabards blew in the breeze off the coast.

Once they were well on their way, Ombree darted across and back into the trees. Lankin followed close behind. I crouched at the edge of the forest, ready to dart across when a shrill woman's voice carried on the sea breeze. Shortly after, a lady in her finery rode past on a chestnut horse with a gentleman on a brown and white paint alongside while she related the town gossip.

I waited until I couldn't hear the lady any more before I hopped up and started across. The sounds of hoofbeats and armor drew closer again from the inland direction. I glanced that way, which turned out to be a near-fatal mistake. I stumbled over the cobblestones and went down, stinging my hands and knees with fresh scrapes.

My heart thudded hard as Ombree and Lankin hissed encouragement that I get back up and join them. I pushed off from the ground. The patrol drew closer as I rushed across and down the shallow slope into the trees.

Ombree caught my arm as I went past and pulled me down. He leaned closer and said in a growly whisper, "Stay down and stay quiet."

I nodded and twisted around to watch the road. The patrol rode past again, headed this time for the city. When the noise faded, Ombree let me go. I got back to my feet and brushed off the leaf litter.

Lankin stepped in front of Ombree. "The patrols never come back through that fast. Who did you cross?"

Ombree turned Lankin around and gave him a shove. "Never you mind that and just keep walking."

That whole first day, we stayed off the roads. Even when we came to the coastal road heading south, we kept parallel to it but well inside the trees, which slowed us down considerably. But Ombree wanted to take no risks. The fire seemed to have spooked him a little. We traveled until after nightfall. I expected Ombree to find a place for us to set up, and make back some of the money we'd lost, but we traveled by moonlight for a while then stopped. Dinner was half of our remaining food, and then we bedded down for a somewhat chilly night.

In the morning, I was the first one up, which was typical for me once I was older than fourteen, but after tending to the horse, there wasn't much else for me to do except wait for the others to get up at midmorning. Breakfast was what remained of our food. That meant we had to leave the relative safety of the trees, but we could make better time.

Just like three years ago, Ombree rode his palomino and Lankin and I jogged alongside. The trip was easier for me this time than our first jaunt from Andrea to Tsillis. The ease with which I could run surprised even me. I didn't need half as many rests. About midafternoon, we came upon a small town. There was no wall, not so much as a fence, but a handful of small, wooden buildings huddled next to the road with several footpaths leading inland.

As we neared, a sharp whistle from somewhere in the trees brought a group of men armed with sickles, pitchforks, and knives out of the building. They blocked the way. We slowed and stopped a stone's throw back.

One man, the only one with a halfway decent sword, stepped forward. "That's far enough. State your business."

Ombree slid off his horse and handed the reins to me as he stepped forward. "Food. We just want to buy some food. Then we'll be on our way."

"You're getting nothing here. We got the word about a man on a palomino and two boys from Tsillis, so you be on your way."

Lankin gripped the hilt of his sword.

A clicking noise and the soft, almost inaudible slide of metal past leather came from the trees to my left. I nudged

Lankin in the ribs with my elbow and jerked my head toward the trees. Light glinted off metal, and Lankin let go of his hilt.

"We mean to pay a fair price for the food, of course." Ombree bounced his purse on the palm of his hand, jiggling the few coins it contained, while he took in the town with a sweep of his other hand. "It looks like this town could use the income."

The leader pointed at us with his sword. "I said you'll get nothing here. Move on."

Ombree reclaimed his reins and swung up into the saddle. We cut a wide path around the town with the townsmen staying between us and their homes the whole way. The lurker in the trees kept pace, too. Our shadows stopped following us when we rejoined the road on the other side of the town.

Lankin heaved a sigh. "How far are we going to have to go before we get beyond the reach of whoever it is you crossed?"

The only answer from Ombree was a glare.

By nightfall, we hadn't yet reached a friendly village. The two others we came across met us with armed men and an order to go around. I was also pretty sure there was someone in the trees watching at the first one. By the time we reached the second, trees had given way to scraggly shrubs.

Ombree dismounted and hobbled his horse a distance away from the road. "This looks like a good spot."

"For camp?" I asked. "For work."

Lankin rolled his eyes. "Who's going to be along this road? We're not even near a town of any decent size."

"Who said anything about stopping travelers?" Ombree gave us both a look and shook his head. He spoke softly enough to be heard no further than the three of us. "Please tell me you've actually managed to notice that we're being followed, that our extra shadow raced on ahead of us to each town and then waited for us to catch up."

I looked back the way we'd come. "I noticed someone in the brush at each town. That was the same guy?"

Ombree groaned. "Yes, boy, the same one. With you two on foot, he was able to get ahead of us each time." The volume of his voice dropped by half. "Get camp set up and make plenty of noise about it." Then he spoke louder. "I'm going to sleep. You two get the camp set up." He stretched out on the ground. "I think we can chance a fire. No sense freezing to death tonight."

While I started taking care of the horse, Lankin collected twigs and hacked branches off shrubs, all the while complaining loudly about getting stuck with the chores all the time. Under the cover of Lankin's laments, Ombree rolled up to a crouch and disappeared among the brush.

I finished with the horse about the same time Lankin got the fire going. He continued to gripe about the lack of a decent dinner and our teacher's poor leadership skills. Noise of a scuffle back from the road a ways drew my attention. A man gasped and groaned, then all fell silent. Lankin stopped his complaining as Ombree strode back to the camp with a sword, a purse, a cloak, and a backpack in hand. He led a rust brown horse with a white spot on her forehead.

"It was a Tsillis patrolman." He shoved the backpack into my chest. "See what's in there."

I didn't have to ask about what happened to the patrolman. The next morning, while Ombree and Lankin slept, I gave the man a decent burial. The grave was shallow, but I couldn't let the body rot in the open.

At the moment, I hid my regrets about the man's death. After fumbling with the clasps a couple times, I opened the pack and found a cylinder full of matches, a whetstone, a canteen, and–most importantly as far as I was concerned– dinner. Hardtack and jerky didn't make for a very exciting dinner, but it did fill the hole. The canteen was full of water, which washed down the dry hardtack fine.

Without the patrolman warning every town we came to, we were able to buy provisions in the next one. After that, things returned to business as usual. Lankin and I tried riding double on the spare horse, but that didn't work too well. Lankin insisted on controlling the horse with me riding behind him. There wasn't a way to get comfortable, and I had to either hold onto Lankin or try to stay balanced. If the awkwardness wasn't enough of a problem, the horse wearied too quickly. I couldn't blame her. Neither Lankin nor I were exactly small, although he was shorter and leaner than I was. We both walked again for a while to give the poor horse a break. Then after that, we took turns riding the second horse. We traveled until after nightfall. If we were near a crossroads or a larger town, we set up on a curve and lightened the load of anyone who came by and looked like they carried something of value. If we were near a smaller town, Ombree and Lankin would disappear the moment camp was set up, sometimes sooner. They invited me to come along the first few times, but I refused, citing fatigue. After my birthday, I wanted no part of their evening entertainments. I'd like to tell you that my reluctance was due to virtue, but at that time, I in fact just didn't want a repeat of the total embarrassment I felt on my birthday. Virtue came later, thank the God.

We were on the road for almost three months, always heading south along the coast. As we traveled, the weather turned much hotter during the day, but still turned cold at night. We began traveling at night and resting during the day in whatever shade we could find. Then the road headed upward into the foothills of a ragged mountain range, providing a relief from the extreme daytime heat. As we continued and crossed through a mountain pass, the weather turned wet. Rain fell so often and so heavily that I never entirely dried out. Fires had to be sheltered in lean-tos made from sticks and broad leaves that were over an arm's length from tip to tip and as wide as an average man.

The wildlife changed as well, going from the small birds and animals we know well to more lizards and snakes then again to brilliantly colored frogs and birds and large cats the size of a big dog. The humid, hot environment seemed to favor bigger animals. In addition to the cat, there were more insects, some as large as my hand. The hum of their wings never let up. I slept with one eye open the night I saw a snake that was longer than I was tall and as big around as my thigh. The plant life, too, underwent a change from forest to grasses and shrubs to cacti and finally back to a forest again. These latter forests had trees that seemed to rival mountains for height. They were draped in flowering vines. The damp places had strange plants with hinged leaves. If any insect touched them, the leaves slammed together.

As we traveled, Ombree told story after story of trade caravans that stretched from one horizon to the other, each cart loaded to the brim with the incredible riches of far off lands. He never mentioned exactly where it was we were going, but he spoke constantly of trade routes, traveling merchants, and great wealth to split among us. When he wasn't speaking of the wealthy merchants and caravans that went for miles, he described beautiful, exotic women. Lankin hung on every word and couldn't get enough details.

During all this time, Lankin no longer mentioned Uncle Haelin, not even when he'd had too much to drink. However, he did speak of our pact often, always out of Ombree's hearing, but now the reasons were entirely to get revenge on Rory-Galstaff and to demonstrate the might of the Iron Mountains, proving that the men of the Iron Mountains were just as good as the Andreans, better even.

One morning, I was taking care of camp chores when Lankin woke up.

He snickered. "Aren't you the diligent little worker?"

"Gives me something to do while you two sleep half the day." I dug two apples out of the backpack and tossed one to Lankin. "Uncle Haelin—"

Lankin snorted and mumbled, "Uncle Haelin."

I frowned and jabbed my finger at him, suddenly feeling very protective of my uncle's memory. "Maybe you don't remember, but he died protecting us."

"Your uncle died because he was an idealistic fool." Lankin's eyes narrowed as he leaned closer. "If he had just taken Guffey's offer, he would have saved us and himself."

"Guffey's offer would have condemned an innocent man."

He laughed, almost choking on a piece of the apple. "Grow up, Therin. There are no innocent men."

At the time, I wasn't sure how to answer that. Lankin had a point. I certainly wasn't an innocent man and I knew it. I'd never met a man innocent in the eyes of the God, but how could that justify saving oneself at the expense of another? Now, older and wiser than I was then, I know how I would have answered that. But I went silent and never brought up my uncle to Lankin again.

Nearly three months after the fire, the walls of a huge city crept over the horizon. At the crest of a hill, I stopped and stared at the city situated near a body of water on the west that stretched further than I could see. A long, broad road headed from the city to the east and disappeared over the horizon. From our height, a long caravan occupied the road. Wagons rode down the center sandwiched between horsemen.

"You see, boys? Did I lie? Just look at that beautiful caravan." Ombree beamed his most disarming smile. "Just imagine what one of those wagons contains.

I pushed my rain-dampened hair back from my face and stared.

Lankin snorted. "And just have a look at their escort. You think the three of us will do any good with that kind of opposition?"

"My boy, we just need a good strategy." Ombree drew Lankin into a one-armed embrace. "We'll observe, we'll learn, and then we'll strategize. Just you wait. In a week, maybe two, we'll be living life as it was meant to be lived."

He turned toward the city. "And there, boys, is our new home. Great Portage."

I knew something of geography, certainly major features like Great Portage, and my mind's eye brought up a map image from my days in school. The Iron Mountains was on the extreme northern edge of that map and Great Portage at the far south, just above the Southlands that were at the very bottom of the chart. The realization weakened my knees. I was half a world away from my home.

⊨ Chapter 8 ⊨

That night, we camped outside the city wall. Unlike Andrea, there were no small villages directly outside the walls of Great Portage, simply an area where the thick jungle trees had been cleared, leaving clear lanes of fire for the city archers. Our camp was within their view but they did not seem to find us in any way significant.

Well, more accurately, *I* camped outside town. Lankin and Ombree left their things with me and went inside the wall to some kind of exotic entertainment Ombree gushed about, available only in this foreign land. I didn't see them again until midday. When they did arrive, they brought along a lunch of roasted chicken and a roasted plant I'd never seen before, with grains along the outside of an inner cylinder that Ombree called a "cob." These were a welcome change from the jerky, nuts, and stale bread we'd been living on.

After we'd eaten, Ombree had us break camp. He and Lankin rode the horses while I walked alongside. The city walls were wide enough for eight men to walk shoulder to shoulder all the way around, and the main gate to the north was big enough to admit twice that many marching in ranks.

Once inside the city, people stared as we passed through. In many places in the Western Bond, you can walk from one town to the next faster than you could get through Great Portage. The size of the city itself made me feel very small. After seeing so many different people from so many different lands at the Tournament of Swords and having spent the time we did in the port city of Tsillis, I thought of myself as an experienced traveler, but what I saw before was nothing compared to Great Portage. I'd seen, and fought bouts with, Southlanders of course, so I wasn't surprised to see them so close to their homeland, not a hundred miles further South. Their dark skin, broad noses, and tightly curled black hair stood out among the men and women of the Bond I was more accustomed to seeing. Their clothing was usually a knee- length skirt made of leather or brightly-colored material and a collar made of an animal pelt, pale yellow with black spots. I was shocked to see the women. Many of them had a brightly-colored skirt and a bead necklace and only thin cotton fabric to hide their usually ample bosoms. Lankin openly stared at them. I kept my eyes on my boots, trying to think about what the God would want, but in truth I peeked up from time to time.

The Southlanders were hardly the only exotic people in the city. Many tribes from the lands of the Kings of the East traveled there. Ombree said their eyes are slanted, but when I looked that isn't true. They have a flap of skin on the inside corner of their eyes that narrows their eyelids on the inside. The eyes themselves are the same shape as anyone else's, though I never met one whose eyes were not brown. Ombree also said their skin is yellow and it is true that some few of them look a color close to yellow. But none are exactly so and most of them are in fact a light brown.

The people of the East wore many different costumes, multiple styles of the impossibly smooth fabric called "silk," but some wore leathers and furs and wools. Some rode short stocky horses and were armed with excellent short bows. Some rode long-legged stallions. Wavy swords hung on their sides. They wore elegant silks and had very long moustaches and no beards.

There were Hindians of many sorts there as well, from the southern reaches of the East. Their skin color was as dark or darker than the Easterners, some as dark or darker brown than even the Southlanders. Eye color matched the Southlanders, but with the same shape eyelids as you or I and the same nose shape and same straight hair. A people I first mistook for Hindians were in the area as well. I don't know their proper name, but I found out later they were native to the region, while all the rest had come there from somewhere else. They were darker-skinned than even the most tanned of our people but not nearly the deep brown, almost black of the Southlanders or the darkest of the Hindians. Some of them had skin with a tint that was nearly red. Their foreheads angled differently, sloping back at a steeper angle. They kept their glossy black hair very straight and long and were in general shorter than people from the Bond, almost like Easterners, but they were bulky with muscles (unlike them), had no inner eye fold, and no facial hair. And I never saw any of them wearing silk.

There were other tribes and customs and clothing and languages that I hadn't seen before and haven't seen since. On that first pass through the city, I didn't know where to put my eyes. When I looked at people we passed, I felt rude for staring. But when I looked away, I felt I had to be insane to ignore them.

The buildings and tents were as varied as the people. Most were stone and intricately carved with terrifyingly grotesque faces of men and animals. Others were domes made of reeds and sticks. The most interesting were white wood or stone with brilliant red supports. They had roofs with upward curving corners that extended out beyond the building's walls.

When the sun was halfway to the horizon, we exited the heart of the city eastward. Beyond a low inner city wall on the east, more people were camped between two walls running parallel with one another that went from west to east. Son, Great Portage is built at the narrowest strip of land between the vast body of water that separates the very West from the very East, what we call the Western Sea but the Easterners call the Eastern Ocean. On the west side of the Great Portage is that ocean or sea I just mentioned and on the east is what we call the Midearth Sea. Goods of trade from east and west and north and south flow through this city like no other. Swords from our province flow south to the great continent of the Southlanders, which lies beyond the knowledge of mapmakers of our land. Hides and furs flow north. Silks and delicate handcrafts come from the Far East. Spices and oils arrive at the other side. Among many, many other things that traders pass through the Great Portage, far more things than I was able to understand at the time or to remember now.

"The Great Portage" is not in fact the name of a single city, but what really are two cities, one on the western end, where we had entered the port at the Western Sea, and one on the east, where the port for Midearth Sea lies. Between these two cities runs a pair of parallel walls between the east and the west, allowing transport of goods between the oceans inside the protection of these walls that run the seventy miles from coast to coast. The entire strip of land is administered by a small collection of powerful families, who charge armed convoys to enter either of the two ports and license them to pass between the walls. The common city government between the walls and the two ports does not in fact defend the city. Convoys and caravans accept responsibility for themselves to defend the long walls as they transport trade goods. Most of the shippers provide their own escort based on their own nation's armed guards, mercenaries, or military. But some few shippers are too small to furnish their own protection, so they hire teams of mercenaries that assemble under the approval of the city government. Who will work for anyone for the right price.

Past the inner protection of the western city center of Great Portage, which as a city with permanent buildings more faded out between the walls than clearly ended, there were collections of more portable structures in clusters between the walls, where convoys assembled in preparation for the crossing and where mercenary teams lived permanently. Toward the southwest, there was a collection of circular buildings, like tents in the way they could be collapsed and carried, but more stable. I would have thought them permanent structures except that a group of olive-skinned men with cloths wrapped tightly across their heads were disassembling one. South of that, there were cone-shaped tents made of hides and long timbers. These, clearly, were meant for people on the move.

Ombree led us back toward the east, removing us from the cleared fields nearest the port into a cluster of vine-shrouded trees. A large black bird with a white face and an enormous yellow beak watched as we passed. The bird snatched a small piece of fruit off a nearby tree and swallowed it whole.

"So, what do you think of it?" Ombree grinned.

I couldn't find my voice. The variety of people and their clothing—or lack of clothing—was too much of a shock.

"It, uh—" Lankin cleared his throat. "Um, it's very overwhelming."

After a good laugh, Ombree reached over and clapped Lankin on the shoulder. "You'll get used to it. We should be here long enough. We'll sign on with a mercenary caravan and make a little honest money while I scout out the route. Hopefully what was true when I was here before is still true. This place is ripe for the picking for someone with enough courage and ambition. You saw those caravans, didn't you? There's enough in just one of almost any of those wagons to keep us living right for months." He leaned closer. "And no patrols to dodge. Every caravan here is a law unto itself."

We eventually came to a clearing, not long before the sun went down. A building with the upswept roof corners sat overlooking a stream. A couple outbuildings of different architecture stood off to the side.

Ombree stepped down from his horse and drew his sword. "My old stomping grounds. Back then most people didn't know these buildings were here. Let's see if somebody's figured it out." He stared at us expectantly for a moment then added with a smile, "Feel free to draw your own swords, too, boys. You don't want your old master to face any potential intruders alone, do you?"

We drew our blades. I felt my heart pounding in my throat. Ombree nodded at Lankin and he pulled back on the door, which swung outward and creaked loudly from rusty metal hinges. In a light step, Ombree rushed inside, Lankin followed close behind, and I brought up the rear.

The inside of the large building smelled of rotting wood and urine. The house interior had a wide open main room with a fire pit in the center and a low, knee-height table near it. The floor was covered with a straw mat. There were three smaller rooms along the two sides and across the back, separated from each other and the main room by walls made of wooden frames and paper turned moldy. The doors into these rooms slid on tracks. Some old clothing molded in a corner in the main room and dirt was strewn across the floor. But other than that, the place seemed livable. There were no signs of any recent occupation.

"Here we are," said Ombree as he sheathed his sword. "Our new home. It's not much, but it'll do for now. The last time I was here, I eventually worked myself up to staying in the West End, in a house that made this kind of place seem like a shed."

"So, why did you leave?" I'd meant the question as pure curiosity, but I no sooner said it than realized how Ombree might take it.

He still smiled, but the laughter left his eyes and his next statement came out forced. "Itchy feet, boy. Sometimes you just have to move on. And whatever other reasons I may have had are none of your business."

Of course there was more going on than simple wanderlust, and given our reasons for striking out to the south from Tsillis, I had a pretty good guess. I resolved not to get too attached to this place. We might not be staying long.

We stepped back outside and he passed the horse's reins to me. "You two get those horses dealt with and meet me inside. Bring all our equipment."

That made it sound like we would have several trips to make, but once we'd tended the horses and put them in an outbuilding made of rough-hewn logs, Lankin took half the pile, and I took the other half, and neither of us were overburdened.

Ombree came out of the back room. "You can just set our stuff down right there and pick your rooms." He grinned widely. "Don't even have to share this time."

While I set the equipment down, Lankin dropped his and walked into the left room then came back out, frowning. "That one's yours. That dumb stream will keep me up all night."

There's a stream in the bedroom? I walked through that door half-expecting to find a river running through the room, but the sound of the nearby stream trickled in through the narrow windows near the ceiling.

The room was small, hardly large enough to lay down in, and it had no furniture of any sort, but it would be better than sleeping under the stars. I spent an uncomfortable night on the hard floor, sweating in the humidity and swatting large insects that entered through a small hole in the wall. It rained partway through the night, which seemed to suppress the insects a little. But made the humidity worse.

In the morning I was already getting up when I heard Ombree call out. "All right, let's go!"

I stepped out of my room, surprised he was up so early. "Where are we going?"

Once the horses were saddled, we headed back westward, toward the built-up portion of the city. The house we stayed in technically was part of Great Portage, but obviously the parallel walls running seventy miles encompassed plenty of bits of territory that nobody was able to pay much attention to.

Just like the day before, I walked alongside the horses. Lankin had claimed the second horse as his in sort of the same way that Ombree divided our spoils by deciding what he wanted and leaving us with the rest. The slow change from Lankin my friend to Lankin the true disciple of Ombree I'd barely noticed at the time, so gradually did the changes happen, but I did feel a strange sort of unnamed grief, almost as if I'd lost him.

In a way, I did. The man he had become by the time we lived in Great Portage was not the boy I'd grown up with. They shared a name and little else.

Outside the low city wall protecting the West End of Great Portage, a large collection of horse-drawn wagons were gathering in the open fields we'd passed through the day before. Men on horses milled around, some in black leather and chainmail of the Andrean cavalry, some in the rawhide armor of the far northwest coast of the Bond, some in silks of the East, some on the squat horses and armed with short bows of the eastern wildlands, and in many other combinations of styles and costumes, turbans and robes, axes and furs. Furthest from the city, four large, gray- skinned beasts were gathered. They had legs like tree trunks and long noses they could move in all directions, but which they used like an arm shooting out from the end of their face.

Believe it or not. I even witnessed them using these long oddities to suck in water from a stream and put it into their mouths. White spikes stuck out of the corners of those same mouths, which otherwise were without visible teeth. They fanned themselves with big, floppy ears.

"Elephants." Ombree pointed at the gray beasts. "Think of them like really large horses that can flatten you if they get mad enough."

I followed the others to the front of the caravan, keeping my distance and a wary eye on the elephant beasts. They seemed calm enough, but being near such a bizarre animal of that size put a tremor in my hands.

The elephant in the lead had a Southlander riding in a box-like saddle made of reeds on its back. He was a tall, thin man. His black hair was graying near the temples, and a faint scar traced a curved line across his left cheek.

Ombree stood up in his stirrups. "Cebo!"

The Southlander leaned on the edge of the box. "Ombree, you old jackal! You are still alive? And back in this part of the world again?"

"Can't stay away! You got some honest work for me and the boys?"

The Southlander's eyebrows shot up. "Honest work? Since when was that your desire?"

Ombree placed his hand on his heart in mock sincerity. "I'm a changed man, Cebo."

"Oh, so you say." Cebo's smile went a little tense for a moment. "Well, we can always use outriders, you know that, and who are these boys? Not sons of yours. That seems unlikely."

"Oh, no, not mine. Sword students. This is Lankin and Therin." He pointed to each of us as he gave our names.

"No horse, Therin?" Cebo asked.

"He hasn't been able to afford one yet," Lankin chimed in. I glared at him, but Cebo spoke before I could say anything.

"Afford one?" Cebo looked me up and down. "More like he has enough manners to not wrestle you off yours. An elephant, that one is. Strong and steady until you rile him up, so, you'd do well to watch those barbs." He turned back to

Ombree. "I will have to confirm this with the boss, but I believe we have room for all of you."

"You not running your own mercenary crew anymore, Cebo?"

"No. I've been Han Chang's man for . . . twelve year now."

"You working for an Easty, Cebo? He must pay you very well." Ombree smiled disarmingly, but I saw a twitch in his eyebrow when he used the word "Easty" that I'd come to recognize as a sign of genuine anger.

"Yes, he pays well. And is an honest boss. Let me speak with him." Cebo prodded the elephant with a staff and the huge beast turned and moved back along the assembling column in footsteps that surprised me with their silence.

"I never cared much for the slant-eyes," muttered Ombree as he sat back in his saddle. "Except their women. Oh, their women are incredible."

"The girl I had night before last was amazing," my onetime friend said. "Are they all like that?"

"Yeah, even better. We'll have to get one for Therin."

"You two disgust me," I said.

Lankin laughed but Ombree faked a grin, eye twitching.

The conversation went downhill from there until Cebo returned. "You two will join the outriders." The Southlander said pointing to Ombree, "You know the way of it, so I'll leave it to you to show Lankin. The usual arrangement for payment: a silver a day and your food. Drinking in the caravan is forbidden. Agreed?"

"As always," Ombree said.

He tapped Lankin on the shoulder and the two of them rode off leaving me standing there among the elephants with a man I had only just met.

Cebo attached a rope-and-stick ladder to the edge of the box and rolled it down over the side of the elephant.

"I could use another set of eyes up here. Come on up. I believe Han Chang will join us soon."

I took a small step toward the elephant as the huge head turned toward me. Its large eyes, relatively small for its massive head, seemed to look into my very soul in a way a horse never does.

"Do not mind Bheka. He is in a good mood today." Cebo waved me forward.

Trembling, I grabbed the first rungs and climbed up, all the while keeping an eye on the elephant. He didn't seem to mind my weight or the awkward way I half-kicked him in the ribs as I climbed. I didn't mean to, of course, but the ladder rested against the elephant's curved side. When I was high enough, Cebo helped me into the box-like saddle. It was only a few feet square, but it had a canopy over our heads.

After a brief time of Cebo looking behind him for the signal, a short, blocky man walked forward and climbed the ladder up to our spot on the elephant with practiced ease. He wore a conical helmet with a spike on top and scalemail armor. He was only as tall as my shoulders, but as proportionally bulky as I am. His face was light brown with reddish cheeks from sun exposure, a thin long mustache under his nose, and the corners of his inner eye strongly folded inward. In fact, it was at that moment I realized the eyes were not as Ombree said they were.

"I am Han Chang," he said simply.

Cebo pulled the ladder back in and rolled it up. The three of us were rather crowded in the basket, meaning each of us were physically touching one another in one way or another the entire time. Neither of the other men seemed to mind. I couldn't help noticing that neither of them smelled like me, nor like one another, either.

Shortly afterward, after looking over at Han Chang and receiving a nod, Cebo picked up a horn hanging from his belt and blew a long note. Bheka and the other elephants started down the road. Their strides were long and the box wove from side to side. I gripped the side of the box and held on.

Cebo chuckled and slapped my shoulder.

Smiling a careful little smile, Han Chang said, "You get used to it. I remember my first ride when I came here more than twenty year ago. Very upsetting."

Cebo asked with his face forward, steering the elephant, "So, how did you fall in with your master Ombree, that old fox?"

"I needed to learn how to use a sword, so I asked him to teach me."

Han Chang watched me carefully as I spoke. The answer was pathetic, and I knew it, but I didn't feel comfortable enough with either the old Southlander or the man of the East to tell them the whole tale.

Chang nodded slowly. "There is more to it than that, I think, but that will do for answer for now."

As we traveled, the two men told me stories. Some were personal. Some were clearly meant to teach lessons. One of the biggest surprises was to hear that both of them had fought in the Dragon War, on opposite sides. But neither seemed to hold that against the other man. There were many ways in which each of them reminded me of Uncle Haelin, and that reminder saddened me, but at the same time made the ride with these men the best time I'd had in a long time. I began to enjoy talking with them, and they didn't seem to mind at all.

Near sunset, Cebo blew his horn again at Han Chang's direction and the elephants stopped. We camped that night and while the boss inspected the rest of the caravan, Cebo showed me how to care for such a large animal. Sentries, who had spent the day sleeping in the back of some of the wagons, went on patrol for the night, some of them archers taking responsibility for the sections of the walls on either side of us. The walls were much closer together here, not even a bowshot a part.

Ombree, Lankin, and all the other horse riders joined us around the campfire, and some of the men in the caravan played music on small, wooden flutes until Chang sent everyone to bed. I lay awake thinking about Uncle Haelin and home and eventually drifted off to sleep.

The next day, we were back on our way shortly after dawn. Again, I rode with Cebo. This time Han Chang rode further back in the convoy. We were silent for a while and I watched the terrain drift by. The elephant's swinging gait no longer unsteadied me, and I was a much better watchman.

Cebo leaned against the edge of the box and studied me. "What grieves you, little brother?"

The question startled me. "Um, grieving?"

"Perhaps I am mistaken." He launched off into another round of tales, some instructive, some personal.

When he paused about midday, I turned toward him and nodded. "My uncle, Haelin. I've been thinking about him. You remind me of him in some ways."

"Ah. How is this?"

So, for the first time in a long while, I spoke of my uncle. Sometimes with a smile and sometimes with tears. Cebo didn't seem to mind. I spoke of how things were before the tournament then later at the tournament and then finally after the tournament and how I came to be with Ombree. The sun was setting as I finished.

"You have had a difficult road, little brother." Cebo gripped my shoulder more firmly than I thought someone so slight could manage. "I fear it will get more difficult before it gets better, but with a teacher such as your Uncle Haelin was to you, I believe you will come out a good man in the end, with the blessings of the God."

My brow furrowed as I turned to him. "Thank you." I didn't fully believe him, but his small comment gave me a tiny ray of hope that perhaps my life would be different one day.

During the second day, we reached a place where the walls ran into some high hills. The pathway had been carved out among the hills, so that the convoy walked along the ground, towering cliffs about us. The cliffs narrowed the path so that only one elephant or wagon could pass at a time in places. The walls themselves actually came to an end at this point, but the cliffs were full of trails designed to give our archers access to each side of the convoy. I saw them taking their places up on high before we even entered the narrow passage, Han Chang having paused us until the higher reaches were secured. This passage was not more than ten miles long but took more time to pass through than any of the other ten miles of the voyage. After the hills faded away again, high walls on either side of us protected the convoy once more.

At the end of the third day we reached the east coast, where boats waited in a huge harbor near a city about the size of Andrea, the so-called "East End" of Great Portage. The caravan stopped within an easy walking distance of the docks. Cebo and some of the other Southlanders left, and when they returned, the wagons were unloaded onto a few different boats. Han Chang pointed his men in various directions. The mercenaries actually provided some of the labor to unload the wagons, which Ombree told me later is not normal and which Cebo told me is part of what made Han Chang's mercenary crew such a success at what they did. Like my uncle, Chang believed in doing the best he could at whatever task given him.

That night I stayed in Cebo's tent and didn't see Lankin and Ombree at all. The next morning, Cebo left again. When he returned, Chang organized us into a long line of men spaced out within easy reach of each other from another boat to the now empty wagons. Half of us faced the other half, so that we were able to unload a boat and pass baskets and small crates from man to man without twisting or taking a step as the wagons in the freelance convoy got restocked with goods for the trip back to the West End. The goods moved quickly down the line, and a pair of men kept rotating the wagons through so that in the end, they were all loaded again. The caravan left the next morning and headed back through the Great Portage, this time going to the West End, where Chang directed the goods be unloaded from the wagons and reloaded in other boats at the grateful direction of the shippers. The mercenaries were all paid afterward, six silver coins for me and six each for Lankin and Ombree. The next day, Ombree and Lankin lightened their purses in the taverns of the West End of Great Portage. I spent some money on supplies but found a place to hide the rest where I hoped my companions wouldn't find it.

In the early afternoon, once Lankin and Ombree had finally began to stir, the three of us were seated on the floor at the low table in the main room, eating disinterestedly at flatbread I'd purchased two days ago, now quite stale. Ombree gestured, waiving a triangular hunk of bread in his hand. "It's just as I thought boys. They haven't changed the pass between the hills at all. I'd heard they'd widened it. Thank my lucky stones they didn't."

"So?" muttered Lankin. "Clearly you're thinking of hitting a set of wagons when they're passing through the hills, where you can get just one wagon at a time. But what good will that do you? Sure, you can get a wagon, but the archers on the hills will just shoot you down."

"Ah, know so much do you now?" Ombree smiled and smacked Lankin across the face with his left hand in a manner intended to look playful. The loud impact of palm on cheek made it clear that the blow when beyond horseplay.

"Ow!" said Lankin. But then he laughed, rubbing his reddened cheek, still scarred from the tournament and when he first met Ombree. "You old bastard!"

Ombree chuckled and then gestured again with the flatbread. "What you don't know, smartiebritches, is that Chang and Cebo run one of the better mercenary convoys. Some of 'em don't run with archers. Or more often, they don't slow down the train of wagons to make sure the archers are up on the hills before passing through, trying to get the passage done in two days instead of three. Also, some of the national convoys, the ones that provide their own troops instead of hiring local talent, can be pretty sloppy at times. Though most of them stay sharp. Disgruntled mercenaries lingering in the area have been the main source of actual robberies in the Great Portage passage, usually right outside East or West End. The City Fathers really frown on that and actually do more with their licenses to keep that sort of thing from happening than you'd think. So the national convoys usually know that not hiring local teams can invite trouble. That means they either hire locals, or they come out armed for dragon. Usually but not always. With the proper selection of convoy, robbing a single wagon without having to worry about archers will be child's play. We just pick one that doesn't have any in place."

"If local mercenaries are the main cause of robberies, why did they build the walls?" I asked.

Ombree looked up at me, a sharp expression in his eyes. But then he smiled. "Used to be the local tribes hit the convoys a lot. The walls were built to prevent that. Now they probably do more to keep mercenaries from running off with a wagon in secret, since the gates to the outside roads all go through either West End or East End, both of which are loaded with armed men who don't want a robber to succeed. Unless they are the robbers themselves, that is." He grunted at his little joke.

"So how do we get the goods from a wagon we rob over the walls?"

"Now that there, Therin," he popped his triangle of bread into his mouth and continued talking while chewing, "Is an actual intelligent question. Getting over the walls is a bit hard but wouldn't be too bad with proper ladders. But if we hit a convoy in the hills, we can haul the goods up one side and down the other with ropes and pulleys. We'd have to take it overland after that and definitely would not be able to cash in anything we take at either the West or East End of Great Portage. But there are other towns nearby, especially on the Midearth Sea coast. We might be able to get away with this only once if we're seen, so it's important we get new clothes and wear masks. We'll have to assemble ropes for the hills and make a few other arrangements. Should take maybe twenty gold or so. Not too big of an investment."

For the next few weeks, we hired on with different caravans. Some of them were known to Ombree, but some were not. Ombree and Lankin always worked as outriders, but my job changed with each trip. Sometimes I rode on an elephant to help keep watch. Sometimes I rode with the driver of a wagon. A few times, I even slept during the day and became a nighttime sentry. We never rode with the same caravan leader twice. After the trips, we always had a long discussion day after we were back home. Ombree focused on the strengths and weaknesses of each leader as well as the route they took. He and Lankin still wasted money, but not all of it. We began to assemble rope ladders and other supplies we'd need for the job.

One day, about a month after we'd ridden with Cebo, Ombree nodded once. "Let's be quick, boys. We need to collect our supplies and head out fast enough to get ahead of the next caravan. Let's go."

We hurried around the house and gathered up the supplies we needed, along with our weapons and Ombree's sledgehammer. Poles attached to the sides of the horse saddles and linked to one another behind the horse allowed them to drag burdens behind them. Our rather large amount of rope went back there. Then we headed overland, meeting up with the main road a few miles east of the thicket of jungle where our hideout was. I jogged the distance while the others rode. By the time we reached the narrow foothills pass, just before sunset, my sweat-soaked clothes stuck to me. Fortunately, Ombree had brought plenty of water for me to drink. At the narrowest point on a curve that came just before the actual narrowest part of the pass, Ombree dismounted.

He looked at Lankin and me. "You boys need to get the rope up on these hillsides. String the rope bridge across the gap up top, so Therin on the right can cross over the top of the ridge to the other side after he releases the rock slides.

Lankin, prepare the rope and pulley on the left, that is, the north side, down to where the wagon will pass, here, to haul up the treasure. Put the rope ladder and pulleys down the north side of the hill so we can escape out that way after we've taken the goods. Hammer all the ropes down with rock pins, like I showed you. Therin, use the rope netting here and here–" He pointed to two spots along a natural ledge below the hilltop "–to accumulate loose rock you're gonna break off with the sledgehammer tonight. That way all you've got to do to make the rocks fall in the morning, is cut the netting. The next caravan should be coming here around midmorning; you'll want to have all the pounding done long before they arrive, so they don't hear you. You want to have enough rock on either side to create enough of a rockslide to block the road on either side of one of the wagons I'll identify in the morning. We want the caravan to have to come to a halt through here, making it hard for any outriders to get back to the one wagon we're gonna hit." He spun and pointed at Lankin. "Do you have all of that? I'm leaving you in charge."

"What, you're not gonna be here?"

"No. I've got an appointment in East End." He grinned, "Don't worry boys, I'll be back by midmorning. Any questions?"

Lankin stood staring at him, his hands on his hips, his mouth open. "Appointment? Do you mean with Samarra? Is this a good time for that? If you ride hard all the way there and back and you'd barely have two hours with her."

Ombree replied with a smirk. "It's always a good time for *that*. And it's more like four hours with her, but don't worry, I'll keep it to two to be sure to return on time. You boys can do this. Don't worry, you've got everything you need. Anything else?"

"What direction is the convoy we're going to hit coming from?"

"From West End. Anything else?"

"Uh, yeah, how about the fact it's about to go suddenly dark out here?" The sunsets in that far south land indeed seemed to come very quickly, son, plunging everything into darkest night. (The days felt hot like summer, but the days were not long like summer days in our province.)

"It's a full moon visible early on tonight. You didn't know? It'll give you more than enough light. All right, time for me to go." Without further discussion, Ombree mounted up on his horse and galloped away.

Lankin and I managed to climb our respective hills and string up the rope bridge from one hilltop to another across the pass and to hammer in the rock pins supporting it before the sun went down. I did not succeed at laying out the nets that would contain the rocks for the ready-made rockslides before the sun fell. While the moon was indeed full, thick clouds covered the sky and it was only on occasion the clouds broke enough for me to see the nets well enough to get their placement right. It took hours, I don't know how many, before I was ready to begin pounding rocks. Almost immediately after I began to smash off pieces of naturally soft rock (I thanked the God they were soft), it began to rain. In that land the rains are warm, so I wasn't freezing, but I found it very difficult to maintain my footing on the hillside with water rushing down. It was nearly impossible to continue the pounding, but I did manage some.

In the early pre-dawn hours, the rain finally lifting, I could see the rocks I had accumulated were nowhere near enough. I was exhausted, but I kept up a pitiful rhythm of hammer blows. Soon, Lankin joined me. "Holy heavens, Therin! You haven't got the rocks pounded out yet?"

"No. Did you get all your pulleys and the rope ladders finished?"

"Yes, but it took all night. The rain made it really hard."

"For me, too, Lankin."

"Here, let me take the hammer." He and I then switched off with the blows. A bit of rest did me a lot of good—my strength returned. Perhaps two hours after dawn, everything was ready. Just after we finished, Lankin and I sat on the ledge that contained the rock nets, on my side of the divide, panting hard.

At that instant we heard hoofbeats coming from the east. Ombree arrived, his horse lathering so hard the poor animal was at the point of death. He dismounted, ignoring the beast.

"Boys, did you finish everything?" he cupped his hands as he called up to us.

"Yes," I replied wearily.

"We may have a problem," he shouted up at us, dropping his hands.

"Such as?" demanded Lankin, wiping sweat from his brow. "Toss down a rope for me and pull me up and I'll tell you." We had some length of rope with a grappling hook that had been designed to help me climb up to the ledge where I built the ready-made rockslides. I hadn't actually used it, having climbed the rocky face of the hill freehanded, because we'd been so pressed for time. (My side was not as steep as Lankin's.) Lankin and I tossed down the rope and pulled our swordmaster up to our ledge.

The first thing I noticed was Ombree smelled strongly of mead. His eyes were bloodshot red. "Um, I think I may have been spotted in East End. There may be someone after me."

"What do you mean, spotted?" asked Lankin. "You go there all the time!"

"Well...uh, I may have let it slip...in the enthusiasm of the moment...something about what we are doing here."

"You're kidding me!" And then Lankin let loose with a string of vulgar language I will not repeat.

Ombree's sullenly apologetic mood shifted as fast as stepping from bright sunlight into a dark cave. "Listen, kid!" he shoved Lankin. "I don't know for sure anyone's coming. I'm just warning you in case they are. This operation is still on!"

He looked around the ledge. "Where's your camouflage? Didn't you chop some bushes to bring up here to hide behind? If a wagon driver sees you standing on the ledge by these rocks, they are gonna know something is up. And where are your masks? Can't you boys do anything right?"

I started to say that he'd never mentioned camouflage, but Lankin snapped before I could open my mouth, "Listen here, planning genius! We had unexpected difficulties! IF you had been here, you could have helped—"

"You wanna taste my blade, you young punk?" Ombree cut him off and put his hand on the hilt of his sheathed sword.

"Yeah, maybe I do," said Lankin in a much quieter voice than before, putting his hand on his own hilt.

"Whoa, whoa, wait a minute," I started to say. I didn't finish because at that moment the lead riders from the caravan we were waiting on appeared around the curve on our left. We saw them and they us, not two hundred yards away. I heard a voice shout back, "Archers!"

While the voice calling for archers still echoed among the rocks, we heard the pounding of horse hooves coming from the opposite direction, from the east. A squad of four Eastern horsemen appeared. When they saw us above, these squat men with short legs and powerful arms leapt off the

216

top of their horses' backs onto the rock wall below us and began climbing up with a speed I'd never witnessed before.

"Time to go!" shouted Ombree, running for the rope bridge (how he had expected us to camouflage that I never found out). By chance, the Eastern riders were climbing up not far from the furthest east of the nets Lankin and I had filled. Lankin pulled his sword and cut the net. Rocks tumbled down, impacting one of the horsemen, who shouted out in pain. I don't know if he lived or died.

"Come on!" shouted Lankin, sprinting after Ombree up the slope of the ridge above our ledge. Running towards the spot where the rope bridge was attached on our side. I ran after him.

Just after I scrambled up the ridge, I looked back. Two of the Eastern riders had already attained the ledge just below us. And four horse-mounted Andrean archers on their tall black horses galloped our way from the direction of the convoy. The Andrean horse archers dismount to fire their longbows, so as they pulled their horses to a halt, I knew I only had a few moments before I'd be in serious trouble.

I was maybe five yards short of our rope bridge, Lankin just starting across it, when both of us saw Ombree pull his sword as he stood at the other side of the bridge. He hacked at one strand of rope. Lankin hastily jumped back to my side.

As he sliced the other rope, he shouted, "Sorry boys!"

Then he ran in the direction of the other rope ladder, the one Lankin had strung down the north side of the hill, making his escape to the freedom of the jungle.

An arrow impacted a rock right next to me. "Over the ridge!" Lankin shouted. We went over the top of this steep hill and half jumped and half tumbled down into the jungle on the south side of the passage that men had carved out of the hillside as part of the Great Portage.

It was really a miracle of the God we survived the long tumbling fall into the jungle.

I found to my surprise once I got all the way down that I'd been shot through the left thigh with an arrow, which had nearly passed all the way through my flesh to the left side of the bone. My tumbling down the hillside had broken off the feathered end. Huddled in dense undergrowth, Lankin examined my wound.

"Can you walk?"

"I don't think so."

"Well, we'd better hide then." We crawled deeper into the underbrush and waited for nightfall.

More than once we heard men tramping through the undergrowth shockingly close to our hiding spot, looking for us. In the late afternoon, we heard a voice shouting down from the top of the hillside, "We know you boys are out there somewhere. Come out, and I promise you a fair trial. We know what you did was because of your master! We will show you mercy!" The voice was Cebo's. I never knew why it was him looking for us, though I suppose he may have been watching Ombree from the time he first saw him back in Great Portage. Honest operators have no love for robbers. He shouted at us for maybe an hour, but we never replied.

We did not come out of hiding until the sun went down, by which time the men looking for us had given up. Lankin managed to push the arrow in me all the way through. I managed to keep quiet as he did so. I bled, but while the pain was intense, I could walk after he was done.

We never saw Ombree again.

Mercifully the nearly-full moon could be seen for most of that night as we struggled toward the jungle, headed east toward the Midearth Sea coast.

"Now what do we do?" I whispered after several hours of silent travel.

Lankin ran his fingers through his hair and shook his head. "We're done here. Ombree won't be stupid enough to come back. He's long gone. Time for us to head back to Andrea. Time to face the prince."

"Are we ready? I mean, do we know enough?"

"I do. I'm ready to show that prince the value of the Iron Mountains." Lankin nodded once. "It's just a matter of us finding the right route there. We may have to take a boat, at least to get north of the East End. Do you have your money on you?"

"Yes, I finally decided to keep it on my body at all times."

With a chuckle, Lankin said, "That explains why Ombree couldn't find your finding place. The old bastard!"

We kept pushing east through the jungle all night, seeking a route to travel to Andrea via the Midearth Sea.

⊣⊦ Chapter 9 ⊨

ravel to the coast of the Midearth Sea was slow. Finding the route wasn't too difficult. We kept the wall in view but stayed far enough in the brush to avoid being seen. Along the way, we camped wherever we were when night fell and foraged for food along the way. The frequent rains there meant plenty of plants had fruit. I recognized some of them from the market.

The hike wasn't as hard on me as I'd expected at first. After an initial burst of pain as we got going, a numbness settled in until after we would stopped for a rest. I came to both look forward to and dread stopping for a break. By the end of the first day, my leg had begun to swell, particularly around the injury. The skin was too warm and bright red, and the wound drained a dense, yellowish-white fluid. The next morning, I had a mild fever. The swelling grew progressively worse until it was the swelling, and not the actual wound, that made it hard for me to walk. On our third day of travel, I felt weak and woozy, chilled and overheated at the same time. The skin of my leg was so tight, I thought it would split open on its own. I could no longer walk without help, and Lankin became my living crutch.

At about midmorning of that third day, the wall made an abrupt corner outward. We turned with it, keeping it in sight but staying in the brush. Toward afternoon, it turned again, parallel to the original path, and we followed it to the coast. We passed through a marketplace, really just a set of tents and temporary pavilions with vendors who had their wares spread out on tarps or small tables. I remember thinking how odd it was to find a market in the middle of the jungle, but I realized later that we had actually made it to the edge of the East End. At the moment we arrived, I noticed little more than the crowds around us and the ground. My head hurt and the sunlight was too bright. Things I should have recognized made no sense to me. Even with Lankin's help, I stumbled when crossing over the ankle-high beginnings of a new foundation for an extension of the wall that would eventually enclose the marketplace.

Lankin was almost dragging me by this point. I was so dizzy, I couldn't even keep my uninjured leg under me reliably. He stopped at a merchant's booth, but I didn't have the presence of mind to notice what the vendor had for sale.

"Excuse me, but d—" Lankin began.

The merchant waved his hands at us and backed away. "Go on! Go on! Take your plague and get away from here."

"It's not plague, sir. He's injured, and I think it's swollen up."

The merchant backed to the far side of his tent. "Go away!"

"But—"

"Go!"

We continued onto the next one, but the crowd was several people deep. The ones after that were the same. Finally, he came to one with no customers waiting.

"Excuse me, sir, but do you know where we can find a physician?"

The merchant, an Easty I think, stepped over his tarp loaded with small, shiny objects and crouched next to me. He looked at my leg without touching it then drew a breath through his teeth. "That's a bad one. I'm new to town myself, so I don't know where you'd find a surgeon, but most ship captains know a remedy for things like this. Not like you can find a physician or a surgeon in the middle of the ocean. The dock is very near now. Find a captain of a big ship, and he'll set you straight."

"Thank you."

A handful of tents further and we came to a long ramp. Wooden docks had been built along the sandy beach but further out into the water, so even the largest boats could dock without running aground. Well beyond even the furthest pier, a breakwater that was part natural and part constructed of large rocks protected the docks from rough water. Most of this I didn't notice until later. I was only vaguely aware of Lankin half-supporting, half-pulling me up the long ramp. The incline wasn't very steep, thank the God. He passed up a number of very small boats, not big enough for more than two people. They were sort of egg-shaped but pointed at both ends. Some were rowboats, and others had brilliant sails.

We continued down the pier, passing a number of other boats and then a long expanse of nothing.

"Where we goin'?" I asked, surprising myself by how brittle and slurred my own voice sounded.

"The biggest boat on the end. It's flying an Andrean flag. I'm thinking we can solve two problems at once: find help for you and passage to Andrea."

I nodded. The walk to the end of the pier seemed to take longer than the hike from the mountain pass, but we made it. The dragon figurehead on the boat had bold, brilliant paint. There was no one loading or unloading, but there was a tall, dark-haired man on the deck smoking a long, thin pipe.

"Sir?" Lankin called.

The water under the pier made a soothing noise as it splashed against the boat. The gangplank creaked as some-one rushed down it.

"What happened to him?" the man asked.

"We were attacked as we made our way toward town. Therin was shot by an arrow."

"Clean through?" He prodded my leg with his long, thin fingers, like stabbing knives.

"Yes, sir. I asked a merchant for the way to a physician, but he said to find a captain of a large ship."

"Good you did. I can tend this, but I won't do it for free, any more than a surgeon would."

Lankin adjusted his hold on my shoulder. "We've got money, and if you're headed to Andrea, we'll work if that's not enough."

The ship captain slid my free arm over his shoulder. "Yes, I'm headed to the Port of Andrea. We'll see what we have and what it will take."

They hauled me up the gangplank and onto the deck of the ship.

The captain turned toward the front of the ship. "Forward. Sickbay's in the forecastle."

Sickbay turned out to be a small room in the front of the ship. A hammock was hung there, and Lankin and the captain helped me collapse into it. I closed my eyes.

The captain tore what was left of my pants leg out of the way. "Hmph. That's a nasty infection. When did this injury occur?"

"Three days ago. We've been making our way to East End ever since."

"Well, all you can do is all you can do, I suppose. Back in a moment." The sound of footsteps retreated then returned what felt like a year later.

"What is that?" Lankin asked.

"A polinox star. It'll get the swelling down and help with the infection and fever some."

I opened my eyes as the captain unscrewed the lid of a jug containing what looked like a yellow-striped, black blob. He pulled it from the jar, and it unfurled, revealing seven thick, black tentacles radiating from a central disk. The creature writhed in his hand.

Gasping, I tried to push myself up with my arms, but my elbow slipped off the side of the hammock.

"Easy, boy. It just might save your life and will take less of your flesh than the surgeon would have." The captain set the creature on my leg. "It'll sting a bit, but you'll grow numb to it."

The polinox wrapped its bitterly cold body around my leg. A sharp pain stabbed my thigh but then slowly began to fade away. I flopped back onto the hammock, grimacing in pain. "All right, that's half the deal as good as done." The captain went to a cupboard built into the wall and rummaged around until he found a large, thick container made of clear glass. "And here's the rest."

The container had a dull gray flakes in it, not too unlike the lichen that grow on the rocks near the house. "What's that?" Lankin asked.

"You probably wouldn't want to know, but it should take care of the infection." The captain scooped out some and mixed it with water. He gingerly moved the polinox legs out of the way before he painted the mixture on the two holes in my leg. "There you go. We'll just have to reapply that a couple times a day as the swelling goes down. Looks like we're not too late."

"He's going to get better? Really?" Lankin leaned closer to look at the polinox.

"I can't say for sure, young'un. I've seen men recover from worse, though. Though others have died from less. But between the polinox and this–" He held up the jar of gray flakes. "–he's got as good a chance as anyone can give 'im." The captain never did tell us what was in the jar, but later, when I was able get up and move around again, I found one of the sailors scraping something off the hull and putting it in a jar just like the one the captain had. The sailor quipped that the hull was now mold-free and sickbay was restocked.

"What do I owe you?" I asked.

"We'll settle the account once you're back on your feet." The captain smiled at me then turned to Lankin. "You said you two are headed for the Port of Andrea? I'm headed that way by the end of the week."

My eyelids were heavy. I struggled to stay awake, but lost that battle. When I woke up some time later, everyone was gone. I could hear people moving around, but no one stopped in, and none of the voices belonged to Lankin. The swelling had gone down more than I would have thought possible, but when I shifted on the hammock, the walls of the little room seemed to move. I tried to pass that off as my unfamiliarity with boats, but I didn't dare try to get up. I wasn't sure what would happen with the polinox if I did try to get up. I didn't want to upset the thing in case it had a meaner side to it.

Light came only from a lantern hanging nearby. There were no windows in sickbay, so I had no idea how much time had passed or what time of day it was. All I could do was lay still and wonder where Lankin had gone. As different as we had become, I still wished he'd stayed around, but I couldn't be too upset with him. He'd taken care of me and brought me to someone who could help, when he could have left me in the middle of the jungle and gone on alone. I have no doubts Ombree would have done exactly that.

My only visitor was the captain. He came in now and then, brought food, repositioned the polinox, and then repainted the dark gray medicine on the injury. One time, he brought me a book about the Dragon War. When I finished the book I restarted it, but it helped pass the time.

I was surprised about how little I had actually known about the war. Surprised also that even though I knew many battalions from Iron Mountains province had fought in the war and thousands had died, the book only mentioned us twice. Once briefly in defending the Andrean king when his griffin fell, as my uncle had said, and the other time as the only units who supplied themselves across a desert I'd never heard of and fought to defend some remote oasis against huge numbers of Eastern infantry. Rescued by Andrean calvary, actually.

Most of the book talked about Andrean units, though Southlanders and others were mentioned. Clearly the Andrean military was much larger and more powerful than I'd ever realized. And it was against Andreans—into the very heart of their capital—that Lankin and I planned to go. For the first time it occurred to me that even if we killed the prince, we would probably die afterwards. Though—how could we even make it past such a powerful army?

I had just finished reading the book for the second time when the captain came in. He checked the polinox and the holes in my leg and smiled. "Well, that's done it. Swelling's gone. You are practically healed. How do you feel, Therin?"

I propped myself up on my elbows. "Fine, I think."

"Then let's get this polinox back in his jug, shall we?" He picked up the container he'd brought the polinox in and lit a candle.

When he brought the candle close to the polinox, it uncoiled from my leg and rolled away from the heat like a multi- armed ball.

Captain caught it and plunked it back in the jug. "There you go, Polly. All ready for the next time." He nodded to a chair nearby. "Your friend brought you some new clothes. Get yourself dressed and join me on deck. We'll be heading out soon, and we need all hands for that."

As soon as the captain had left, I sat up and swung my legs off the edge of the hammock. Reddish indentions marked my leg in the shape of the polinox. Where the central disk had been, there was a thin, V-shaped cut about as wide as my thumb. I carefully prodded the area. The cut didn't seem to go very deep, but it was numb. Keeping a hand on the wall for support, I stood and slowly, carefully transferred my weight to my injured leg half expecting it to collapse under me. It was wobbly, but it held. I walked from one end of sickbay to the other a few times until I felt steadier on my feet.

The clothes Lankin had brought for me were sturdy but not very fashionable. The brown material would hold up well and the stitching looked excellent. As I undressed, something seemed strange, like I was missing something. Where had my money gone? Thoughts of Lankin taking my pouch swarmed my thoughts. I patted myself down then sorted through the clothes on the chair. My money pouch fell and hit the floor with a muffled jingle. I picked it up and frowned. It should have been heavier. I pulled the drawstring open and dumped the contents into my palm. Half my money was gone. I didn't have to wonder where, but I hoped he'd just spent it on my clothes and the captain's fee for my care. I had a suspicion, though, that he'd paid himself for his troubles. I gritted my teeth and dumped the remaining coins back into the pouch. Pushing my anger aside, I reminded myself that he could have left me to die in the jungle. He hadn't. My life was worth half my money at least.

I dressed and found my way out of the sickbay, through the forecastle, and onto the deck.

When I got there, men and boys–many younger than me–were crawling around the ship. Some were high up on ropes that looked like several ladders tied together. Others were lined up along a hefty, long rope on the deck and pulling the sails up using pulleys.

The ship was smaller than I remembered, though not at all small, but then a fever does confuse the mind sometimes. Over the course of the trip, I took the measure of the ship. I could take almost fifty full steps from the bow to the stern and twelve steps across. There were three tall masts. Both the front of the ship and the rear were raised above the main deck. The front section, the forecastle, was the crew quarters and, of course, sickbay. The aft section, the poopdeck, had the wheel on the top and the captain's quarters below. Several heavy pegs the length of my forearm were scattered around the lower deck as well as on the top of the forecastle and poopdeck. Near each one was a large wooden crate. Once we were underway, I found out what the crates held and what the pegs were for. Each one held a ballista, a sort of over-sized crossbow, that mounted on the pegs.

The captain noticed me as I walked toward him and pointed me toward one of the ropes on the deck. I joined the end of the line and helped pull the sail up. The first time I gave the rope a tug, the Hindian in front of me turned around flashed a smile missing several teeth.

Once the sail was up and secured, the captain set me to winding the rope around a huge spool. By the time I had that done, the next sail was up, though not yet unfurled, and I got busy coiling that rope, too. As I finished coiling the last rope, the captain came over.

"Where's Lankin?"

I shook my head. "I don't know. In town, I think."

How could I know? I'd been confined to sickbay for the last few days, drifting in and out with a fever.

The captain looked up at the sky. "Well, we're ready to get under way, but I told him noon, so I'll wait until then, but no longer."

"Yes, sir. Thank you."

He took me below decks in the forecastle and showed me to a hammock stretched out between a pair of poles. There were some dozens, maybe even a couple hundred, others just like it, all arranged in pairs, one above the other. The captain said one hammock was for me and the one above was for Lankin. I had nothing to leave there, so I counted berths from my space to the ladder leading up to the deck and then went back up top.

I went to the rail nearest the dock and looked up and down the length of it, as far as I could, trying to remember what Lankin had been wearing so I could pick him out of the crowd. Most likely, he'd bought new clothes. I couldn't imagine that he'd kept the garments that had torn on the tumble down the mountain pass. The sun crept higher in the sky, and I began to wonder if I should leave for Port of Andrea without him—or apologize to the captain, pay him if Lankin hadn't already, and disembark.

Behind me, some of the men pulled up one of the gangplanks and secured it.

The captain joined me. "It's time, Therin. Are you joining the crew for this trip or going ashore to catch another ship with your friend?"

Rapid movement of something dark on the docks caught my eye. I looked closer and found Lankin weaving in and out of the crowds. I pointed. "There he is."

"Good. Could use another strong hand."

Lankin raced up the gangplank. At the top, he leaned forward with his hands on his knees and puffed.

"You were nearly left behind, Lankin. I recommend you keep from being late in the future. Get that gangplank up here. It's time to get underway." The captain headed up to the poopdeck at the stern of the ship.

I rushed to help the men pulling up the second gang-plank but ended up standing there watching, afraid to get in the way. As soon as the second gangplank was stowed, the captain signaled men on the docks to cast off.

One of the sailors, an older man with tanned, weathered skin and sparse blond hair, slapped my shoulder. He spoke, but whatever the language was, I couldn't make sense of it. I followed him anyway and helped him with a two-handled crank that wound up a massive chain bearing a tremendous weight. Getting the crank started took a lot of strength, but once we had the wheel moving, the chain came up more easily until a loud clunk told us we were done. The sailor held his side of the crank with one hand–which released a lot of the weight to me–and grabbed a rope secured to the deck. The other end had a loop, which he slipped over the end of the crank. That took the weight off of me. Then he came over and secured another rope to my side of the crank.

The boat headed out of the port. Not knowing my way around a boat, I stayed with the sailor and helped him with whatever he did. We spent a lot of time adjusting sails until we were outside the breakwater and well away from the East End of Great Portage. By then, I was weary, but I wasn't as sore as I expected.

I found Lankin at the rail and joined him. After a moment's thought, I decided not to bring up my lightened purse. Money isn't the most important thing.

"Good to see you up and around," Lankin said.

"Thank you for looking after me and bringing me here. Really. I know it wasn't easy."

He clapped my shoulder. "Couldn't leave you to die. What good would that be?"

We watched the water for a few minutes until Captain hollered for the first mate.

I glanced up to the poopdeck. "Y'know, I wasn't sure you were going to make it before we cast off."

"You'd have waited for me." He smirked and ran his fingers through his damp, blond hair.

The certainty of his words didn't sit well with me. Would I have waited for him? Probably, but something bothered me about the way he assumed that. At the time, I wasn't sure how to answer, so I just shrugged and agreed.

The trip was routine, except at the end. The first mate blew a piercing whistle in the morning to get everyone out of bed. After a breakfast that looked a lot like dinner, but with a bitter dark drink called "qofwah" instead of spiced wine, we got busy on the day's work, and when we ran out of that, our time was our own until some time after dusk. Then we ate and went to bed because the morning would bring the same. Aside from the captain, there were only a few sailors who spoke any language I knew (clearly they were not for the most part, Andreans), so I spent most of my time with them or with Lankin.

Chores on the boat amounted to food preparation, mopping the deck, adjusting sails, and mending ropes and sails. The sailors often sang while working and timed movements with the song. By the end of the trip, I had learned them all. We didn't see much of the Captain unless he was on deck issuing orders. He, for the most part, stayed to himself in his quarters under the poop deck. The first mate handled most of the business on the deck. When we weren't busy with chores, we sat around on the deck or in the forecastle playing dice or cards. One of the sailors taught me how to whittle, as you've seen me do from time to time.

The seas weren't entirely calm on the trip. Here, my strong constitution saved me. I didn't suffer from sea sickness even once, but Lankin disappeared below decks a few times, trying to get as close to the keel as he could where the ship's motion wouldn't be so noticeable. Captain gave him things to do down there, like checking traps for rats and mending things. On deck, the sailors joked about him, mocking his illness, calling him Lankin the Landlubber.

At the start of the trip, our meals were a piece of bread, roasted meat, potatoes or carrots, and qofwah or spiced wine.

As the trip progressed, the meat became stewed and then jerky. The bread became a kind of flat, round bread with dark patches on the surface, sort of like a pancake but not sweet. Later yet, it became hardtack. When Lankin couldn't join us on deck, I brought food to him and ate with him before I went back topside to earn my passage.

Once a day, each of us was given a green sour fruit. On the second day, I tried to pass up the offer, but he insisted they were necessary if I wanted to avoid an illness much worse than seasickness.

A young Southlander snickered as the captain walked away. "Not too likely to get that sickness in the two weeks we'll be traveling, but why risk it, eh?"

I wish I could say that I got accustomed to them by the time we reached Andrea, but when we disembarked, I was glad to be done with them.

We were well into the second week when a boy up in the crow's nest yelled something. His voice had a note of panic. The cry was repeated by a couple other men and then by the first mate. Captain cursed. He started issuing orders that didn't make any sense to me. Lankin and some of the others came out of the forecastle and dispersed across the deck. He joined me and one of the sailors we could talk to.

The old sailor grabbed us both by the arm. "Boys, you do as I say, when I say, get me?"

"Yes, sir. What's happening?" I followed him to the rail.

He pointed toward the horizon. "Storm. They come fast and hard out here, but you keep your head, and we'll be fine." I turned a glance toward the dark clouds. They seemed so far away, and yet everyone was acting like they were our certain doom. My guts unsettled.

"Take it easy, boy. We ain't sunk yet. You just do as I say and stay close."

I nodded once and pushed my fears out of mind. "Yes, sir." He tied a rope around his waist and secured the other end to a loop on the deck then handed Lankin and me others. Once those were secured, we rushed to bring the sails to half their height so the wind wouldn't tear them to shreds, but we didn't get them all down in time. In spite of our efforts, the lower sail on the mizzenmast and one of the shrouds tore.

The captain had turned the ship to take advantage of the wind. The storm winds drove us, but the waves grew bigger and the storm approached faster than we were making distance. When it was clear we wouldn't outrun the storm, the captain issued an order the first mate repeated. As we brought the sails all the way down and tied them, Captain turned the ship to hit the waves straight on. That seemed odd to me, almost against reason, but the sailor explained that if we aligned ourselves otherwise, the waves might have capsized the ship. They washed over the deck as water pelted us from above. The rains felt warm at first, but the harsh wind chilled me. My teeth chattered, and I kept close to the old sailor who was telling me what to do. I was terrified of being swept out into the ocean.

One of the waves crashed onto the deck. Men all over the boat were swept off their feet and slid over the timbers to the ends of their ropes. Over the sound of the storm, men yelled something I couldn't make out, and anyone nearby rushed over and leaned over the rail. I searched the deck. No sign of Lankin. I looked at the rope he'd tied around himself. It hung, pulled taut, over the edge of the rail. The old sailor was nearby pulling on another rope.

I gasped and ran to the side. I saw Lankin clinging to his rope, swinging back and forth and fending himself off from the side of the boat.

"Hold on!" I yelled.

Gripping Lankin's rope, I pulled him up hand-over-hand. The weaving of the ship threw off my balance, and I lost my footing once, slamming hard into the railing when Lankin's weight pulled me forward. I braced myself a little better on the hooks bolted to the deck and tried again. Two other men joined me. One helped pull the rope. The other hung onto me and helped me keep my balance. When Lankin reached the height of the rail, I caught his hand and helped him aboard. "Thank you." Lankin stumbled against me and hung on.

He was pale and gasping for breath. I steadied him. "You're welcome."

The ship creaked and groaned, and I feared the old timbers would splinter. But as hard as we rocked and shook, the boat held together.

Then as quickly as the storm came, it passed. The rain dwindled to nothing, and the winds died back.

I thought that maybe, once the crisis had ended, the captain would have us set the sails again, but instead, he ordered an extra measure of fortified wine for every man on deck and gave us the rest of the afternoon and evening to rest, warm ourselves as best we could, and relax. We didn't get back underway again until morning, and even then we were short the lower sail on the mizzenmast until we'd sewn up the tear. There were other repairs to be done. The railing had split in a couple places and the shredded shroud had to be replaced. The dragon figurehead had suffered, too. The left ear was gone. All that water had also ruined some of our supplies.

Meals for the last three days of the trip were shorter rations of everything except limes.

On the third day after the storm, long before the day's chores were finished, the boy in the crow's nest hollered again, and whatever he said brought a cheer. I guessed he'd spotted the shore.

If I hadn't been busy with mopping the deck, I would have raced to the front of the ship for a look, but by the time I'd finished, the first mate was giving instructions, and I joined the others with bringing the ship into the docks. Then everyone, even the Captain, participated in unloading the cargo. My legs felt weirdly unsteady on land, but I wasn't alone. Everyone else on the crew also stumbled and wove as they tried to move.

With the task finished, the captain paid everyone their wages, including me. I assumed that meant that at least part of my missing money had gone to pay for my care. The entire crew dispersed to the taverns near the docks. I went along with them for some food and maybe a little camaraderie, but as the night wore on and I wearied of tavern songs and seeing everyone get more and more drunk, I paid for a room and went to rest. Sleeping on a bed that didn't swing with the motion of the waves didn't feel natural anymore, but I dozed off before too long. When I woke up, I wasn't surprised to find Lankin still gone. He was no doubt in some woman's bed, but I knew he'd be back sometime around midmorning. We still had our quest to complete.

⊶⊩ Chapter 10 ⊫

As I expected, Lankin did reappear at about midmorning the next day. I was waiting for him outside the tavern.

Port of Andrea wasn't the huge city I'd expected. The docks were there, of course, and built a long way out into a harbor. Which was protected by a long, thin barrier island extended into a breakwater. Adjacent to the docks were huge storehouses and establishments that catered to sailors of all ranks. A marketplace, somewhat makeshift like the one outside East End, occupied a wide space just behind those storehouses and taverns.

I had expected that the prices here would be lower than most places because of how close we were to the source of the goods, but the merchants hawked their wares at half again the going rate elsewhere and claimed, correctly or not, that their "rare" goods came from foreign lands, which supposedly justified the price increase.

There were things in that market that I'd only seen in other places like Great Portage, but even the typical sorts of goods were being sold for far more than anywhere else. In spite of the prices, a number of people were eagerly lined up.

We only spent money on the foodstuffs we needed for the hike inland to Andrea. Then we set off north along a cobblestone road. Along the way, we encountered other travelers by foot and wagon and even some small caravans. They were nothing like the massive, elephant-led groups of Great Portage, but they were good-sized. When Lankin eyed one of them greedily, I was afraid he was going to suggest we rob one, but he didn't mention it, and I didn't raise the subject.

I thought that Andrea would be within a day's hike from the port. It certainly looked like it on every map I've ever seen, but as the sun started toward the horizon, there was no sign of the city walls. A recently-built walled town protected by Andrean regulars provided lodging for the night, but it cost twenty gold pieces to even enter through the town wall, let alone pay for any of the amenities inside. The wealthier travelers routinely paid this, but the travelers of lesser means and even some of the caravans passed around it to a spot where an area cleared of forest on the side of the road beckoned. A number of travelers from both directions set up camp next to the road. We joined them. I had to go pretty far afield to find wood for a fire.

Just like the Great Portage caravans, these smaller ones had sentries keeping watch. Isolated travelers set up their own camps, some of them banding together in small groups around a single fire. After we'd passed the last of them, Lankin and I stepped off the cobblestone road and set up our own camp. Dinner was half the provisions we'd purchased, washed down with a little water mixed with cheap Andrean sour wine. I stretched out next to the campfire and watched the stars appearing in the darkening sky.

Lankin leaned closer to me. "Y'know, we could do a little business here tonight, once everyone's gone to sleep. Just have to pick a person or a small group and wait for them to fall asleep."

"Too many people around." I shook my head. "Too much of a chance of getting caught. We're almost to Andrea, we have everything we need to get weapons and armor and get the job done." I'd never been fond of Ombree's occupation, but after the disaster in Great Portage, I wanted no more of that lifestyle, no matter how much wealth someone in theory could gain.

"Listen here, Therin," Lankin shook his head as he spoke, "We are not out on a coward's mission. What we need to do requires bold action, including supplying ourselves. Maybe you'd better rethink whether you really have the salt to do what needs to be done."

While he was still speaking, the sounds of horses' hooves, jingling tack, and creaking armor came closer. I sat up and watched a patrol of Andrean soldiers ride up. They dismounted and spread out among the campers, walking up and down the short expanse of road as if they were looking for someone.

I exchanged a glance with Lankin then stretched out next to the fire again.

He rolled his eyes. "Never mind."

The patrol stayed in the area all night, remaining particularly close to a small caravan with the royal crest emblazoned on each wagon. As the sun rose, the patrol left and the caravans weren't far behind them. I got up, ate my share of what food remained, and watched the people going by. Lankin woke a little earlier than usual.

I passed him the bag of food and broke camp while he ate. We were on our way shortly after, and weren't nearly the last ones to go.

The morning was cool but not chilly. We walked swiftly, dodging around other travelers and catching up to the slowest of the caravans as the Andrean walls came into view a bit after midday.

After Great Portage, Andrea looked much smaller than it had four years ago. Impressive, but kind of limited, even though it was one of the largest of the cities in the Western Bond. As we walked through the gate, memories of the tournament and Uncle Haelin returned in a flood. That one tournament I'd pleaded my uncle into training us for, that had been the beginning of everything we'd done since then. We'd come back to finish it, but some part of me couldn't imagine what would happen next, if it really would be over, even if we did manage to get into the palace and kill Rory-Galstaff.

Our first stop was a weaponsmith. There wasn't time to commission a sword, but he had some already made. None were imported Iron Mountain blades, which irritated Lankin, who wanted to make a statement by us both carrying blades from our province—I still had a practice sword with me that I sharpened. And the prices for new blades were quite high, so we could only afford him buying a new one for himself. As if to compensate, when we went to an armorer a few doors down, he focused on getting me armor instead of getting any for himself. There was no full armor available for purchase that would fit someone my size, so I was only able to get a few pieces, all leather. I walked away with an empty purse and a gorget, bracers, and greaves. Lankin wound up doing a little better, finding a studded leather doublet that fit him well. With the swords belted on and the armor hastily fitted to our bodies, we left the shops.

The sun was setting but before looking for somewhere to stay, we wove our way through the city using the palace spires as a guide. We came around a corner and onto a long, wide street. A row of trees had been planted in a long stripe that split the road down the middle. More trees and statues of Andrean noblemen lined one side of the street and ladies lined the other. I went to the nearest of the statues, the last in the line, and read the plaque.

Lankin joined me and snorted. "So, this is our current king."

I looked up at the face of the statue and compared that to the memory of the man I remembered from the tournament. "When he was our age, maybe. He's a lot older now."

The next monument on the way to the palace was the previous king, so immortalizing the royal line one king at a time. We strolled down the lane, pausing from time to time to look at a statue. The one closest to the palace showed Andrea's first king, who'd taken power long before the Western Bond had formed.

The palace was a large granite building with tall, thin spires in every corner and a moat surrounding it. A wide area full of flowers and statues surrounded the palace. The bridge over the moat was up, and the nearby guardhouse had at least twenty armed men in it. Others patrolled the perimeter.

I leaned closer to Lankin. "Any idea how we get in?"

He blew out a breath and waved for me to come along. We followed the roads around the palace, stopping now and then to look. The guards kept a wary eye on us, and I hoped we looked more like curious visitors than would-be assassins.

As we came around the back of the palace, the caravan we'd seen before, with the royal crest on it, was just driving away from the palace grounds. Outriders and sentries were piled into the backs of the wagons or went on horseback alongside. A grin spread across Lankin's face as he slapped my arm with the back of his hand. "I know how to get in. Come on!" We followed the caravan back out toward the market. They pulled into a large stable in the corner of town. The men on the wagons tended the horses. Then the apparent leader, a tall dark-haired Andrean, stood at the barn's door as men lined up to receive their pay. We waited until the last few workers were paid before we approached.

The caravan leader slid the rest of the coins in a drawstring purse and tugged the cord. "What do you boys want?"

"A job, sir." Lankin glanced back at me. "I'm Lankin, and this is Therin. We've worked as outriders and sentries on caravans, and we're looking for work."

The Andrean hefted the bag of coins. "What's your experience?"

"Great Portage. We made several runs with various caravans."

"Did you now? I happen to know some of them. Name a leader and describe him."

I stepped forward. "Han Chang, an Easty. Smallish but strong. And Cebo, a Southlander with a curved scar on his cheek. Actually, Han is the caravan master and Cebo works for him now." I went on to describe a few of the others I could clearly remember, too.

"Well, I suppose that'll do." He looked us both over and blew out a breath. "Fine. We're headed back to the port in two days. You be here at dawn the day after tomorrow, and you have a job for this run only. If you do good work, we'll see about the next time." He turned his back on us and walked away.

Lankin grinned. "Great. Now we just find somewhere to lay low for a couple days, go with this caravan to the coast and back, and when it unloads in the palace, we're in."

I walked with Lankin back toward the center of town. "They won't notice when we don't come out?"

"Did you see how many men there were?" He snickered and shook his head. "Who'd notice two fewer?"

I wasn't as certain as he was, but I didn't have anything better to offer. We went to an inn and paid for two nights. Lankin ate dinner with me, but then announced he'd be going. I might not have known exactly where, but I knew why. Once I'd finished, I went upstairs to my room and picked up a piece of wood from the scuttle on the hearth. I spent my evening whittling until I was tired enough to sleep. The next day, I explored the city like a wanderer from another land. I watched people going about their business, bought food for our journey, and wasted time in shops.

When I walked down a street in a wealthier part of town, one of the patrolmen followed me several steps behind. I entered into a glassblower's store and all conversation stopped. The shopkeeper and the few patrons there all stared at me. I hadn't come to cause any problems. True, I wasn't there to buy anything either, but there is no law against walking into a shop and just looking at the merchandise. Clearly, I wasn't the clientele they had in mind. With the money I had in the pouch around my neck, I could have bought one of their gold- or silver-decorated bowls for their asking price, but that didn't matter. I was not dressed as a nobleman, so they wanted no part of me. In all my travels, son, I've met good people and bad people in every social class and from every nation. It's not a man's appearance you should judge, but his actions.

Their stern glares made me a little self-conscious, but I stayed and looked at the glassware on display, keeping my hands clasped behind my back so no one could accuse me of taking anything. The patrolman who'd been following me came in and went over to the shopkeeper. They whispered, but I couldn't make out what they were saying. I had a good guess, though. Before someone decided to throw me out, I left.

The sun was nearing the horizon again, so I made my way back to the inn and had dinner. I turned in early so I'd be sure to wake up in time to get to the caravan by dawn. I didn't expect to see Lankin until morning. In fact, I was fairly sure he'd be running up to the caravan as it was getting ready to pull out, so I was surprised to wake up and find him sleeping in the padded chair by the fire. I woke him, and we ate breakfast before heading out to the stable where the caravan was housed.

We got there before the caravan was ready and helped hitch the horses. The leader assigned drivers to the wagons and then put another man on each one. Extra men were told to stay alongside the caravan and watch for trouble.

Our first stop was a set of storehouses near the edge of town where we loaded crates into the backs of the wagons. They didn't use the same efficient method that Cebo and Han had arranged in East End. Instead, we each got a crate from the storehouse and carried it to a wagon where a man standing in the back took the crate and stacked it with the rest. The caravan, although much smaller than Han's, took all morning to load. It was past noon when we set off of Port Andrea.

By nightfall, we'd reached that widened area next to the road. That's where we camped. As before, a patrol arrived and kept watch on the caravans, paying the most attention to ours. The next morning, we set out early and arrived in Port Andrea by day's end. The wagons unloaded to a storehouse and reloaded from a boat before we drove them to another big stable.

At dawn the next morning, we set out again and made it to the camping area right on schedule. The trip had been pretty routine so far. I almost felt unnecessary, so when men started hollering in the middle of the night, I jolted awake and took a few moments to make sense of my surroundings.

"Stop him!" a deep voice yelled.

Lankin and I were camped furthest from the road, but Lankin's place was empty. Someone barreled past our camp, headed away from the road. I jumped to my feet and took off after him, catching only a glimpse of dark clothes and blond hair. Lankin? Would he really have wrecked our chance to get into the castle so he could snitch trinkets from the caravan? At the time, I wasn't sure. I kept telling myself that it couldn't be Lankin. He wouldn't have been so foolish. I told myself that Lankin was taller and thinner than the man I was chasing, that the clothes were cut wrong, but at the same time, I had doubts.

There was a loud crack like breaking a stick and the man I was chasing stopped and fell backward. He made no effort to rise. I caught up in a few strides and crouched, careful to duck under the now broken tree branch he'd hit at a full run. The man was similar in stature and clothing to Lankin, but the face, now bloodied by the collision with a tree, was too broad and pockmarked with scars from an old disease. I blew out a breath. I might not know where Lankin had disappeared to, but at least I wasn't going to have to choose between turning him over to the soldiers or trying to come up with a good excuse about how he got away.

The soldiers arrived moments after my discovery. One of them drew his sword.

"Wait." The other caught his arm. "Take him back for a trial."

The first soldier shrugged away from his friend and drove the sword through the man's chest, just left of the center. "I saw him take something out of that crate." He leaned over and pried a metal figurine out of the dead man's fist. "He's guilty, and now we don't have to worry about him getting away from us."

Both of them walked away without a word to me. I'd seen enough death by then so I wasn't entirely shocked by what happened. But still, it seemed very wrong. Nor did it bode well for what would happen to Lankin and me if we were caught trying to enter the palace.

The ground was too hard to dig a grave without a shovel, and there wasn't enough light for me to find enough rocks to make a cairn, so I left the body. I returned to camp and spent some time staring into the fire before I dozed off.

At dawn, the caravan master woke everyone. Lankin was back but offered no explanation for his disappearance last night. There might have been a good reason, perhaps even one not involving theft or a woman, but I didn't ask.

We were on our way as soon as we'd broken camp and hitched the horses. The Andrean patrol headed out ahead of us and soon left us behind. As expected, we arrived in Andrea at midday and wove through the streets until we came to the back of the palace. A bridge was lowered across the moat, and we started unloading much the same way that we'd loaded. Lankin and I made one of the last trips in and let the others go in ahead of us so we'd be last. We dropped off the crates and took a couple steps toward the back of the piles.

A balding little man in a heavily beaded doublet entered the storeroom. "You two, door's the other way. Make your delivery and go." He opened the first crate as servants rushed into the room.

I leaned closer to Lankin. "This is never going to work." We had no choice but to leave. On the way back to the stable, I wondered if we could still find a way to save our plan. If we hid earlier in the unloading process, we'd still be found when the servants came in to do the unpacking. Hiding in a crate would be no good. The guards had spotted a man taking a fist-sized figurine out of a box, never mind emptying one and climbing in. Then, too, the crates would weigh too much, mine particularly.

Maybe it would be easier to wait until Crown Prince Rory- Galstaff was out of the castle. The only problem then would be getting around the soldiers that were sure to follow him. We might even be able to kill the prince from a distance. Later, when Lankin and I were alone, I planned to make that suggestion.

At the stable, we parked the wagons, tended the horses, and lined up to get our pay.

When we got to the caravan master, he handed us our money. "You two wait a minute."

Lankin and I exchanged a glance and stepped aside while the master paid everyone else.

He hefted his bag of coins and smiled. "You two were the ones who chased down that thief."

It wasn't a question.

Lankin stammered. I hadn't told him about that night. "Yes, that was us." I turned toward Lankin. "You remember.

That blond-haired fellow in black swiped a figurine from a crate and ran right through our camp. We were on his heels until he smacked into a tree."

His eyes widened. "Right, right! How could I forget that?" The caravan master nodded.

"Thought so. That figurine was more important than you know. Stopping that thief prevented a great deal of embarrassment for the royal family, and the king wants to thank you personally. Tomorrow afternoon. So get yourselves cleaned up and dressed decently, and meet me here tomorrow after breakfast." He looked us over and then fished a couple more coins from his purse. "Decent clothes, boys. You're going to see the king, not spend the night in a farmhouse."

"Yes, sir," we said at once.

The caravan master turned away from us and left. We immediately went looking for new clothing. Lankin went straight to a store that sold used clothes. As usual, he found something suitable that fit him pretty quickly. There was nothing at all that fit me. In the back of the shop, he changed into his new clothes, and then we went to the wealthier part of town where I'd been a few days before.

Lankin walked a step ahead of me, which made me feel like a servant. But I didn't get the same hard stares I had when I'd been there on my own.

We came to a shop with a sign over the door that read "Gilded Needle" and stepped inside. Rolls of fabric in colors I didn't know were possible were on display on shelves around the edge of the room. Ready-made clothing formed stacks on the tables running down the center. A chest-high table stretched across the back of the room. Two men sat behind the table. The older one was sketching lines on black material with a piece of white chalk. The younger one feverishly stitched two pieces together.

The younger one looked up. "Good afternoon, sir. What can we help you with?"

I looked at Lankin. They meant him, apparently. In my "farm boy" clothes, I didn't rate attention.

Lankin stepped back even with me. "I need clothing suitable for court for him. Something already made, if that's possible. Time is short. We have an audience tomorrow morning."

"Oh!" The younger man came around the table as he looked me over. "Tall, broad-shouldered, hmm."

"Bottom of the last pile at the far end of the table. The brown and green will do, I think," the old man said without looking up from his chalk drawings.

"Yes, yes, I'd forgotten that." The younger one hustled to the end of the table and moved things aside until he reached the bottom of the pile.

He picked up dark brown trousers and a doublet with green embroidery around the edges. The material was silk as fine as any I'd seen in Great Portage, and it certainly looked large enough to fit me. The younger man held it up to me.

"Yes, that will fit him fine," the older man said, still focused on his chalk. "A little loose around the belly perhaps, but not noticeable to most."

I paid more for those garments than every other article of clothing before or since combined. Lankin muttered something about his own new clothing looking too dingy by comparison, so he found something else that he liked, white silk with red beadwork, and bought that as well.

Across the street, the cobbler outfitted Lankin with a pair of boots that fit with a little straw stuffed into the toes.

For me, there was nothing even close, but the cobbler was able to polish my boots enough to make them look relatively new. We started for the inn where we'd stayed the night before.

"You have to tell me the whole story of what happened, in detail," Lankin said.

At the inn, we had dinner and paid for a room. I expected Lankin to disappear as he so often did, but instead he came upstairs with me. We sat by the fire and talked. I told Lankin about chasing down the thief, all the way to the part where the soldier played the role of executioner. Lankin didn't volunteer anything about where he'd been at the time, and I didn't ask.

Lankin leaned back in his chair and laced his fingers behind his head. "Once we're inside the palace tomorrow, we'll just have to find a way to get away from our guide and find Rory- Galstaff."

I stared at the fire for a few moments. "I've been thinking about that. What if—"

"You're not having second thoughts about our oath, are you?" he asked.

I sat up straighter. "No, not second thoughts exactly. I'm willing to go through with it. Though, if we go straight into the palace, from what I saw of the man who stole the figurine, we're sure to be killed. Whether we get the prince or not. I'm thinking that it might be, well, survivable, to get to the prince if we catch him outside the palace. Then instead of all the protection of a guarded fortress, we'll just have his personal guards to deal with. We might even be able to take him out from a distance, with a crossbow bolt or something. Maybe nobody would know it was us. We might…actually survive."

He jabbed his finger at me. "Killing him is not the point. He needs to know the merits of the Iron Mountains, and it's the sword, not some coward's arrow that will show it to him."

"Look, I'm just trying to find a way that isn't suicide."

"Tomorrow's audience with the king gets us in. Then all we have to do is get away from our guides and find Rory-Galstaff. I'll take care of everything from there. Believe me —if I can get us in, I can get us out." He flopped back in the chair and stared at the fire.

We stayed silent for a long time before I went to bed. I didn't sleep much. I realized I didn't actually believe Lankin. Though maybe it didn't matter. The tournament from four years before kept going through my mind, particularly that final bout when my uncle died to protect us. If he died, perhaps that's what I needed to do as well.

At some point, I fell asleep and woke when Lankin jostled my shoulder.

"We'd better get going. Today's our big day."

I took a deep breath and blew it out. After a few minutes to wash up, we ate breakfast downstairs. Normally I like to eat, even bland food. But nothing tasted good to me. I forced down my meal and we left.

The caravan master came out of his house as we approached. He was dressed in black. A blue sapphire the size of my thumb joint adorned a gold chain around his neck. Another half that size glittered on his hand.

He looked us both over and nodded. "You did well." He gestured for us to follow. "You are not of sufficient rank to ride a carriage into the palace courtyard, so we will walk."

The way he said that made me think that maybe he was of sufficient rank, but we kept a brisk pace and stayed in the wealthier parts of town. At the palace guardhouse, the caravan master produced a small piece of parchment and handed it to one of the guards, who pried the paper open, studied it, then waved us through.

Our boots made hollow-sounding clunks as we crossed the bridge. The distance from the end of the bridge to the main palace doors felt longer than the way from Port Andrea to Andrea.

When we arrived, a man standing by the door opened it for us. The foyer had a gray and white marble floor and a sweeping staircase up to a second level. Gauzy blue material hung from the ceiling around a gold statue of the current king. Once inside, the balding man from the storeroom met us there. The caravan master produced his paper again. The balding man led us to a nearby room with thickly padded chairs and paintings of the royal family.

"The two of you gentlemen will wait here, please." The balding man turned to the caravan master. "Your Excellency, the king's minister wished to see you as soon as you arrived. This way, please."

I walked around the room and looked at the pictures while Lankin went to the door we'd come through.

He went to one of the chairs and sat. "Guards in the foyer and no other way out of here."

"I see," was my only reply. I went to the next picture, one of the queen holding a baby, probably Prince Rory-Galstaff. The baby's hair was certainly blond enough.

After I'd looked at paintings enough, I sat in a chair near Lankin and sank down further than I had expected. My stomach was all jittery and my mouth had gone dry.

"The king regrets the delay, but important business has come up," a girl said.

I startled, almost knocking myself to the floor.

The girl, maybe half my age, walked over from a direction that had only the wall and a few paintings. She carried a tray of two crystal glasses that sparkled in the light, a pitcher of water, a pitcher of wine, and a plate full of fruit.

"He wishes for you to be comfortable while you are waiting." She set the tray on a low table between me and Lankin then darted back toward the wall.

She pressed a spot on the wall. A small section between two of the paintings swung open, and she darted through. It closed behind her, leaving no trace that it had ever been there.

Lankin chuckled. "That's how we get out of here."

"We don't know where it goes," I said.

"Who cares? It gets us out of here and away from the guards. Then we can find the prince and finish our task." Lankin stood and waved for me to follow.

At the wall, Lankin pressed where the girl had and the wall section swung open. We squeezed through the space and into a narrow, undecorated corridor lit by sconces along the wall. There was no room to walk side-by-side. In fact, my shoulders brushed the walls. We'd only gone about twenty steps when a servant came out of a side passage.

The man's jaw dropped. "You're not supposed to be in here!"

"We're not? Oh, sorry. Our mistake." Lankin pointed back over his shoulder. "That way, right?"

I started back the way we'd come, but the door into the little sitting room opened and a guard stepped in.

Without taking his eyes off us, he turned his head. "Found 'em. In the servant's corridor." He jabbed his finger at me. "You two, out. Now."

There was no choice.

⚔ Chapter 11 ➤

Within moments pounding metal on the stone hallway revealed the presence of Andrean Royal guardsmen. Five men in Iron Mountains chainmail with Andrean longswords and helmets (and no shields) met us at the hallway. Lankin drew his blade and thrusted at the nearest one.

"Whoa, Lankin!" I found myself saying. But I drew mine, too, and found a furious guardsman with a sergeant's red sleeves hacking away at me. I backed up and parried. I'd returned none of his furious blows, but none had touched me either, and the other guards seemed focused on Lankin. Then I heard pounding feet from behind me. I ducked behind a decorative column along the way, giving me the chance to glance the other direction down the hallway.

Another ten or so Royal Guards were charging us, their swords drawn.

I dropped my blade and raised my hands, "I surrender!"

The Sergeant of the Guard who'd attacked with the sword punched me just below the left ear, knocking me sideways and making my head ring. One of the new guards approaching, raised his sword as if to cut off my head, but the Sergeant stepped in front of him and punched me in the gut. I know how to take a punch, but something in the back of my mind told me not to take the punch as well as I could. I let myself crumple to the floor. The Sergeant grabbed me by the hair and shoved me face down on the cut stone floor. Another guard, probably the one ready to kill me, kicked me in the ribs.

"Who are you and what are you doing here!" the sergeant roared in the same ear he'd set ringing.

"I'm a traveler!" I answered, truthfully in a way, but not to the point.

"From WHERE?"

"Iron Mountains Province!"

"What are you doing in this palace, Mountaineer?"

This was a question I felt most reluctant to answer as you can imagine, son. I stammered. I got kicked in the ribs again. I've imagined since what it would have been like if Elin had been with us. He would have no doubt announced, unashamed, "We are here to kill your prince!"

I, not the fully honest boy I had once been, but not a habitual liar either, tried to split the difference between a lie and the truth. "We came on a personal mission. Which… which we do not wish to discuss—but we mean no harm to any of you!"

They tied my hands behind my back, very tight, and hauled me to my feet. The five men took me back down the hall toward Lankin. He'd retreated back into the narrow servant's corridor in order to reduce the number of guardsmen who faced him at the same time. In that narrow, dimly-lit hallway, a massive servant from the Shos Hillcountry (who'd been carrying a barrel of ale on his shoulder), had tackled Lankin from behind.

They hauled us back down to the ground floor of the castle, into the courtyard, which contained a permanent gallows. A man wearing an Andrean official's robe approached us from a door along the upper right corner of the courtyard. As he neared us, I realized I recognized him. But Lankin said it first.

"Look, if it isn't Guffey, from the tournament." He said this loudly enough that Guffey himself heard, now not twenty paces off.

"That's Magistrate Guffey to you, whoever you are."

"You've moved up in the world," Lankin observed.

"His Majesty always recognizes and rewards competent leadership," drawled the Midlander in reply. But his eyes studied us intently as he spoke, as if the words themselves were much less important that some secret hidden in our faces. After a long pause, his eyebrows raised and he said to me, "I know your face. You're kin to that Dragon War veteran who died in the tournament several years back."

Confronted with this level of recognition, actual honesty seemed the only way to reply. "Yes. His nephew."

"Grew a bit of hair on your face, did you? That's why it took a bit to recognize you. You're bigger, too. My handling of that little incident actually favored my eventual advancement. But at the time, his Majesty was not pleased at *all*." He paused, apparently in mid-thought, and looked us both over again. He waved his finger at us and tsk tsked, "Now this here wouldn't be about some plot for *revenge,* would it?" He looked at both of our faces, but mine probably was the one that gave it away. He suddenly straightened himself. "Why, that *is* why you boys are here, isn' it?"

Lankin, trembling slightly with rage, answered, "I challenge your prince, Rory-Galstaff, to a duel to the death. For the sake of the honor of Iron Mountains Province!"

Guffey laughed. "Why that's quite a statement, young man. You may have noticed you've been brought down to the royal gallows. I suppose you could say we're about to do you a great honor. At least you won't die as common criminals. An assassination attempt on the royal personage is punishable by hangin', of course. But you won't spend one minute in the local jail. Very nasty, that place."

Turning to the dozen guardsmen who surrounded us, he casually added, "Bring them up here." To the platform he meant. Where the hanging ropes draped down.

From the third level up on the balcony, an angry-sounding voice called out, "What's going on here?"

Guffey looked up and cupped a hand over his eyes to prevent the brightness of mid-morning sunshine from drowning out the image of the figure in the shadows. "Your Majesty. We've captured some intruders with the intent to kill your son and heir. We were about to execute them."

"Why would they want to do that? Did Kung Tzu send them?" said the voice. It did not wait for a reply. The sound of boots crossing a stone floor clicked our way as the speaker walked to the nearest stairway and descended toward our level. Once at the ground of the courtyard, the figure approached us and we could see this was the King of Andrea. He wore a robe of what must have been mink, rich and luxurious, with silk trim in the blue favored by Andrean nobles. But other than that, it was undecorated, as if it were bed clothing. As if he'd been ill or napping during the day. So much for his "other" business.

"Where are they from, Guffey? And what is the issue?" It was at that moment I realized the caravan master probably would disavow ever knowing us, for his own safety. If he ever reappeared at all (which he did not).

Lankin didn't wait for the magistrate to answer the king's question, "We're from Iron Mountains province, here to avenge its honor, after your son killed one of our helpless old men!"

"Old man? Ah. Well, there's only been one of those I can recall my son killed. I remember that day. I was most displeased with the outcome. Until Guffey here made it plain to me the incredible pressures he was under."

"Pressures from an old man? Your Majesty?" I felt glad Lankin remembered to add the last two words.

"Young man, at what point have you earned the right to address our majesty directly?" The king's eyes narrowed as he said this. "You were about to hang them, were you, Guffey?"

"I was, your Majesty."

"Stop. We think there may be a vital lesson in this." The Andrean king, federal head of the entire Western Bond, turned to the Sergeant of the Guard who had pummeled me in the ears. "Javvon, please fetch my son the heir from his bedroom chamber. Bring him down here."

"At your order, your majesty." Javvon charged off at a run. "Guffey. We wish to be dressed. Send my valet. Hold these two and detain my son when he arrives. When we are ready, we shall take action in regard to what happens to each of them." With that, the king walked away. He never even looked back.

So we stood below the platform, the gallows that might still hang us. I couldn't help thinking how the coarseness of the rope would rub harsh across the skin of my neck, like a burn. The wait stretched out long. Lankin and I said nothing. After Guffey quietly sent a guard to run into the castle (to fetch the valet I assume), he said nothing.

The fall morning air, which had not seemed particularly cold earlier, began to chill me very much. It occurred to me I'd spent so much time in the jungle that my sense of what is and is not cold had changed.

It couldn't have been minutes before Prince Rory-Galstaff entered the courtyard. He stood in a corner of the square area back and to the right from where we were, some fifty paces away. As far away as he could be in this enclosed space. We waited for what seemed an awfully long time. The guards would not allow us to pace to stay warm and the cold irons they clapped on us made the experience especially miserable. I longed for the day to grow warmer.

It probably was about an hour later that His Majesty appeared again. He remained up on the third level, hidden by a glaring sunlight from the east that felt almost without warmth. So I couldn't see him very well, but I could tell he was up there and he clearly had changed clothing to something much more elegant. A glint of light from his crown sparkled as he sat in a chair provided for him.

A man standing beside the king walked down the side of the third level toward the stairway. He appeared out of the stairway in the courtyard and approached the prince to speak with him briefly. Rory-Galstaff followed him as he strode towards us.

"Unchain the mountaineers," the man commanded the guards. At that moment, when he was walking to the side of the gallows not twenty paces in front of us, I recognized him.

He was the Andrean swordmaster who was in the ring with Prince Rory-Galstaff the day my uncle died. His left hand was wrapped around an enormous two-handed sword in a gem-encrusted scabbard.

Once we were unbound, Guffey, who'd been standing above us on the gallows, moved down the ladder of the platform to stand beside the swordmaster I'd seen before. The man addressed Lankin and I. "I hear that you have challenged the prince to honorable combat. Are you serious in this intention?" I paused, knowing our actual intent had been otherwise.

Lankin did not, "Yes. This is why we entered into your castle stealthily—to have the chance to challenge the prince, to avenge the name of our province, which your Prince Rory-Galstaff defiled!" I suppose the formal language Lankin attempted to use came from the knowledge he was speaking in the presence of royalty.

"Sounds serious," replied the swordmaster without a trace of artificial flowery language. He turned to me, "And you?"

"Some of us…f-from the tournament where my uncle was killed. We swore an oath that we would avenge him. I have sought to fulfill that promise since that day. So yes. Me too."

"The Fourth Battalion Volunteers veteran? The man my age? He was your uncle?"

"Yes," I answered, flushing in shame when the man spoke of my uncle. (My son, of all of the moments of my life, I regret this moment as much as any other. Because I should not have felt shame.)

"I fought in that same battle," he said, his jaw working with emotion. "I honor your uncle. And all the men of the Fourth Battalion." He paused a moment, then turned his head upward to the figure seated in shadows on the third level, "Your Majesty, with respect to your faithful servant Guffey, I believe he was mistaken as to the intent of these two young men. They came not as assassins, but on an issue of honor. The most they have done is trespass on the royal estate, which is punishable by a jail sentence, not by hanging."

For a few of my heart's pounding beats, silence ruled in the courtyard. Then the voice from above called out, "We concur. You have my permission to conclude this matter as you wish. Only bear in mind our previous discussion."

The swordmaster turned his eyes back on us. "So what will it be then, boys? A jail sentence for trespassing, or honorable single combat, for which you will face no punishment if it should be that you manage to win? Death, of course, if you lose."

Again, I paused while Lankin did not. "That's no choice at all, Andrean dog! We came for combat!" Lankin lunged forward, but four of the guardsmen held him in place.

The swordmaster turned his head toward the prince. "It is impossible for a man not to have enemies. The past will not let itself be forgotten. No matter what you do or do not do, someone will always be out for your blood. Now the past has come for you. You must decide what to do about it—if you do not defend yourself, it will kill you without mercy." As he said this, Lankin was growling and struggling to escape the guards, as if to illustrate his point. I stood rather numbly, not certain what I should do. If there was anything to do at all.

The prince looked at Lankin, a bit of color coming to his cheeks. The swordmaster pressed the impossibly long two-handed blade to his chest. It was still in its scabbard.

The swordmaster looked over his shoulder at Lankin, "Stop squirming. It's undignified for such a contest. We will release you and give you back your sword in a moment."

He turned back toward Rory-Galstaff and took hold of the scabbard of the enormous two-handed blade. The prince, slowly, as if reluctantly, grabbed the sword hilt from where the pommel was, which was over the top of his head. The swordmaster pulled free the scabbard, first pulling it his direction and down as he did so.

The prince changed positions as the blade came clear, from it pointing downward to diagonal across his body, the blade far taller than his shoulder (which reminds me now of a spearman at port arms, though the diagonal of the weapon rests in a different plane in that position).

The blade was exceedingly long. Taller than the prince. But nearly as thin as the Andrean rapiers I'd seen in the tournament so long before. I marveled at the craftsmanship of the metal, having some idea how difficult it was from knowing a bit about my uncle's work to make a blade that long, which would not bend or break under its own weight. (Now I know that this particular brand of blade is worked over with special magical incantations to strengthen it. Andrea has three specialties of magician that do nothing but work the spells required to build these two handed swords, the type used by griffin riders.)

Lankin had been carrying the blade he purchased in Great Portage, while I'd carried one of the Iron Mountain practice swords that I'd sharpened. The Sergeant of the Guard offered him each of our two swords at that moment, apparently not remembering which blade had been mine and which had been his. To my surprise, Lankin picked my sword instead of his. Iron Mountains pride, I suppose.

As soon as the sword touched his hands, the guards behind him having backed already, my friend lunged forward, roaring in anger as he charged.

The prince leapt backward and swung his blade downward, putting its tip between himself and Lankin. Though two-handled, the point reminded me very much of the rapiers the Andreans had used in the tournament. The blade, though stiff, was that narrow.

The tip caught Lankin's shoulder. He immediately backed up, but a spot of fresh blood spread across his white tunic.

Lankin's entire mood shifted. Neither my uncle's nor Ombree's sword training recommended charging an enemy in rage. He swatted the long blade aside, kept his eye on it, and charged forward to close the distance to Rory-Galstaff. The prince swung at him and he parried, continuing to close. The prince had to run, leaping backward, to keep Lankin out of striking range. My friend charged again, alert, parrying the prince's blows. As the prince lunged back a bit too late, a swing of Lankin's blade caught Rory-Galstaff in the shoulder, nearly in the same place where he had poked Lankin.

Now the prince began moving the blade with more purpose. It was harder for Lankin to parry, but he managed. Normally a blade of that length, while it has a great advantage in reach, has a disadvantage in the length of time it takes to swing it. But this special weapon was so light and thin that in spite of its length, it was only a tiny bit slower than Lankin's ordinary blade. Lankin of course had to close to have any chance to win. The prince would have been able to skewer or slice him easily enough if he had fought without skill, but Lankin proved adept at knocking aside the prince's blade and moving forward so the prince had to jump back to prevent his own death. Since jumping backward is harder on a body that running forward, and clumsier, it first seemed it was only a matter of time before the prince would trip and Lankin would finish him.

But the prince didn't trip. He swung the long blade with power, Lankin parried and parried and tried to close. The prince lunged backward. Over and over and over.

"One blow! One blow is all you get!" the Andrean swordmaster shouted at the prince. "You cannot play on griffin-back. Kill him!"

Feeling ashamed at my silence, I called out, "Get him, Lankin!"

"One blow! One blow!" the swordmaster continued to shout.

After just a few minutes. Lankin began to sweat…while the prince seemed mostly unfazed by the strenuous swinging of his massive sword. I could not help but notice that his slender arms showed wiry muscles as he moved, his balance remained very good, in spite of his one stumble. Watching them, I slowly realized that we'd made a mistake in thinking our time with Ombree had prepared us to face the prince.

What had the prince been doing this whole time? Sword training it seemed, with this new, longer blade. Sword training, perhaps for hours, every single day, day in and day out. Not robbing caravans, not drinking, not chasing women. Training.

Lankin began to tire and slow down. You might think that would have pleased the swordmaster, but he grew angrier over time. From time to time he interjected things like, "Why are you playing with this Mountaineer? He means to kill you! You have ONE blow to stop him. One blow!" Several times I heard this same phrase repeated from the third level, from the royal figure seated in shadows, "One blow!"

The expression on my friend's face changed. His face that had flushed red began to whiten. But he continued to parry, to charge, to fight. But he charged forward more slowly. The tip of his blade no longer got anywhere close to touching the prince. Some part of me realized that Lankin had only had one good shot, when the prince stumbled. Which he had wasted by going for the shoulder to avenge his early small wound. Instead of slashing his throat as someone truly fighting for his life would have done. The thing the Andrean swordmaster said about "one blow"—it had applied to Lankin, too.

Eventually, puffing harder and definitely slowed, Lankin called out, "Give me a sword like yours then! A long blade," he panted. "And I will kill you like the insect you are!" At these words the prince changed tactics, driving forward more aggressively. Now Lankin had to back up as he parried.

"Oh will you?" He thrust twice and slashed twice, each time parried by Lankin. "You're sure about that?" The prince had now begun to sweat just a bit as well, but was nowhere near as soaked as Lankin.

"Yes," said Lankin through gritted teeth.

By the way, it's perhaps worth noting that outside of tournaments, real sword fights do not usually last a long time. Not in my personal experience. In a few heartbeats, usually, one opponent gains significant advantage over the other. A few blows, or just one, and it's over. A battle between two opponents that lasts more than a minute is very rare. This one had already stretched on for much longer than five minutes. Much longer than the time of a single round at the Tournament of Swords.

"Drop your blade!" called the prince. "And I'll drop mine. Then we can switch!"

"What do you think…I'm stupid?"

Suddenly the prince lunged back. And dropped his very long blade flat on the ground. "Now you drop yours," he said, his hands raised.

Lankin paused a moment, his eyes round in surprise. He took a deep breath, clearly thinking over his options. The Andrean swordmaster shouted at that moment, "What are you doing! PICK UP YOUR SWORD!"

This moment hung suspended for what seemed much longer than what it really was. Lankin's eyes narrowed and his brow scrunched together. Then he charged the prince with a shout, swinging the sword from our province, the sword that my uncle had provided.

The prince leapt backward, unable to recover his two-handed battle sword. Lankin was on him in a heartbeat, swinging a blow that would have perhaps decapitated Rory-Galstaff. As he had retreated, the prince pulled the long dagger from his belt. As Lankin swung at his neck, he used the dagger to twist aside the power of my friend's blow, expertly, deftly. Then before Lankin could recover, he plunged the dagger upward into the soft tissue at my friend's upper throat, upward in a flash of skill and power, upward until the handle stopped in place under his jaw, the blade of the weapon all the way through Lankin's brain. My friend's whole body stiffened. Then he fell.

"Good, prince!" boomed the swordmaster's voice. "It took you far too long, but you have learned well. Your enemies are treacherous. You can only count on having one blow to destroy them. One blow!"

From the third level I heard slow applause of a single set of hands clapping. But the actions of these men barely registered as I rushed forward toward my friend. If I called out, "Lankin," or if I said anything at all, I don't remember what it was. I remember as I ran, the prince, not without an angry look at Lankin, pulled his dagger free and backed away. Blood, dark blood, gushed from the upward slit under the jaw, which began not far above my friend's throat apple. Lankin's eyelids were open, the whites showing as the eyes themselves had rolled backward into his skull. His body squeezed and relaxed in unthinking twitches, especially his legs. He wet himself and I smelled him losing his bowels, his body, no longer alive, but not altogether dead, unable to retain its waste. (This is what death looks like, son. I'm not hiding the truth from you.)

I wept, I know that. I wanted to hold him as he died but I was also disgusted and horrified by his death throes. I believe I did call his name as I hunched over him. Soon, within only perhaps ten heartbeats (which seemed to last horrifyingly long), the major spasms ended, replaced by tiny tremors in his legs and hands. And my friend Lankin was gone from this life forever. If he was received by the God, I have no way to know it directly. I know I did not pray over him, as I should have done.

I looked up at the prince, who had moved past me to recover his two-handed long blade. He stood by his swordmaster, frowning and breathing hard, his face white. His face faded away as my eyes brimmed with tears. This moment also seemed to stretch long, but probably ended in mere heartbeats.

I stood, wiping my eyes. My uncle had told me once there is no shame in crying, but it's not going to help you to cry when there's something you need to do. "Cry later," he said. So I tried to apply that bit of wisdom, wiping my nose, wiping my eyes again and again.

The swordmaster stepped towards me and said in a firm but not unkind voice, "Now it's your choice, mountaineer. You may also face the prince in honorable combat. Or choose a jail cell for trespassing instead."

I looked at the prince. He was sweating and panting a bit still. I was, other than devastated, fresh. And I would not ignore the lesson of the Andrean swordmaster, the one Lankin himself had ignored. If I got one blow, I would use it.

But my hands were shaking badly. And as much as I tried to wipe away the tears, they kept coming. And to be honest, son, fully honest, I felt fear to fight the prince, who had killed both my uncle and my best friend. I had a reason to fight, but a reason not to fight as well. I paused.

As I answered I trembled (son, I'm not proud of my fear, but I have committed myself to telling you the truth), "No. I won't fight. Send me to jail."

Guffey, who had been silent during the single combat, who stood not ten paces behind the swordmaster, smiled at me in way that made a chill run down my spine. "Oh you're gonna love your time in our luxurious Andrean prison. But I wouldn't be expecting to ever find your way out, if I were you."

⚔ Chapter 12 ⚔

The guards chained me and threw me onto the back of a wagon. I found I could remember very clearly what I had overheard being said to my uncle about the Andrean prisons. I felt a sense of dread about going there. But at the same time, there was a guilty sense of relief that I had not been killed. That what had happened to Lankin had not happened to me.

I prayed to the God out of my guilt in babbles that didn't have much meaning, on my belly, my face down, hands over my face, tears pouring through my fingers. I had now twice witnessed someone I loved be killed by Prince Rory-Galstaff. Twice, and though I was revolted and horrified, my main thought was a sense of relief. But that sense of happiness to be alive provoked a powerful guilt, mingled by fear of what would happen next. I prayed and prayed as I bounced down the rough lane to the prison in the back of a wagon, face down, weeping, feeling no peace in my prayers at all.

The wagon tipped downward for a bit before coming to a halt. I looked up, wiping tears from my eyes, suddenly afraid of looking weak. The wagon was in a courtyard lower than the general street level—I saw stone buildings on four square sides around us at a higher level than the stone wall in front of me. The sunken courtyard, paved in rough stone, led to a gate that clearly went below the city street level. A rank smell, like a mixture of sewage and bread yeast, assaulted my nostrils as I faced the rusted iron gate of the prison.

A guard hauled me forward. A city official, dressed in a grungy gray Andrean-style tunic that went down to his knees, began reading to me from a scroll, as I stood just outside the gate. Prisoners pressed forward into the gate, around twenty of them, which had double doors and a rounded arched top. They started calling out to me saying things like, "Fresh meat! Here we are meaty! What a pretty boy that is! Come on, sweetheart, give us a kiss!" and many other things, some much more obscene, all in voices calling out at the same time. The thing my ears picked out more than anything else was the term "fresh meat" or "meat."

A tremor went through my legs as the official droned on, "…as it is not proper to feed criminals at the public expense, your family members are entitled by the mercies of the law to bring provisions to you. A letter will be provided if needed. Do you have an address in the city of relatives who will provide for you?"

"FRESH MEAT, FRESH MEAT" some of the prisoners began to chant, louder than the official, who had his back towards them, some ten paces in front of the prison gate.

"Uh…n-not in the city, no. I'm from Iron Mountains province."

"A notification will be posted at the court plaza on your behalf." Several prisoners laughed very loud after the official said that. "Can you write?" he added as if could not hear them.

I indicated I could and I scrawled out a crude note, not even knowing what to say. I put something like, "IF YOU ARE FROM IRON MOUNTAIN PROVINCE, PLEASE, A PRISONER NEEDS YOUR HELP." And I scribbled my name below that.

The guards with me drew their swords and I noticed there were some other Andreans with swords on hand, apparently the prison guards. They drew swords as well and ten of them put themselves in a defensive line as a prison guard opened the gate. Two guards grabbed me by either arm as two others with naked sword blades shouted at the prisoners, "Back off!" Some part of my mind noticed that the swords the prison guards carried were forged in our province. Unlike the blades of the Andrean nobility. Some little voice in my head wondered if my uncle had inspected any of their blades. The guards threw me in and slammed the gate behind me. Many rough hands reached my way, but I ran forward as hard as I could, my size allowing me to yank several men with me who managed to get a good grip on my arms. Fortunately, they did not tackle my legs and I lost them as I charged down a narrow hallway with shallow rank water over the floor. A single light from a hole in the street above shone down. I plowed forward toward it, running as hard as I could from shouts of, "MEAT!" and "Come back!"

The twenty or so at the gate charged after me—I heard their feet splashing in the muck—but only a few at a time could pass through the hallway. I reached a corner where the hallway turned right. Light filtering down from grates above revealed more prisoners coming my way, grinning with blackened teeth and shouting in glee.

I took my stand at that corner and hit the first man to the right of me with a left cross, as hard as I could. His head snapped backward and he fell into the muck, his eyes rolling back into his head. I laid out the man right behind him with a left jab, flattening him just as much, even without the power punch. Someone coming from the other direction I gave a right cross. His skinny body flew backward, his feet lifting clean off the ground.

Suddenly the prisoners charging my way began to backpedal. The ones in front did, anyway. The ones in back kept pushing, still shoving their comrades forward, men suddenly reluctant to come near me. I knocked four more prisoners in a row unconscious before the mass of men from both sides halted themselves.

I suppose I have Ombree to thank for the boxing lessons that poured forth from me at that moment. He taught me how to use my power, which gave me what I needed at that moment to stop those men dead in their tracks. Though the truth is that if I had never sought the revenge that led me to follow Ombree, I would never have been in the prison in the first place.

A long pause came about, one in which my breathing poured out hard and my legs trembled and I felt like wetting myself from fear but did not do so. I held my big fists up, in good boxing stance, ready to clobber the next man who came in range. Several of the prisoners reached down to their fallen comrades, to lift them out of the water, but most stood there in the dim light, illuminated in the light beam coming down from the street, several paces to my right. I saw whites of surprised eyes in both directions. I panted and trembled. The ragged silence was interrupted by a single set of hands, clapping, from the direction of deeper into the prison on my left. A single voice spoke out from the same place as the hands, "Impressive. I haven't seen anyone get past the welcoming crew in years. Not without satisfying them first. Well done." Prisoners began to move aside and I realized the figure was coming forward. Soon, not so close as to be in easy punching range, but closer to me than anyone else, a slender Andrean with a neatly trimmed beard stepped forward.

My eyes continued to adjust to the dimness. Flickers of white were now visible in his neat beard. His clothing was in no way tattered or common even. His demeanor demanded respect, as if he had been a nobleman.

"I am Gaspar," he told me. "A man of some importance here." Something told me he'd understated how important he really was there. "You have a talent which I would like to employ. You will find I reward those loyal to me. While those who oppose me…well, let's say their prison experience is less pleasant than it otherwise would be. Do you understand me? Or must I employ coarser language?"

"I understand." But what I said next I don't understand. Not to this day, son. Was it the rush of my immediate victory? Was it that I'd become ashamed of backing down from a fight, especially after refusing to face Rory-Galstaff? Or was it some leftover commitment to standing alone for what is right, the way my uncle taught me? But whatever the cause, I added, "But I'm not interested. You wanna do something about it, feel free to take another step forward!"

He smiled at me. A smile that was not in any way nice, kind, or even amused. His cold dark eyes met mine and he said, "Oh, I'm sure you could knock me flat like these other men. But you'd be dead by morning. Isn't that so?" He looked to his left, the direction I'd come in from. The men who'd been unruly and uncontrolled before cowered back from him. Their voices rang out in a disjointed chorus of things like, "Oh yes. Yes, sir. Of course sir."

"Kneel," he told them. And every one of those depraved brutal reprobates did exactly that. Immediately. He glanced behind him and added, "You, too." And every last one of those prisoners got down on their knees in the muck of rancid water.

"You still of the same opinion?" Gaspar did not raise his voice. I realized he didn't need to.

I breathed hard for several heartbeats and my thoughts grasped that I could not stand in the corner forever—I could not even stay awake forever. I needed someone to protect me and standing right in front of me was my obvious best chance. I opened my mouth and the words that came forth were, "I am. I can take care of myself. Sir."

He stepped forward and grabbed hold of my cheek, as if affectionately, but harder than even the most enthusiastic grandmother would ever do. "Standing on your own. How cute." His tone became what you'd use in addressing a small child. "Well, I'll give you some time to think it over. Maybe a few days." He tapped my face, a near slap actually. Then he walked away, back through the crowd of men. After he disappeared from my sight into the darkness, his voice called back, "None of you are to harm him. He's mine until I say otherwise."

Then the men who'd chased me backed away. I pressed through them, going deeper into the prison.

I don't know, son, how much trouble Gaspar's statement may have saved me that first day. I wandered around the place, which was really a piece of a sewer that had been separated off from the rest of the system by thick rock walls. It took less than an hour to walk every passageway available to me. I later learned Andrea has five such prisons, all underground, all linked to the sewer system to one degree or other. I'd been taken to the one with the most notorious criminals, the very worst of the worst. So some of my prison mates enjoyed saying about themselves.

I realize our sewers are quite different. In our province we often use iron pipes to haul human waste away from places people live, into deep underground chambers. But in Andrea, the city had been built up over its waste removal. The system was made so that what was washed into a gutter at the street would fall down into a river of muck below. The muck flows out of the city, but sometimes gets blocked up with leaves from trees or other debris. So the system had always been made so that men could descend stairs and clear narrow points. The system led downhill into the river leading to the Middle Earth Sea.

The section of the city over our heads had been cleared of old buildings. A process of new construction was underway. In the meantime, relatively little human waste from above came down our way. But we prisoners produced our own waste, naturally. And when it rained, which happened three times while I was there, water in the lower reaches stacked up, forcing men to press together at the entrance gate for there to be enough room that no one was in danger of drowning. I found it terrifying the first time to go back up to the gate, where the terrible men waited, but in fact the press of flesh from all prisoners made it so they could not do what they were accustomed to doing. There was simply no room to do more than growl or grunt.

Lower down the water from rains and prisoner waste drained between a gap in the floor and a solid granite wall. The gap did not drain quickly, so there always was a pool of rancid water there, filled with mosquitoes. The weakest of the prisoners congregated there. Weakest, because when families brought packages of daily food for their loved ones, they came to the gate and left them there. Some families insisted their relative come to claim the package. But in either case, the food always went to the strongest men at the gate. Even if a man received bread directly from his wife, he knew his duty was to smile at her and thank her. Then he would be robbed, beaten, or worse if he resisted. He'd be given a bite or two to allow him to stay alive and that would be all.

Such men without power who had families who cared for them had a special name in that prison. The other prisoners called them "cows." The food their loved ones brought was called "milk." There were specific ways to stay alive in that terrible place. One was by being a cow. Another way was to please the men at the gate. I don't want to say more about how to please them than that. A third was by being an enforcer of the order—by being one of the strong men that kept Gaspar and his close associates well-fed, even though most of them had no one come to bring them anything. This was the position Gaspar had offered me.

Once again I thank the God for how things turned out as I entered the prison. It was not impossible for me to have joined those men. I might have, in order to stay alive. I can say my honor would have prevented me, but in truth, I found it harder to keep myself to what I believed was right than I ever realized. I could have given in—but circumstances prevented me.

During that first day, as I explored the cells of stone cut underground, a voice called out to me. "You must be the one who made quite an entrance today."

Instinctively, I raised my fists. The room I'd walked into was as dark as night. I stood at the entrance to the chamber, the one deepest in the prison, a shaft of light from above not far behind me. From deeper in a room that stank of sewage and mildew the voice had come. I said, "Why? Do you want some, too?"

The voice laughed. "No, not really. Though I do know how to defend myself well enough. If it were necessary, I could kill you."

I lowered my fists and took two steps forward. "But it's not necessary, I suppose?"

"No. I don't think it will be necessary at all. You seem like the kind of person who, like me, only fights to defend yourself."

"I've fought for other reasons before."

"Oh? Such as?"

At that moment it hit me how much I deserved to be in prison. I'd entered that Andrean jail with a sense that injustice had sent me there. Even though I hadn't really thought about it, that's how I felt.

And even though I cared more about the death of Lankin than my imprisonment, I had this strong sense I had been cheated, that Guffey had taken a form of revenge on me for inconveniencing him for my justified desire to repay my uncle's death. Revenge is not a good motive, son, but I had convinced myself it was good, that my cause was just, that throwing me in prison was an unjustified punishment for something I'd done for good reasons.

But at that moment, I realized the actual reason I stood there. All the men I had robbed, the people I had fought as they rightfully defended their property, they were the reason. They were why the God had allowed me to go to that prison cell. Not my desire for revenge. Not Guffey. Not anyone else. Me—my crimes—put me there.

THE BOND OF THE SWORD

I paused in that moment, horrified in the realization of my guilt. After a time of silence, I started to wonder how to answer the still lingering question from the stranger in the dark. Before I could come up with anything, he added, "Well, whatever else you've done, you made a big mistake in not killing the men you punched today. I'm not saying you could have easily killed them, unarmed as you are. But each man you hurt today will be coming after you again. You damaged their reputations. They will believe that they have to kill you."

I raised my fists once more. "If they come at me, I can do to them again what I already did."

"Perhaps. Though they would plan more carefully how to attack you a second time. They'd use weapons. Oh, there are weapons in here. Mostly improvised knives. They'd be stabbing you right now, probably, except Gaspar told them not to. He's giving you time to see how horrific the prison really is. Then he'll offer to save you from the worst of it— if only you'll help him. Haven't you already had people tell you how terrible it is here? How you need help to survive?"

"Yes. Several."

"They're telling the truth. Even if they work for Gaspar. The part they are not telling you is that you don't have to work for him."

"I agree with you. I don't need him. Or anyone. I can take care of myself!"

"Oh, really? Is that what got you into prison in the first place, taking care of yourself? But let's just say for sake of argument you without weapons can outfight a whole crowd of prisoners who have weapons. What happens when you fall asleep?"

"I don't have to sleep."

281

"Yes, my friend, you do."

I stepped deeper into the dark, my eyes adjusting continually. The first thing I observed was the pool of water against the granite wall I already mentioned. But then I began to make out shapes next into the pool, in what I didn't realize then was the deepest and most remote corner away from the entrance. Four shapes were in one place there.

"I suppose I do have to sleep. But I can stay alert while I do."

"That gift is quite rare. Are you sure you have it?"

I paused. No, I didn't really have any such gift. And I knew it—I would eventually fall into a deep sleep. But I didn't want to directly admit that. For all I knew this stranger would be the one to attack me while I dreamt. "So what do you suggest I do about it? Join Gaspar's men?"

"That's one answer. Or you can join us."

"Here? By this pool of filthy water? In total darkness?"

"Yes, here by the pool. The darkness isn't total, but I suppose it's close enough. Gaspar doesn't want this spot, so he and his goons leave us alone here. Mostly. There's one of us that receives packages. We fight our way up every three days to collect them and return here to split the food among us. I don't suppose anyone will be leaving food for you, will they?"

"No, I don't think so. Nobody who cares about me knows I'm here—I'm from Iron Mountains Province. Come to think of it, I'm not sure anyone cares for me at all, anywhere." But then I realized my mother must still. What pain I must have put her through!

"Too bad," said the voice with genuine disappointment. "You seem young enough—and handsome enough—that somebody would be interested in what happens to you."

282

"Sorry to disappoint. Does that mean you don't want me in your little gang anymore?"

"No. We still want you. Our regular battle to the gate and back for the simple right to eat has drained us lately. You see, I used to be the one the animals feared the most. But I've been wounded…I'm not as strong as I used to be. We all would gladly sacrifice some of our food to have you join us." I stepped closer still and my eyes adjusted more. The speaker, I realized with a shock, was an old man in a loose robe, leaning on his side. His eyes and mouth showed the stress of obvious pain.

"*You* were the one they feared?"

He laughed briefly through his hurt. "My name is Kalway. I'm a sorcerer. Of sorts anyway. My specialty is heat magic. These are the simplest of spells really, but I'm quite good at them. I can cook a man's brain in his skull before he realizes he's dead. Though usually it's easier to catch their clothes on fire and let 'em run."

Son, such magical arts really do exist. Some people in our province say they are only legends, but they are not. They are just extremely uncommon—you are much more likely to see rain falling on a sunny day than meet a wizard or see magic in action. Though under certain circumstances you'll see them more than others. Like during war.

What I said at the moment was, "*If* you can do that, then how is it that anyone could wound you?"

He ignored my cynicism. "Gaspar is a magician, too. A lesser one though, like me. Not one of the great power masters—or I doubt very much he'd be here. He specialized in levitating and moving objects. He sent a small dagger flying at me, aimed for my heart. He had hesitated for a long time to attack me, because both of us know my specialty kills a man more quickly than his. But he picked his timing well. He had me distracted. And himself hidden, so I couldn't immediately strike back at him. I have to see my target to strike at it. Whereas he can send an object flying without looking where it's going."

I considered this for a moment. What he just said made a lot of sense. The fear Gaspar inspired in other prisoners did not at all seem justified by any physical ability I'd observed in him. I cleared my throat. "So...how is it he didn't kill you?"

"I moved. Jumped back actually. The knife buried deep in my gut—it was painful to remove. I've cauterized the wound more than once. But the harmful vapors in this place continue to attack it." (Cauterizing is a way to clean a wound by heat, usually by heating metal in a fire and touching it to the wound. Kalway of course didn't need to light a fire or heat metal to do that.)

"Hmm. So you want me to join you? What happens to us if you die? I don't think I can replace you."

A brief laugh barked from him. "One minute you're saying you can take care of yourself and questioning how a weak old man like me can fight anyone, the next you're wondering how you can live without me? You're quick to change your mind, aren't you, mountaineer?"

I considered the point while drawing in a deep breath. "Ah, no. Not usually, sir. But in this case, yes."

"I suppose I ought to thank my lucky stars for that." I didn't know if he using sarcasm or not.

And so I joined them from that point forward. Kalway, ironically considering what my uncle had done, had been a sword maker. He'd been responsible for welding thin strips of rare light metals that created the very long light swords of the sort I observed Rory-Galstaff use to kill Lankin, a work which required a precision that only magic could perform. What he did to wind up in jail he never told me. But when I eventually mentioned Guffey in telling my story, he became very angry. So I think that particular official probably had something to do with it.

The three others in our group were Evrend, an Andrean who'd been a keeper of the Andrean king's gold accounts and who did not hesitate to say how Guffey had lied about him for the purpose of making himself look better—to move up in prominence among the royal servants. In fact, he hardly ever stopped talking about it. Evrend also had a wife and family devoted to him, who brought him ample food packets every three days. Ample packets for one man—though of course what he got had fed four before I arrived, five with me.

Sarmok had been a member of the Royal Guard, who admitted to me once in vague terms that he had killed another guard in a dispute over a woman. Rence, who talked even less than Sarmok, had been a petty thief, part of Gaspar's crew, who had fled to Kalway's protection when some conflict among their gang had caused several of the members to swear an oath to kill him.

When it came time for us to go to the gate, Sarmok and I walked up front, shoulder to shoulder. He was not quite as large as me, but he'd had a great deal of combat experience. He also was very cool under pressure and good at killing men by single blows that not even Ombree taught me. Evrend lent his shoulder to Kalway, virtually dragging him behind us. Behind them, Rence scrambled backward, his sharp eyes and ears alert to surprise attacks. Kalway burned anyone he pointed out.

Our first trip up, two days after I joined the group, one day after I shouted to Gaspar I wouldn't join him, perhaps the memory of the beating I'd given some of them made the men at the gate hesitate (the ones Kalway consistently called "the animals"). Or perhaps Gaspar still hoped at that point I would change my mind, I don't know. But that first time was almost peaceful.

After seven times I stopped counting how many trips we made upward. Gaspar himself stayed out of our view. More than once, fast flying objects whirled at Kalway from nowhere. Never at any of the rest of us. Gaspar knew Kalway was the key to our survival. Not Sarmok. Not me. Even though he and I did most of the fighting.

As much as we did nearly nothing when not fighting and tried to stretch our rations, the food we received was not enough. I grew weaker over time. All of us grew weaker.

Mosquitoes attacked us—Kalway boiled the pool next to our spot more than once to kill them. He also boiled the water we drank. But this weakened him. Day by day, no matter what the rest of us did, he grew weaker.

I saw my death coming, slowly, eventually, inevitably. My skin began to hang loose, while the men at the gate seemed to grow bigger and stronger relative to me every time we went up. I dreamt at night of food, more food, any kind of food. I wept and cried to the God when I thought no one else could hear me, begging his forgiveness for having stolen the hard-earned work, the bread, from other men.

I thought of my oath I'd made, too. I begged forgiveness both for making it and for breaking it. It wasn't Guffey who had really put me in that prison—it was myself, my own evil, my own foolishness.

I would not have known it was my ninety-ninth day except Rence told me later, after we heard the noise of shouts and fighting from above. Not the ordinary sounds and screams of a new prisoner learning his first lesson from the animals, but metal on stone and boots marching, shouts of "Clear the way!" Soldiers coming down into the jail, as Kalway had told me they did from time to time. Shouting something else I did not recognize at first.

The words were: "Prisoner Therin of Iron Mountains Province!" I realized with a shock.

I didn't know if I should call back to them or not. "Do you suppose it's Guffey, finally decided to execute me? Should I hide?" They all knew my story. I didn't realize it then, but I had proven to be almost as talkative as Evrend.

"Don't be afraid," said Kalway's voice, very weak. "At least you will see the full sun in all its glory. Let yourself rejoice in that. And perhaps your God will show you mercy."

I stood, took two steps towards the sound of the guards, then looked back. "What will happen to you?"

"We'll have one less mouth to feed." The dying sorcerer smiled at me one last time.

Then I walked out of there, not looking back.

Rence walked with me for a bit, chatting more to me more in those last two minutes than he ever had before. His last request for me was that I pray for him. Son, I often wonder what happened to those men, though I'm afraid I know. Sometimes I do pray for them.

I met the guards in one of the corridors, under a shaft of light from above. Then they roughly seized my hands and tied them behind my back. Someone shoved me forward from behind as armed men surrounded me on all sides and escorted me out of there with naked blades.

The animals had cleared away from the gate, so even before they let me out, I saw a flash of red hair. With a shock I recognized Arta, taller, her body fuller. Next to her was her father, his own blazing hair now full of white. They, I found out, had paid the price for my freedom.

I was released.

Part Three

The Bond of War

⊣⊩ Chapter 1 ⊨⊢

he hastily scrawled note I'd written before going to jail, that's what Arta had seen. She'd told her father.

He'd quietly sought my release, not even knowing who I was for certain. Through official channels, the royal court were those who had to release me because I had been charged by the royal family. Officially, they would not even consider my release.

Unofficially, Alkin knew the man to bribe to get me out of there. It cost him a lot of hard-earned trade goods. Later, on the way back, once I realized how steep the price had been, I asked him, "Why?"

"We've been looking for you. Both you and Lankin, ever since Elin made it back."

"Elin made it back?" I don't know why, but this shocked me nearly as much as Lankin's death.

"Yes, and he told us what you and Lankin were trying to do. What all of you had sworn to do. And how you planned to do it. It made us sick to hear it. Everywhere we've traveled, we'd looked for any sign you may be around somewhere. I went to Tsillis three times. But you'd departed already.

Or for all I knew, perhaps you were dead. But we hoped, both of us, that you were still alive."

"Both of you?"

Arta walked in front of the oxen pulling the trade goods at that moment, twenty paces in front of us as we walked behind the wagon, bringing back a very meager supply of nothing but grain. She couldn't hear me right then, but what she thought of me mattered more than anything else in the world at that moment. My feelings for her had changed very much during the three days we'd already spent on the road. She was no longer an irritating girl that I may have cared for in a way I could not explain. Her body had become a woman's and her compassion for me when I'd told her my story, especially how Lankin had died, brought tears from her that my own soul had already expressed earlier. And I'd replied with deep tears that gushed out of me once again.

I had wept with her, she in my arms and I in hers. And when she released that embrace, the shy recognition of her beauty, the joy of release from prison, and that unbelievably sorrowful but comforting shared touch, a touch not just of our bodies, but the sharing of soul grief, linked me to Arta in a way I had never known was possible. I fell passionately in love with her.

I have not plainly said what you must already know by now, son. Arta is your mother and Alkin, your grandfather. I didn't say so plainly because perhaps you might have wondered if there had been another Arta. Or perhaps you were surprised at how I first saw her as an annoying girl, even though she interested me at the same time. Perhaps you wondered how my feelings changed so much.

Now you know. What you may not have known is how my uncle's death was also the central grief in her life. She had helped treat him between the rounds. She understood his courage and cheered for him to win. Then she watched him die as brutally as I did. She understood in her bones why we had decided to avenge him—but feared more than anything that we would wind up dead like him (which of course, is exactly what happened to Lankin). She had pushed her father over the years while we had been gone. She had insisted on coming with him—she had searched and searched and never given up on finding us.

Your mother, son, saved me. By her compassion, by never giving up, by always searching—eventually, she found me. Her devotion to me has been—astonishing.

In spite of that, I once accused her, years later, after the war, after I'd been hurt, before I managed to walk correctly again. I said, "I bet you don't love me at all! Not me, not really. If I had died and Lankin had come back, you'd have been so glad to see him, you would have married him instead of me—it's not me that's important to you at all!"

She threw her arms around me when I said that. And cried and cried. And held me. And told me how glad she was that I'm her man, that I was her only one and that I always had been the one she cared about most. I cried too, after that. I regretted the words I spoke to her at that moment as much as any others. Yes, she loved me and never gave up on me. No matter what. Not now. And not then.

Once Alkin understood the story I told him on that road, the story of how Lankin died and Guffey's role, he feared to bring me back to Rogin. Because Guffey could look for me in that prison at any time. He had built up quite a reputation in the city as the king's enforcer. From what Alkin had heard about him, he would not hesitate to come back to our province and destroy me, and if necessary, others in my village, if he realized I had departed.

So I went back with him and Arta instead. I'd grown so much and my face had gotten hairy. Nobody in his town would know me. I called myself, "Trone," a Shos Hillcountry name. I pretended to be from there. I certainly was big enough to convince people I was one of them. I also told people that I'd lived in Tsillis, which was true enough, one of the refugees who'd fled there from the Hills, which was partially true, since I was a refugee of sorts. Though I implied I grew up there, which was a lie. Your mother never cared much for this falsehood, but your grandfather felt it was needed. To please him and out of genuine fear of Guffey, I went along.

Nobody in Rogin, not my own mother, knew that I was alive. This random stranger, the man I claimed to be, a tradesman in his own right, supposedly from far away, married Arta the local girl. It isn't common for our people to marry outsiders, but it does happen sometimes, especially in the trader families. So I was accepted in the town of High Crossing. I passed myself off. I hid. I felt shame at hiding so much that life would not have seemed worth living at all, except for the indescribable joy that your mother brought to me every single day.

That joy, incredible as it is to say it, began to wear a bit thin after our first year of marriage. I wanted to have something to do to get me out of the house. But going out with Alkin would have raised the risk of me being seen by someone who might know who I am. So I needed to stay in High Crossing. After a few months of grumbling, I found an apprenticeship with a bow maker in the city.

Our traditional weapon in Iron Mountains has always been the bow. Ever since the ancient days, when the first settlers of the Iron Mountains were hunters, who only discovered the iron later. Swords and other gear we made for sales elsewhere, but bows we made for ourselves. And our bows have always been made by hand. It wasn't the type of work I enjoyed. Parts of the process I found easy, mind you, chopping the yew tree and cutting the logs—though even at that basic first phase I began to make mistakes. I'd swing the ax too hard sometimes and put a crack in wood that an expert bow maker could have used. Or I would saw crooked or miss my mark in various ways.

The situation got worse when it came to carving the bow wood by hand or stringing out the animal tendon for the bowstrings. My hands have always been too clumsy for that kind of work. Try as I might to be careful, I often made mistakes. I had no real talent for the job at all.

Valinin, the man I'd been apprenticed to, had been in the same battalion of Iron Mountain volunteers as my uncle, the 4th. He did not know him well, because they were in separate companies and never actually stood side by side in combat. But he told me how he recognized my uncle's face in my own. He knew who I was, but he agreed to keep my secret.

Eventually I realized my position there had nothing to do with any estimation of my skills and everything to do with my trademaster's loyalty to my uncle—or better said, to their unit, to the survivors of that unit. I was, after all, rather old to be a new apprentice. I had no experience at all and I certainly wasn't any good. But Valinin was unfailingly kind to me, praising any success I had and overlooking my failures.

I should have been happy I suppose. But I was miserable. I wanted to be good at what I did in my own merit. Not someone who benefits from special treatment.

One day though, my mind wandered back to a metal bridge just outside the East End of Great Portage that I'd seen an elephant walk across. The metal bent under the weight, but snapped back in place after the elephant passed. Metal under a lot of pressure stays bent usually, but some types of metal have a lot of spring to them. I sat at my workbench, staring at a piece of yew that would have made a wonderful bow—in hands other than my own.

I felt a hand on my shoulder. I met my two eyes to Valinin's one remaining orb, which shone bright with his genuine affection for me. His black eye patch covering his missing right eye had little flakes of sawdust on it. "Is something wrong, son?" he asked me.

"Sir, has anyone ever thought to make a bow out of steel? And the string…out of steel wire?"

Valinin rubbed his beard and smiled at me. "Hmmm. I don't think so. But maybe we could give it a try."

He took the idea and ran with it. He was the one who brought in the steel inspectors from the nearest plant, the one in Alandria, the gentlemen who knew exactly how to make wire and what kind of steel would give the greatest spring—strips of steel, actually, thin strips bound together. I helped, some, but between the steelmen and the bow maker, they were the ones who created what is common to us now, the steel bow of Iron Mountains Province.

I'm saying this because I imagine your mother says I invented the steel bow, but I didn't really. I just had the initial inspiration. Valinin made it happen.

But the steel bow becomes important to this story. Because steel is much more resistant to dragon fire that yew or sinew.

⊹ Chapter 2 ⊱

I remember the morning the rider thundered through town, the Andrean messenger. Everyone noticed his horse, the steam rising from its flanks. The single rider, no other travelers accompanying him—unlike in Tsillis, this was as much a rare event in our mountain towns back then as it is now.

The rider thundered past, his brow furrowed in concentration, his long dark hair swept behind him as he spurred on a horse already exhausted. His red sash proclaiming his role as member of the Messenger Corps as he headed toward Alandria, home of the Elder Council.

I saw him myself, briefly. But I heard much more detail and description on the floor of the steel bow factory Valinin and I had established. What I knew about the properties of steel from my time pursuing the arts of the sword was not inconsiderable. My specific role at the factory was the inspection of completed bows, but that task didn't prevent my ears from hearing all about the rider.

I remember that day for another reason, one much plainer than the Andrean messenger. Valinin and I had just concluded that it is not necessary for a bow of steel to be unstrung when stored or not in use. Our steel would resist rust with proper treatment and our wires did not seem to stretch the way sinew eventually does. That morning I was verifying this, inspecting the bows left strung and made the previous month, ensuring they still functioned properly.

Valinin recalled over our lunch of cheese and onions that he'd seen another Andrean messenger charge through the town once before, when he'd been a young man.

"So what was it all about, back then?" I asked.

"His Majesty the King of Andrea requested the Council of Elders to honor the oath that joins them to the Western Bond."

"Did they?"

"Of course. You *have* heard of the Dragon War, haven't you?"

"Of course I have. So what happened after that?"

"After that?" Valinin chuckled at the question, but as he continued his face settled into a stony mask of inexpressiveness. "We went offta war, that's what happened. Me, your uncle. And many others."

Something about that expression stopped me from asking any other questions that day. Two days later, we heard the town criers shouting. "War declared! Elder Council honors the Bond! The Kings of the East have crossed the Heavensfoot Peaks into the Western Lands!"

Many more things were said about what had happened, including Kung Tzu having ten times as many dragons as he'd had in the last war, that villages were in flames across the Bond, and many more details. I did not recognize these bits of news as rumors, but Valinin told me, "Look, early on in a war, everyone says all kinds of things and hardly any of it is actually true. Don't let these things bother you. You'll sooner or later find out what you need to know."

Before the declaration of war we'd sold our bows to private customers, men we persuaded with some difficulty that our weapons were superior to what they'd always used. After the war was declared, one week later, a scribe representing the Council Treasury came to the shop. He asked a lot of questions and looked around at our work. Two days later a shipment of gold came in. We'd been asked to produce one thousand steel bows for the battalions of volunteers that were beginning to form.

My life story would have been different if the rider had come at a different time of year. But it was early fall when he charged past. Some places like the Great Portage or Andrea itself have weather that allows people to work all year round. But as you know, our province closes down over most of the winter, other than the factory work that happens underground, which we ship out every spring.

So there was time to build bows before the volunteer battalions marched out. And time for the volunteers to train. And plenty of time for me to think, even though I had more than enough work to do, work I was much more suited for than traditional bow making, work that should have been fulfilling.

But in fact, I felt sick. Great Crossing had a recruitment post, where boys and young men eagerly lined up for their chance to join one of the volunteer battalions. I walked past this post in the morning on the way to the bow factory from the wing of your grandfather's house, the one your mother and I shared (this was before I built the house you know, son). I walked past it again in the evening, when work finished for the day. Even if I left late, when the sun had gone down, young men congregated there. Bards sang war songs outside praising our heroes of the past and men drank hot tea in weather than soon grew cold, so steam would rise in little clouds from the great silvery steel kettle holding hot tea that volunteers gave out to the young men in line. They drank from tin cups, steam rising, as I crunched though the snow on the ground, my head hanging down, returning to the woman I loved more than my own life, as if doing so were a punishment, as if stepping into my household was like entering into the Andrean jail the God enabled me to survive. Well son, perhaps my writing is growing rather poetic as I think of these events. It wasn't that bad, really. Not entirely. My love for your mother made life worth living. But it did bother me that other men were pledging to defend the country at the same time I was expanding my business. Me making money off a war about to happen, but me not putting myself at risk. It seemed wrong to me. Very, very wrong.

More than once, as I walked past the station, I heard these somber lines of the Dragon Song:

The Fourth stood firm and strong
While dragon swirled fierce and long
The fiery flames melted every shield
But the firm Fourth would never yield

These words in particular made me think of my uncle. His sacrifice. The one that came before the one I witnessed myself.

At home, at the dinner table Arta and I shared with her parents and their other three children that still lived at home, after several weeks of such suffering—I announced, "I've decided to join a volunteer battalion."

Alkin looked up at me through his bushy eyebrows that had once been red but had turned pure white. "I see," he said, then carefully took another spoonful of steaming tuber soup, watching me. Berta, your grandmother, dabbed her eyes with the corners of her napkin. Your uncle Lanin cheered, "Hooray!" and Lana and Raspin clapped their hands.

Arta, the one whose opinion mattered to me more than all the others, looked down at her soup. She, like her father, continued eating. But her eyes would not meet mine and the pale skin of her face flushed very red with an emotion I knew had to be strong, but I did not know what it was.

I waited, watching her take one spoonful of soup after another. My heart beat hard in my chest. Would she see my desire to leave as a betrayal to her? Would she think I didn't care about leaving her alone?

After what seemed a very long time, the redness began to leave her cheeks. Arta looked up at me and said in a clear quiet voice, "I've seen sacrifice. I don't want that to happen to you."

"I don't want that to happen to me, either. But how can I stay here and do nothing, when other men go out? How can I make a living off selling weapons if I am afraid to face what it means to use a weapon I sell in a war?"

Her eyes dropped again, "So you want my permission, do you? Or my blessing at least?" Then those lovely crystal blue eyes met my own, waiting.

I breathed in and out. Then I answered, "Yes. Of course."

"Very well. You can have it. But only if I get to come with you."

"What?" I felt my own face flushing.

"I get to come with you. As a healer."

"What?" This time it was your grandfather who said it.

Her eyes turned down to the soup again. She took a bite before answering me, ignoring her father. "Yes. If you want my blessing, you can have it only if I come along as a member of the Healer Corps."

"But dear, you can't—"

"Yes, I can!" her fist slammed the table, jostling soup bowls; she shot up out of her chair, her reddened face blossoming anew. Then she took a deep breath herself. And sat back down, turning her attention to the soup bowl again. The discussion did not quite end there, but it didn't linger longer at the table either. Your mother had declared what she wanted. And it so happens I got what I wanted— or better, what I felt I needed. Your grandparents didn't like it, not my decision and certainly not hers, but they didn't resist much either. Berta cried and Alkin rubbed his hands, but that was about all they did.

The next day at the factory I told Valinin of my decision. Our bows were selling so well that the original bowmaker's shop had proven to be too small. The man who took me in as his apprentice had bought the bakery that had been next door, and masons we'd hired were laying bricks that morning to create a new wall in the small gap between the two buildings. I'd taken him aside from his supervision of the workmen to tell him of my decision and why.

He studied me very carefully as I spoke, his single unpatched eye shining as if ready to tear up, but the rest of his face showed no other expression. Once I finished, I waited for some answer through his silence, feeling sheepish, while chisels and hammers rang in the background from the new doorways workmen pounded into what had been outside walls.

Finally I broke the silence between us, "Well, what do you think? I believe you'll easily be able to run this operation without me, sir."

He cleared his throat, then his reply came just above a whisper. "Well, that might be hard. Because I was gonna put you in charge. I've already volunteered myself."

"You have?"

Louder now he said, "Don't sound so surprised. Yes. I got asked by Norrin of Alandria, who's been selected by the Elder Council to command the battalions. He told me they were looking for experienced men from the last war, men who could still march and fight. There aren't very many of us left in that category. I'll be an officer, one of the battalion commanders. Or perhaps a second, if they have enough officers to afford that luxury."

"I see. Then I can't leave, can I?" The weight of the thought bowed me down. I so much wanted to go—looking back on that time, it's contradictory, but I see myself both as a fool for wanting to leave so much. And I'm also proud of me. Yes, it's an honor to serve. But eagerness for combat shows a lack of understanding.

He studied my face again. By then he knew my background well. He'd asked small questions here and there in a patient way and I'd talked. Maybe that's why he knew this meant more than me just wanting to join others in service. This was a desire to undo my fear when Lankin died. A chance to stop hating myself from the way I'd been helpless to do anything when my uncle died. Now was the time for me to take my own risk in turn. Now was my chance to repay.

He put his hand on my shoulder and said in a gruff tone, "Well, I've got a nephew in Rogin who can take over the business for us. He'll screw everything up I s'pose, but not so much there'll be nuthin' left when we get back."

I smiled at this and my heart pounded in my throat.

"Can I go to the station now then? Before all the slots are filled?"

"You don't have to go at all, in fact. Norrin asked me to keep a look out for other potential officers. I think you qualify. So you don't have to sign an enlisted contract."

"How can I possibly qualify? I have no military experience at all."

He snorted. "How much experience do you think the rest of the boys signing up have got? You've got a lot more experience fighting, if not actual combat experience, than average. Besides, in my day, they made anyone with sword training into an officer right off. That's because in our formations, officers walk behind the lines with swords, while the rest of the men carry spears or bows—"

I interrupted. "I know that."

He shrugged. "Then you meet the first qualification of an officer. Swordsmanship. The rest you'll learn by experience. We're gonna train 'til springtime."

"Can the war wait until then?"

He tilted his head, like a dog puzzling over an odd noise. "Chances are, the war's not goin' anywhere, Therin. It'll still be there when you arrive."

"That's not what I meant. I mean, if we've been invaded, won't us waiting until spring give the enemy the chance to win?"

He chuckled. "All your uncle taught you and you still don't know very much, do you? Maybe you didn't listen too well. We're hardly the only troops in the Bond, you know. 'Sides, the Heavensfeets will be unpassable in winter. Kung Tzu will only be able to advance so far without spring reinforcements and supplies."

"Oh," I said.

And that son, is how I became an officer in the 4th Battalion, Iron Mountain Volunteers. From Valinin, who felt loyalty to my uncle, even though he hadn't seen him in decades.

We did train through the winter, though as an officer I had it better than the enlisted men. The men had to sleep in tents out in the field, to practice making camp and keeping formation. They let officers go home to our wives on weekends, except for special exercises. Though sometimes when I got home, Arta wasn't there because she'd be doing her own training with the Healer Corps.

Nearly six years had passed since I first asked my uncle about the Tournament of Swords. At nineteen I was hardly a grown man, let alone an old one, but I'd been married for almost two years, was responsible in part for a growing business, and now was an officer in my uncle's old battalion. I certainly felt grown up.

But my devotion to the Fourth had a childishness to it. I felt thrilled to see the hammer and sword on our battalion flag and had a pride in the unit that echoed from my childhood. The "Fearless Fourth," they called us. We were as fearless as we could be. Dragonslayers, the songs said, and I believed it nearly as much as I had as a child.

As the second officer in the battalion, my main duty was to follow Valinin around, learn from him, and take his place when he wasn't available. I also would be in charge of the troops that supported the battalion, the supply boys, healers, and engineers.

Not all nations in the Bond apprentice officers like that —the Tsillians have a special school that their officers attend —but most other provinces appoint nobles into the role of officers. Since we don't have a traditional nobility, the ability to use a sword seemed as sure a sign of being suited to becoming an officer as any other. And imitating an officer with more experience is a great way to learn how to do the job—assuming the one teaching you knows what he's doing.

Valinin had never been an officer himself, but he did know a lot about leadership. He'd been promoted from a Line Soldier, through the ranks of Squad Chief and Line Chief, all the way up to a Detachment Chief. As such he'd commanded fifty men, a fourth of a company. Back when he'd served, there had been more men with sword training, so all of the company commanders and most of the detachment chiefs had been appointed as such instead of rising through the ranks. But so many had died in the first Dragon War that swordsmanship had become nearly a lost art among our people. So all of our detachment chiefs were former enlisted soldiers, as were some of our company commanders. Of our four companies, three of the commanders were men of experience from the first war. The fourth was a young officer who had an assistant commander, who happened to be somebody I'd never expected to meet again. Elin.

I met him in the second week of my command. I was walking next to Valinin across a snowy field. We were headed up to the recruiting post. He'd directed me to write a letter to the station manager about ensuring the recruits we got were in top physical shape (some men with missing fingers from the ironworks had slipped through the system —this task had been delegated to Valinin by Norrin). I often helped Valinin with letters of this sort, since he'd never been much of a writer.

As we walked by the line of men at the station, not even looking at them, one called out to me, "Therin, is that you?"

I glanced over at the line and blinked twice, hard. His hair had changed to a light brown and the voice had also lowered, in a body taller than before—though still not my height. But the face was nearly the same. "Elin?" I asked.

"Therin!" he exclaimed and before I could do anything else, he embraced me at that very spot in the snow, slapping me in the back, with dozens of men nearby.

"I'm…not Therin," I stammered, not returning the hug. As he pulled back I tried to give him my adopted Hillcountry name. But at the moment of shock I couldn't even remember what it was.

"What do you mean you're not Therin?" he asked, his eyes as open and direct as ever.

That son, began the death of my false name and identity, the one I'd maintained even as I became an officer in our army. I had first joined up under my made-up name. (It was a terrible mess to straighten that out in the paperwork afterwards, but that's not part of this story.)

"Where's Lankin?" Elin asked, looking behind me as if expecting our old friend to come along at any minute.

I couldn't believe how much that simple question choked me up. I couldn't speak.

Valinin, next to me, didn't know Elin by his face and hadn't heard me say his name as we met. "My officer apprentice does not give out that information to just anyone, not even to old friends."

I gripped my old friend's shoulder. I managed, "Uh, Elin…" My eyes watered.

"This is Elin?" asked Valinin, a step behind.

"Um," I said, wanting to explain, knowing I needed to explain. It's always surprised me how tongue-tied I can get when my emotions run high. As opposed to how words flow for me when writing. That is, words flow when every-thing is quiet and calm.

Elin studied my face. "He's dead, isn't he?"

"Yes," I said, wiping tears from my eyes.

"Did you ever face the prince?"

I nodded affirmative, still wiping my eyes.

"The prince has a lot to pay for." Elin's mouth set with a determination I recognized from his youth.

"Maybe there's other things that matter more jus' now," said Valinin softly.

Elin really looked at him for the first time. "Yes. There's the war, of course."

The corners of Valinin's mouth turned upward in the faintest trace of a smile. "You've had a bit of sword training, haven't you?"

So that, son, is how Elin became an officer, even though he had no previous combat experience.

⊶ Chapter 3 ⊷

As the dark days of winter began to grow noticeably longer, something unexpected happened at home. I walked into the kitchen, ready to leave early from a Restsday break to go back out to training on the drill field, hoping to find a wedge of cheese or crust of dry bread to munch on as I left. What I found instead was Arta, your mother, her head lowered over a bowl of porridge—one she was crying over.

"What's wrong, dear?"

She looked up at me, tears streaking down her beautiful lamplit face. "I made this for you," she glanced down at the porridge bowl, "But you can't have it."

"Why not?" I began to ask but before I finished the second word the smell reached my nose. Your mother had vomited into the bowl. "Oh, I see…" My voice trailed off.

"No, you don't see at all!" she sobbed, fresh tears flowing from her eyes in big streaming globes full of yellow flickering light.

"Are you sick?" I immediately felt stupid at the question —of course she was sick. "I mean, is it bad?"

"No, no. I'm not even really sick," she moaned, eyes back down at the mess inside the bowl.

"Then why are you crying?" I asked, shocked and confused. Her eyes met mine again. "Because I'm pregnant."

"You're pregnant?" my voice lifted in excitement. I stepped around the table and my right arm flew around her as I lifted her and kissed her cheek. "That's wonderful!"

She shoved me away and even in the flickering light I saw her cheeks flushing fully red. "No it's not!" she bellowed.

"Shhh, you'll waken your family, dear. Though perhaps they'll be excited to wake up to this news," I said, quite without a clue as to what was going on with her.

"Oh, I'm sure they will be! Especially the part where the Healer Corps won't let me deploy now that I'm pregnant. They'll be overjoyed to hear their little girl is safe!"

"Oh," I said, beginning to understand. I sat in the chair across from her at the table and leaned forward towards her. The anger had disappeared but her tears kept flowing. "Can you move that thing away from your face?" I asked about the bowl.

"Yes." She shoved it aside. She wiped tears from her eyes but her head still hung low.

"So you don't want to be safe while you're pregnant, is that it?"

"Sometimes I don't think I like you very much. This is *not* a good time to tease me."

"I'm sorry. But…um, I definitely want you to be protected. Especially now."

She looked up at me, her eyes intense. "Well maybe I want the same thing for you. I've seen a man slaughtered before. Maybe I want to come along to make sure it doesn't happen to you."

She was thinking of my uncle in the ring, of course. I reached out for her right hand, but she pulled it away from me. "Please, Arta, let me comfort you."

"I don't want to be comforted! I'm afraid of what might *happen* to you."

"Well...perhaps you shouldn't be so concerned. My uncle survived the war, after all. Many men did. I'll just be one of them." I'd already seen enough of hardship at that point in my life to realize that I was not immune from it. I knew there was no guarantee I'd come back alive. But I wanted to comfort her.

"He survived, but you know he wasn't a whole man afterwards, right?"

"What do you mean? He was very much wholly a man."

"I mean he wasn't able to father children afterwards. That's why he never married after the war ended."

I paused. It was such an obvious reality. But I had never before considered—I'd never even asked—why my uncle had never married, when so few men returned from the First War and there were so many widows desperate for a man in its wake. "I never realized that."

"You might be able to see why that would really matter to me. I want you back. Whole." Her mouth smiled just a little.

"Hmmm. But there's no guarantee that you going with me would ensure that, is there? It could mean that you'd just witness me slaughtered out on the field of battle, like my uncle, but me this time. There are many wounds beyond what a healer can fix."

She nodded and wiped away tears again. "I know. Believe me I know. But...I felt much better about you going if I could go, too. I want to *know* that everything that can be done to bring you home safe is being done.

I want to see to it myself!" And the tears, which had nearly stopped flowing, returned in a gush.

I moved around the table and put my arms around her. I did my best to reassure her, but it was not easy.

So son, now you know the beginning of why it is I was not with you when you were born. Though that itself is its own story, your mother's story, which I believe I will need to include.

⊶╟ Chapter 4 ⊨

everal months later, Spring came as spring always does. A bit late that year.

By the time it did, all of us were pretty sick of training. Sick of standing outside in formation in melting snow—that's one thing about the military. I always thought I was partial to cold weather, because I enjoyed going out to toss snowballs in weather too cold for other boys. Well, maybe I'm better at handling cold than average, but when I got cold, I went inside to warm up. Guess what happens in the army, when you're outside training and you get cold and long for just a few brief minutes by a fire to add a bit of heat to your bones? Do you suppose your commanders give that to you? No, they don't, not until all tasks are completed, until all training is done. Training meant a lot of standing in formation in the cold, shivering. At least as an officer I got to walk up and down and rub my hands together.

It wasn't two weeks after the snows melted that we marched off in our column formation, heading back down a road I knew from experience leads toward Andrea. Our people cheered us from the windows and on the streets as we left the province, followed by wagons full of provisions, many of which had been donated by our patriotic people.

But Arta was not the only young wife weeping from the side of the street as her soldier left for war, one measured and drilled step after the other. Though she may have been the most bitter about not going herself.

We did not actually go to Andrea itself, but passed far north of it on a road I'd never taken before, one that ran north of the Shos Hills even. Heading east, due east.

At a city called Ogreton between mountains east of the Great River and the Eastern Desert, we linked up with the main body of the Bond Army. Units came from all the places of the Western Bond I'd seen represented at the Tournament of Swords.

Iron Mountains Province provided four battalions of volunteers (with more to come later), some 3,200 troops, not counting support specialists, but this proved to be very little among the total army. On the plain east of Ogreton, where in fact some of the armies of the Bond had yet to join the main army, the field of camped soldiers was so wide it covered from horizon to horizon. No one, at least none of us from our province, actually knew how many troops the total amounted to. Valinin estimated 200,000 persons, though likely not all of that number were fighting men.

Our component of the Grand Army marched with military troops alone, including our military blacksmith repairmen, waggoneers, and supply specialists. Even our Healer Corps were technically part of our army—and that includes the healers who were women. But that was not at all true for the majority of the provincial armies. Many had what you call "camp followers," often consisting of wives of some of the men, who did laundry and made food and many

PART THREE: THE BOND OF WAR

other legitimate tasks—but some of whom also provided
services Ombree would have been eager to use. But there
were others, too, not just "followers" of that sort. Civilian
blacksmiths and tailors, bakers and brewers, leatherworkers
and more. There was a tremendous buzz of excitement,
especially from those of our troops who had never been out
of the province. Many of us wanted to go out and see what
there was to see and do what there was to do (though of
course others distrusted nations other than our own and
wanted to remain in our own camp).

Norrin, the overall commander of what collectively was
called the "Iron Mountains Brigade" (but in theory we were
supposed to fight as separate battalions, not one battle
formation), wasn't too keen on our troops getting into
trouble. Men could only go out as approved by their
commanders, in groups of six or more at time, with an
officer or senior enlisted man among them, with a limit of
the total number of our troops being away from camp being
set at 100 at any given moment. Our battalion took our
allotment of 25 and divided it into four groups (three of 6
and one of 7) that could go out in the morning from sunrise
'till noon and another set of 4 groups that went out from
noon until sunset. But the restrictions applied the most to
the enlisted men. Because I was an officer, and an officer or
senior man had to be with each group, I went out and about
every other day.

Some of our men had money and wanted to buy
souvenirs for home. We limited but allowed that. Some men
wanted to get too close to some of the camp followers. We
didn't allow that at all. Most men wanted to try exotic food
or drink and we allowed that—though sometimes we
regretted it when a culinary experiment did not go well for

314

one of the troops and he'd be puking his guts out on the way back. Or dealing with it at the other end later on.

We dug latrine pits on one side of our area and the engineers made a water well on the other (with a separate latrine area for the women in the Healer Corps). We built a low rock wall for ourselves around our perimeter, with a place to remove mud-splattered iron boots. Our squads did shield and spear drills and shield chaining and unchaining exercises. We didn't have an archery range or space enough to make one, but archers practiced close-range attacks.

We waited at Ogreton for more Bond troops to arrive for over three weeks. It got pretty boring for the most part. Even going out was mostly boring after a while. There were only so many new things to see within easy walking distance.

Toward the end of the three weeks, I was out with a group of seven. We'd just come from a booth of Northwest Passage fisherman, who had traveled over a thousand miles to sell us smoked fish—which was delicious, by the way. As I was walking, we passed another group from one of the other battalions, a group of ten or twelve, us walking in a round cluster on one side of the street and they in a single file line on the other.

The fourth man down, the only one of the group with a sword strapped to his hip (thus, an officer) instead of a long dagger belted to the black chainmail that distinguished our province, waived at me. I waived back, but kept walking.

He called out to me, "Therin, is that you?"

I turned my head, stopping at the edge of the rutted muddy lane that passed for a street, which was packed with little wooden booths covered with canvas tops. The face looked familiar to me, but I couldn't quite place it.

The figure across the street commanded his troops, "Halt!" then began walking my way. (My men stopped themselves without me saying anything.)

"It's me, Elgin."

"Elgin?" My mind struggled to remember who that was. But then I placed him. He'd been a pudgy kid on the sword team. Next youngest to Elin, probably. He'd thinned out a lot as he'd grown up. "Elgin! Good to see you. How are you?" This was followed by a handshake that turned into a hug, us slapping each other on the back in the middle of the muddy road. Other than Elin, he was the first member of our old team I'd run into.

He ordered his squad to follow us the rest of the morning as we wandered around markets while I told him about what had happened to Lankin, Elin, and I. His reaction to our desire to avenge my uncle caught my attention.

"Avenge him?" he said. "Why would you do that? Or why would you go after the prince—he wasn't the reason your uncle died."

"Er, excuse me, what are you saying? The prince killed my uncle. Of course."

He stopped mid-stride and his dark brown eyes met my own. "Therin, your uncle died on purpose. To set us free from the tournament. Didn't you notice the way he goaded the prince? Your uncle didn't talk to people like that. He practically begged him to kill him."

My mouth opened and stayed open a heartbeat or two. Then I closed it. I shrugged my shoulders, at a loss for words. He made sense, but it was hard to accept I'd been wrong about something so important. Finally I found my voice as I realized something, "Hey, wait a minute!

How would you know anything about that? Weren't you back at our camp?'

"Oh, that. I was kinda sneaky as a kid. Especially good at taking food that wasn't mine, actually. Thank the God I don't do that anymore." He patted his flat belly. "But yeah, I snuck out and made my way to the stands. A place apart from you, Elin, Lankin, and Arta. I was pretty sure none of you ever saw me. What happened to Arta by the way?"

"She married me," I grinned as I said it, even though I was still thinking about my uncle.

Elgin slapped me on the back and congratulated me and asked a few questions about our family, but soon the subject returned to Uncle Haelin. "Your uncle. What a man! Who knows what would have happened if they had made the three of you fight. And if he'd refused, they'd have thrown us all in jail. Would any of us have survived that?"

I imagined our team of soft, untrained boys pushed into the Andrean prison I'd known. "Probably not." Or, if we had survived, we would have been so beaten down and abused that our fate would have been not much better than death. Maybe worse even.

"Your uncle, I've never known another man like him," he added. "To this day, he's my hero."

At that moment, son, during a conversation which continued for over an hour after that, I recognized in myself that I had stopped seeing my uncle as a hero after I trained with Ombree. Maybe even before that. I'd begun to see him as weak, as a victim. But that's not what he was. Sure, he was in a desperate situation, but he chose the way to take out of it. He goaded the prince on. His death wasn't an accident—he'd died on purpose, for us. For all of us.

Elgin said another thing that stuck with me: "Your uncle would have been surprised and hurt that you tried to avenge him. He died for you, and all of us, so you could live. Not so you'd ruin your own life and the lives others in a quest for revenge." We parted a while after he said that, each back to our own camps.

Our brigade set off after the Tsillian army joined us, a bit more than three weeks later. Not that marching is ever much fun, but it got considerably less fun after that. So many other units from Bond were ahead of us that made use of ox carts or were mounted on horseback that the road got pretty well covered with animal droppings. Not to mention human waste that some of our fellow members of the Bond didn't feel as bad about leaving alongside the road as we would. The road of muddy manure.

As we pressed further east, there was also dust, a lot of it (you'd think the manure would keep it down, but it didn't very much), from the wagons and hooves before us. And also hard winds whipped over the short grass plains just north of the Great Eastern Desert, dotted with occasional cattle-raising villages, both day and night, When the winds blew up from the desert south of us, as they did about half of the time, the air was incredibly hot and as our road angled a bit south, blowing sand increasingly came with the heat. If you want to know what it feels like, grab a handful of sand and go to one of the sword furnaces at Rogin where the oven is hot and the billows are blowing hard. Have the billowsman steer the outtake pipe at your face as he pumps air, and then throw up the sand in front of your face so the hot wind blasts it into your skin. That's what it was like where we marched at the edge of the desert.

After all that marching, as the Heavensfoot Mountains began to show themselves over the eastern horizon, delaying the rising of the sun. We still had not seen any sign of the enemy army. Not that we expected to yet. The mountains were like a solid wall of blue, topped by white even in early summer. The sudden stark enormity of the mountains, no sign of foothills, is quite different from the round, naturally-forested mountains filled with iron ore where we come from.

Valinin attended meetings of the Iron Mountains Brigade battalion commanders every other night. I did not attend that meeting at that time but was at the company commanders' briefing held the next day and I got the results of the information shared by Norrin through Valinin. Sometimes we'd have representatives of commanders of other Bond units, in addition to news and orders from the general command of the Andrean Crown at times (some part of me wondered if the king himself were really there, or just one of his generals representing him).

So I knew our general strategy. Kung Tzu had crossed the Gateway to the Gods pass (also called the Southern Pass) and pushed south along the mountains until he hit the Midearth Sea. He'd followed along the coast, attacking, supplied both through the pass and by his fleet, following along on the Midearth Sea coast. The Western Bond fleet was supposed to attack the Eastern fleet while we were to come north of the enemy, through the desert, down along the mountains to block the Southern Pass, while a second army, smaller than our own, was to face Kung Tzu's men at the west side of the Tassappi peninsula, which had been conquered by the eastern armies. The emperor would be forced to retreat to the pass when his supplies were cut off, only to find a massive army blocking his way back to his supply chain and a smaller one harassing him from behind.

Over two months after we began our march, after we had left behind the grasslands and had crossed a corner of the desert back to the small patch of livable land right in front of the towering Heavensfoot peaks on our left, we heard word of the Eastern army.

By the way, crossing the desert, during late summer, had been an amazing feet of organizing enough wagons hauling water and a massive usage of hay for the animals to continue pressing through the sands, using native guides to avoid the deepest drifts. It was a feat in some ways greater than everything that followed, though not as interesting to read about and one in which I took little part, other than making sure our own supplies were secured and our wagons properly employed and our men camped every night and during the hottest part of the day, marching as the sun set until it was too dark to keep moving, then again at sunrise and on until the morning began to get hot.

One day I was in our battalion command tent, writing a letter to your mother. I wrote many letters and we had plans for a rider from the province to eventually catch up with us and collect our posts to return to the province with them. But as of then my letters, all of them, remained in my possession. Valinin opened the tent flap. A glass-and-iron lamp burning with oil imported from south of Tsillis cast light within the tent he and I shared with several clerks, a tent containing three field tables and chairs, along with scrolled requisition requests and reports and four cots. He paused for a moment before coming all the way in. "I have news."

"Oh, what's going on?" His entrance was unusually dramatic, so he had my attention.

"Our far forward scouts say they've spotted Kung Tzu's army in full retreat."

"Why would he be retreating? Wasn't the fleet supposed to wait for another three weeks before they attacked? And wasn't that attack, assuming it won, supposed to be the first sign of trouble for the emperor?"

"Yeah, that's the plan I heard," Valinin commented stoically. "But that's not what's happenin'. He musta had spies who reported our movement, that's all anyone can figure."

"So what are we gonna do about it?"

"We're striking tents two hours before dawn and making a forced march south."

I whistled low. "We're gonna try to beat him to the pass? How far off is he?"

"We don't know yet."

There's a lot of that in warfare. I know this not just from my own experiences, but also from stories I've heard from men like Valinin. There is a lot of not knowing what's going to happen next. Or thinking one thing will happen but something entirely else does. There's also long stretches of time in boredom without much to do, though I didn't find marching as boring as it was tiring. Since you wanted to know what war is like, you should know about those parts, too.

We pressed hard for three days straight, with breaks of only an hour at a time. Our brigade was able to keep this discipline better than some of the other contingencies. Maybe because they depended on camp followers more, I don't know. Maybe because our wagons had axles and wheels enforced by iron. "Three days" sounds like nothing to say it. What it meant was already conditioned legs, already toughened men, dropping from exhaustion. Already deeply tanned faces blistering in an afternoon heat that we had up until that point avoided. And men falling out from lack of water, even though our supply troops worked with great success to ensure every man in our brigade had water on his person.

After the first day we even shed our armor and loaded it up on the supply wagons that had been emptied out. I'm sure it helped. Our battalion had 102 men drop out. The Healer Corps came along behind us at a slower pace and picked them up after we passed by. So only four actually died.

We covered around 120 miles on foot those three days, through the dry rolling plains next to the mountains, when we came to a village along a stream. The people there raised camels. They also raised oxen for food with very long hair (strange that animals that looked so much like they were made to live in the cold could survive in a place that's so hot in the summer). Andrean cavalry, which were the only unit ahead of us Mountaineers at that point, thundered through the village without stopping. We stopped alongside it as our supply boys haggled for meat, which they paid the villagers for in silver.

While we were there, with our sweat-soaked clothes caked with dust and our faces streaked with sweat, we must have made quite an impression on the villagers. The people came out, dozens of them, no, hundreds, and brought us water they carried in animal skins. And gave us little sour cheeses to eat, along with dried, salted meat. We could not understand their language, but some few of them spoke Common with an Andrean accent. Their eyes had the same inner fold of the man I'd known in Great Portage, Han Chang. These were Eastern people, even though they clearly lived on our side of the mountains and were part of the Western Bond. The name of the village was Walu.

We paused about two hours there, refreshed by the kindness of the people, then pressed on as the night began to fall. The moon was three quarters full, which is really quite a lot of light once your eyes adjust, far more than you would think it is, since I know you are used to carrying a lantern with you when you go out at night. You get used to actual darkness to a large degree, but even so, we faced the danger that hidden holes would break wagon wheels or men would trip and fall. Those among us with the sharpest eyes led the way for our battalion, which was in the lead of the whole brigade. Elin was among those out front.

He described to me later what I heard jumbled and second-hand at the time. The men in front heard the thundering roll of cavalry moving at a trot across the plain (well, I'd heard it, too, further back, therefore not as soon). Horses can't run constantly son—when they have a very long way to go, they walk most of the way. Trotting or galloping is something we'd never seen any of the cavalry do in the dark up to that point, I guess because of the danger of a horse breaking a leg in some shadowed hole.

"Are you Mountaineers?" called out the lead cavalryman, Andrean cavalry of their famous Green Lancers Brigade.

"Yes, the rest of the brigade is behind us!" Elin called back.

"I recommend you turn around, hillybilly—we've got about ten thousand Easty cavalry hot on our tail. About half of them *longma!*"

"*Longma?* What's that?"

"Easty dragon horses. They're tall, long legs. They move fast!" By then the rider had trotted far past Elin.

He immediately ran back and found Valinin, who started shouting orders, including sending Elin to report to Norrin, our overall commander. We were a bit strung out, too far from one another; it was dark; we didn't know where the tail company was. Only the wagon-mounted troops were wearing their armor. Andrean cavalrymen, many more than us in numbers, kept moving by us on our left flank, back towards the main army, hundreds of horse hooves at a time making a dull continual roar—a sound I'll never forget from the war. It took several hours for all of them to pass us.

In the meantime a runner found tail company and the men struggled to figure out which sets of armor were their own. Senior men shouted at juniors and juniors shouted back and the whole thing was a jumbled mess. Companies got mixed in with other companies, but as a battalion we did manage to form a line, shields in front. "Chain your shields together!" shouted Norrin to all of us, which was unusual. Usually he did all communicating through the battalion commanders. But not that night.

Norrin, unusually tall at nearly seven foot, stood out in a crowd. That night our overall commander towered over everyone as his voice bellowed out commands, the force of his words and his height commanding our attention, putting us into action, as his balding head shone in the moonlight.

Our battle-shields are designed with hooks in the back. A chain running behind the front line of men, hooked up together, helps a shield wall stay strong. Horses charging into chained shields will not break the wall. Dragons, well, that's another matter…

That night, not five minutes after the last of the Andrean cavalry had passed, the first of the Eastern riders thundered towards us. These were some dozen regular horses, no sign of any dragon horses.

"Brigade, take aim!" shouted Norrin. Around half of our archers actually had their equipment on them. Only around half of these were ready to draw their bows. When Norrin shouted, "Shoot!" I'm pretty sure not everyone did. But something like 500 arrows hurled at the dozen riders in their flared-out Eastern armor. Even though a lot of the aiming wasn't very good, I think all of the enemy were hit. Only two managed to gallop away. (They sure moved fast on the way out, though.)

A cheer broke out among some of the men. Norrin roared: "BATTALION COMMANDERS, straighten out your troops! Get your companies in order! That was just the beginning of the beginning of a fight!"

"Pathetic!" shouted Valinin at our men. "Archers, where are your bows?" We scrambled to fix our screw-ups as tremors hit the long muscles in my legs, whether more from excitement or from fear, I don't know.

But as we finally formed up correctly, even in the pitch black (the moon had disappeared behind some clouds), and finally found our wagons with the rest of the bows and made sure all of the men had at least a few arrows, while the shieldmen and spearmen held the chained-together wall. While at the same time we got almost everyone into armor that at least halfway fit right.

While doing all of this, we did not see any other troops at all. When the dawn rose, we saw a handful of horsemen in the far distance, facing our way, obviously watching us. I don't know for sure what happened, but apparently Kung Tzu's commanders felt running into armored infantry in formation meant they had run into the main body of the Bond army. Which they were not ready to face.

We continued to improve our position, getting all our supplies and equipment straight. Tail company even began digging a ditch around the left flank, which was exposed. Valinin stopped shouting orders to everyone and worked through the company commanders again. By mid-morning we received orders from the Andrean command. We were ordered to retreat back to the main army. Because we in fact were miles in front of everyone else and would have been slaughtered if Kung Tzu attacked with all he had.

Gear we packed back into the wagons in better order this time. And, of course, we wore our armor. (Though some troops had grabbed the wrong sets in the confusion. It took days before everyone had back the custom-fitted chainmail that our military blacksmiths had made for each man out of standard sizes.) We marched back battalion by battalion, company by company, in sight of each other.

We passed by the village of Walu. The people waived at us and smiled as we marched by. We camped for the afternoon a few miles to the east of the village and slept, intending to do so for just hottest part of the day. I woke up after sunset and I have never heard such mass of snoring. Blaring elephants or roaring bears do not make so much noise. But I was so exhausted, I was easily able to fall asleep again.

Two days of regular marching later, we met up again with the main army, Andrean cavalry passing us again on the way out, this time in the early evening, the sun still up, just before we arrived back.

As soon as we got back to the Bond army, we received news that the Eastern Army had stopped advancing our way and continued to retreat back to the pass. Weeks later we'd hear that the naval attack had been a success, but had come ahead of schedule, because of some admiral's ambition to show off the navy. Kung Tzu's supplies by sea had been cut off. This is why he retreated. Not because of anything we had done.

When we received the order to go out again towards the Eastern Army, we saw plenty of sign that both horsemen and infantry of the East had come a significant distance towards us. Some of their units must have actually passed us, far on 4th Battalion's right or left flank without us even knowing.

When we reached Walu, smoke rose from the roundish huts the people used as homes. Second battalion arrived first and passed through without saying anything to us. But they hadn't been to the village before, unlike the rest of us. They saw bodies of villagers stacked in tall piles along the roadside. Some of them, especially children, had been butchered and eaten.

It was late evening when we arrived and Valinin had us camp next to where Walu had been. Elin's company got the task of looking for survivors. He took four men with him to search the area himself. Other battalions searched on their own initiative as well. Seven people were found. Seven. Out of perhaps a thousand villagers.

One was able to say in broken Andrean that the Rysshurian contingent of the Eastern Army had done this to them. Because their scouts saw that we had come through and the villagers had waved at us in a friendly way. They saw Iron Mountains-minted money and some of our trade goods in the village, so they knew they'd helped us. So they tied up the men, raped the women, and ate some of the children while forcing their parents to watch. Then they killed everyone else and stacked the bodies as a message for us when we came back through.

My uncle had warned me how cruel war can be. But he hadn't given examples. We were shocked, all of us. (By the way, not all Easterners are like the Rysshurians—their cruelty is infamous. And they don't have folds in their eyes, either, so nobody can blame that for how they are. But I hadn't heard about Rysshurian cruelty at the time—and I thought I knew a lot about the world before then.)

A lot of the men and junior officers, Elin among them, pushed for us to chase after the Rysshurians for what they did, to pay them back in kind. This messaged reached Norrin. He approved.

It was an insane idea in a way. We had no idea how many Rysshurians there were and didn't know how far away they were. We only knew they were infantrymen, so we had a chance to catch them. Our battalion happened to be younger overall, especially in leadership positions, than most the rest of our units. So Norrin selected us.

Valinin spoke with me that night after coming back from his commander's tent. "He's approved the plan," he told me. "Two companies will split off, hope the Rysshurians are trailin' behind the rest of the army, and see what we can do."

"Two companies, from our battalion?" I suddenly sat upright from leaning over the field desk.

"Yes, us," and he explained why. He added, "It'll be your command, Therin. I'm still draggin' from our last forced march. I won't be able to do another one so soon. A mission like this will have to be younger men. We'll re-organize the companies a bit. I'm putting you in charge."

I swallowed hard. "Very well. I guess that makes sense. But I don't think I'm ready for command yet."

His answer surprised me, "You're right. You're not. But the company commanders know what they're doin'. You just have to coordinate 'em and listen to 'em. Besides, who is more ready than you? Elin? He'd certainly try, but in some ways he don' have a clue."

And so it wasn't even with two whole companies we set out. Those older, or with foot problems, we left behind. By my decision, we also left behind the chainmail, wearing only under linens and shields, carrying our bows and arrows and supplies on our backs. No tents. No wagons.

We began our march that first night just over an hour after we got word about tracts of pressed-down land showing what direction they'd gone. Elin put himself out front with some of men with sharper eyes to watch out on the trail as we moved by night. We knew, vaguely, it was possible that our company could be surrounded by the whole Eastern Army and killed. But somehow we didn't believe it could happen to us.

One of the villagers, a boy of eleven who knew how to track and spoke a few words of Andrean, led us. I couldn't see the difference, but he said he was able to track the Rysshurian footmen separate from all the rest of the trampled ground in front us.

We followed their trail. After only a few miles we reached a campsite. The village boy spoke with Elin and the men in front, but I heard later what he said. "Camp here night," and he held up his index finger.

"They camped the first night here?" asked Elin. The boy nodded *yes*.

Their progress was not particularly fast. We were gaining on them.

The Rysshurians branched off in a more westerly direction from the main body of the Eastern Army as both armies marched south. Perhaps because they knew that the passes over the Heavensfoot Mountains still remained the great prize in this mass of maneuvering armies. We all moved south, but southeast, towards the passes. So perhaps they knew straying west would be safer for their infantrymen, who seemed as exhausted as we had been. It seems they wanted to avoid enemy contact. Or perhaps the Rysshurians intended to come around behind Western forces, hoping we'd press too far east, not realizing a separate enemy unit was seeking to ambush Bond soldiers from the rear.

We marched all night and as the sun rose, I gave the men a rest break. Our route had crossed no water as of yet, which concerned me. What we could carry would be gone by noontime if we didn't find more. Though of course we were aimed west, away from the mountains. Headed back into the Great Eastern Desert, instead of the grasslands and forests right in front of the Heavensfoot peaks.

I caught up with Elin resting with his back to a boulder —the entire area was filled with rocks and boulders and some scrubby trees. "Say, can you ask our guide about water? I'm concerned we'll run out. Better us divert in the direction of water and be able to keep going, than follow the exact path of Rysshurians and run out."

He smiled at me, "Good thinking. I agree. But Po Tal already told me we're headed towards water. Or a good place to find a well anyway."

"Oh, good."

We moved throughout the day, though not especially fast in the heat. The number of footprints declined in a large measure. Everyone realized that we were following a single unit now, maybe one no bigger than a battalion. One with no horses or oxen or wagons at all. We did run out of water in the early afternoon, which concerned me. But by evening we'd hit the second campsite of the enemy, one with a well dug in a fold of land by a hillside. They'd covered it over, but sloppily. After only a few minutes work, a few men digging with their daggers and open hands cleared it again and got fresh water.

We rested for several hours, replenished our water, and set out again. The night was clear and cloudless in a way it only occasionally is in our province. The sky sparkled with stars and as I marched near the middle of the two companies, what we were doing seemed out of line with nature itself. Were we really going to hunt down the enemy and kill them, out under this beautiful starry sky, the handiwork of the Sky Father? But I knew that we would, in fact, do just that.

As the Eastern sky began to turn a salmon pink, the air seeming dryer with every step, we came to the tents of the enemy, the Rysshurians. Their sentries were asleep in place. Son, I could tell you exactly how we killed them, but to think of that time makes my heart sick. I will say we caught them sleeping of course and many—most—died without even knowing we were there. But some of our men, enraged by the horror that they had seen at Walu, took it on themselves to torment those few who were alive and awake as the sun rose in the east. I was at the western edge of their camp and this began on the east side.

Yes, they had done terrible things. But that was for the God to judge, as my uncle taught me. It was enough for us to kill them, in their sleep, to prevent their evil deeds from happening again. But to torture them—it was worse than wrong.

Elin and I stopped the men involved, but then it fell on me to hand out company discipline. I faltered. I did not want to hurt my own men, even those who had violated the law of the God, who had fallen into the cruelty my uncle had warned comes so easily in war. Elin was furious and the other company commander looked at me strangely, but I ignored them. I gave no punishment.

We marched back towards our battalion, the stroke against the Rysshurians accomplished. Po Tal, the boy who had guided us, laughed in glee at the bodies of those who had slain his people as we left. Their cruelty had bred more cruelty. It could make a cycle that would continue forever, unless someone stopped it.

I felt sick inside, but I marched on. Because it was my duty to do so.

⊣⊢ Chapter 5 ⊢

I took us two days of marching southeast to link up with the Bond Army. Another two days to find our brigade and battalion.

I never described in detail to Valinin what happened. I just told him we "accomplished our mission" with a grimness that it seemed he recognized from the way he studied my face.

Shortly after that, Kung Tzu surprised everyone I knew by ordering a full retreat back across the mountains. The officers at our battalion officer meeting and those at our brigade meeting puzzled over our maps, wondering about the reports that Eastern troops were crossing the pass back through the Heavensfoot Mountains. (Valinin began taking me to the brigade meetings from that time forward.)

I remember once Norrin shaking his head. "Why would you deliberately dam yourself up behind the mountains, so that breaking out is virtually impossible? It makes no sense." The reason I heard much later was that Kung Tzu heard that the Andrean navy and other Bond forces had landed shipborne marines on the other side of the Heavensfoot

Mountains—an admiral's ambition, yet again. These troops had marched northward in a move to seize the inner approaches to the passes leading into the Western Bond. If they had succeeded, they would have cut off the Eastern supply lines and possibly forced the surrender of their entire army. In the end, they didn't succeed in taking the passes, but Kung Tzu feared they would, which is why he ordered his retreat. Several months went by before we ever heard about the marine landing. Which again illustrates a general truth—confusion about what's really going on is as much a part of war, at least the way I experienced it, as anything else.

Our marching came in shorter bits. The overall army command decided to use cavalry to chase after Kung Tzu's forces, Andreans and Tsillians leading the way. So we were held in reserve. We went from one campsite to another, over ground well trampled, edging south and east, but the view of the Heavensfoot Mountains barely changed from day to day. We made camp, used up supplies, made sure the men kept their perimeters and maintained their equipment. Some of our soldiers learned to play the Andrean dice game "Sharps." While I wrote letters to your mother in my free time.

Most of the Eastern forces steadily retreated over the mountains, but a delaying force of their own cavalry spent their time avoiding the Western horsemen while at the same time making them think they were massing for an attack. (I got the chance to talk to some Andrean cavalry from time to time as they passed near our formations.) From a strategic point of view, their actions in protecting their army while keeping their total killed and wounded low was brilliant. But that's not how we talked about it in our tent meetings:

"Damn, those Easties are pure cowards!" (Your mother won't appreciate the curse word I just used son, but soldiers sometimes use bad language—I try to avoid it, but I use it sometimes, too.)

"Why don't they stand and fight?"

"They're afraid to face us, that's what it is!" And other foolish talk that really had more to do with frustration than reality.

But after I don't exactly remember how long, the situation changed. We heard at our meeting that they'd formed a line and the cavalry had retreated behind it. Now the chance for a real battle had come.

Norrin pointed at the map, "See the main pass here? The Eastern infantry have dug a trench in a giant semi-circle. Around the trench are wooden stakes and no doubt other man traps. Behind that are the Eastern infantry, including plenty of their crossbowmen, ready to shoot at anyone working to cross the trenches."

"Sounds like a death trap," said Valinin with a sly smile. "Since you called us in here in such great excitement, can I assume that means we've been selected to do something about this mess?"

Norrin glared at him, "I swear you old veterans are the worst..." his voice trailed off as he muttered this. Then he grinned and started over. "Yes, Valinin, yes, we have been selected to lead the Bond Army across the barrier."

I felt an incredible nervous excitement. *Finally, we'll get a real battle.*

Valinin's response was different. His smile was gone but he nodded. "I suppose we're better armored than most Bond troops. They think we can make it through the crossbow fire."

Norrin nodded, adding, "That's right."

"And that we can fill the trench with rubble while we're under attack? That happened a couple of times with mountaineer troops in the first war."

"Right again."

"And then next I suppose we're supposed to fight our way through the stakes and traps and create and hold a corridor for the cavalry to come thundering through? To save the day yet again?"

"Are you sure you didn't go the big meeting while I stayed behind here, waiting to get briefed?" Norrin's voice showed both amusement and annoyance.

"Some things are predictable when you've got some experience. So what happens if Kung Tzu uses his dragons against us? While we're out there in front? The whole plan dependin' on us, and the Easterners can see it as clear as we do?"

"The griffins and their riders fly in and drive the dragons off."

"Uh huh," Valinin replied with clear skepticism. But then he placed his right hand over his mouth and looked down at the ground.

There was a lot more in the meeting after that. Maps rolled out and unit markers placed on them—4th battalion's was an "X" shape—enemy dispositions discussed, requisitions for needed supplies and troop equipment required planned. The action was designed to engage the entire Iron Mountains brigade, all four battalions. We would be the point of the lance, as the Andreans say, to drive the Western forces through the lines and "crush the Eastern bubble" on our side of the mountains.

Valinin said little and when he did, he immediately put his hand back over his mouth. I think the session lasted something like four hours.

I felt like I was ready for battle. I was so tired of trudging through horse droppings where the cavalry had gone ahead of us, facing blowing sand when the storms blew hard from the west, and came to hate the blazing afternoon sunshine, even though our early mornings were usually freezing cold. I had volunteered, I had trained, and I wanted to prove myself. It's true that I'd seen the horrors of bloodshed already...but some part of me genuinely believed this would be different.

And in a way it is. War isn't criminality or a blood match between men. War was defending our homes and families— and keeping our word. Though also, the kinds of things my uncle talked about.

After we got out of the command tent, while I was walking back with Valinin, I noticed he still had his hand over his mouth.

"What is it?"

He dropped his hand. There was a crescent moon, enough to see where we were walking more or less, but not nearly enough to see his face. But his head turned my way, "What is what?"

"What is it you're forcing yourself not to say?"

"Hmph. I obviously think it's better not to say."

"C'mon, Valinin, tell me. How bad can it be?"

"How bad can it be? Funny you should put it that way. That's exactly what I'm not sayin'."

"C'mon, what's the worst that could happen. The dragons show up and griffins don't?"

"Yeah, that could happen."

"Then I suppose we all get burned to death." I said it lightheartedly, like a joke, because I never really thought any such thing would ever happen to us.

"Oh, that comes out of your mouth so easy, my young friend. Just wait until you're seein' it with your own eyes."

I laughed nervously. "Well, it's not gonna happen anyway. The griffins will come."

"And what if I told ya the battle 'tween griffin riders and dragon riders is by no means equal? The dragons win much more often than not."

I'd never heard that. I said so.

"What, do ya think the things you hear 'bout war are really all of them the exact true things? Did any of the war songs mention slogging through horse apples?"

Of course they hadn't.

A question weighed on my chest. My heart beat a number of hard thuds as we walked in the darkness before I managed to ask it. "Was my uncle a coward?"

"Why wouldya even ask that? No."

"Did you really kill a dragon? The fourth battalion, I mean? While the Andreans ran? While the king, then a prince, was crying in a ditch?"

"Um—sorta. We'd been ordered to retreat, so had everybody. The Andreans did run, but they'd been ordered to fall back. So. Same orders we had. But we went forward anyway, the God help us." A quick, bitter laugh passed through his lips, almost like a bark. "Damn, we were stupid."

"Why?"

"Therin, I don't really wanna visit the whole scene in my mind again to paint the entire picture for ya. Part of it though was to save the prince in that ditch. He had the royal banner; we knew who he was. So did the dragon and its rider. And other dragons. They went after him. We couldn't let that happen."

"So you did kill a dragon?"

PART THREE: THE BOND OF WAR

"Yeah. It only cost five hundred men or so." The world "only" was thick with sarcasm. "And I mean killed right then. Plenty more were burned bad and died over the next few days."

I thought that over for a moment. Five hundred out of eight hundred. A sobering thought, but I couldn't really wrap my mind around what that would look like. I continued with my earlier idea, "Was the prince really standing there crying?"

"I think so, but I don' know for sure. The first of us to reach him said he was. Your uncle was among 'em. Weeping over the broken body of his griffin, they said. Though I think your uncle pitied him for it and didn't hold it against him at all from what he tol' me. I was one of the ones in the rear of the advance. I led the prince, now king, back to Andrean lines. Me and four others. With my own eyes I saw his face when he looked at our losses, at our burnt bodies on the field. Yeah, he shed some tears then, I know that for sure, even if he didn't before. But don't believe the God would hold that against him." Even in the dim moonlight, I noticed that Valinin's own eyes welled up.

I walked in silence for a while, thinking over what he'd told me, not sure if I should say anything else. As we passed the outer sentry, indicating we'd crossed into our battalion's zone, meaning we were about to be in the midst of our men, meaning we wouldn't be able to talk freely anymore, I found the words coming out of me: "So now you think we're set up for the same thing this time. Don't you?"

"Well. Things are never 'xactly the same 'tween past and present. But sometimes they dance to the same tune. But I shouldn'ta told ya that. Only the God knows what'll happen when we get out there. *That's* the real truth."

Even then I knew from my own experiences that what he said was true. Nobody knows for sure what will happen. We guess, we anticipate, we try to imagine, we pray and ask the God, but none of us on earth really knows. I knew I couldn't know for sure, but I had the sinking feeling that what he'd said about the battle plan going bad was gonna come to pass. But I was too busy to brood. That night commands needed to be issued to the company commanders, who spoke to their section leaders after that. After that, Valinin had me arranging the movement of supply wagons while he reviewed the order of battle.

In the dark of the early morning, with a hard cold wind blowing down from the north, we struck tents to lamplight and the men loaded them on the wagons, the ones I'd directed the wagon commander to bring forward. We set off on the march with the sun still thoroughly hidden behind the towering Heavensfoot peaks to our East. But we put out our oil lamps and marched on in the light of the moon that was waxing up towards the half as it set in the west.

It would take more than a day to march to the position where battle was to be joined. We stopped for brief rests every two hours. The men were issued only water and dry rations to chew on the move.

In the blazing afternoon sun, it was easy to see to our right the blackened iron armor of the marchers of 2nd Battalion and to our left marched the 3rd. An unexplained distant dust plume to the left of third had to be 1st Battalion, our 4 groups marching in parallel towards our goal.

The sweat ran down the back of my neck and stirred up dust mingled with it, covering me in grime. My mouth chewed grit and our smell, which must have been awful at any time to anyone truly clean, rose up enough that even when I was used to it, I could smell it. I've heard people say there is a smell of fear. I don't know I've ever smelled that. But the odor of thousands of men marching together towards the battlefield under a sky aglow with sunshine too bright, oranging radiance increasingly to our backs as the sun set, as we marched due East—that I *have* smelled.

As the twilight sun cast our long shadows forward, the wind finally had died down and we could see in front of us better. We crossed over a long, low rise and our eyes lit upon the sharpened stakes of the enemy positions, still far away from us. The sheer multitude of cut and sharpened wood gave the ground an appearance almost like brown fur. Beyond the stakes masses of men, blackened by distance and dimness, also stood. And clusters of horses. And other, taller mounts. Behind that were tents in bright reds and yellows, the tops of which shone in the glint of the setting sun in a way that no Western tent ever would.

I felt like pausing, standing there to look—and for the first (but by no means the last) time my eyes scanned the skies for flying dragons. I saw none. But the march kept moving forward, down the ridge into the valley that lay just before the first steep foothills leading up into the towering Heavensfoot peaks, a valley cast into shadow by the ridge we'd just crossed.

In the not-full darkness of a sun just set, us down below in the valley did not set up tentage. The wagons rolled forward from the rear and we distributed water and hard rations and blankets. We set an area for the men to dig a ditch latrine and put sentries on the alert. We established a watch rotation and in general, we prepared for the morning.

3rd battalion and us were toward the front and first and second were partially behind and a bit further out.

They would support from the rear and follow up when 3rd and 4th hit the barricade by first morning light.

Time had been allotted for us to sleep, four hours, but I couldn't. Not because the ground was too hard or the blanket not quite warm enough, no, those things hadn't bothered me before.

Long after the sun would have risen if there had been no towering mountains to the East, while it was still dark because of them, by hooded lamps we arrayed ourselves in battle position. The company commanders with my help issued oil to their sections in drums that teams of four would use with the steel and flint strikers to light them—we would burn part of the wooden barricade. Axes, shovels, and picks were also issued, the plan prepared. Then the lamps went off. And we waited.

My mouth got so dry at first. From the nervousness, I guess, but the wind was dry, too. But I found it simply was not possible for me to remain nervous forever. Not completely so. Some of us joked with one another in low voices. In the pale glow that began to show over the mountains, you could see the still and very pale faces of some of our men. I think a few of them were trembling, though others were looking for a place to pass urine. Each of us in our own world, even though at the same time in the same place and under the same circumstances.

After, I don't know, perhaps an hour of waiting, Valinin put his hand on my shoulder and nodded, giving us a silent start. I turned to the company runners and because the light was bright enough, they knew. I didn't have to say a word. They ran out and in minutes, once the commanders had been alerted, the battalion began to move forward. My heart pounded hard in my chest and throat.

The battalions train independently of one another, so we were not all exactly the same. But in Fourth, we all had been trained in archery to some degree. And our unit had been issued the steel composite bows Valinin and I had manufactured. He paid the supply for the arrows out of his own pocket (the council of elders had paid for bows, but not the arrows that matched them). But as we marched we were in an order where the bowmen were inside the outside line, which was made up of shieldmen. Just inside the heavy rectangular "block" shields we issued, the kind you can stand behind that we don't carry at all times, were spearmen with round shields on their arms of the type we normally use. Behind them came the rows of bowmen, bows and arrows at the ready, shields strapped to their backs. Further in we had the senior men and officers with swords and shields (really to enforce discipline among our own men more than fight, though we could fight with swords if need be— though each and every member of our formation carried a long dagger for close fighting if it came to that) and with them the engineer crew carrying the pioneer gear—the axes, shovels, and picks—slung over their shoulders or held in bent arms. Each man carried his own basic supply of water and food and of course all of us were in the black chain armor and helmets reinforced in key areas with plates of metal that our province is famous for crafting. We carried these supplies because we had no idea how long it would be after the battle began before we got resupplied from the wagons again.

All that gear is heavy. Sure, we trained with it and had marched thousands of leagues with it on our backs, but as we made our shuffling run towards the enemy pickets, about two hundred yards in front of us, none of it got any lighter.

But we kept moving, shuffling forward, rasping breaths squeezing out of our iron-armored bodies. The ground leading up to the enemy pickets was quite sandy, actually, with patchy grass, which I hadn't expected. We kicked forward, the sound of falling sand accompanying us, and that of clinking metal. And hard breathing of men. There was no talking among us at all. Not a single word.

Someone in the front row shouted, "Arrows!" and we all took to our knees without bending forward, faces covered with metal-gloved hands or shields (the outer men easily covered themselves with their block shields), whatever we had available, which was our standard bolt-and-arrow defensive position. I had my issued round shield up partway but was still looking forward over top it. It was my job to look forward—I was an officer.

The man who shouted must have had good eyes. The sun was shining in the direction of the East, so the arrows fell out of the glowing sky in a high arc. I didn't see anything until they had almost impacted.

Three arrows buried themselves in sandy ground about fifty yards in front of our lead row. Only three, several hundred yards in front of me (because I was near the middle of our rectangle formation, not the front). I may not have seen them at all, but each of them had a broad ribbon attached to their rear, a ribbon I'd soon learn was made of silk. Each ribbon was pure white.

I remember the ribbons, three yards or so long each, so wide, thin, and light, twisting in the air, curling as they fell, as if resisting being drawn away from their Eastern masters, or as if fighting against whatever it is that brings all falling things to the ground. Behind me, Valinin blew into the signal pipette two short blasts and one long, ending our signal-less advance.

That particular code meant halt in place until further notice. I had no idea why he'd violated the orders commanding us to maintain noise discipline as long as possible.

"Runners," Valinin shouted. "Find leaders of other battalions! The enemy's just signaled a request for a truce, so we can have a little chit chat. Last I knew we're required by treaty to oblige. Let 'em know we need to halt 'til further notice. Make sure they get the message. Go!"

It turns out the runners were unneeded. Third was only about four hundred yards to our left, a bit north of us. They'd heard Valinin's whistle blasts from the pipette. First and Second hadn't heard, but their orders were to halt in a supporting position until we'd breached the hasty barrier of sharpened stakes and traps the enemy had made. (By the way, this is battlefield trivia, but we had been taught to make a hasty barrier by digging a broad ditch on the outside and stacking up the excavated dirt in a mound, requiring an enemy to go down into the ditch and then up onto the little hill to face us. But the Eastern army dug pits and a ditch and laid stakes while spreading the dug up dirt evenly. That's because they had lots of crossbows that fire more or less straight on—putting a mound in front of themselves would only block their own weapons.)

The runners came and went anyway, wearing only light chain without plates that covered head and neck and body core, arms and legs only covered with fabric that had been hand painted to make it look like chain. I won't report to you every little message we received, or the confused expectation at one point that we were going to ignore the enemy request and charge forward anyway.

At first my heart pounded with the changing confused orders but I eventually realized we really *had* stopped for quite a long time—especially since Valinin had given the order to rest in place. I drank some water and thought about the fact we'd need to bring more water forward if we were going to be out here all day. And we'd need to dig a latrine ditch soon and other practical things I'd learned to think as the second in command.

After about three hours an enemy force moved forward toward their broad-but-low barricade. They began to take down stakes, horsemen in their strange armor made of large overlapping scaly plates—something like a pine cone made into metal and put on a man—watching men working. The workers, men with conical straw hats and plain linen clothes, who wore their hair in a single braid behind their head, moved about with their strange carts that had a single wheel in front and handles behind. They seemed to be able to carry a huge amount of material in these carts and their hands worked quickly in removing stakes and lifting up many metal objects that looked like the Eastern equivalent of bear traps. Making me feel a bit of relief that we'd been stopped.

The voices of the men began to rise and I shouted out, "Keep it down—low-voice only!" We'd trained on noise discipline and the men knew what that meant. But I had to issue the command several more times.

Eventually a runner came to Valinin, his long limbs churning through the sandy ground between our battalion positions. He was one of those long, lean guys who seemed like he could run forever, but the sheer multitude of messages and sandy ground showed their effects in his sweaty brow and hard panting. "The Eastern army is sending a party to discuss a truce. All battalion leadership requested to attend."

"Wanna come?" asked Valinin.

"Battalion leadership? That sounds like you."

"Psst," he said, continuing in a mock conspiratorial whisper. "Our battalions are independent trained as you know. Leadership is who we say it is and I say you're parta leadership. So, you wanna come?"

I went with him but we did not walk directly over to the meeting. A flurry of other messages came in a confusion that took up time, but achieved no real purpose. Eventually we left and we ran into the 3rd commander first, just after we left our formation. Then we decided to gather together as an Iron Mountains element before meeting up with anyone else. Second joined us, but we couldn't find First. In the meantime, some horsemen came forward, some from the Andrean Houseguard. A rider without armor, in magisterial robes, was in their midst.

"Hmmm. Maybe we should go over there," said Valinin. "First B will have to figure it out on their own."

There were seven of us representing battalions 2, 3, and 4 who joined the riders. Once we were there we realized 1st had somebody on horseback already there, a liaison who spent most of his time with the Andreans. Norrin was also there, on horseback.

By the time we arrived, the Eastern delegation had nearly passed through the pickets. All our Western eyes looked east as the ever-rising sun shone behind a delegation mostly dressed in white silk, while we Westerners were mostly in black leather and metal. The unarmored rider in magisterial robes commented to no one in particular, loud enough for me to hear him well, "Well, don't they look special." The way he spoke caught my attention far beyond any meaning found in the words themselves.

Because the voice itself I recognized. It was Guffey's.

⊸╟ Chapter 6 ╞⊸

The meeting with the Eastern representatives lasted about four hours. Two things stand out in my mind from the meeting. The first, how I maneuvered myself away from the center of everyone. I struck up a side conversation in a low whisper with the representative of 1st battalion and kept his horse between me and the representative of the Andrean king and therefore the entire Western Bond, who was indeed Guffey. He was not much visibly older than when I'd last seen him, but clearly heavier. Obviously he'd continued to move up in rank since I'd known him.

Valinin looked at me like he wondered what was going on. I mouthed, "I'll explain later." From that point on, he covered for me by pretending like I wasn't even there. He didn't have a speaking role in what happened next anyway. He'd been called as a courtesy, like the rest of our Iron Mountain battalion leaders, since he was one of the leaders of forward troops.

The second thing that stands out was the person of the Eastern representative. In all white silk with a high collar that was itself red, embroidered with a small golden dragon, he had flowing white hair and a long flowing white mustache.

Such an appearance could have matched almost any high official of the alliance of the Kings of the East. But he introduced himself by the simple title of, "Kung Tzu, Emperor."

The man himself, Kung Tzu, had come forward to represent his side. His introduction was greeted with open-eyed shock from some of those on our side, with skepticism that this was *really* Kung Tzu by others. Guffey dismounted his horse when he heard that and offered a half-bow, while saying, "Guffey of the Midlands, Chancellor to the King of Andrea." Kung Tzu also dismounted, then stepped forward and astounded everyone by shaking Guffey's hand, Western style.

Most of their conference was in low voices that did not carry our way. I did hear enough to realize that Kung Tzu spoke Western without a translator, though he did have a strong accent. He also wasn't particularly tall, standing up to Guffey's chin, who stood maybe up to my nose. But there was a certain something about him. A dangerousness that transcended his physical size, a menace that was evident even though he was very courteous.

Eventually from the Western side wooden chairs were brought forward so the main parties could sit, along with a large umbrella to shade them from the sun. A small table with a porcelain container of a hot tea of some kind with elegant white cups was brought from the Eastern side. I couldn't hear them as they talked, which made the conference seem even longer than if I had taken part in it. They sat what seemed like forever and drank a lot of tea.

Eventually Kung Tzu stood from his chair, the sun now shining in his eyes from the direction of the West, his squint adding to the effect of his inner eye fold, making his pupils invisible. Guffey half bowed again and the Emperor shook his hand again. Both men mounted on their horses and the Easterners turned around. As Guffey mounted his horse, while he swung his leg around to the other side of the steep Andrean saddle (two Andrean cavalrymen on the ground had helped him lift himself upward), his eyes glanced around the area. They rested on me for a moment, his eyes boring into the inner depths of my being. A look of puzzlement crossed his face, as if he should recognize me but couldn't quite. Then he shook his head and turned his horse backward and rode away, along with the rest of the men on horseback.

We foot soldiers remaining, all of us from the Iron Mountains, trudged back to our respective battalions. On the way back, I asked Valinin, "What happened?"

"The emperor brought up doing a prisoner exchange. They mostly haggled details of that."

"For four *hours*? That's something you could do in maybe four minutes."

"Kung Tzu used the meetin' as a delay tactic, that's clear. He's got a coupla hundred Western prisoners he'll release in the mornin'."

"Guffey went for that?"

"He sure did, though he's got his own reasons I think. Though I don't know for sure what they are. Maybe some of the prisoners are from the royal family, since there sure are a bunch of 'em…say, he's the same fella you told me about, the one that was at the tournament, isn't he? And later. Right?"

"Yes."

"Hmm. Well, I can't say if he was doin' a good job or not. It depends on your pointa view. More interesting to me was Kung Tzu. I've never seen him so close before."

"You've seen him before? He didn't look that old to me."

"Oh sure—they say the Easties age better'n us. And they say it was him flying the great gold dragon over the battlefield where I stood as a common soldier, a beast bigger than any of the other dragons. I've seen it flyin' before and seen the rider up top, with a golden dragon embroidered across his chest. But I was nowhere near close to him. Thank the God for that!"

"Why? Is the golden dragon worse than the other ones?"

"Well…I don' know for sure. But they say that unlike every other dragon, the golden one never runs out of fiery breath. We woulda never killed the red dragon we fought if it hadn't run out of fire. Which it did. After a while."

By then we reached our battalion. Our mission was to guard the border until we received the prisoners in the morning. It was a long night; I still didn't sleep very well.

In the morning, as the glow of the sun lit up the towering mountains to the east, clusters of Western men stepped forward, their hands raised high. Most of them had been cavalrymen of some kind or other, mostly Andreans and Tsillians. Funny, I had never heard that any of them had been taken prisoner.

Later in the day, orders came for us to fall back. That's when I first realized the battle we'd prepared for wasn't actually going to happen. Not with us fighting it anyway. It may sound foolish for me to say so, but I was tremendously disappointed.

Our next set of orders didn't come for an entire week. That week stretched long, generally boring, with no battles of any kind happening anywhere during that time. Why, I never knew.

We made camp while other Western units moved forward. We did stand to every morning, every armed soldier at the ready as the sun showed itself. We practiced marching maneuvers in our camp area in the afternoon. We received more supplies and requisitioned others. We played games like Sharps at night or had prayer meetings arranged by the battalion lay chaplain. And we waited.

When the orders finally came, orally by messenger sent from Norrin, it was that our Iron Mountains element was to be divided. First and Second battalion were to stay at the bulge, the expected site of battle. Third and fourth were to march north to cover an obscure pass, one we were to protect on a "just in case" basis. But this pass was too small to be considered a reasonable threat for an Eastern invasion. Anyhow, they were still retreating back over the mountains. It took a week to march northward, each step taking us away from both the bulk of the Bond Army and the only known enemy positions. Our two battalions were joined by the Andrean Reserve Guard, which was a cavalry unit made almost exclusively of men who were fifty years old and older who had fought well in other units during a long military career and who were "on call" in this unit in the case of war. We were also joined by a contingent of Southlanders, not all the Southlanders in the Bond, but a good proportion of them. And some Shos Hillcountry Militia, who were a rowdy, poorly-armed bunch, notorious for enjoying all forms of fighting—especially fistfights. And brewing their own hard liquor. Not necessarily in that order.

During the march I wondered out loud why these particular units had been thrown together. "I don' know for sure," Valinin replied. "But among the units who don' do full-time, all the time training—that is, the militia units—the ones they're sending have the reputation for being the toughest fighters."

"Even a bunch of Andrean old men? And their nags?"

"Hey now!" he laughed. "Some of us ol' men still have life in us."

"You know what I'm saying," I grumbled.

He laughed again. After a few moments marching in silence, the wind whistling across the plain, the massive wall of blue mountains on our right, I asked him, "What do you think that means?"

"Hmm. Prob'ly that they think holding the pass we're going to, is serious enough to commit some good troops. But not serious 'nough to commit the best. Which means, I think, they don' believe Kung Tzu will try to use the pass, but they wanna be sure."

"What's it called, Eagle Pass? Did anybody ever use it in the First Dragon War?"

"Nope. Not that I know of. Too narrow."

"Great," I grumbled. And sighed.

He laughed again. "Young men are all alike. Not 'nough sense to know when ya catch a lucky break."

The Andrean reserve cavalrymen led the way. At a certain point, in a spot with green trees and grass and folds of rolling hills before the towering mountain range and no sign that any living person had ever dwelled there, we turned inward, eastward, and marched towards the ever-rising mountain range, the sun over our heads at first and increasingly at our backs.

We camped in hills that suddenly collided into the front of a much steeper mountain range, not at all getting gradually larger. These peaks towered so high, so suddenly, it was quite a surprise. It was nothing like the Iron Mountains, son, which are in many places beautifully covered with green pine trees. Only the lower reaches of the Heavensfoot mountains had trees. Craning my neck to look upward before the sun finally disappeared to the west, as it casted my shadow forward in stretched long form, the upper reaches of just the first and lowest of these mountains reached well past the height where trees can grow.

The night was unremarkable. I slept well and arose not particularly early, but the sun nonetheless remained largely invisible, hidden behind the mountains. The first place it shone through, in almost a curtain of light passing between the peaks, marked the first time I witnessed the location of the so-called Eagle Pass.

By the time we struck camp and marched there, trailing the Andrean reserve cavalry and their horse droppings, the sky above was aglow with pre-dawn light. But still, the curtain of light shone through the pass brighter than its surroundings. I remembered turning between columns of mountain rock at the entrance to the pass— that unlike most passes was a very dramatic and obvious passage, that wound up climbing in a snaking path upward between peaks. Valinin muttered as he looked to the side of the entrance, "That's odd."

"What's odd?" I asked.

"It's wider on bottom than top."

I looked. It was. I stepped closer—the pass was about 20 paces wide at that point. It wasn't nearly as wide about ten feet in the air. I blinked in surprise. "There are tool marks here."

"You mean like somebody made it wider? With picks?" he asked.

"Yes. Something like that. Not that it's all that wide anyway."

"Hmmm. But it ain't as narrow as I heard it was either. And if somebody widened it, what did they do with the rocks they moved? They should be 'round here somewhere."

I rubbed my chin, thinking that over. Valinin and I had stopped marching forward and Elin's company came to a halt beside us before entering the pass in columns of three, which the entrance to the passage could comfortably hold. Valinin absent-mindedly waved them forward.

"They must have hidden the rocks," I concluded. "That's the only explanation."

"Yeah. And somebody from our side musta noticed. Hence us marchin' up this pass now. Because it looked suspicious."

"Right." There seemed nothing else to say. We resumed the upward march into the light, the sun high enough not to be directly in our eyes but still plainly in front of us. It made me wonder if it truly was possible to walk all the way to the house of the sun, as in the nursery rhyme:

Jackin and Jilla walked east and run
Straight into, the house of the sun

The resemblance of the pass to a gate faded as it continued to curve upward and we could no longer see the entrance. The Iron Mountains are a relatively narrow range. If you go past maybe three or four peaks, you are through the pass. Not so the Heavensfoot Mountains, at least not there. So after a while it seemed like we were just on a road that went through the mountains—a road that in most places was wider than the entrance that somebody had widened.

It became clear as the twisting road continually climbed why this was called "Eagle Pass." Soon it seemed we'd be as high up as the legendary Kingdom of the Eagles.

We marched an entire day and camped in a ring canyon on the south side (a "ring canyon" is one with only one way in and out, with mountains circling around, like a boxing ring), one filled with scrubby pine trees.

After starting out again in the morning, by late afternoon we reached another place where rocky cliffs came close together, another spot where the pass resembled a gate. As our column marched up to it in the afternoon sun, the thin air in the high mountains making breathing and marching harder, part of me wondered if on the other side of this gate lay the Lands of the East. But no, it couldn't be. We'd gone up and up and never down. The pass would have to go down to enter the plains of the East. Some of the Easterners might live in high mountains, but surely not all of them did.

Past this gate, the ground descended into a valley of sorts. It astounded me how dry and dusty the place looked. From the ridge our road went downward some several hundred paces, then reached brownish hills of dirt and rock, scarcely without any trees or grass or any sign of life. The valley wasn't truly wide, but it was by far the widest spot we had gone by in the Eagle's Pass. Several miles off in the distance I saw where the road went up again out of the valley through another formation that looked like a gate. But the path must have gone downhill after that, since the mountains behind that end of the valley seemed somewhat smaller than the ones behind us. Our journey had taken us to this remove vale at the highest point in the pass, supposedly in the land of the eagles. Though I never actually saw any eagles there.

I already knew by then that a high valley was to be our campsite—it makes for more dramatic storytelling for me to not mention that fact, not until already describing our arrival at the place. The commander of the Andrean Reserve Cavalry, the overall commander of our little army—his name was Reynaldo (he was actual nobility, a duke)—divided us up into two groups at this point. The 3rd Battalion of Iron Mountain troops would move forward to hold the end of the valley in front of us, backed by the Andrean Reserve right behind them. We would camp at our end of the valley, along with the Southlander contingent and the Shos Hillcountry militia.

Down in the valley it seemed a lot bigger than it had when we were standing on the ridge observing it. I heard that it was five miles long and a mile wide at the widest. Though most of it wasn't that wide. A long, narrow round shape, like the bottom of a canoe, that's what the valley at the top of the pass looked like. The mountains rose up brown and dirty, rocky in places. The trees visible were in small clusters at certain points on the high mountains around us. Down in the valley some strips of browning grass could be found at the lower reaches of hillocks that looked like great mounds of dirt, like the dirt had been washed down a river and dried off to the side somewhere. But there was no sign of any river. The very highest peaks to our north still had snow on them, as did some of the ones to the south. So you'd think at least some snow would have melted and found its way down to this dry dirty bowl. But it sure didn't look like it when I was there.

Valinin went to a meeting of leaders of our combined force while I assisted the company commanders place their tents and with the distribution of our supply wagons. Our supply chain to back home was now far too long to easily maintain, even with supply masters making local purchases along the way whenever possible. We had enough foodstuffs to last 7 days, longer with rationing. Which for all I knew would be good enough. We had no idea how long we'd have to stay in the pass. For all we knew, we could be ordered to strike camp tomorrow.

My boss and friend returned after the sun had gone down. I already knew one of the things he was going to tell me, because I'd seen myself that the Southlanders had very few tents. The temperature had been fairly warm during the day but dropped down sharply at night. One of the sentries reported they were huddled together in a great mass of bodies, trying to stay warm.

"We need to share every spare tent we got," he said.

"Maybe we can do more than that. Maybe we can double up our men and let them use the excess."

He raised an eyebrow at me, "Don'ya think that's goin' too far? First we take care of our own, then anybody else."

"That's not what my uncle told me you old-timers believe. But, if you want, let's think of it in terms of what's in our own interest. Every last Southlander who freezes to death out here is one less to fight by our side, should it ever come to that."

"Hmmp!" he rubbed his beard as the sound came out of his nose. "Fine. You can tell the men in the mornin'. I think it's too late to move everyone around t'night."

"But we can deliver the spare tents tonight."

He looked at me and chuckled. "Sure, you wanna do that, I'll let you. But you can roll the supply masters outta bed yourself and make delivery of the tents right alongside 'em. If you really care that much about it, you should be willin' to put your own shoulder to the work."

Maybe it was the thin mountain air that pulled me in the direction of saying it could wait until morning. But then I thought of my own terrible time huddled in a prison, cold. And my uncle giving out swords at a tournament that seemed very long ago. "Fine," I answered.

The supply tents were the best ones in the battalion. Not only were they the newest and without any patchwork, they had wood floors the supply boys assembled as a base above the ground, while the rest of our tents mostly had canvas bottoms. I pulled the string that undid the side of the supply master's tent flap and pushed my way through. "Marin? Time to get up!"

Marin, a man in his fifties with a perpetually flushed face, a big belly, and disordered gray hair and beard, answered from the darkness, "We under attack?"

"Yes!" I replied, "We are under siege from a dire lack supply!"

Marin did not laugh at the moment and not when he understood what was going on moments later. But his supply boys, all in their teens, seemed to think what I said was hilarious, because throughout the darkness, during the time Marin got out of bed and pulled on his boots and threw a blanket over his shoulders, the boys in his tent chuckled softly. Then as we walked to the supply wagon, boys from the other tent joining us; I heard my words repeated more than once with laughter. I didn't find it all that funny myself. Once the spare tents were identified, four whole ones and one partial used to make patches, I led a procession of the supply boys moving the tents in the direction of the Southlander camp, an oil-burning lamp in my hand. They weren't far, less than one hundred paces behind us, that is, mostly uphill, from our camp. I felt grateful for my lamp, because the ground was strewn with rocks and I couldn't see any fire from the Southlander camp telling me where it was. Clouds blocked out the stars and the moon hadn't risen, so the night was like having your head wrapped in wool. Except much colder.

With the hooded lamp lighting up a circle of ground maybe three paces wide at my feet, it must have been easy to see me coming. Several dark figures stepped my way. I first saw them by the reflected whites of their eyes. As they came closer, I saw that one had a sword of dark iron strapped to his leg—an Iron Mountains sword.

To my surprise, as I raised the lamp enough to see the swordsman's face, I recognized it. "Koto!"

"How do you know my name?" he asked in very good Andrean-accented Western.

"We…we were at the Tournament of Swords together. I fought you."

He stepped close to me and his eyes peered into mine with evident hostility, as if I were an enemy telling lies, some form of trickery. But after staring at me for a less time than it took me to draw in a breath and exhale, his face changed, softening, though not all the way. "Ah, yes. I remember you. You did not have a beard then."

"No. I didn't know how to fight with a sword then, either."

His eyes widened for an instant. "Are you saying now you know?"

I chuckled. "Well, I'm better than I was, that's for sure."

And some part of my heart wanted to tell him the whole story. How I'd trained to kill the prince. How I'd failed. And now, by the inexplicable acts of the God, I was a subordinate commander in our army, no longer the scared and clumsy boy I used to be, not entirely, anyway. And some part of me wondered if he had won the tournament after we left. But there was no time. "Why do you go to our camp?" he asked. I realized this is why he had come out to face us, why the two men with him had their wicker shields strapped to their left arms and a steel-tipped spear in the right. It was nighttime. Who comes out on legitimate business at night?

"It's cold," I answered. "We brought some tents to help you stay warm."

He stared at me again, this time his eyes narrowing, evaluating me. "Who says we need your help?"

I paused a moment. "I notice the sword you carry with you. Is it one of the ones my uncle gave to your team at the tournament?"

"I have carried it since that day, yes." He paused, touching his hand to the point of his beardless chin. "Your uncle was the leader of your team?"

"Yes."

"I saw how he died. He was a great man."

I blinked back hot tears, astonished at myself after all that had happened I was still able to feel sorrow and loss over that old man. I felt grateful for the darkness that covered my face. Finally I managed to say in a calm voice, "He certainly cared for us. For everyone."

"And now you wish to be like him," Koto stated it as a fact instead of raising his voice in a question. "For your sake then I will say this—tents are good, but blankets would be better."

I felt stupid. *Of course.* Tents would keep in some heat, but mostly have the virtue of shutting out rain, wind, and snow. But it wasn't windy, raining, or snowing up here. Just cold. Blankets would have been a better choice than tents. "We will...first give you the tents. Then come back with the blankets we can spare."

"You may drop the tents here. We have men who can carry them."

So we returned and I looked for extra blankets. There were none in the chests designated for them. I instantly realized that the extras must have already been claimed. Distributed by the supply masters, no doubt, but without authorization. As I thought about it, I realized there seemed to have been many more blankets than people in the supply tents. I held the lamp up and examined the faces of the supply boys around me. Their eyes looked downward, and not just to avoid the brightness of the lamp.

"Where are the extras?"

"Well, you see, sir…" began one of them.

"No, I don't see," I replied, though not in a harsh tone. We went to the supply tents and found ten extras right then. I realized there must be more, but distributed out among the men in general. I decided to find those in daylight. Two supply boys I made carry five blankets each. I had them fold them first before I walked back with them towards the Southlander camp.

At one point one of the two said to me, "Sir, we got this. Let us deliver the blankets and you can go back to bed."

I imagined the two of them traipsing back to the supply tents the moment they were sure I was out of sight. I didn't say this to them though, because it didn't seem good to accuse them of wanting to do something wrong without evidence.

So instead I answered, "Nah. I know that one Southlander guy. I'm hoping to see him again." Which was actually true, son. To lie is shameful before the God, but sometimes there's no point in telling the whole truth.

We passed on the blankets to shivering Southlanders and I did see Koto again. But just briefly that night.

The next day we did some consolidation of goods and came up with another ten tents and twenty-six blankets.

It seemed like nowhere near enough, but the Southlanders were grateful. I later heard that instead of setting up the tents they would huddle in large numbers under the canvas. The clothing they wore was still minimal, as if they were still in the lands of the South. The Southland chiefs expected their warriors to simply endure any cold that might come—but they didn't usually face the cold of high mountains. Still, in spite of their lips turning gray and their shivering, their bare chests covered in gooseflesh, I never heard any of them complain, not once. I suppose if we hadn't provided the blankets, they would have simply died off from exposure in small numbers every night. Quietly.

Normally, they would send runners out to gather wood and build a bonfire. That's what they'd done in the ring canyon we'd camped in on the way up. But there was no wood up at our narrow valley at the top of the pass. The brown dustiness and almost total lack of vegetation was astonishing. There were only a few patches of dried grass in the curves of some of the large dirt mounds that passed for hills at the canyon bottom.

It may surprise you to hear me say this, son—I know the war songs of valor, if they mention equipment, only mention weapons—but one of the biggest things an army needs are the things of ordinary life. A place to sleep, warm enough clothing, food to eat, and water to drink.

That's true though the Andreans drank more wine than water and the Shos Hillcountry militia brought barrels of whisky they would mix with water to make it last longer. We had some barrels of beer, but we'd have just one mug after supper—far less than the Andreans or Shos people would have. They'd have strong drink with every meal.

Since our province has long survived from making iron goods and exporting them and bringing things we need back in, we actually have a lot of experience with supply. For distant travel we bake special hardtack and jerky and dried fruit that stores well. We run water wagons to local sources of water and know how to filter purify it for drinking through the reeds of the lastaria plant, which has pores too small to see and which captures everything foul except a few kinds of poison. We keep plenty of extra supplies like tents and blankets and even extra weapons. We always had plenty for our men to eat, plenty to drink, and an acceptable place to sleep.

Other armies in the Bond varied a lot. I already mentioned the Shos Militia brought whiskey (and brewed new hard liquor whenever they got the chance) and the Andreans brought wine. The Andrean main body of forces brought lots of other things, too. They had special pavilions with silk tents and minstrels to play by night and plenty of women following, some as washers, cooks, and cleaners, and some in the profession not legal in Iron Mountains Province. They brought food, but generally elegant fare, ducks for roasting and boars and all manner of fruits and spices to add to their meals. That is, that's what the great lords of Andrea brought.

Their lesser men-at-arms would either be fortunate enough to find a place at a great Lords table, or they would often do without. The Andreans units often did not even have a single commander! The richest of their lords would dispute with one another as to who should be in charge and on a temporary basis one or the other would be in command for a certain engagement or battle. But that could change with each battle and it wasn't uncommon for them to disobey one another, which shocked me when I heard about it.

The Shos Hillcountry people were like us in many ways as an overall fighting force. They would elect a single commander, who they usually obeyed, unless they were really drunk (which happened fairly often). They shared all their supplies in common. But they didn't have much of anything really. Their whiskey wagons, drawn by donkeys, were the main supply they carried. They'd look for local water and mix it with their whiskey. If there was no local water, they'd drink more whiskey. They'd trade some along the way for food (as we did sometimes as well) or hunt wild game. Their weapons came in a great variety—bows and arrows, spears, slings, clubs, daggers, maces—so did their armor, but it was mostly leather and padded cloth. They had a reputation for loving to fight. In fact, before arriving at the pass, we'd heard rumors about them clashing with another army from the Western Bond forces almost every week, though only a few times with us (they seemed to especially have trouble with Andreans). Maybe it was as much to get rid of them as to help us hold the pass they were sent along with us, I don't know.

The Southlanders, unlike the rest of us, had no supply system at all really. Many of them had chains of gold around their necks they would trade for, say, a cow. If they ate a cow, they would eat all of it accept the hides and bones—even the bones they'd boil and break open to get to the marrow and the hides they'd make use of, too. Their shields they made from stretched dried raw cowhide. For water they would dig wells by stabbing daggers in the ground and scooping dirt out by hand. By a river or lake they'd never take open water directly—they'd dig near the shore until water seeped through dirt as a means of purifying it. They slept on the ground without blankets or tents. If it was cold they huddled together or built a bonfire. They did do some hunting, but mostly it seemed they would simply go without much of anything. They always obeyed their commanders (who were always relatives of their king or lesser chiefs) with perfect discipline —maybe that had something to do with the fact that when they were offered wine, beer, or whiskey, they would refuse to drink it. They believed very much that a man should be able to endure hardship while remaining in control of himself.

The Andrean Reserve Cavalry were different from their main forces. Their funds came from a group of their war veterans who paid money to help those of them who had been wounded for life in previous battles. This group also funded the purchase of horses and equipment for a regiment of horse-mounted men-at-arms, which they filled with men from their order of old veterans still fit enough to ride and fight. Not a one of them were younger than fifty. To conserve money, they purchased their equipment together, so it all looked similar, unlike most of the rest of Andrean units. The Andrean nobles paid the bulk of the money to sustain this group, but usually did not join it. If they were fit enough to fight, they preferred to fight under the name of their own houses—so the unit in the mountain pass with us was from the men who had been impoverished warriors in their youth. There only one true nobleman among them— since he was the only one, he had unambiguous command— Duke Reynaldo.

A lot of complaints came up through the chain of command about us taking extra blankets and giving them away. Packing the tents full wasn't popular, either. It seemed like we'd probably be up in this pass a long time, at least until the Autumn snows shut the pass down, and nobody wanted to give up anything we might need for survival if the weather got colder.

"Tell 'em they'll be glad enough for the Southlander spears if it comes to combat," answered Valinin. "There's no point in them dyin' up here from the cold in the summer."

When the Hillcountry militia heard what we'd done for the Southlanders (how they heard I don't know) we had a request come from them for food and water. And any extra weapons we could spare.

"Well, we've gone'n'done it now, haven't we?" said Valinin when the request reached him. "Whadya think?" he asked me.

"I think we can hardly support one ally and deny the reasonable requests of another."

"Hmmp!" He scratched his head before continuing, his scowl softening, "Yeah. But water is almost outside the bounds. There's not much to spare. Weapons and food, yes. Water? We need to do somethin' 'bout water."

"I agree. For now the water wagons are going back to that one stream in the ring canyon we passed and hauling the water up here. But the barrels at the rate we fill them is barely enough to support our battalion. The God only knows how 3rd battalion and the Andreans are getting water—"

"I've gotta request for water from 3rd right here," he replied, lifting a parchment message square from the table with folding legs in his tent he used as a field desk.

"We can hardly support that, can we?"

"Barely. With water rationin'. We're gettin' to the point we'll be drinkin' our own piss soon enough."

"So what do you want me to tell the Shos boys? No?"

"Ya know, the Southlanders must be short on food'n'water, too."

"True, but they haven't asked for anything."

"Not that they would…they're prob'ly ready to heroically starve to death…" His voice trailed off as he looked down at the request from 3rd Battalion.

I chuckled. "Well, thirst would get 'em first. Though I did see them digging a well."

He looked up at me, eyes widened in interest, "Really? Did they find any water?"

"I saw some damp sand, that's it."

"Hmm. They put pieces of cloth in the sand and soak up what they can and pop the pieces into their mouths to suck out whatever moisture they find. I seen 'em do it in the first war."

"Better than nothing, I'm sure."

"Yeah, but nowhere near good 'nough." He scratched his head again. "Let's say 'yes' to the Shos request for weapons for now. Set aside a third of our hard tack for both the militia an' the Southlanders. Split it between 'em. Then, my bright young friend, I need you to solve our water problem. Let the Shos boys know we're workin' on it and if that's not good 'nough, tell 'em they can use their empty whiskey barrels to help us haul water up from the ring canyon. Make it happen."

"Yes, sir." I saluted him sharply. He didn't usually make me salute and he didn't really like it.

"Hmmp! Get goin' you!" his voice was gruff, but he grinned at me afterward.

Some representatives from the Hillcountry militia came by our supply section to pick up the weapons we made available, after our runner delivered them the message. It was funny because they didn't come with a wagon or cart or anything. They just sent ten really large men who turned over their crude round wooden shields like little tables and we piled on them extra swords, spears, spikes, some helmets, some suits of mail, some bows and even a few axes from the pioneer gear (Valinin had decided we couldn't spare any of the arrows).

One of them, the biggest of the bunch, was over two and a half yards in height. He had no shield, but merely stuck out his arms to receive his portion of weapons. I found something awfully familiar about his face...then realized with a start I knew him, too. He was the Shos Hillcountry boy I fought back at the Tournament of Swords.

I looked directly into his pale blue eyes. "I know you."

"From the tournament, I reckon," he answered, the voice coming from the massively wide and tall body surprisingly high-pitched.

"You remember me?"

"Yep." His freckled baby-smooth pudgy face revealed none of his thoughts.

"You've grown. A lot."

"Well. I was ten years old. So."

"You were ten?"

"Yep."

I had to catch my breath. "You must be still *growing.*"

"That's what my ma and pa say. I still got a little bit to go to be as tall as my pa."

"Really? Is he here somewhere?"

"Nah. He's older and Ma is young. He lost a leg in the last war an' can't fight no more."

"What's your name?" "Danl."

"Danl of...or son of...?" "Just Danl."

"Danl the baby giant if you want." The Hillcountry man next to Danl, who had a graying beard down to his chest, laughed hard after saying it.

Danl's face flushed a bit at that. "Just Danl," he said.

"Very well...Danl, why is it you don't have a shield?"

He shrugged. "Ones we make don't even cover my whole arm."

"Um, I think I can do something about that. Wait here. I'll be back in a few minutes with something for you."

I gathered up one of the camp smiths from the supply section and requisitioned one of our tall rectangular side shields. He and I carried it back together. They're tall and heavy and had been added to our equipment list after the First Dragon War, in hopes they'd be of some use against dragon fire, even though they were so heavy.

We got to Danl and saw the other nine Hillcountry Militia had already left, taking all the weapons with them. The smith adjusted the fitting on the shield so Danl had it strapped to his arm, like one of our round iron shields or the Shos' wooden ones. The side shield, tall enough to cover a man with it planted in the ground from head to foot if he hunched over a bit, seemed a lot smaller on Hillcountry giant's arm. Its weight didn't seem to bother him at all.

"Can we get you another weapon? A spear...or mattock?"

"Nah. This sword'll do." He pointed to the Iron Mountains forged sword on his belt.

"Was that one of the ones my uncle gave away at the tournament?"

"Yep." And without any further comment, Danl turned away from us, walking in his long slow pace back to the Hillcountry position behind both us and the Southlanders in the pass.

That same day we made a trade with the Hillcountry Militia on food. They promised to share with us a portion of their hunted game (they were sending men down to the ring canyon to do that), while we gave them three-quarters of a lot of hard tack.

Still, our water situation was bad. We wouldn't last a week without finding another source, hopefully one closer.

Valinin, considering the problem, told me the next morning, "Therin, take some men from Rogin company (which was 2nd company) along with pioneer tools. See if ya can help the Southlanders dig their well deeper. That might take care of our problem."

Elin was the commander of Rogin company, so I decided to ask him to help me directly. I'd seen him some during our long march from the Iron Mountains to the Heavensfoot peaks, but their company stuck close to one another usually. Meaning I'd hardly seen him apart from the times I've already mentioned. So I thought it would be good to perform a task together. For old time's sake.

He and I and a work squad of ten approached the Southlander Camp. Before we got there, it was easy enough to see a crew of their own working on a new well, a bit downhill from their camp (that is, closer to ours), to the left (southward) of where we were walking. I said, "Let's go see how they're doing."

Koto stood watching around twenty Southlanders working. Only four were digging, but the rest were scooping away dirt and carrying it several paces off, to two different piles. Only Koto wore a sword and only he watched the work instead of worked himself. I realized must be some kind of Southlander nobility, since all their commanders were and it was evident he was a sub-commander of some kind. I realized at that moment that I was almost completely ignorant about their nation and how they do things.

I knew a few things, but not really very much. I didn't even know a single word of their language.

Fortunately Koto spoke Western. As I walked up to him, I said, "Would you like some help? We've got shovels."

He looked at me for a moment, evaluating me. "The problem is," he said slowly, "not our lack of tools. It is the location."

"Oh? What's wrong with the location?"

He smiled at me in a way not quite friendly. "You don't dig wells, do you?"

"Um, no. Not usually. Engineers usually do that."

He nodded at my acknowledgement and stretched out his arm towards the terrain behind my back. "Look out at this valley." He paused while I turned to look. "You see the shape? Narrow between ranges, higher on either side where the passes enter the valley? Like the hull of a boat?"

"Uh, yes, I see that."

"When the snow melts in spring and soaks into the ground, it still flows under the dirt. Where does it go?"

I paused a bit before realizing he actually expected me to answer that. "Er, to the bottom. I guess."

"You guess right. And where is the bottom here?"

I studied the high mountain ranges on either side of our narrow valley and perceived for the first time that both ends, both where we were and where 3rd Battalion was, were higher in elevation than the center. "It's in the middle of the valley. Are you saying that's where you can find water?"

"It is the best place," he replied.

I turned back and looked at him, doing an evaluation of my own. "So why…aren't you digging a well there?"

His eyes widened. "That isn't our assigned sector!"

I chuckled. "Well, yeah, but that doesn't mean you couldn't request to go over there." I turned to Elin, "Which of your men would you pick as a runner? We should ask Reynaldo if we can dig a well there."

Elin breathed in deep before saying, "Sir, shouldn't we run this past Valinin and let him decide to send a messenger to Duke Reynaldo? Or not? As per the chain of command?"

"Oh, yeah. What was I thinking?" I answered. "Who would you send as a runner to Valinin?"

"I'll go myself," he said. "In the meantime, the men with shovels can help see if there is any water at this site here. If that sounds like a good idea to you, sir."

"Uh, it's a great idea. Go ahead."

Elin scurried off. He sure could run fast for a guy in chain armor. I asked permission for our guys to dig at the well site by the Southlander camp for a while. Interestingly, even with much better equipment in our shovels and picks, we could only dig marginally faster than the Southlanders. They were better organized. All we found was some moist ground—the valley was just that dry.

It took about two hours before Elin came back. "Lord Reynaldo gives his permission for a mixed force of Southlanders and Mountaineers to go dig a well in the center of the valley."

After Koto checked with his king, our ten men with shovels led by Elin and me went with the twenty or so Southlanders who had been digging at their campsite, led by Koto. The Southlanders started off at a run but I immediately called out, "Koto! We're not running there in armor!" So they marched with us—they really enjoyed running though. Sometimes they'd take off in short sprints in small groups and come back. Though they did it in a systematic way, as if scouting ahead.

We marched a quarter-mile-an-hour pace in spite of feeling winded in the thin mountain air, higher even than the very tops of the Iron Mountains. With the irregularities in the terrain, it took us about an hour to hit the center of the valley. The sun shone down on us as we arrived, nearly directly overhead at that moment in the high thin air, lending us warmth in the midday that made it hard to believe how cold it had been at night. A deep fold lay in the terrain there, a depression that we could not see from our place back at the valley's entrance. The floor of this depression was coated with tall grasses, most of them brown. But there was a particular spot, lower than the rest, where a small patch of small, green trees grew, their leaves waiving gently in the breeze.

"There," declared Koto as he pointed. After we descended down to the spot, this small patch of trees around us, we had this strange moment where neither group knew who was going to dig. But Elin said to one of the men with a shovel, "There, like the man said. Start digging." So he began and three others started digging in the same place. As they scooped out shovelfuls, Southlanders moved the clumps of dirt out of our way, making two piles like they did with their own well, both a bit uphill in either direction, since we picked the lowest spot we could find.

The first shovelful came up moist and it wasn't long before our guys were knee deep in muddy water. "Now what do we do?" I asked Koto.

"Dig some more," he said. Then he said something to his men in the deep tones of their language. Some still stayed nearby to gather dirt (6 in fact) but the rest set about gathering large field stones. There were none nearby, but they proved willing to sprint around the area looking for them. They must have good eyes.

As our men dug deeper in muddy water in a pit widened enough for four men to work (this takes moments to tell but took several hours to do) Southlanders started piling stones around the perimeter of the pit to build the exterior of the well. When it became clear our guys didn't really know how to do that and were in the way, two of us came out and two Southlanders went in, working on the stones.

Elin, who still wasn't the tallest guy in the world, even though he'd grown, had taken his own turn in the pit. His men had complained about working in armor, but he wouldn't let them take it off—instead, he showed them himself how it didn't really get in the way. He was wet and muddy up to the bottom of his neck as he stood next to me. I remember him getting a thoughtful look on his face, his eyes rolling up. "You hear that?" he asked me.

"Hear what?" I replied.

"Sounds like…someone blowing a signal whistle, a long ways away."

I called out to the men in the pit, "Hey stop digging! You're making too much noise."

Koto issued what was clearly an order in the Southlander language. I don't know what he said, but I assume he repeated my words. Every one of his men halted in place. And we all listened.

"It's three blasts in a row," said Elin with certainty.

I listened a bit more. "Three in a row, with a pause, then repeated." All of us Mountaineers had been trained as to what that meant. Attack imminent.

Where in the sky and earth from? I wondered. I glanced around. I'd seen it before, but I realized a rocky outcropping about 50 yards from us was the tallest natural feature at the bottom of the crevice. Maybe from the top of that we'd be able to see what was going on. We didn't even know if it was 3rd Battalion or 4th signaling. We were about halfway between each.

"There!" I pointed and started running. I started moving before Elin, but it wasn't long before he passed me. A moment later, and Koto rushed past us both.

The outcropping looked to be made of a single massive rock, three times taller than a man, that somehow had been cleft, so that boulders intermingled with dirt and some few spiny plants had fallen down on either side from the ruin of the still-intact core of stone. This rock was a sort of outpost at the bottom of the depression, the top of which was still below the folded curves of the east and west heights that rose above the sunken ground.

We scrambled to the top of this rock, which had been a bit south from where we'd been standing. So all three of us climbed the north face of this massive rock, facing southward. A few paces before reaching the top, Koto began shouting to his men in Southlander. I glanced back and saw his men leaving the well, marshalling as a group, taking their spears in hand, facing south. I wanted to see for myself what Koto saw, so I, who had just hit the bottom of the outcropping, climbed upward.

"Beastmen!" shouted Elin, now at the top himself. Coming over the southern mountain ridgeline!" Beastmen are creatures of the Far East I thought were legendary, something halfway between man and bear—or man and ape maybe. They are said to live in high mountains like the Heavensfoot ranges. My Uncle Haelin mentioned fighting them in the First Dragon War.

"Form a line!" shouted Elin, "Facing south—there are hundreds of them!"

I realized in a detached way this made strategic sense for Kung Tzu. *Of course! If they live in the mountains, they can take the mountain pass by attacking the middle, isolating our forces at either end.* As I got near the top, behind both Koto and Elin, who both were studying the enemy coming our way from the south (the mass of which I was still not high enough to see myself) something told me to turn around.

When I did, I saw dozens of black shapes coming down from the top of the chain of northern mountains that defined our valley in this high mountain pass, just like Elin and Koto had seen them coming from the south. If I had not been on the rock, I would not have seen them, because from the rise in land and the trees at the well site would have hid them.

With a shock of horrific realization, I saw that large clusters of moving black were not just crossing the mountain peaks. They were much closer than the mountains. And charging, full speed, straight in our direction.

I felt this strange sense that what my own eyes told me could not be real. Perhaps because I had imagined being in battles so many times as a child that the very idea of battle had become imaginary to me, not quite real. But at the same time, that same disbelief in my mind was overlaid with an enormous pounding of my heart by my body. My mouth turned dry and it seemed my eyes could only see what was directly in front of them, not to what was the right or left. And I could not think of anything the senior officer in such a situation should say to encourage his men, nor of any clever commands that could save us all.

My voice only managed one word, "Look!"

From behind me, I heard Elin exclaim, "The God save us!" And then, after a short pause, he shouted down at the men,

"Up here! Get up here, all of you!" Immediately afterward, Koto's voice yelled words in a similar tone in Southlander. And all of the men at the well, the Southlanders and Mountaineers alike, ran as fast as they could towards our outcropping, fifty yards or so southward, out from behind the small cluster of trees.

Everything seemed to happen very slowly. It seems the God made any man capable of seeing the world differently in a time of grave danger. Many of my memories are like fixed images, like paintings that capture a single instant, quite different from regular memories of motion and action, in which time seems normal. I have a memory, a fixed image, of one of our men struggling to get out of the well, while two Southlanders were reaching down to haul him out.

The running of our troops seemed so slow—and now the black shapes of the beastmen were much closer, right after them. But they ran slowly, too.

"Therin!" Elin shouted from behind me. I turned. A black shape behind me loomed over my old friend and junior officer. I have a clear memory of Elin pulling his sword out of the beast's belly. But no memory of him stabbing it in.

I pulled my own sword from its scabbard and stepped forward, upwards to the top of the rocky hillock. That much my training ensured I would do, even though my thinking mind had no notion of any clear plan. Some part of my mind, not thinking at all about what was right in front of my person, realized Valinin must have seen the beastmen coming. It would have taken all the whistles blowing at the same time for us to be able to hear them. It never even occurred to me to think they could be under attack as well— or that 3rd Battalion could be.

As I reached the top, as a beastman of the far Eastern mountains finished scrambling up the south side of our rocky hill. As he swung a massive club at me, my mind thought, *That was wonderful of Valinin to warn us, thank the God!* At that exact instant, my lead foot slipped on a piece of loose stone. This random act of the God probably saved my life. As I slipped down, I fell to my rear knee (the left). The beastman's blow, which by instinct I brought up my shield to meet, instead of hitting me full on and breaking my arm and shoulder and most likely hurling me down the hillock, hit the upper part of the shield, mostly glancing off. Part of its force also glanced my helmet as it went, just a small part of its force sending my ears ringing and my eyes watering.

The beastman drew back for a second mighty blow, its nearly human face snarling, surrounded in black fur, not at all like a beard because its upper lip and sloping chin were bald of hair. I braced myself for the next attack. And at that moment, my uncle's voice came into my memory: *Don't trade blows with him!*

I lunged forward before he finished his swing and stabbed at the beast's right knee, a diagonal blow across my body with my dominant hand, one of the attacks my uncle taught me. The beast howled and bent over, its blow striking the ground. I back slashed at its neck, one of the follow-up blows my uncle had said to use in combat, but not the tournament. I did not take its head clean off in one blow. It howled and bled in a gushing fount in a way that reminded me of the worst moment of the tournament, my uncle's death. I took pity on my enemy with a second blow that finished the decapitation. It fell backward, into fellow beastmen lunging up our rock of safety, leaving a gush of hot thick blood in my face and down my chest.

I glanced sideways and saw Koto next to me on the left and Elin on the other side of him, holding the ridge of our rocky outcropping, all three of us wielding Iron Mountains-forged swords. Before I could think, another monstrous man was upon me, roaring in rage, a full head taller than me. Coming uphill presented his head and face, but I stabbed him as low as I could. I did like my uncle taught me. It worked. A strange thing about the beastmen—you could stab at their heads and they'd weave away. Stab or slash at their upper bodies and their matted thick fur seemed to deflect much of the force of the blow. But aim for the legs and then they felt the pain. Then they opened up for a killing blow, every time I did it.

It was on that outcropping I realized, what kind of sword fighting had my uncle known? Tournament fighting? Fighting other swordsmen for sport? Or for banditry? *No. He knew how to fight in war. A war like this war. He knew how to fight this enemy. That's why he taught what he did.* It was what he taught, not any of Ombree's instructions, that saved my life.

To my right a cluster of Southlanders stabbed and thrust their sharp spears. Behind my back, partway up the rocky hillock, facing the enemy from the north, the ten men on engineering duty fought with shields, shovels, and picks. They probably would have all perished almost immediately, except over a dozen Southlanders stood behind them, stabbing, stabbing, and slashing, with their increasingly bloody steel-tipped spears—most of the metal for which was made in our province and traded down a long path through Tsillis, on a path I'd accidentally traveled in a life that no longer seemed to be my own.

The bit there, the engagement where they rushed upon us, surprising us, was bad for the men down below me.

Four of them were dead in less time than I can hold my breath. Though "dead" is not really the right word, son. Unless a man's head is instantly removed or smashed to nothing, a mortally wounded man is not "dead" but dying. That's something the war songs leave out, except for recording the last stirring words of dying heroes. There's a fixed moment in my mind of glancing back at the four men down below. One had his head obliterated in what had to have been an overhead club blow, his skull driven down between his collar bones and flattened sideways, having gushed underneath his caved-in helmet. The other three were broken, fallen back, howling in pain.

The beastmen howled, too, and I realized how quiet they'd been running up on us. *How had they managed that? And how had they known we were down low where we couldn't see them crossing the ridgeline?* My mind kept having thoughts and observations like that, things you think you would not waste time thinking about while fighting for your life. But you do—or at least I did. I've asked other veterans and many had these kinds of thoughts like I had, but some did not.

And many thoughts were much more random than that. The bodies of the beastmen began to pile up near the top of our rocky hillock on the south side and near the base on the north. I'm not sure how long that took, but it seemed at the same time an eternity and an instant after I first pulled my sword. I glanced behind me again and saw the three men who had been wounded before now lay silent and motionless, the skin of their faces and hands now turned gray. The piled up beastmen bodies especially helped the men on the north side, because it slowed the momentum of the enemy charge. And as I turned forward again, my eyes caught a glimpse of the blue sky overhead. *What a gorgeous, clear blue sky it is,* I thought. And then I stabbed a beastman in the knee and sliced open his neck.

Again, suddenly, after I don't know how long, things changed. A beastman with fur that was silvery gray all over his head and shoulders, with a streak of silver down both the center of his chest and down his spine, roared from the top another tiny hill at the bottom of our depression that was about thirty yards east of our own and significantly lower. At this roar, the mass of the beastmen stopped their advance as suddenly as it had started. Their battle howls and roars, the sound of which I will never forget, a sound like a wolf's high pitch with the growling of a bear, also stopped. As they stepped backwards, the grizzled beastman roared again, this time in what I realized had to be words, even though he still sounded nothing like a man.

As they retreated, the beastmen grabbed their wounded and dead by the legs and arms, pulling them out of the way. There was a pause in which none of us seemed to know what to do. "Come up higher!" shouted Elin to the men on the north side. Koto shouted in Southlander at nearly the exact same moment, apparently giving out a contradicting command, since his men went *down* after our retreating enemy and jabbed sharp spear points at them, harassing them as they left. But soon enough he called them back.

Now, the leader of the beastmen, who might have been their king, issued more commands and pointed. The beastmen had been charging straight at us as they arrived, so that we never had more than four or five at a time to deal with. But now there were hundreds of black shapes all around us, on every side. I could see from their king's gestures and pointing and from the beastmen falling in closer together, that they planned to rush us from all sides all at once, in close order. Which would surely overwhelm us.

I felt this fear come over me. This certainty that all of us would die. I prayed without speaking out loud, *The God of heaven and earth—please, may it not be too painful.*

But as I looked around, I realized another sound was in the background, getting louder. Hoof beats. Coming from the south—I looked that way and saw dust rising. What had been terror in a moment turned to joy—Andrean cavalry were coming.

A deep-voiced shout from the north wheeled my head around. At the top of the sloped ground leading to our depression were frozen in my view a row of dark shapes, charging down. A moment passed before I realized it was the Southlander contingent, apparently all of them, charging into the massed horde of beastmen. *How did they outrun the horses?* my mind wondered. But shortly afterward, Andrean cavalry topped the southern side of the depression.

The beast king bellowed—or had been bellowing before I realized it. When the beastmen swung at them, the Southlanders were quick to dart in, stab in, dart out, stab stab. Seeing them made my mind think of a swarm of angry bees. Each of them were shouting in his own rhythm as they attacked, too, making a rolling noise not altogether different than the droning bee wings, though in a much deeper tone.

I heard horses squealing and whipped back my head the other way. Some of the Andreans had charged into the mass of the beastmen, who hadn't run for their lives like men would normally do when horses charge into them. The bodies of horses bowled over several rows of the massive creatures of the east before losing forward speed—when that happened, both horse and man were smashed to pulps by down-swinging clubs. That's why the horses were screaming. And that is one of the sounds that comes to mind any time I am near a neighing horse, or even a braying donkey.

The Andreans a bit back from their first men responded fast to what was happening. They galloped around the mass of beastmen, slicing through stragglers to their formation, circling, slashing with long swords and impaling with lances.

A body of them thundered up the slope of the depression to the west as if they were going to charge against the Southlanders but they stayed north of them and wheeled around to thunder towards the beastmen, staying at the edge of their group instead of charging right in, slicing and impaling those on the outside of the beast-man formation as they thundered around them in a circle. One of the riders wore armor gilded with gold, which I knew to be their leader, Reynaldo. Duke Reynaldo, as rich as any of the noblemen of Andrea, who chose to fight with the reserve calvary instead of under his own flag.

The beastmen fell back into a confused, compacted mass, being torn apart bit by bit on both sides. So no one was attacking us on top of the rock. We watched this for long, amazed moments when Elin turned to me and shouted over the roar of battle, "Your orders, sir?"

"Uh…well…what do you think?"

"I think we're missing out on the fight!"

I'd been so eager to fight, son, so you might think I would be eager to keep on fighting. Actually I wasn't so eager anymore. But Elin asked me, so I had to say something. I had no idea what to say, but I had learned a little something about command.

I put it back on him, "They're your men! You lead them into the fight—I'll be right along with you!"

So he did, he ordered them. Koto, who had been watching us, commanded his own men as well. We Mountaineers were still checking our wounded and forming up at the top of the rock when Koto and his men ran down to join the other Southlanders.

"Come on!" shouted Elin, "These beastmen are late for their appointment with death!" He waived his arm forward and started scrambling down the south side of the rock. An uneven line of six men, including two with broken arms who moved forward anyway went in parallel with him to his right (that is, trailing off to the west). I followed after the line, a pace back.

I'm not sure why I glanced upward about halfway down, but I did. A serpentine shape twisted in the sky far over our heads, dropping downward towards us. I'd never seen one before, but I knew exactly what it was.

At first my mouth couldn't say the word. I was too shocked. But my voice finally yelled: "Dragon!"

⊣⊦ Chapter 7 ⊨

f I understand anything about storytelling in the Andrean style that I'm loosely copying (loosely because the style is for fiction and this story is about truth), now is the time to heighten the anticipation of what will come next by changing the subject. Though of course your mother's story is not exactly changing the subject. She also was in the war.

Soon after I left Iron Mountains province in the spring, your mother experienced some…womanly bleeding, which made her think she'd lost you before you were born.

Immediately after that happened, the next day, she went looking for the officer she'd been under in High Crossing, Larin of Alandria. He'd left with our battalions, but his second was still in High Crossing, Aarin.

Aarin knew why your mother had a medical exception from service (though she was still in fact technically enlisted) and from what she tells me was pretty astounded that she'd come back to him as quickly as she did after a miscarriage.

As astounded as he was and as many times he asked her if she was fine and sure about what she was doing, he put her back on the active roll. The Healer Corps from Iron Mountains had proven to be so effective in helping troops during the First Dragon War, even though our means are entirely non-magical, that the Andrean crown requested the province provide extra healers to support Andrean and other troops not from the Iron Mountains.

Aarin had the role of recruiting an entire military hospital of healers, as directed by the Council of Elders, along with three direct support companies. They needed every volunteer they could find (and they not only accepted women volunteers, they encouraged them).

Arta has said her main drive was to be near me and do what she could to save me if the worst should come. She was disappointed that the forces the Healer Corps were recruiting would not be going directly to support Iron Mountain troops. But in her mind, going to war to support anyone at least did *something* to ensure I would live. Because every healthy soldier in the Western Bond would be one more to help me fight the Armies of the East. And who knew if one of them might help me in some way?

Iron Mountains had really only sent out support healers in teams before this, the largest group being a company of four teams and a supply and support section. The hospital was a new idea, supplied with a new factory putting out metal litters and steel surgical instruments, importing cloth from other provinces for bandages that clasped closed with metal fasters. And steel windlasses for tourniquets, along with other things.

Supply wagons went out every week with new equipment and food for our troops—equipment of all kinds, not mainly medical. This cost our province quite a lot—contracts were drawn up to repay loans taken from Tsillian bankers, the details of which probably don't interest you.

What I think does is that your mother looked at these supply wagons each week, thinking if she could stow away in one, she could be transported all the way to where we were. But she couldn't think of a way to do it without getting caught.

Still, every week, wagons would leave and she would long to go with them. Medical training and assembly of medical gear continued, but in her mind it was all *too slow. Too slow.* Six weeks passed before Aarin judged the first two new medical companies ready to travel. Arta went out with the first, now trained in what they called "Second Aid," which was mostly cleaning and cauterizing or suturing wounds men had suffered a day or so beforehand. More serious wounds that could not be fixed by this kind of treatment alone would be directed to the new hospital.

The companies set out on the same road I'd taken months before, due east, but then they shifted southeast, closer to the coast than where we had gone. By then it was evident to Arta that she was in fact, after all, pregnant. That whatever was the cause of the bleeding she experienced, it was not due to losing you. Her belly grew bit by bit every day.

But she did not want to tell anyone. She didn't want to be sent back—after all, she was already on the way. And even a pregnant woman can help those in need, right? And perhaps, somehow, she might make a difference in the war—she might be able to help me and other men who needed it. Those were her thoughts.

The medical wagons moved faster than the combat units (when not doing forced marches)—they used draft horses, not oxen and horses are significantly faster. They also did not stop to wait for other Bond forces or march with numerous camp followers. Still, it took just over a month for them to come close enough to the Heavensfoots to see them on the horizon. Another week to cross along the southern edge of the Great Eastern Desert, lined up as though they would go through the Southern Pass (though that was controlled by Eastern armies).

They received messengers long before then that Kung Tzu was in full retreat back toward the pass. Unlike us, they had moved every single day without a halt, except at the moment they received that news.

In the desert, which they were on the edge of, the late summer days grew extremely hot, but the nights dropped down to a much colder temperature. So much, that many of the healers on the trip wore extra clothes to ward off the cold and some also kept those extra clothes on during the day, taking off outer layers and tying them around their waist, because they were on the move so much they didn't want to lose their things.

But as they finally halted in one place for some days before getting word to move on again, women and men healers alike looked for shady spots to lay out during the hottest part of the day, taking off as much clothing as possible to be able to better endure the heat. Which made it abundantly plain that Arta was *not* taking off her extra clothing. Which caused someone to approach her.

"So you're pregnant, is that it?" Arta's section leader, Greda, asked this.

Arta paused a moment. "I don't believe in telling lies, Greda. But I'm not telling you."

"I see. So what am I supposed to do with you? Send you back?"

Arta was laying beneath one of the wagons, while most of the women in her section were under a low, thorny tree in the area. She propped herself up on her elbows. "If I'd wanted to go back, I would have told you months ago."

Greda, who had walked through blazing sunshine to talk to Arta away from the others, wearing just a thin linen underdress, sweating in the sunshine, nodded her head. "I see. So you're letting yourself become a burden on all of us, instead of going back home where your family can help you give birth." (Greda said this without anger, matter-of-fact.)

"Have I been a burden on you? Have you, or has anyone else had to do my assigned tasks?"

Greda's head tilted sideways. "No. Actually no. You are one of the people in the section I never have to worry about. You always do what you're supposed to and then some."

"Let me stay," Arta pleaded. "I'm not about to change. I will do everything I can to help everyone. Even once I give birth."

Greda scoffed. "It doesn't work that way. Once you have the baby, everyone will know. I will have to send you back with the next supply wagon, no excuses or getting out of it."

"Does that mean I can stay until I do give birth?"

"Why would you want to?"

"I do…because I do. My husband…I…I want to help save lives for a long as I can, to help in the war in any way I can. At least let me save someone if the God allows me. Before you send me back."

"You're crazy, you know that?" (Again, Greda said this completely deadpan.)

"Maybe. But I can help, at least for a while. You know I can."

Greda shook her head and breathed a deep sigh. "All right. We don't know what's going to happen next, so we may need you and you're doing good work so far." She took another breath before adding, "How far along are you, about six months?"

"I don't know for certain. Maybe?" (She was in fact closer to eight months.)

"Very well. I'll keep an eye on you and I'll keep my mouth closed about your secret. The minute you can't keep up, you're getting a ride back with the next supply column. Understand?"

"Yes, yes, thank you!"

"Don't thank me, thank your recruiter," Greda said with a smile.

Soon, the company received orders to travel northeast, to take a position halfway between the Gateway pass and another pass where troops would eventually go, a pass which Arta hadn't heard the name of (it was Eagle Pass, of course). The second company was ordered further south, to support the mass of Western forces arrayed against the Southern (or Gateway) Pass. The 4th Battalion in fact marched right past the 2nd Medical Support Company on the way north to Eagle Pass at one point, but I thought nothing of it.

The 1st Medical Support Company, Arta's unit, set up tents along a route between the two passes, at a crossroads. East of our route towards Eagle Pass, so we never saw them.

Though at the very edge of Western Bond lands, some small villages were out that way, filled with people with Eastern eyes and hair, even though members of the Bond. The medical company spent their time there treating illnesses the villagers suffered from.

Once, an older woman who said she'd learned to speak Western during the last war told Arta their lands used to belong to one of the Eastern kingdoms. That Kung Tzu wanted to take back lands that had belonged to his great-grandfather. "But of course, we like Andrea king better," she added with a grin. Arta wondered if she really meant it.

Days dragged out and it seemed nothing important would happen, which Arta didn't like at all. She didn't want to waste time. She wanted to be saving lives, especially near the end of her pregnancy. Her unit was too far away from all the action, which did not please her.

Arta's company was put in position at a desolate, little-traveled crossroads to cover any unexpected contingency of unusually high casualties. As backup medical support. Just in case they were needed.

Back in the high valley of Eagle Pass, my own shout of "Dragon" was the only warning I heard from anyone before a massive ball of flame landed in the middle of the Southlander contingent. I have a fixed image in my mind that comes to me sometimes at night, along with other things, when I wake up in a sweat. It's of the bravest men I've seen anywhere, running from the burning center of their formation, the whites of their eyes showing in their shock and horror. Though maybe they ran because their chief commanded it as the flames came rushing down. He did shout something. There was no chance to ask him what it was afterward. He'd been in the center of their unit, and he was instantly transformed with dozens of others into a standing flaming torch made of flesh and blood after the fireball impacted. I remember that, too.

Dragon fire is beyond any other kind of fire I've ever seen elsewhere. I suppose it's magical, at least in part. Like Kalway's magic, but also made of real, burning matter.

After incinerating the Southlander king, the dragon then twisted towards the cavalrymen, launching at them multiple smaller balls of flame in rapid succession. It was nothing like some of the paintings of dragons you see, which have the four stocky legs, like a dog bred to fight bulls, and massive spreading wings, like a griffin. Those dragons are legendary as far as I know.

No, the body of the dragon was more than anything like a snake, one that seemed to swim effortlessly through the air, twisting its body from place to place as it did so, like a serpent bouncing off rocks as it rushes through them. From far off, any wings were completely invisible, though they hummed faintly like insect wings, and its eight legs in four pairs of two were tucked up close to the body, difficult to see. It really did look like a serpent that could slither through the sky. With a grinning mouth, shooting searing flame.

Its face was not much like a serpent's, though it had scales. The mouth was wide and the nose short and the eyes very large, with slit pupils. Like a cat's face, the fangs included, without fur, but with something like cat's whiskers trailing from its mouth. A frill in the place of a lion's mane was at the base of the skull, where it connected to the snaky body, a body of dark red for that dragon, with a belly of orange-yellow. But the frill was made of yellowish, solid bone. Immediately behind the frill sat the dragon rider, who was strapped in with a saddle made of black leather.

My sense that what was actually happening could not be really true, could not be truly real, increased. I stood there on the side of that rocky outcropping, with my mouth open, in shock, as the dragon hurled balls of flame, its head jerking back and forth as if it were a cat spitting up furballs at the clusters of galloping Andreans. The horsemen dispersed out of anything like a combat order. Horses with riders scrambled all directions, but mostly towards the eastern end of our valley, where they'd started the day (I later heard they had trained to do that, based on their experience in the last war–they'd practiced dispersing in case of dragon attack and reassembling at a rally point).

Of course they were not fast enough to outrun the death that fell from the sky. But sometimes the fireballs missed— and if they hit, it was only one or two horsemen that exploded into flames at a time. Only one or two men and their horses screaming in agony for a very brief instant before their lungs were destroyed.

I realized Elin was shouting something at the men—"To the well! To the well!" My senses came back, at least a bit. And I realized *Yes, yes, low ground with water. Good!*

Elin went directly over the top of our rocky outcropping for the purpose of charging down in the direction of the well on the other side. I and the men followed him up. Down below us, I saw Koto and a cluster of Southlanders, their well crew and more, sprinting around our hillock, clearly going the same place as us. As I reached the top of the rock, I realized I didn't know where the dragon was. I scanned the sky in what soon would become a habit. I spotted it—zooming down from the south east. Straight my direction. I hit the ground on the top of the rock, flattening my body, face down, trembling. *The God help me!* my mind said without words passing my lips.

I heard this powerful deep throbbing sound over my head and felt air pushing down on me. I rolled partway over and saw the back end of the dragon hovering—*hovering*— over me. Its wings became visible to me at that moment, what I couldn't see before. They were in pairs down the length of the body of the dragon, how many I don't know. At least ten pairs, maybe more. The wings were small compared to the length of the beast's body, which was something like fifty yards long (I was looking from the rear towards the dragon's head—the head had gone right over me as I lay on the ground, then halted beyond having passed me). The wings were smaller than a man's arm, but they beat very fast, like a hummingbird's. I later found out that the dragon rider flew down near to the beastman king and shouted out to him in the beastman language. But all I saw at that moment was a suspended dragon's body in the air, slithering back and forth sideways as it hovered, directly over my head, it's body thicker than an ox's, its wings beating in a roaring hum, close enough that if I had stood up, my head would have impacted its belly.

As suddenly it had come, the dragon and the rider flew off, chasing more Andreans. I noticed the rider wore the protruding overlapping plates of armor common in the east, but his were colored red. I also saw the beastmen, now that their Western enemies had been cleared out of their way, they began to sprint eastward, towards the end of the pass where 3rd Battalion was stationed. The side closest to the Eastern Kingdoms.

At the time, I barely noticed that. I rolled down the side of the hillock facing the well like a tumbling rock, bouncing hard on the ground and not caring in the slightest about any damage I may have done to myself at the moment. I sprinted for that well as if it somehow had the magical power to make someone safe. As if.

At the well, everyone wanted to be *in* the water. But with over twenty Southlanders at the site, eight Mountaineers, and one Andrean who'd lost his horse somehow, it simply wasn't possible that all of us would fit. Koto and Elin were barking orders and men from both armies were cycling in and out of the well—as if getting soaking wet and muddy would save you. As a tactic, I suppose it was better than nothing.

Except for the fact that any cluster of men in one place made a tempting target for dragon fire. And there we were, all clustered together in one place. Under that small stand of scrubby trees.

I don't know who saw it first, but there was shouting and pointing. I turned and saw this reddish beast with a feline face and a serpent's body slithering through the sky. Its mouth was open; its eyes wide. Like it was happy, grinning because of what it was about to do. It was zooming towards us through the depression that cut across our mountain valley, a place that stands out more in my memory than any other location I have ever been.

"Get down!" shouted Elin. "Koto, get your men down!"

At Arta's crossroads, almost a week before I started digging a well in a high mountain valley, a large mass of Shos Hillcountry militia passed by her company, on the way to the little-traveled pass. They stopped for water to mix with whiskey and flirted with the Second Aid providers, most of whom were women.

Some of the Mountaineer women enjoyed the attention and flushed and laughed. Some did not enjoy it, Greda and Arta included.

Shortly after they departed, the magical liaison from the signal tent, Dario of Aneas (a village in southwest Andrea), came out into the courtyard in the middle of all the tents and entered the command tent to speak to Freda of Widow's Creek, the medical company commander.

When he came back out, a grin spread across his youthful, light brown face. "Ladies...and gentleman," (he added "gentleman" for the one other man in sight) "Strike the tents, we've got orders to move out!"

So they took down the tents and packed gear. Arta worked as hard as anyone else, though she felt awkward and tired and too hot and had to use the bathroom more than anyone else. Then they marched north—well, walked and rode in horse-drawn wagons—towards what they would learn was Eagle Pass.

Arta walked for a few miles, but Greda saw her and rolled her eyes, then ordered her up into a wagon. The sun had just set when they arrived at the entrance to the pass, the dramatic opening in the mountains that was wider at the bottom than the top. They camped the night there, Arta sleeping fitfully in a wagon seat, barely kept warm enough by a coarse wool blanket provided by trade with Shos people. She spent two hours on guard duty in the middle of the night, but that benefited her, because she peed before and after, pregnancy denying her much space to hold water in her body. Which meant she slept better when not on duty.

When morning came her hands were cold, but she warmed them by the fire Dario set ablaze by magic. Heat magic wasn't his specialty but he could do enough to light afire twigs damp with dew. (His specialty was moving objects, like Gaspar. Which was normal for signal specialists assigned to Iron Mountain province, because they used the Flying Letter System.)

Long before the sun rose above the towering peaks, in the pre-dawn glow, after a hasty breakfast of hard biscuits and beans, the medical company moved into the pass.

They, like us, traveled up until they reached the ring canyon. But unlike us, their orders told them to stay there.

They set up their tents, again doing hard work moving stuff. Which is a large part of almost anyone's military service. But the women with Arta were mostly factory-working girls, not of the merchant class, not daughters of Elders, so they were used to hard work. They had strong hands and backs. (Unlike us boys, the girls did not all go to school together at that time, so the divisions between them were bigger.)

To her credit, Arta kept up with them in the work, though she began to feel waves of pain pass through her gut after a while.

She realized that many must have known she was pregnant, even though she wore loose clothes and nobody said anything. But Arta was a bit of an oddity as a merchant's daughter. She kept to herself, mostly, and kept quiet. Sometimes she'd hear women around the campfire laughing in what sounded like a mean way as she walked by. As if they thought she believed she was better than them. When in fact, she was afraid of being sent home if everyone knew she was pregnant.

Dario was one of the few people to show her kindness on a regular basis, maybe because it didn't bother her that he was a foreigner. He did things like offering to bring her water. Maybe the women gathered around the fire laughed about that, too—about he and her supposedly doing things they didn't actually do. Arta wasn't sure–maybe that's why they laughed.

Greda though treated her in a matter-of-fact way, the way she acted most of the time about almost everything. Which meant, as long as Arta could work, Greda was satisfied with her performance.

Arta slept in the same tent as Greda, her entire section there together (the four men in the company, including Dario, had their own sleep tent, separate from the women). She spent that first night in the tentage just set up in the ring canyon on a mobile cot made of canvas-and-steel, under a single wool blanket but now warm enough because of the tent, feeling the strain of having worked hard. Spasms crossed her middle and she silently prayed to the God that her baby would be well.

She also prayed she could make it through the night without peeing more than once, since going out of the tent meant opening the flaps, which meant letting cold mountain air inside, which would make the women in her section angry. That prayer was answered, but meant she was the first one awake in her section. Though most days she was the first or one of the first to awaken.

After making use of the marked-out latrine area, she directed herself back towards her tent, well aware that some Shos Hillcountry troops and a handful of Andrean Reserve Cavalry were also in the ring canyon with the medical company. She wouldn't want to accidentally stumble into one of their camps in the pre-dawn darkness.

She saw though that the warming fire in the center of the company's tents had been lit. Which probably meant Dario was up. She steered herself towards the fire.

When she arrived, he was sitting on a large rock set up on the perimeter around the flames, his hands held out in the direction of the blaze. Arta sat on a rock opposite the fire from him and warmed her hands, too.

"Good morning, Arta."

"Morning, Dario. Did you need to use magic this morning, or did flint and steel light the tinder?"

"Flint and steel. It takes more time than using magic, but doesn't give me a headache." He grinned, his normally dark brown eyes reddish from reflected flames.

Arta nodded. "I suppose it sounds funny for me to say so, but I used to think of magic as something a person could do without work. Like free power. Why else call it 'magic'?"

He chuckled. "No, there's no such thing as free power. Everything comes with a cost. Though some costs are higher than others."

She smiled, "Sounds like life in general."

"Yes. You could say magic is just a very unusual aspect of ordinary life."

Arta didn't know what to reply. She liked Dario. Maybe more than she wanted to. She didn't want to encourage that feeling by talking more.

After warming herself a bit more, she got up from the fire. Not long after, the company cook got up and started preparing breakfast porridge. Arta helped her draw water from the stream.

Through that day and the days that followed, drawing water from the stream was the main event for Arta's company. Empty barrels came down, moved by a combination of our battalion supply boys, Shos militia, and Reserve Cavalry. They filled up at the stream, where members of the medical company helped (Arta sometimes helped, but Greda scowled at her when she did), then the water containers were hauled back up the pass.

So Arta knew from the talk of those who delivered water that 3rd and 4th Battalions were up in the pass. With the healers assigned to our battalions supporting us.

She fantasized about leaving her company, sneaking up higher into the pass and joining the group of battalion healers.

That way she could be on hand to save my life. She knew of course that her personal involvement would not guarantee I would live. But she still had this deep feeling she needed to be there—that my life depended on her being there somehow.

Arta observed the teams of Andrean Reserve Cavalry riders at their post in the canyon. Riders didn't just help with the water barrels, they maintained stations of riders throughout the pass, including in the canyon, so that in case of an emergency they could get word to the command by horses galloping to other horses in a relay team, down the pass and into the lowlands, all the way to the Bond headquarters post. Since walking became harder for Arta day by day, she imagined that perhaps one of the riders would take her up the pass, if only she could befriend one of them.

She offered them bits of food and conversation and helped brush down several horses. They responded with serious formality in the way of most Andrean knights, but she thought they were warming up to her after several days. Note Arta managed to help these men while still doing her section work while still quite pregnant. Which tells you something about what your mother is made of.

One of them, Alfredo, a man who had been a common foot soldier promoted to lesser knighthood because of courage on the battlefield during the First Dragon War, politely asked her on day four if it was normal for Mountaineer women to go to battle while pregnant.

She stopped visiting the Andreans after that. She didn't want her pregnancy to become a common topic of discussion. Still, she no doubt was less involved in the conversations and actions of the Medical Company than many of her fellow company members. She frequently found herself looking in the direction of the entrance to the ring canyon, where the

Andreans stationed themselves (the medical company was at the side of the stream and Shos militia between the other two groups).

So on the sixth day she observed it as it happened when an Andrean horse lathered from hard running entered the canyon and the horse and rider on alert took off immediately, headed lower down the pass. The Andrean Reserve relay messengers, riding hard.

The medics had just eaten lunch and still needed to clean their mess kits. But Arta knew the heart of the message, even before Alfredo shouted at them and at the Shos militia, loud enough to hear across the whole canyon: "Battle up in the pass! Beastmen attacking! Get ready!"

Right after that, Freda shouted at the medical company, "Prepare to receive casualties!"

Women jumped up, abandoning the metal plates and utensils of their mess kits. Arta whispered a prayer to the God, her heart pounding in her chest.

⚔ Chapter 8 ⚔

After Elin shouted his warning to get down to Koto, the dragon zooming towards us, our men and the Andrean, understanding the command, flopped their bellies onto the ground. A few of the Southlanders did, too. But most stood upright, not understanding, while Koto had to repeat Elin's command in their language.

At the same time the dragon's head reached our rocky hillock, its grinning mouth closed and its head cocked back. Elin ran out in front of the Southlanders, shouting, "Down! Down!" Waving his hand downward.

The bright ball of flame hurled out of the dragon's mouth, flying forward with a speed like that of an arrow or crossbow bolt.

In that slow motion moment, time dragging on impossibly long, Southlanders began to drop to the ground while Elin turned to face the dragon's breath, shield up, as if to stop an arrow. The ball of flame impacted the shield. It had some sort of stickiness to it, which my mind captured circling around Elin, coating him in fire. He fell to his knees, still holding up the shield. Like the chief of the Southlanders, he didn't make a sound.

"Elin!" I shouted from the ground. I got off my belly and crawled on my hands and knees towards him as fast as I could, like a dog. Then I saw the dragon pull back its face again, mouth closed. Ready to spit flame again. I froze in place.

Instead of attacking, it jerked upwards, hissing. A single man on horseback in gold-inlayed armor, thundered underneath it, charging our way. Lord Reynaldo. The dragon avoided his attack by zooming up.

Reynaldo held one of the light, very long and thin swords I'd seen before—or a person that used to be me had seen one, in the hands of the prince who killed my onetime best friend. Reynaldo held it upright and I saw darkness at the tip of the blade from his upward slash at the dragon's belly as he passed under it. So he did manage to slice it somewhere and drew a little blood. I remember that particular moment very clearly, even though my war memories are sometimes not at all clear; sometimes I've had to talk to other men who were there to build a picture of what really happened.

Since I started crawling towards Elin again, I did not see Reynaldo wheel his horse around. I'm told he waved his sword at the dragon and its rider, challenging it. Buying time for his men to disperse, I suppose. The dragon, which had by reflex flown much higher than even the extended range of the Andrean Lord's exceedingly long blade, flew backwards, away from him. Several hundred yards southward (which only took it moments to reach), it lowered its body downward again. To the height of a man on horseback, hovering near the ground. I'm told it then launched itself forward. The Andrean noble in reply spurred his horse on, man on horseback with a sword charging straight at a dragon and its rider.

For me, my world consisted of reaching Elin. To my astonishment, he was still alive, faintly calling out, "oh, oh" even though smoke rose from him, even though his shield glowed red at the upper rim, and the mud still caked on his lower body had hardened into a burnt plaster. The mud saved him more than the water, really. But his upper body had been cooked, as if over an open flame, the skin above his chest roasted black but his lower body and lower arms, protected by the mud, steamed, but not all the way through. I will never forget what he smelled like. A smell not unlike burnt pork.

"Elin!" my mouth uselessly said as I crawled up to him, "Are you all right?"

"Ah," he somehow said through lips blackened and cooked. "I been better."

A clod of dirt kicked backward from Reynaldo's horse as he galloped forward. It struck my helmet, alerting me to the world outside of myself. I looked back and saw the horse charging towards the dragon, full speed. At the same time, Elin said something to draw my attention, drawing my eyes back down. "Disperse…the…men…disperse." And then his voice fell silent.

I looked up. And instead of doing my duty, I watched a horseman in gilded armor charge straight at a dragon, his sword forward, yelling a battle cry. The dragon roared in response—loud as thunder, angry as a bear. The dragon zoomed straight at Reynaldo, as if it intended to crash into him, weight of horse and rider into a dragon's weight, head to head. Instead, at the last instant, it popped upward, above the line of Reynaldo's stallion, the long sword blade swinging at air. And then its open, grinning mouth snapped down and ripped off Reynaldo's head, helmet and armor notwithstanding. I know this sounds incredible but I was

THE BOND OF THE SWORD

there and I'm telling you that the Andrean lord's body continued onward, charging forward on horseback after he lost his head, blood spurting from his neck, for how long I don't know.

I don't know because then the dragon continued forward after killing the commander of our combined Western Bond force in the pass—which meant it was flying straight at me. At us. I turned my head, shouting, "Disperse! Disperse!"

The warning came a little late. Some of the men were already reacting on their own, especially the Southlanders this time, which means Elin standing in the way of the earlier blast no doubt saved many of their lives. How many of those only died later, I don't know.

This part brings to mind the secret of how to survive a dragon attack. Son, the main way to survive a dragon attack, is not to be in the place it's attacking.

I was forward of the men clustered near the well, under the little stand of trees, at Elin's side, so the three fireballs the dragon reared up higher to spit—they would come down at an angle towards the men on the ground—missed me. I remember looking up as the third ball of flame flew from that grinning mouth high over my head, dripping red with fresh blood (my face was in the dirt for the first two) and feeling the shock as it hit men at the well, not me. Screams erupted behind me and the few small trees exploded into pieces in a blast of flame, but I barely noticed that. The dragon had my full attention.

I'm alive either because of coincidence—because it didn't bother to come back after me. Or because the God spared me. Why He would spare me, I do not know. But on the battlefield, it's hard to escape the thought that you've been taught in our scrolls is true—that every living person has a certain appointed time to die, a time to meet the God, and there is nothing anyone can do to prolong your life one heartbeat beyond your own destiny.

Instead of destroying me, the dragon flew up and eastward, towards the end of the pass held by 3rd Battalion, leaving me alive. And ashamed, because while it fired those fireballs right next to me, I wet myself.

The dragon's flames, they came out as some sort of fluid that could surround the victim of dragon fire. But it wasn't like pitch that sticks and burns for a good while. No, the dragon's breath burned much hotter, but burned out faster, too. Unless it caught something else on fire. Which in fact, it usually did.

So as I turned back to the well after the dragon flew off, the trees only stumps now, it was to men not only burnt but still burning. And worse. Son, I've told myself I will tell you the truth about what things looked like and what they were like. Because you deserve to know—because...I don't want you to be a fool like I was, loving war, thinking it was a grand game. War is no game. And I don't mean to say a war isn't ever worth fighting or that only bad men fight. No, that's not what I believe at all. But war includes people deliberately trying to kill and mangle one another. There's nothing nice about that—nothing beautiful. Even though war has real heroes.

So as much as I've tried to tell you the truth about the war and everything I saw there, as much as I will keep on trying. I don't want to tell you everything about that moment. It's too much for me right now.

But I realize you can tell from the sequence of events here that what I dealt with next were dead and dying men, both of the well crew and the Southlanders there.

Two of our men had dispersed on their own far enough away to escape uninjured. They came back around to help me, as did a number of Southlanders who were in the area, who had rallied after the beastmen ran off and over half an hour or less, had rebuilt their formation. I had learned a few things about medical treatment of the wounded, but in truth there was not much I could do, except try to get them next to a bit of sloping ground where they could have something under their heads with their legs elevated at the same time, so vital humors would flow back into the body. Though moving them itself was horrific.

After I thought I moved everyone, I looked around to see if I had missed any bodies hidden in the black-burnt grass. Almost by accident, my eyes chanced upon Elin. And I noticed his chest rose and fell—rose and fell. He was still alive! I walked up to him, "Elin?" He said nothing. I knelt beside him, "Elin?" and I touched him, lightly fear of damaging his flesh.

His swollen eyes without eyelashes opened and he spoke. As he moved his mouth, the blackened lips began to bleed. He said in distant tone, "Oh, I must have fallen asleep. I'm sorry."

My mouth worked, trying to find words, finding none. But then, from behind me came Valinin's voice, gravelly at that moment, "That's all right, son. You've done a good job. Take all the rest ya need."

I turned and stood up, "How…"

As my voice trailed off, he spoke. "Therin…I walked right up on ya and ya didn' know it. Ya need to clear your head, son. Men's lives are still at stake. They'll need leaders if any of 'em are gonna come outta this alive." He said this to me in the quietest tone of voice, almost a whisper.

"Yes, sir," my voice rasped back, tears flowing from my eyes.

"Wipe your face, soldier," he used the same quiet tone, kind but firm. "Your men will need to believe in you. Or you're gonna see a lot worse than what ya've already seen."

"Yes, sir," I said, wiping. I hadn't even known when I'd begun crying.

"Follow me," he turned and started trotting towards the rocky hillock when we'd taken our stand, which already somehow seemed very long ago. It had been a different era, back in the olden time of "Before the Dragon."

Valinin glanced to his right, up the sloping wall of the depression. I followed his gaze and to my surprise the 4th battalion stood there, the first ranks of each company in order visible to me. As they returned my gaze, some faces were stoically expressionless, some had eyes wide in shock and horror, some met my gaze in a way that showed compassion and empathy. I worried for a moment if anyone would see the wet outline of my urine, but I glanced down and saw I was covered with grime and dirt all over my front. To my relief, I had no telltale marker of having laid on the ground and lost my piss while a dragon killed men who fought beside me.

"What are you doing here?" I called out to Valinin.

"Came forward to help Third! But it might be too late."

Shortly after that he reached the rock formation I was on earlier and began scrambling upward. I followed him. From the top he looked eastward. So did I. We saw that the beastmen had surrounded the 3rd from behind (to their west) while other beastmen attacked them from their front.

By then the Southlanders had finished forming up again and they took off, running in formation towards the backs of the beastmen far ahead of them. As if the dragon and its attacks didn't matter at all. East, where 3rd Battalion held that end of the valley by themselves, because the Andreans were no longer at that far end. The Southlanders were only a few hundred yards from us at that moment.

From the other side of the rock, the southside, a solitary Andrean in armor, separated from his horse, joined us. His helmet was removed, cradled in his arm, showing his silvery beard and hair framing his otherwise dark features and near-black eyes. A naked sword was in his other hand, the right. Valinin reached out his hand. The Andrean paused a moment, shifted the sword, then shook it.

"Valinin, 4th Battalion commander."

"I recognize you. Fernesto, knight second order, esquire." An echoing roar of the dragon, thunderously loud even from several miles away, cut off whatever Valinin would have said in reply. Even several miles away, it was easy enough to see its twisting red shape and flames flying from its mouth. We also heard the roar of men shouting and beastmen roaring and metal on metal. 3rd Battalion was fully engaged. Andreans galloped across the battlefield, dispersed, but mostly charging towards the ongoing battle. As were the Southlanders. Valinin had come forward to join them—that made sense to me at that moment.

"Shouldn't we advance, Valinin?"

"Let's watch a minute more and think about our plan of attack."

As fireball after fireball flew from the dragon's mouth and each time was greeted by screams we could hear *from miles away*, I asked, "Valinin, how long can a dragon do that?"

"Depends on age," he said. "Older can go longer. The golden dragon can go forever, I heard said. But I'm thinkin' this one will run out soon."

As if he were a prophet of the God, immediately after he said that, the fireballs ceased. Valinin sighed in relief. "Thank the God! At least now 3rd's got a chance."

"Will the dragon keep fighting?" I foolishly asked.

"Of course it will," said Fernesto. Valinin glanced at him and added, "Yeah. It'll hover low and tear off men's heads like a bird pulling worms outta the ground. You may not believe it can do that, but it—"

I interrupted, "Oh, I know."

Valinin looked at me, meeting my eyes, and whatever he saw there caused a look of pain to cross his face. Briefly, because he looked away, down at the ground, before saying, "Well, we gotta march forward to join 'em. The Shos boys can hold our end of the valley. Between all of us Mountaineers, the Southlanders, and the Andreans, we should be able to stop the beastmen and kill or drive off the dragon and still hold the pass. We move forward."

"I will go with you," announced Fernesto.

It was then, at that very moment that I saw in a flash of shock that another dragon had just flown into the valley, crossing the mountains near the eastern end. And immediately after the second dragon came a third. Some instinct told me to spin my head around—and from the western end, a fourth dragon flew in.

Preparing to receive casualties meant first that everyone be in position, nobody off fetching water or anything. It also meant pulling kits of second aid gear off metal shelves and arranging them next to canvas-and-steel cots which also had to be set out. To receive the wounded.

Some of the healers in Arta's unit panicked a bit after receiving the order, tripping as they fumbled to get items in place. Freda, the company commander, called out, "Calm down, do your jobs! We don't know how long before we see the wounded or how bad it will be. For now, the first aid teams have this under control as much as anyone can. Just keep doing as you've been trained!"

After a quarter hour, the essential set-up had been performed with Greda and other section leaders supervising (this gear was normally kept in tents to protect it from rain). After that, over the next half hour or so, everyone, the majority of whom were women but also the men, fidgeted in place, not wanting to engage in ordinary conversation when they knew lives were on the line. But it's just not easy to remain on high alert very long when nothing is happening.

Samna, a woman in Arta's section, announced in a loud voice, "Thank the God we're doing this! I didn't want to clean my mess kit anyway." Women and men laughed.

A hard pain passed through Arta's belly. She drew in a slow deep breath and tried to act as if nothing was happening.

Freda glared at Samna and announced, "Speaking of that, someone really should clean all those mess kits. Looks like you've volunteered."

Samna shrugged, not completely surprised. "So much for prayer!" A few chuckled at that.

Freda, a tall woman with gray eyes and silver hair pulled back in a bun, replied with a sharp: "Looks like Samna needs some helpers!" That cut off the snickering.

Arta, releasing her breath as smoothly as she could, announced, "I'll help."

Samna shot her a surprised glance, her brown eyes widening.

She was among the women who routinely laughed as Arta walked by their circle of friends. (Arta merely wanted to get away from almost everyone else for a bit—not wanting everyone to notice her pain.)

The hardest task of cleaning the kits was keeping track of which kit belonged to whom, because they were assigned to individuals. But Arta picked up the kits in section order, Samna following her lead. They asked when uncertain what item went with which person. They took multiple trips back and forth to the stream, washing the small metal trays and tines, spoons, and knives in water, then putting cleaned kits back into sleeping tents, on the assigned cot of each person. Arta had her head down at the stream, scrubbing one of the last kits when Samna's voice announced in a tense, low whisper, "There's a dragon in the valley."

"Where…" she started to ask. Her voice dropped off as she looked up. A large blue beast, serpent-like, hovered over a mountain in the ring canyon, in the opposite direction from the canyon entrance…the direction everyone else in the company faced as they waited on alert for casualties.

The blue color nearly blended in with the sky. The beast was lowering itself, straight down, like a supply lift in a sword factory, down towards the mountain. Maybe a mile away, but in clear, unobstructed view.

After a moment of astonishment, Arta drew in air to shout a warning. Samna held a sunburnt-on-top hand up to her mouth. She whispered, "Don't! It can see us. I'm sure. Dragons got good eyes, everybody knows that."

The hand transformed Arta's intended shout into a loud whisper, "We have to let Freda know!"

Samna whispered with urgency as the two of them leaned over the gurgling stream in the canyon, dark brown locks of hair cascading down her sunburnt face, "What exactly is she gonna do about it? Call one of our battalions for help? They're hours away by foot. And last I heard, busy fighting beastmen."

"There's a ballista on the lead supply wagon. We could shoot at the rider!" Arta still whispered, but not exactly quiet.

Samna's own whisper grew louder, her breathing more intense, "Listen, you might wanna risk your own life to be some kinda hero, but I can't imagine you'd want your baby to die—" Arta shot her an astonished glance—"yes, we all know you're pregnant, but obviously you don't got the common sense the God gave a rock, because you should be back home now—"

Arta held her own sunburnt hand in front of Samna's mouth and matched her volume and tone. "Shut up!" Samna's eyes widened again, but she held her peace.

Arta continued, "I'm here for a reason. I'm not sure what the reason is, but I know there is one—and you don't need to know anything about it. Now this is what we're going to do. We are going to take the mess kits back, which the dragon must have already seen us with already, if their eyes really are as good as legend says. We're gonna act normal, that makes sense, because you're right, we don't want to give it a reason to attack. Then we are gonna walk over to Freda, just like we were carrying mess kits back before. Then we're gonna tell her what we've seen—she's our leader and she needs to know."

Samna breathed twice fast then nodded her head. Each woman stood straight, the last mess kits in their hands.

Arta cast her eyes towards the dragon at that moment —now it was near the ground, midway up the mountain.

Two tiny dark shapes leapt off the dragon's back onto the dusty brown mountain slope, but she didn't dare watch any longer. She and Samna turned and walked back to Freda. On the way, another hard pain passed through Arta's gut, which caused her to bend over a little bit, but she kept walking, holding her belly, breathing deep breaths through the pain.

By the time they reached Freda, the pain had passed.

While the company in general faced the entrance to the pass, Freda's head was turned back towards Arta and Samna as they approached and her eyes kept flicking between them and something over their heads. She, unlike most of the women and men in the company, was not sunburnt, but her face still showed red in the cheeks. So Arta understood that Freda had already seen the dragon.

Freda, who had been a front-line healer during the last days of the First Dragon War, raised her voice, "Ladies and gentlemen. Remain calm. Stay in place. In fact, wherever you are right now, sit down."

A host of puzzled faces looked Freda's way but the company obeyed her order, though a few were already seated. Even Samna sat down, so only Freda and Arta remained standing. Freda's eyes met Arta's for an instant before she added, "There's a dragon and rider in the valley. Don't look for them! Don't look! Keep your heads and eyes forward. And keep your voices down, people! The dragon is halfway trying to stay hidden. That's probably good. Maybe that means it won't attack. If they're attacking, they don't care who sees them. But if they're trying to stay hidden, we're gonna let them, so the God willing they leave."

Her eyes locked onto Arta's, "My own eyes aren't what they used to be. What did you see?"

Arta breathed in deep before answering, "As you said, I saw a dragon in the valley. Blue. Almost blends in with the sky. It lowered down and landed on the mountain for a moment. I think it left two men there. I haven't looked back since."

Freda's eyes flicked upward for a moment. "It's gone back into the sky. It's flying east. Most likely towards the valley where 3rd and 4th Battalions are."

"Oh the heavens!" Arta replied. "Maybe we should shoot at the dragon now, with our ballista. Our men need our help!" Various shocked faces turned Arta's way. She ignored them, fixed on Freda.

"We're not a combat unit, Arta. All of us getting killed doing something foolish like that would mean none of us would be alive to help the wounded. There's likely to be plenty of wounded." Freda's face spasmed as she said that, but she didn't tear up like my uncle would have. Freda was tough.

Freda looked around at the company with steely eyes before adding, "However, it's bad that men are on the mountainside. Sometimes dragons would drop off Rysshurian mages during the First War. A few times—only a few, thank the God. Thank the God too that the talent to kill with magic is a rare thing.

But when it happened, they went into areas behind the lines, where the mages would kill as many support people as they could, people like us, which is why we have the ballista, for dealing with that...so after the dragon leaves us—pray the God it does without attacking—we'll need to get ready the few weapons we've got, including the ballista. We can kill the mages, though it won't be easy—but in the end, they're only human. So we might be fighting for our lives soon, ladies and gentlemen. But not yet, nobody move yet! The dragon has to leave first. I pray the God, it will."

A woman's voice began sobbing, Arta couldn't see who.

"Stop!" Freda ordered. "We don't have time for crying. Yes, it'll take the mages a while to get close enough to attack, but it won't take long. Half an hour perhaps. Minutes at the soonest, if they run up to where they can see us good. You can cry when it's over. Or when you're dead." Her eyes lifted upwards, searching the sky for the dragon. "Stay calm, stay where you are. I'll give the word."

Arta glanced upward and saw the dragon was already behind Freda's head, over halfway across the ring canyon, headed east.

Freda did not give the word. Her eyes suddenly turned cloudy and the skin of her face crinkled and blackened in an instant and she fell over, her body stiff and straight, like a tree chopped down by a woodsman. Some instinct told Arta to hit the ground and lie flat. She hit hard, hurting her belly. The smell of Freda's burnt flesh assaulted her nose and she swallowed back vomit, rolling slightly to one side to get off her belly a bit, fighting against throwing up. She wondered if she peed herself—wetness spread down her upper thighs. Screams erupted and some members of the company jumped up from the ground and ran in panic. Though others stayed seated where they were in shock, not doing anything. Many of those who ran fell right away, obviously cooked in the head in an instant by heat magic, which Arta knew about from my prison experiences. The magicians on the hillside picked them off from further away than Freda had thought possible, leaving bodies dropping all around Arta, right and left.

After the mages first targeted people running, then those seated and not moving began to fall over. Maybe a dozen medics died in the first minute. Arta didn't move from where she lay on the ground—except her lips, just above dirt, moving in prayer as pain rolled through her belly in a massive wave.

The few Andreans in the area must have realized what was happening. A trio of horsemen galloped towards the mountain on the other side of the canyon, Alfredo among them. The number of screams from the medical company diminished as the horsemen charged at the mountain. Shouts and cries after that indicated a large number of medics had made it to the tents, where they called out for others to join them.

"No, no!" shouted Greda from behind her somewhere. "If you're down on the ground, stay down!"

After Arta couldn't say how long, but what must have been less than a painful minute later, Greda shouted from outside her field of view, perhaps from a tent: "Anybody see the dragon?"

Arta, still on the ground, dared to look up into the sky, her belly still in the dirt, spasming in pain. "It's just leaving the canyon!" She then lowered her head back down, fearfully aware she was still in the open. The only thing protecting her from death was the fact she must have already seemed dead.

Greda's voice rang out from behind her. "All right! The mages don't seem to be able to hit us if they can't see us. Pick up that cot, ladies, that one! Let's drape some blankets. Yeah, like that! We're gonna make ourselves a cover to carry with us and get ourselves over to that ballista. Arta! Don't move! We're coming your way!"

Arta imagined the mages employing some sort of spell that let them see from afar. It was the only explanation she could think of for what they were doing, because she knew they had to see what they attacked. She didn't even want to breathe, let alone reply, even though she'd already searched for the dragon, but she replied, "Understood!"

Soon she heard Greda call out, "At the full step! One, two, three, four; one, two, three, four." The voice calling the march approached her way. She didn't turn her head back until the sound was close. Behind her, Greda, Samna, and two other women had a cot over their heads, upside down, Greda on the left end marching them to keep them lined up together. A number of wool blankets were tied to the cot legs and draped backwards, dangling down the back of the cot, effectively keeping the marching women invisible from the viewpoint of anyone behind them on the mountainside.

Arta realized she couldn't see the mountain behind them, so she stood, facing them. Water ran down her leg. She had no idea if she'd peed in the terror of the moment along with her fall or not. Or maybe her water had broken—but it wasn't gushing out like she thought was normal.

But something more urgent for her was on her mind: "Where's Dario? We need him to signal we're under attack! And there's a dragon in the area!"

"Halt!" Greda called before replying, maybe three paces in front of her. "I had a mind to get to the ballista first. Would be nice to shoot back at whoever's killing us." A hint of emotion—anger—crept into Greda's tone. But only a hint.

"They're way out of range, I think. Somehow they're shooting from afar."

"You sure they didn't use magic to somehow get close real fast? Did you see them?"

Arta opened her mouth, then closed it. Maybe that was what had happened. She shook her head *no*, because she hadn't seen them.

During the moment she pondered the issue of where the mages could be, she noticed among diminished shouts from the company the sound of horse hooves. Right after the sound, two horses, without riders, galloped back in the direction of the Andreans near the entrance to the canyon, running to the left of the medical company. Alfredo's black mare wasn't one of them. She realized the mages must have killed the few Andrean cavalry who'd rushed to defend the company—maybe Alfredo was still alive, but it seemed the other two riders were not. Or maybe they killed Alfredo's horse, too.

Shouts and even screams of burning men erupted from the Shos Hillcountry camp in the canyon, less than a hundred yards away. Arta looked that way—canvas tents burned, men pouring out of them, abruptly awakened from afternoon naps, some with burning clothes. It seemed instant death by cooking heads wasn't the only option their attackers had.

"The blankets!" said Arta.

"Wool doesn't burn easy," replied Greda, "But we need to move, before they notice us."

"Dario, we still need Dario! He can guide a ballista bolt after its fired!" (Arta did not in fact know he could do this. The idea came to her in the moment.)

"He can? Right then, where is he?"

Samna, pointing with her left hand (her right held onto the cot), "There—facedown."

Ten yards away, Dario's legs stuck out from under a body fallen over him. "He might be alive," said Arta.

"We're headed that way," ordered Greda. "Fall in under the cot, Arta! One, two, three, four; one, two, three—" they marched over to the Andrean down on his face. There, Greda and Arta slipped out from underneath and pulled Lisna's body off Dario (she was a kind-hearted girl from

Rogin). Her eyes were white, her skin darkened, her swollen tongue pushed out of her mouth—her brain cooked in an instant. Arta barely had time to think about that at the moment—but she remembered later.

Greda kneeled beside Dario and shook him, "Are you hurt?" He didn't reply.

Arta dropped her right hand around Dario's neck and found the main artery there. "His heart's beating!"

"Let's roll him!" When they did, they saw the right side of his face had been partially burned—both eyes were closed. Greda leaned down and slapped his uninjured side. "Dario!" Both eyes opened, but the right looked half-cooked. "Oh, I don't feel right," he said in a low voice, his mouth moving in an odd way.

"We should leave him," Greda said.

"No, no, no, we need him!" Arta reached under his left arm to pull him upright. It was strangely limp.

Greda scoffed but without another word helped Arta pull him up, so he was standing. It turned out his left side had almost no strength but Arta put his limp arm over her shoulder and with Greda's help, they helped him limp over to the ballista.

Arta's belly squeezed tight. She breathed hard through the pain, bent over.

Samna called out from the cot covering them from behind, "Arta, are you giving birth?"

The reply came through gritted teeth, "Not now I'm not!"

Samna offered to help, but Arta roared in anger driven by pain, "You can't drop the cot!"

They limped and struggled and almost made it to the ballista when the smell of burn hair assaulted their noses. "The blankets are on fire!" shrieked the girl next to Samna.

424

"Stay calm!" snapped Greda. "They won't burn well."

Which was entirely true—but the blankets did burn for long moments, leaving a thick smell of burnt hair.

By then another crew of medics, following Greda's example, was at the ballista with a cot-covered in blankets, which they were heaving upwards, gray smoke and the smell of burnt hair rising from their blankets, too. Women grabbed blankets and moved them, crying out in the pain of the fire, but still holding onto the blankets, maintaining a barrier between them and the mountainside.

Dozens of Shos militia had charged the mountain, a number of them falling to the ground dead, trying to stick to the scrubby trees and large rocks between them and it. Arta barely had time to process what they were doing, but it seemed the mages didn't spend much time focusing on wool blankets because of the militia. Soon, many bushes and small trees were on fire in the canyon.

Two women, one Samna (the other Edna), were turning the crank handles that pulled back the ballista's bow, preparing it to shoot. Greda leaned over in the wagon and peeked around the blankets that other women held. "I see two tiny dark dots on the mountain. Black against the brown of the mountain. I suppose that's them. Like they're not even trying to hide!"

"How far?" Samna grunted as she asked the question, cranking hard.

"Not sure. Almost a mile, maybe. Maybe less."

Samna whistled low, "You must have good eyes. I could barely see a thing when they jumped off the dragon's back."

"That's gotta be a long, long ways out of the range of this ballista," added Edna, who had popped open a box of ballista bolts. "How far does it shoot, anyway?"

"No more than five hundred yards," said Greda. "About a third as far as we need."

"Maybe it's not really them," Samna said. "Maybe they left something dark up there and are somewhere else."

Greda replied without emotion, "Maybe, but we gotta try." Arta was next to Dario, both flat in the back of the wagon.

"Can you help the bolt go farther?"

"How would I do that?" he asked, his voice distant. "I can't help crank right now, not with my arm like this."

"With magic. Can you lift the bolt and make it fly farther?"

"I don't even know if I can do magic now," he muttered. "Maybe I can. If I can, I can."

Arta shifted to help sit him up and more water came out of her. "Not now, not now!" she cried out. Then to Dario, "See the bolts in the box? Can you lift one with your mind, right now?"

"Um, sure." A bolt lazily lifted up from the box, seemingly on its own.

Edna grabbed it from midair and slammed it down on the ballista in its slot, then swiped brown hair out of her eyes. "All right, let's do it!"

"Wait, wait," said Greda. "He's gotta see the bolt to do that, right? Or doesn't he? If he does, how far away can he see it?"

"Not as far as the mountain," Samna said.

Arta leaned in next to the Andrean mage. "Do you have to see it Dario?"

"I can send it flying without seeing, but I won't know where it's going."

Greda sighed, "That's not gonna work.

Arta said, "Is there a way for you to use magic to see farther, Dar? Can you do that?"

"No, no. I can…I can't do that. Not my…not my magic."

"The God help us!" said Edna.

"There's gotta be a way!" said Samna.

"No, there doesn't," deadpanned Greda.

"There's…what about heat?" said Arta. "You told me once you can feel a fire from far away. If we set the bolt on fire, could you do it then?"

"Like a little point of light with my eyes closed. Oh, yeah, I can do that." His voice had become like a young child's. He smiled wide, one side drooping a bit, grinning as if nothing at all was wrong in the world.

"Can you, can you *feel* the heat of a person's body from far away?"

"I don' know. You'd have to point me the right way."

The women had to maneuver him around, which took time and effort. But after a bit, while Edna was wrapping a bolt in cloth to make a torch, Greda moved aside a no-longer burning blanket, stinking like burnt hair, just enough to expose the mountain to Dario's good eye.

"Do you see the brown, dusty mountainside?" Greda asked. "On the slope are two black shapes, very small. Do you feel any heat from them?"

Dario closed his eyes. "There's a tiny, tiny light from one. The one lower down."

"None from the other?" "No, just one."

"Fine, fine. We're gonna set the bolt on fire and shoot it. Can you make its fire go into the little light, far away?"

"Oh, I dunno. Maybe, maybe."

Edna had already struck a torch with flint and steel. Greda looked her way. "Light it!" Edna touched the torch to bolt and it burst into flames. "Ready, Dario?"

"Ready, Ready."

"Shoot it," deadpanned Greda.

Edna pulled the trigger.

The steel ballista bow thunked and the burning bolt flew. "Light to light," muttered Dario, "Light to light."

"You've got this," whispered Arta to him, while thinking: *Oh the God, may he get it!*

Chapter 9

One of the dragons was red of nearly the same shade as the one we'd already seen. One was more orange and yellow. But the last to cross the mountains was blue, the one that flew in from the west, with a lighter blue underbelly —almost white, actually. The orange and red hurled fire down on the 3rd Battalion position, which we could see, even though it was hard to make out individual people (thank the God). The blue skirted around the edge of the valley, well away from us, and joined its companions in blasting fire down on the 3rd.

Some disconnected part of my mind felt astonished when the blue dragon breathed flames. I guess I was expecting lightning or water or ice or something. But no, it shot forth flames like the rest, though it did so by making a steady stream of fire that flew out in a long line, instead of blazing balls of flame. Ironically its fire was very reddish, while the fireballs spat by the red dragons burned blue at first and faded to red.

It's funny I suppose, but I've told that to certain people before and they looked at me like I was a liar. This is one of the reasons many veterans don't talk—some people see our true stories as lies or exaggerations. Which just isn't worth dealing with. Though there are more important reasons some of us don't say much.

"What do we do now?" I said out loud, trying to hide the rising sense of panic from my voice. Not really to Valinin, but he answered.

"Well…" his pause stretched out long before he continued. "Lemme ask you this, did Elin get hit direct on by dragon's breath?"

"Yes. Straight into him."

"So why isn't he dead?"

I had no answer for this, especially since I'd thought he *had* died. Fernesto said, "Do you think this is a time to stand and ponder? It is time to *act!*"

Valinin glanced over at him. "I disagree. We gotta minute ta think—and this is the perfect time for it." He turned to me again, "So his lower body's dirty, like with dried potter's clay—he'd dug in the well, right, was covered with mud?"

"Yes," I answered, not at all following his thinking.

"So, a little bit of water is no good. It just boils and steam cooks. But mud, wet gloppy clay mud, that allows a man to survive gettin' hit, at least for a little while? Assuming of course, you wet the clay afterward or it flakes off, because once it gets hot, it'll say hot." I nodded but he wasn't paying attention to me, "Company commanders!" he bellowed behind us, "Move your men forward! Into the depression."

He turned to me, "Are ya ready to act like my number two?" I nodded, swallowed, and said, "Yes."

"Good. I'm gonna stay up here and watch the enemy. I'm gonna shout some orders in a bit but I want you to understand 'em and follow up and make sure it happens.

We need crews pullin' water outta your well, haulin' it over to four separate patches of ground with clay in it. They're to make a mud flat at each spot to roll the men in it, everyone, but starting with the tower shield men. There's probably not near enough time, but we gotta try. Understand?"

"Yes, sir."

"Make it quick!" And then he bellowed out his orders, basically what he told me. I scrambled down the rock and started to run to the first company commander, who had started walking to the rock, leaving his formation the nearest to the well, and who had a puzzled expression on his face.

No, I realized. 1st company, closest to the well, closest to Valinin, was the most likely to figure this out first and get it done first. If anyone would really need me, it would be 4th. I ran around the rock, the opposite direction Koto had run to the well. Some small part of my mind wondered what had happened to him as I ran. I hadn't seen him among the fallen.

Never the fastest of runners, I did the best I could. My body ached already from earlier fighting. I decided not to stop at second at all, since I saw Alfrin, Elin's second, had a crew of men digging in a patch of clay. I came to the 3rd company commander, who'd just finished orders putting his men in a defensive square. He was in the center, so I had to push past shieldmen to get to him.

Huffing hard, I asked him if he understood his orders. He said, "No, but I sent a runner." So I explained to him. Including mentioning why. I remember the eyes of the commander, Parolin, growing wide when I mentioned to him four dragons in the distance.

I pushed my way out of third company to see a cluster of eight men running with the four tall metal cans we use to provide company wash water. I saw an area where they'd dumped them out and men already wallowing in mud. I spoke with the 4th company commander anyway; checked in on 3rd again on my way back; checked with 2nd for the first time. Valinin's orders were being obeyed on the south side of the rock.

I ran back to the rock and passed halfway around it. First company, too, were clearly doing the right thing. There was a din of men working, preparing positions, making sure arrows were distributed to the bowmen—and wallowing in mud. The rock wasn't a towering mountain, but I had to shout up it to be heard by Valinin, "How's the battle going?"

He shook his head no and his lips formed the words, "Not good." He gestured for me to join him. At the base of the rock, all the things that had happened when I was on top of it came back to me without words, without images even. I felt a little bit of dread to climb that rock again. I climbed it, but I felt heavier climbing it than I had before.

I reached the top of the rock and looked eastward. Long shapes of some kind of animal with men on their backs running very fast were pouring from the eastern end of the pass, into our valley. Andrean Cavalry had dispersed in all directions, most running back our way. The Southlanders were running back towards us in formation, many with their shields on fire. Some of their men were on fire, too, running in formation, on fire, chased by the blue dragon. My eye could detect no sign of 3rd battalion at first. But then I realized there were scattered bits of men running in black chain armor, running alone, or at most in clusters of two and three, running back our way. There weren't very many of them, and the dragons kept landing on them and tearing into them, then taking to the air again. Though some of the men in black were run over by the long-legged beasts or stabbed by their riders, who used long, gently curved swords and who wore no shields.

Three dragons chasing the remnant of our sister battalion in our direction, one burning Southlanders alive, also coming our way, Andreans scattered again, running, new beasts running after them—even the beastmen were headed our way again. Things were about to get bad. At that moment, I very much did not want to be there. But it didn't matter what I wanted. Perhaps you've heard the saying, "He who lives by the sword is bound by the sword." That means he leaves peace behind if he uses a sword and must *continue* to use the sword, even if he'd rather not.

That's what the bond of the sword is like, son. Once you take it up, you cannot put it down just because you want to. You have given your holy word—you are bound to that word. You are linked in bond not just to your weapon and your duty to fight, you are linked to those you fight beside; as a commander, the bond is to your men, but they also to you and you to your commanders and all of you to your allies. You are in it together—you will live together or die together in a way that is like nothing else, fighting for your life beside someone else. It is not quite love and it is not quite brotherhood; it is both and neither.

I would have liked nothing more than to be at home with your mother at that moment—not knowing she was no longer there. But I could not. I was bound.

"Prepare a battalion volley!" shouted Valinin. This was a command for the archers.

At that moment I realized I'd forgotten something very important. I turned to Valinin, "Sir, permission to secure the wounded men I left by the well."

"Therin, I don' know any of us are gonna be secure here in about two minutes." He said this without looking at me, his eyes still forward.

"Still, I can't leave them unprotected."

Now he looked back at me. "Make it quick! First Company is closest, grab one of their squads. Go!"

I scrambled down that thing halfway between a rock and a hill yet again. I don't remember feeling sore or tired as I went down at all. The mass of 1st company filled the area between the rock and the well. "Make a tunnel!" I shouted. The outer shieldmen, with their tall tower shields, all of whom facing me were at least a little muddy, parted. Past them were the spearmen, past them the bowman, then the inner circle of the company, where the commander and senior sergeants armed with swords stood to direct the rest (the type of formation they were in is called a "square" which means the unit was in tight, with shieldmen facing outward each direction). As I trotted through the middle, I shouted to the company commander, "I need a squad to recover the wounded!"

I wasn't even looking at him as I yelled, I just kept going through the formation to the other side. As soon as I cleared, men hauling water, from 3rd company I think, passed back the direction I came. I glanced behind me and saw the spearmen on the well side of the formation were following me. I hadn't heard the command given.

My mind was wondering where in the world we'd move them. Putting them in the 1st company area would probably get them trampled. Or worse if the dragon attacked. But leaving them where they were would let the enemy cavalry run right over them, which I couldn't allow. So I decided to take them back through the formation and put them up on the sloping ground near the north side of the rock where Valinin stood.

I shouted and pointed where men lay as I ran up to Elin. "We need to go!" When I said that, he sat up and tried to stand. Me and a spearman reached under his arms and lifted him. He yelped like a kicked dog when we did that. "I'm sorry, so sorry!" I said.

"It's all right," he answered, barely keeping his voice under control. As I started to move him, thundering hooves of horsemen jumping into our sunken area. We'd barely gone two paces when eight or nine Andreans thundered into the depression and back up the other side. As a mass, they ran right through where Elin had been, barely missing trampling us in fact. So I guess you could say that I saved his life. In a manner of speaking.

I just managed to get him to the base of our rock, back through the 1st company formation, when the first wave of the enemy hit us (in the end, four wounded men made it to the rock). "Hit us" isn't the right term, because they didn't. Instead, they tried to run around us.

These creatures that Eastern riders were using as mounts, they had bodies like horses, except their legs were very long, as were their necks. The bodies were white and they had short wings to their sides. As they'd gallop, their wings would flap, stretching out their time in the air, making their bounds very long. And very fast, too, though they seemed to move with an elegant slowness, because their limbs and bounds were so long.

I realized after I understood how fast these creatures ran that the Andreans must have turned and run from them before they even got close to them. Otherwise the horsemen would never have reached us before they did.

I felt a brief surge of the anger of betrayal at this, even as some part of my divided mind watched these creatures from the East in amazement.

I eventually heard these are called *longma*, which I heard of once before. Their heads were like dragon heads—I don't mean like the real dragons we saw flying in the air, whose heads and mouths were wide and noses short, like scaly cats. These had a narrow mouth that came to snout more like a scaly dog, but the eyes were large, like a griffin's, and a crown of horns pointed backwards from the tops of their heads. Their bodies were white, but the heads were like gold. I never saw them breathe fire on anyone as a weapon, but as they leaped, tongues of flame curled from their nostrils, as if a small fire continually burned inside them, only released every now and then.

It's funny—and at some point in the battle I was thinking this, too—but their heads were like dragons in Western artwork, like the dragons on the banners some of the Andrean nobles fly. But there aren't any real dragons in the West, not that I ever heard of anyway. Maybe there were once and they're now all dead—maybe those long-dead dragons had heads like that. Or maybe us poor confused Westerners got mixed up in our minds with the different beasts of the Eastern Kingdoms and started drawing *longma* heads on dragon bodies.

They were breathtakingly beautiful in white and gold, in their massive galloping leaps and curls of flame. But they tried to pass our formation sooner than they should have, before we were suppressed, a tactical error. And we were bound to our duty to kill them.

The mass of them, clearly more interested in getting to the other side of the pass than dealing with us, ran *around* the

4th battalion and our squared up companies in the middle of the depression that cut more or less across the middle of the valley. Valinin bellowed the order and 3rd and 4th companies fired arrows into the ones trying to go around us on the south and 1st and 2nd fired into those trying to get past us on the north. I could only see north from where I stood but my mind retains the picture a tumble of snowy white bodies and golden heads, full of arrows, riders tumbling off, armor protecting them only somewhat. Some of the *longma* caught on fire as they fell. Our arrows easily obliterated their elegant, graceful beauty, fast transforming their vibrant life into dead, unmoving objects like the dirt and rocks, but spattered with blood. And burning.

There were so many at the same place at the same time, our arrows inevitably missed some of them, ones a bit further back from the place the arrows fell. At that point, after they had passed the depression, the Andrean cavalry wheeled around and charged into flanks of the north and south columns the 4th Battalion had forced the *longma* cavalry into, though that's something I heard about later rather than saw myself. Using their forces that way, the Andreans demolished all the enemy survivors of our archers. What had struck me as cowardice by the Andreans was actually a clever strategy—as a point of fact, not one of the *longma* made it to the other side of the valley.

Though at the moment, I stopped thinking about them almost as soon as I saw them fall. More urgent matters seized my attention.

All at about the same moment: The Southlanders sprinted back into our depression, at what I later understood was the 2nd Company's location, the blue dragon in fiery pursuit. I saw a red dragon whip its body over the location of 1st Company and draw back its head to spit a fireball. I felt and heard rather than saw something massive impact the rocky hillock right next to me.

At some distant moment later…distant in how it felt, but it really was the very next thing, the heat of the red dragon's fireball made the left side of my face hot—this was the one attacking 1st Company—I later learned the other red dragon was attacking 4th at the same moment. I glanced up to my right because of the sound I'd heard and the impact I'd felt. The orangish dragon had slammed into the top of the rock —right where Valinin had been, the very point from which he directed our troops.

I fell backwards—I don't know at all why. I had enough presence of mind to twist as I fell. I landed next to Elin instead of on top of him, on my right side, facing the orange dragon.

Its mouth, that terrible, grinning cat's mouth, roared down at me and my little assembly of the wounded, so loud that it was as if my head were a brass bell and the dragon's voice smote it with a massive hammer, sending my head ringing. And the sense passed over me, yet again, that we were all already as good as dead. Yet I found myself a certain rage that I should be separated from my wife and baby so soon—that I had suffered so much under Ombree and in prison and being away from home, only to find joy and the God's blessing again—only to lose it once more. There was another impulse, too. I stood as the only guard over the bodies of the wounded I'd just moved. They were *my* men, and I wasn't going to let that damn dragon have them without a fight.

I scrambled to my feet, pulling the sword I'd put back into its scabbard, and yelled back at the dragon. I suppose

I meant to charge up the rock, slashing at the beast's head. It proved unnecessary.

A strange thing happens in battle. Or at least it happened to me (not all the time, it came and went). Your vision becomes restricted, so you look at only one thing, like you were looking down a tunnel or through a pipe. So maybe if my vision hadn't been like that, my eyes only seeing at that moment an orange dragon, maybe I would have realized sooner that something new had happened.

Or maybe not, because I remember the dragon's eyes shifting upward, it blinking in what must have been surprise. Then from nowhere in my field of vision appeared a sword, upside down, hanging from the air, as if swung by one of the God's angels. The sword slashed through the dragon's eyes, flaying each one open.

I lifted my head in astonishment and saw a Bond griffin rider, upside down, the griffin's impossibly long wings tucked into its body as the bird rolled in the air. The griffin rider had one of those very, very long swords of Andrean design, stretched out long—the one that had just struck the blow I'd witnessed. While my eyes were fixed on the griffin, the dragon howled and blindly leapt upward. Its head was tucked down, in pain I guess. Its rider had a sword of his own, of the Far Eastern single-edge design, slightly curved. The rider and dragon flew after the griffin, which righted itself and began flapping its very long wings hard to gain altitude.

I have to admit to spending I don't know how many heartbeats staring upward, watching, in shock. Watching when I should have been paying more attention to my own circumstances. The griffin stroked hard in the thin air, struggling to gain altitude to recover from the steep dive it must have made. The dragon gained on it steadily.

I suppose if it had been able to see it would have shot flames at the griffin, or torn into it with its teeth. Instead, as it closed, it veered to the right side, steered by its rider I suppose. And the dragon rider slashed downward at the wing that was so incredibly long, slicing through it as if it were a stalk of wheat yielding to sickle. The griffin tumbled in a spin.

At that point screams of men from 1st Company finally registered on my battered senses. I turned back to the red dragon that had attacked them, the one actually threatening my life. It had gained considerable altitude from when I last saw it. A griffin streaked towards it, its wings tucked in from its dive from higher up. The rider had the long sword held forward, like a cavalryman with a lance. The dragon, I realized, had another griffin rider in its jaws. And while still mid-air, its serpentine body wrapped around and eight small legs dug into the broken body of a griffin, its beautiful long wings bent in ways the God never intended.

The griffin rider flying in, this one wearing Andrean deep blue, following after his doomed comrade, deftly turned his high speed mount just a little as he spun in. The impossibly long sword reached out and sliced off one of the dragon's wings flapping in a blur before this griffin, too, had to stroke hard to gain altitude, to avoid crashing into the ground. Slowly climbing, clearly easy prey for a dragon as it fought its way up.

Something came back to my mind at that moment, something I would have been better off thinking later. I remembered I'd heard it said to the Andrean prince, more than once, "One blow! One blow!" I finally understood what that meant. A griffin diving in on a dragon gives its rider just one good attack before it has to fly off. Just one blow.

No doubt the dragon over my head would have torn into that griffin as well (losing just one wing didn't seem to affect its ability to fly at all). Except another griffin was inbound on him. This one actually trailed a banner behind it, flapping green and gold with the colors of Tsillis. Before that moment, I'd thought only Andreans were griffin riders.

The banner streaked down from above and across, from north to south, as if it were aimed for the rocky hillock I stood next to. That perception of its motion made me realize I was forgetting myself. And something especially important that had been on top of that rock. *Valinin.*

I scrambled up the rock, my body sore, but it didn't matter at that moment. The dragon had landed on this rock, flat on top of it. But maybe Valinin had rolled off in the direction of 2nd company. Maybe he was still alive.

I found him at the top of the rock. Yes, still alive. This large block of whatever kind of rock it was had a number of fissures, splits in its top. Valinin's body was jammed into one of the larger of these fissures, a small crevice, twisted partly sideways, pressed down into a mold just big enough that his chest, while crushed, wasn't totally so. His head was still intact, but the angle he was jammed into the rock meant he had to keep his head lifted up off the ground. His right arm was wedged into the crevice and his left was bent backwards in an unnatural shape, obviously broken.

His eyes, which I had never realized before that moment were so green, looked upward at the sky. His face showed no pain, though it was very pale, very close to the paleness of death.

"Valinin?" My voice couldn't manage more at that moment. I'd already seen more death than I'd ever wanted to that day, but seeing Valinin like that nearly broke me.

"Hello, Therin," he said distantly. "I'm glad you're still alive."

"I…" I started to speak, but couldn't continue, as choked up as I was.

"Hey, none of that. Or, save it for later. The men will need you. Somebody…has to lead them."

I wiped my eyes and managed an answer, "They need *you*, Valinin."

He smiled. "Well, that's too bad. 'Cause I'm never leaving this rock. Not alive. Not 'til the God restores this life and I walk in the heav'nly courtyards. So it has to be you."

"Don't say that. We'll find a healer to take care of you. I don't know what to do, Valinin."

"Keep the men fightin'. They don' practice… dispersion… like Andreans. If they run, they're dead. They'll get picked off in ones and twos. So they need to… keep 'em in formation."

"Right, right." I raised my body up, still kneeling, and first scanned the sky for dragons. All four were engaged by griffin riders, around a dozen or so. I had no idea how they knew we had needed them, but I thanked the God under my breath that they were there.

So then I looked down from the rock at our companies. We'd made sure the outer men were covered in mud, but by the appearance of the clusters of our men, our lines collapsed into the center from men turned around to deal with the wounded, the dragons had mostly fired into the center of our formations. Except the blue dragon, which had attacked second company; it had mostly attacked the outside tower shield men. I looked out and I saw a wave of black running our way, in somehow even greater numbers than before.

I cupped my hands and bellowed, as loud as I could, "Form your lines, form your lines! Beastmen coming!" A whistler in 2nd company heard me over the screams of the wounded and repeated the order in high-pitched blasts.

Third and fourth and first reformed just in time. The Southlanders took the places of our spearmen in all these companies. I found out later that even in the confusion of the moment, Alfrin had the presence of mind to come up with the plan of bringing the Southlanders into our formations and Koto had the command presence to execute it. Because without any armor, the Southlanders had an even worse time facing dragon fire than we did.

The beastmen hit us—there must have more of them that crossed from the end of the pass where 3rd battalion had been. What they did was strange. They came as a mass that nearly filled the valley. Where they ran into us, they fought us. Where they didn't hit us, they ran around us, not to hit us from behind, but to keep on running for the other end of the valley. Clearly this attack had a specific goal in mind. Taking the pass.

We fought with beastmen slamming into our shields with the fury of their clubs and with dragons hurling flames down on us whenever they weren't busy with griffins. Still, our formations held. However, we were not holding the pass, just a piece in the middle of it.

I didn't hear until later, but when Valinin had ordered the 4th forward, he'd left some of the supply troops and the medical wagons behind and had ordered them to fall in with the Shos Hill Country militia. Even before the dragons showed up, some of the beastmen that went directly over the mountain had tried to make their way past the militia, past the relatively narrow space running into the mountains on the western end of the valley. But those early enemy warriors, while they'd fought with ferocious strength, had come in only ones and twos and the Shos boys had easily enough dispatched them.

A certain number of minutes after more than half of them passed us (how many exactly I don't know), the beastmen hit the ragged line of the Shos Militia at the rock formation that looks like a gate at the entrance to the valley. These men with mixed equipment and limited training, but plenty of will to fight (one of them told me they were low on whiskey and in a bad mood because of it), put their leather and iron and wooden shields and hammers, spears, swords, and pitchforks into the enemy with a shout of rage. For a good half an hour at least, the Shos boys pushed back when they were pushed and took the blows as powerful as a bear would deliver, yes with broken bones and death, but with no shortage of men from behind willing to step forward to replace the fallen, always jabbing, stabbing, and swinging, giving back to the enemy as bad as they received.

But after a while the beastmen stopped hitting them on their whole line at once. From about a hundred yards away, the beast king called out and the whole mass of them backed off the Shos line.

One of the Shos troops named Nane had a crossbow, and a reputation for being a good shot. "Right eye," he called out. As I understand it, the beastman king wasn't all that far away, but he was surrounded by other beastmen... and was moving. Still, Nane made the shot into the beastman king's eye, just as he called it.

When their king fell, the beastmen started this terrible howling, so loud that I even heard it from our separate battle in the middle of the valley. So mournful was its sound, so anguished and heartfelt, that they didn't seem as much like beasts after that.

But while I was on the highest rock in a depression, wondering what could have made the beastmen howl so movingly, Nane is said to have seen something else in the beastmen's reaction. "They're sure takin' it hard! C'mon, let's hit 'em while they're down!"

He then grabbed up a pike and started off in a sprint, running towards the beastmen. He waived others to follow as he trotted off, and a sizable portion of the Shos line went after him. Over half.

Danl, the giant man I'd given a tower shield to, didn't follow them. Perhaps because he didn't feel like running anywhere.

Nane and his cluster of followers did hit the mass of the enemy. They killed a few, but then the entire body of beastmen turned on them, their howling sorrow transformed in an instant into howling rage. The lead element of Nane's group, including Nane himself, were battered into pieces by club blows in moments. The tail part of his group, in shock and horror turned and sprinted away, back to the Shoss line. Fear, just like laughter, can be contagious, son, and the ones who had never charged forward now saw those of them bold enough to run ahead were now running back like a dog with its tail between its legs. They broke, too, almost all of them, running west through the pass, as if they were going to sprint all the way back to the Shos Hills.

Almost all of them sprinted off. Danl roared at them, "Come back here, you chicken livers!" Anyone trying to run past him he knocked over with his shield and roared at them to get on their feet. Some men he grabbed by the collar of their leather or padded armor as they ran by him and physically whipped them around so they faced forward. Some came to their senses after he did that. Though some turned and ran again.

But in spite of his shouting and grabbing men, for a minute or two there was only one thing standing in the way of the beastmen taking the entire pass. Danl. Three of four of the beastmen took him on and he traded them blow for blow, them swinging with their monster strength, him absorbing it in that tower shield and swinging back at them. The shield strapped to his arm did the most damage, but his sword bit as well as he swung with force even greater than the beastmen. It happens to be the case that the fat old supply sergeant who I'd thought very little of, Marin, commanded his men forward and they were the first to fill in the right side of the line beside Danl. Marin stepped up with his boys into the line. He died right there, a father of four and a grandfather, a supply troop, trying to do the right thing at a bad moment. Danl, the supply boys, and some others, by a miracle of the God managed to hold their place until the rest of the Shos Militia rallied, realizing they were leaving men fighting successfully behind them. Which shamed them into coming back to stand again. Soon enough, the pass was as secure as before. Beastmen alone were not enough to break our hold on the Eagle's Pass.

While the battle for the control of the pass raged miles behind my back, the fate of the 4th battalion rested largely in actions we could do nothing about—the air battles between griffins and dragons. Griffins spent a lot of their time fighting to gain altitude, to be able to streak back down on a lightning attack. They probably would have done a lot better fighting at a lower elevation. (That's just me guessing, based on how hard I found it to breathe there, especially when we first arrived. Though maybe the dragons would have even been faster had all of us been lower.)

But as it was, griffins could only attack part of their time in the air. And when dragon riders weren't busy, they were free to hurl fire down on us. Which we could do nothing about, except to continue to get men muddy and try to hold together.

Only minutes after our unequal air and land battle began, griffin riders began to converge on the blinded orange dragon. Their inbound steaks came in pairs, one heading for the rider, one for the dragon wings. One of the red dragons virtually ignored us and focused on attacking griffins in their recovery climb away from his orange kin. The red dragon that had been nearest to me flew eastward, I don't know why. In the meantime, the blue dragon turned its attention on us.

I remember it hovering, spinning in a coil, blowing fire down in its seemingly endless steady stream of reddish orange flame, just over the height of the spears of 3rd company. I had no idea what to do about this. I lay flat on the top of my rock, watching in shock. After I don't know how long of seeing men burn and scream—it seemed like a very long time, but couldn't have been, I scurried back on hands and knees to Valinin.

"A dragon is…hovering over 3rd…breathing…fire. What should we do?"

"Archers shoot at rider," Valinin replied briefly, in calm, quiet voice.

So as I turned back around to order this very thing, I discovered Alfrin was already on it. Archers from second company, their shield men getting hammered by beastmen, their spearmen with the help of Southlanders and swordsmen engaging the enemy from behind the line, some of their men still smoking from dragon flames, the wounded in a heap, ordered his bowman to fire at the rider of the blue dragon attacking third company. Arrows landed in a volley on the heavily armored rider. But even heavy armor has its gaps and so many arrows were launched that some by chance found their way into the man atop the blue beast, into the joints under the arms and at the small gaps between body and thigh and neck and helmet. He jerked backward and his curved sword fell from his hands. He must have been strapped to his saddle, because while his body went limp, he remained on the dragon.

It became instantly clear the strategy of hovering that left us helpless had been the rider's idea. Because free of the rider, the dragon immediately plunged down into the middle of third company. It whipped its body around, mashing men, snapping quick bites that would rip even a man in iron armor in two. The bodies of men squirted under the dragon's weight, like grapes squeezed between merciless fingers. That is another moment engraved in my mind forever, a sight I cannot unsee.

But almost right away, men from third company fought back in hopeless sword stabs and spear attacks. Especially the Southlanders who they'd let into their ranks. I didn't see one of them running away. And our men rallied to them. I turned again back to Valinin to ask what could be done to help them, but before I could, Alfrin shouted orders and the spearmen and Southlanders in the body of 2nd company charged the dragon. Men rushed into the beast, throwing the weight of their bodies into spear thrusts as they ran, like a dismounted version of Reynaldo's cavalry charge. Many times they bounced off the dragon's hard scales, but not always. Especially the men who ran from the rear towards the front of the dragon got their spear tips at least a finger width or two through the dragon's scales and into its body. Facing a dozen needle pricks, the dragon roared, swinging its head viciously, biting at more men. Crushing them, rending them, but men kept coming, especially the Southlanders, but Mountaineers followed after them, some coming from 4th company after a bit.

I saw with my own eyes the terrible glory of warfare. That each man could overcome his own fear and risk his life for other men is a wonder, especially against such a certain death as a dragon in a frenzy. It is a glory, a triumph of the will. But the price of that glory is so terrible, so horrible, that it is not worth it. Not for the sake of the glory alone. Far better to do something else to exalt life and show the courage of our mortal race—climb a mountain, build a bridge over a dangerous river, something, anything. Something that does not involve men's bodies rent in pieces by forces they have no power to resist. And leaving other men horribly disfigured for the rest of their days—and still others with the memories of these events seared into their minds for every day of the rest of their lives.

And so it was that these men, on the ground, with spears, slew the blue dragon. I suppose between the men burnt to death and those crushed on the ground by the dragon's fall and those who died between the dragon's teeth, about a hundred and fifty men died doing so. With another hundred seriously wounded. But this was only the smallest and weakest of dragons sent against us.

Soon after the blue dragon shrieked its last, I looked up, scanning the sky for dragon, as I'd quickly learned to do. The orange dragon was listing in the air, sideways, drifting east. As griffin riders attacked dragon wings, the sound of which grew louder when there were fewer of them, it became evident it would not much longer remain airborne. I prayed, "Oh the God, oh the God, don't let it land on us." Which of course would have made tactical sense for the rider to have done, to try to take out as many of us as possible with its last breath.

Perhaps the rumor I heard later, which says that over time dragons can regrow their wings, which could mean perhaps even their eyes would heal—perhaps that's why the dragon rider tried to escape over the eastern end of the pass. The orange dragon crashed there, several miles away on the mountain slope, two griffin riders streaking after it.

In the meantime, the two red dragons had taken up circling (the one that had left came back), prowling the air for griffin. Of the dozen or so griffin riders, already over half had fallen. Three of these, including the Andrean in the deep blue of royalty, the Tsillian, and another Andrean, were flying towards the dragons, but breaking off long before they reached them, gaining height, streaking down again,working as a team, keeping the dragons circling. This one advantage the griffins had—during their diving attacks, they flew much faster than the dragons could. And they seemed to have an uncanny knack for knowing when a dragon would hurl fire, because if a dragon attacked from a distance, these three riders always shifted in the air, leaving a massive ball of fire to pass by harmlessly.

Back on our piece of dirt, the survivors of the death of blue dragon, spearmen exhausted, many with broken spear shafts, burns from the spurts of flame that erupted randomly from the beast in its death throes, or broken limbs from the dragon's thrashing, were run upon by beastmen, who bludgeoned many of them to death with their clubs.

Even I knew what to do about that, so I shouted an order from the rock that probably could not be heard. But Alfrin had already commanded 2nd Company to close in on the ruins of the 3rd. What was left of 2nd, that is, because they'd suffered losses as well. Fourth ran into the action as well and between them and the Southlanders they reformed their lines, like they'd been trained to do on a flat, peaceful drill field. But they did it over the body of a dead dragon, over the bodies of their dead and wounded comrades, while under attack. I know the war songs don't even mention stuff like forming lines in the heat of battle, but it's more amazing than it sounds.

At about this same time, when the companies formed up again, I heard the howling of the beastmen behind me that I mentioned before. The howling at the death of their king.

When I looked to my left around then (time in a battle is hard to remember right), I saw 1st company had pulled closer to the well. They'd been the special target of balls of flame from one of the dragons. Some men, because of being muddy and getting muddy again (they were the nearest to the well), had been burned up to three or four separate times, though of course they mainly survived by being on the edge of where a fireball landed. As I said, the main way to survive a dragon attack, is to not be there when it attacks.

Their shift towards the well as their numbers diminished, left the wounded men I'd moved, and many other burned and wounded men, largely unprotected. My eyes caught sight of three beastmen advancing along the trail of wounded First had left, bashing the heads of the wounded in as they caught up to them, headed towards the troops I'd moved next to the rock. I came to my feet and ran, jumping off the rock with a shout, straight at the one closest to me. My bent knees slammed into his chest, along with the force of the fall from above—me, a bigger-than-average man in armor. Yet instead of knocking him flat, I bounced off him and hit the ground, while he only staggered backward.

The wind was knocked out of me, but I rolled over anyway, not able to breathe. I lunged forward on all fours and slashed at the right leg of the beastman I'd just rattled. He fell to his knees and I rammed my blade clear through his throat and out the back of his neck. The other two beastmen grunted and stepped my way. I pulled back on my sword but it was stuck in the neck. I put my left hand on my enemy's forehead and pulled back hard on the sword with my right. It came out partway. But now a beastman was on me. I rolled away as he swung a club almost as big as one of my legs. The impact hit the one I'd killed in the head (who was still on his knees) and removed the head clean off the neck. I scrambled up to run, managing to suck in a single painful breath, but the other of the two headed me off that way, his club raised to swing down and turn my head into a crushed melon.

Out of nowhere an arrow flew into him, as if it sprouted from his upper chest, just above his collar bone. It was in deep, only the tail feathers showing. The one who had been about to kill me reached down and pulled the arrow shaft outward. Big mistake, because an arrow does more damage going out backwards than going in at the pointed end—blood spurted from him as he did so and he fell to the ground. In the meantime I turned sideways, with an eye to the other beastman after me. He suddenly arched his back and howled. I knew without seeing it that another arrow had sprouted.

I dashed for my sword, now easy enough to free from the somehow-still-kneeling headless beastman. I finished off the one with an arrow protruding from his back. My breath returned to me completely. I sucked in a complete lungful of sweet air and scanned for the archer who had saved my life. One of the wounded was holding a bow. I ran over to him, my eyes scanning the skies for dragon as I did so.

"Elin? Is that you?"

"Last I checked," said a familiar voice from a face I no longer recognized.

Some of the other wounded with him were screaming and some moaning. Others were very quiet, like Elin himself. "I'm glad somebody gave you a bow. Though I'm surprised you can use it."

"Me, too," he answered. Somebody had also placed a water skin next to him. I gave him a drink and took one of my own, a long draught of what tasted delicious, even though it was muddy well water. I tried not to think about what I'd seen in that well.

Then I looked up, in what was by then a habit, and scanned the sky for dragon. The one red dragon, three griffin riders were playing tag with—that's a rather flippant way to put it, since they were risking their lives and as long as they did so, the dragon wasn't attacking us. But that was exactly the thought that crossed my mind at the time—tag. The other red dragon had moved out of my view—I was distinctly uncomfortable not knowing what had happened to it (I still don't know, because it never returned, perhaps the rumor that circulated later that griffin riders killed it on the eastern side of the pass was true). Things seemed to be taking a turn for the better. Even the number of beastmen attacking us had visibly diminished. The three I'd just fought actually seemed to be stragglers behind their main body.

"It getting quiet," I said, "Do you suppose we've won?"

Elin answered, "You need to climb the rock and look. To see if more are coming."

"Right," I said, as if I understood and it was no big deal. But in fact I didn't want to climb that rock again. I didn't want to see Valinin wedged in that crevice. I didn't want to know if more enemy were coming. So I walked up to it with a sense of dread—the dread being not just fear of what I'd see up there, but the memory of what I'd already seen and done from the top of that rock.

I climbed it anyway, my body seeming incredibly heavy as I did so, like I was carrying another man on my back. When I reached the top, I looked eastward.

I saw the other end of the valley filling up with formations of regular Eastern troops. "Shit!" I shouted, my heart pounding in my chest. My eyes kept looking though, coolly noting what was going on, almost as if my body was in the possession of two different people—one who had emotional reactions and cursed and one who did what he'd been trained to do.

In the distance, I was not entirely sure if they were eastern regulars or not. But whoever they were, they weren't charging us recklessly. They were assembling formations at that end of the valley, for the evident purpose of sweeping through us all to open up the pass. I know your mother won't appreciate me recording exactly what I said just above this, son, because she believes a man should be able to control his mouth. I believe she is in fact right, but the truth is, the curse word I recorded is what I actually said. And then I said that same word a second time.

I turned back to Valinin. My eyes had avoided him on the climb up.

Whereas he'd been placid before, now he was writhing —as much as he could, wedged into that rock. I stepped towards him.

"Oh, it hurts, Therin, it hurts," his voice said. His face had begun to turn blue, because of the difficulty breathing, I suppose.

"I'm sorry. But I need your help. I don't know what to do." I felt shame at asking him while he was suffering like that, but I really did need him.

For a moment, his body stopped its churning. "What's happening?" I told him what I saw.

"You'll be surrounded. Square up…the men, fire lotsa arrows, take out who you can. You got the extras?" He meant the extra supply of arrows. No, we didn't. The supply wagons were back at the other end of the valley.

"I'll get them," I said, finding a sort of enthusiasm to have a purpose, and I got off the top of that rock as fast as I could, also happy to have an excuse to leave it, if I'm to tell the complete truth. I went down the opposite side of where I'd gone up, towards second company. As I went down, two men I recognized as second company men were going up. As I hit the bottom, to my surprise, I nearly ran into Alfrin talking to Fernesto at the side of his formation, both of them taking advantage of the lull in the battle, just as I had done. Fernesto had found a horse somewhere.

"There's enemy forming up!" I exclaimed.

Both men turned their heads towards me with a look of cool disdain. "We know," said Alfrin.

"We need to make a single formation…um, square…with the remnants of first company and be prepared to…um engage with…our archers!" I was finding it hard to think and speak clearly.

"Is that an order, sir?" Afrin asked.

"Yes," I said, "Though I'm gonna leave you in charge. You're doing…a great job at that. I'll go back to bring the supply of extra arrows up here."

"Very well," said Alfrin. He saluted me, his face expressionless. But his cheeks were flushed red. I can only guess he was angry at me, maybe because it seemed I was fleeing to the rear at a key moment of danger. I don't know if that was it, but I think about it now, after the fact.

Was it true? Was I being a coward? Like everybody else from Iron Mountains, I was taught a man should never "show yellow," but the things people do are not always so clearly all the way brave or all the way afraid. I certainly wanted to get a long way from Valinin, which is a kind of cowardice. But I also genuinely wanted to get help.

I sloppily returned salute and turned to Fernesto. "Can you get me a horse? I need to hurry."

"Can you ride?" he asked, his eyes widened in surprise. Andreans know we Mountaineers rarely ride horses.

"Yes. I can."

"Here, take this one," he said, dismounting. He handed me the reins, "*If* you can mount and ride, then I will find another horse for myself." I mounted with ease, even though my body ached, to the evident surprise of Fernesto. For my part I felt an odd sense of relief that at least one thing I'd learned from my time with Ombree actually proved to be worthwhile.

I pulled the right rein, turning the horse, kicked my heels in, and galloped off, back towards the western end of the valley. The Andrean Reserve Cavalrymen were in clusters of two and three, widely separated from one another in broad formations that formed V shapes if you looked at them. They all waited at that end, spread out. The bodies of Longma and their riders and clumps of dead beastmen spoke to the effectiveness of their previous work. Though at the time, I felt anger to see it. They let us take the brunt of the dragon's ground attack and then swept up the residue afterward.

It never occurred to me at the time there might be a lot in common between my anger and Alfrin's.

There were dead cavalrymen along the way as well. And wounded, some crying out for water.

I reached the other end of the valley, a place that had no name any of us knew before we came there, but which somebody, I don't know who said it first, called "the Valley of Death."

At the western end of the Valley of Death, a ragged line of exhausted Shos Hillcountry militia filled in with some of our healers and supply boys, were sweating, wiping their faces, checking their wounded. Heaps of dead beastmen were all around. Some the Western men were on their knees, praying maybe. Or maybe too exhausted to stand. Their eyes, most of them, were staring off into the distance, thousands of yards away. Many of the wounded were asking for water, some begging. Their fellow militiamen gave them whiskey instead.

That's where I saw Marin dead, in front of his boys. I felt guilty for having thought of him as greedy and lazy. Not that he wasn't those things, but his death in combat seemed to make the worse aspects of his nature seem a lot less significant.

"C'mon, we need to move the war supplies forward!" I shouted. *Might as well move them all*, some part of my mind told me. Or at least what was ready to move.

Though actually none of it was ready to move; the ox carts were not hooked up. It took a half hour to fix that, even with Shos militiamen stepping in to help. I was lucky the oxen were alive when I think about it.

We rolled forward with five wagons in the group I led, one of them a healer rig, just the most significant stuff.

Eleven supply troops and healer assistants came with me back towards the eastern end of the Valley of Death.

We tried to hurry them a bit, but ox carts are inherently slow. The healer wagon was pulled by horses, so it could go faster, but they were keeping pace with us. And a fast walk is about the best you can expect from oxen. Since the valley slopes upward at the far end, we were able to see the eastern end of the valley better than if we'd been in the depression cutting across its center. Almost like a riverbed, but with water only at the well.

We saw the Eastern formations marching forward. At their front was the orange dragon, on foot, undulating up and down and a bit side to side as it walked on its eight small legs. I felt a bit of surprise the loss of its eyes hadn't disabled it more. Along with that bit of surprise came a lot of fear. The dragon would hit our formation on the ground, just as the blue dragon had done. *O the God help us!*

As I scanned the sky for dragon, I saw a flash of red on my left, quite far away, past the other end of the valley actually. But my eye also caught a glimmer of gold, on the right side of the clear blue sky above me.

Almost completely free of clouds now, the valley had warmed from the coldness of the night. A bright and cheerful day, as if it were a picnic holiday and we were bringing the meal—except this picnic contained a spot of gold in the sky. Which was growing larger by the instant (while the red one grew smaller and disappeared).

Impossibly wide wings moved up and down nearby the spot of gold. I saw the wings more by their movement as a thin line of darkness against the sky than I was able to really observe them.

As the golden dragon approached and got larger in the sky, I saw the moving wings grow into twins, two pairs of wings of griffins, moving in the same direction as the golden dragons. I hadn't realized none of the griffins were no longer over our heads. Until that moment.

They were chasing the golden dragon—or perhaps following after it, which isn't quite the same thing. As if they'd flown east engaging the red dragon, but now were coming back west.

The golden dragon flew fast as its body wriggled like it was slithering through the sky, like a snake zipping downhill through rocky terrain. Its wide reptilian cat mouth was grinning—grinning as if eager to kill. The griffins were far behind, but gaining altitude as they flapped.

The dragon zoomed downward as it came to the depression in the center of the valley. We were about two hundred yards away from it and the Eastern formations maybe another three hundred further. I had this horrible fear it was going to use the breath that we had all heard the golden dragon can breathe forever, without stopping, on our men in front of us in the depression.

The fear changed its nature when the dragon zoomed right over the depression, hovering low, headed straight towards us at full speed. Growing larger and larger as it raced through the valley.

"Dive!" I eventually shouted by some instinct. I jumped off the right side of the seat in front of the boxy supply wagon, landing flat and hard on the dusty ground. The driver jumped off to the left. The middle seat guy didn't make it out before a ball of flame slammed into both him and the wagon. Unlike a number of the burnt I saw that day, he died within the first heartbeats. The oxen were badly burned and dashed forward for a bit but then stopped moving and bellowed like calves separated from their mothers until they, too, died. But it took around an hour before their bellowing silenced. Their animal cries of pain formed a backdrop to events for a while, audible if I thought to listen for them. I would have ordered them killed to be put out of their misery, but as events happened, I could barely deal with all that happened with the lives of men, let alone the animals.

The golden dragon ignored us past its first strike. It turned back around and went after the Andrean horsemen. Its breaths not only seemed to fall without end, they came more quickly than from the dragons of other colors. The horsemen dispersed, but it hunted them down, much faster than any of them, hurling its deadly breaths with rapid and fatal accuracy. It seemed what had happened to the *longma* had reached Eastern ears. The dragon rider's clear intent was to never let it happen again.

I stared for I'm not sure how long, but then came to myself. I wasn't the only one staring. "Move forward!" I bellowed at the men. "Get those supply wagons *forward*!"

They followed my order. As they did so, our four remaining wagons were whipped forward by their drivers. Actually the medical wagon had taken off at a gallop just before I gave the order to do so. But the other three ox carts took more work to get on the move. I scanned the skies for dragon and saw two shapes with wings folded in, diving in from on high.

I felt a sickness in the pit of my stomach about the two of them taking on this golden monstrosity alone. *The God help them!* passed through my mind, but I didn't really have a lot of time for prayer. I barked at the supply boys while behind me oxen bellowed and horses screamed. By the time the first supply wagon reached the southern side of the depression where 4th battalion made its stand, with me literally pushing on one of the oxen to make it go faster, our men had started launching arched volleys of arrows at the approaching mass of Easterners, now 300 yards out.

It's worth noting here, son, what an unusual thing it is for a military unit to take a defensive position in a depression. It's usually a bad idea, because if an enemy has to come uphill to get you, they have to work harder, while you get good opportunities to attack down on their vulnerable heads. Vice versa when you're downhill from them. Military units all around the world put a pit or moat or something *in front* of their defensive line so an attacking enemy has to go down, then run back up, vulnerable to attack, or traps even, as they do so. But a combination of circumstances fixed our place at the low spot—the well, the mud at the bottom of our line across the valley, the vulnerability of the beastmen to attacks to their legs, putting them at a disadvantage going downhill, the fact the dragons seemed to find it somewhat harder to attack something down low than what was up on the plain or on a hill (only somewhat harder, but still).

Now it came to the advantage of the 4th Battalion in another way. Something nobody planned, but which happened. The Eastern crossbows generally have a longer range than our bows. But they fire them on a flat line, aiming straight for what they shoot at, where we are used to firing in an arc, lobbing arrows into an enemy at a higher angle. So it happened that the Eastern crossbowmen couldn't get a straight shot at our troops, because we were below their line of sight, while we were lobbing arrows into them as a unit.

I'm not sure why I'm saying "we" because I wasn't down in the depression at that moment, though the medic wagon with their pair of horses had already gone down on the south side of the big rock, that is, to the right from where I faced. Me and the supply boys were actually in the enemy line of sight. A certain number of the mass of the Eastern army facing us, by no means all of them, began firing crossbow bolts across the top of the depression at us.

But that proportion, whatever it was, amounted to dozens of bolts whizzing our way in a continuous attack. "Get down!" I bellowed, for once reacting to a danger as it happened instead of staring with my jaw dropped open. The ox I'd been shoving along died almost immediately. But since we were being shot at from near the limit of the crossbow range, there was a weirdness to what got hit and what didn't. The ox on the right, where I was, died almost right away, as I said. The other, though it got hit, never fell, though I assume it eventually did die. It bellowed and bucked and the driver and I had the "fun" of trying to unhitch the wagon under fire, on our bellies, the left ox surging forward and back. The driver took a crossbow bolt that found a natural gap in his armor, where it had not been cinched tight. It passed clean through the meat of the left side of his neck at moment when he lifted his head up to look ahead. It passed halfway through, the sharp tip pointed somehow upward and the feather end down.

"You're hit!" I yelled. "Get down!"

"I am?" he questioned, like he didn't believe me. He did hit the ground though, falling to his side. His right hand reached across to touch the side of his neck and his eyes widened in astonishment. I would probably have just stayed down but that ox kept lunging back and forth and it was clear we could be crushed. Somehow I unhitched the coupling bolt in a pause between the ox's spasms. Then we crawled back to the rear of the wagon. The other two wagons were in line with us, so our wagon protected them. (Unlike dragon fire, the wooden shell of a supply wagon will stop a crossbow bolt.)

Garin was the guy with an arrow sticking though his neck. He was seventeen years old. When we got back to the front of the next wagon, I saw the assistant driver had dismounted and moved forward. He saw Garin and said, "That's messed up! Let me help you!"

This other supply boy, who was Garin's close friend—his name was Udin—reached out fast, grabbed the tail of the crossbow bolt and yanked backward on it. "No don't!" I said. But it was too late.

I could describe in detail what happened after that. My memory captures all too well how Garin bled to death in way not unlike my uncle. But I'd rather skip over these details. We all knew—or at least I thought we knew—that a shaft in such a wound helps seal off the bleeding by the pressure of its location. Only a healer should remove such a thing. I in fact had a half-formed plan in my mind to find one of the saws in the wagon and cut off the ends of the bolt, leaving the middle inside him until some future point, when the healers could take care of him.

Months later, by some miracle making it home alive, Udin would take a section of rope set aside as a replacement for the kind used to lift ore gates, go into the tool shed of the ore processing shop where he worked, and hang himself to death. Though of course, Udin had just made a mistake, under pressure, when none of us felt very sane. If he took his life because of what happened with Garin, whatever shame he felt wasn't worth trading his own life to erase. He should have found forgiveness for himself from the God, as I have struggled to find myself.

At the actual moment, I yelled at him in anger. I wonder to this day if I shouldn't have done that. If that led in some way to how he ended himself. But I can't live in that guilt. It wasn't an easy day for any of us. There is a limit to what any man can do.

After that horror, my mind returned to our mission. Our archers would be needing the extra arrows. We had to get the cart in front of us forward. So we pushed it from behind, having to actually pull it back and to the right first, to get around the dead ox.

When not doing something else, my head would jerk upward and around, as if on its own, looking for dragons. Just as we managed to get the cart rolling forward again, I saw a griffin streaking in, the one with the green banner of Tsillis trailing behind it. Its wings were tucked into its sides and the rider had his sword held high in the air. He twisted in midair, as I'd seen done before, and sliced off not one but two of the golden dragon's wings that beat with the noise of thunder, off the left side. But the dragon instantly reversed direction from its pursuit of a cluster of horsemen and caught the griffin's hindquarters in its teeth and ripped. The eagle claws of the griffin forelegs scratched at the dragon in reply, but seemed to have no effect on the scaled beast. The dragon shook its head and chunks of furred flesh, visible even from my distance, flew into the air. The griffin tumbled downward, its rider separating from it mid-air, hitting the ground hard, his body crumpling as he did so. The dragon, hovering above them, turned the two broken bodies into a blazing funeral pyre.

But as it launched one of its endless fireballs, the griffin in the blue of Andrean nobility streaked in. And sliced off two of the dragon's wings on the opposite side of where the dead Tsillian had struck. A griffin wing peeked out briefly from the western beast's tucked-in bundle and our ally in the air veered off sharp to the left. The dragon fired flame at it, but missed.

I tell this like I was casually watching, but I wasn't. I had my shoulder in the back of a supply wagon and was shoving with all the strength I could muster. Crossbow bolts were still thudding into the front of the cart and I was shouting instructions at men behind me. Screams erupted from beyond the front of the cart along with a roar from what I knew had to be the orange dragon on foot, reaching our front lines. But still, in spite of all of that, I was watching the sky, the great drama in the air, as best I could. All of our lives were at stake, since over time, the golden dragon could effectively kill every soldier on the ground without even risking flying low enough that we could fight back.

But there was more to it than just survival. Now, just one griffin remained, against the dragon all of us had heard was the worst and fiercest of all.

At some point I caught a glimpse of the griffin beating its wings hard and the dragon chasing it. The loss of four wings seemed to affect the golden dragon much more than it had the orange beast I'd witnessed losing wings before. The golden dragon must have weighed more—its body was certainly thicker. It could not gain altitude as quick as the last of the griffins. The griffin and its rider were leaving it behind. I could see it in my mind as I imagined the future, gaining altitude again, plunging in on fast attack after fast attack, cutting the dragon piecemeal until it died.

What I conceived in my mind, like everything else I ever imagined about combat, wasn't what actually happened. As the griffin's wings spread wide in an elegant downstroke, the flames erupted from that grinning dragon mouth, yes, from a distance of what must have been several hundred yards. But this time its aim was true—and a griffin wing at full length is a large target. One of the griffin wings, the right one, erupted into flame. Not the entire wing, just from the middle joint outward. But the griffin immediately began to falter in the air, tumbling downward. Some part of my mind realized, as I still shoved forward on the wagon, that the griffin had been west of us, traveling east, almost parallel to our position, but south of us. Now as it tumbled, the griffin and its rider were spinning to the north. Towards where we were.

The griffin impacted the ground, not twenty yards south of, that is to the right of, our third supply wagon, the one in the rear. It tumbled a bit as it hit and the rider must have hit his head on the ground before the eagle-headed creature with a body half lion, half eagle and its very long ruined wings came to a halt, more or less upright. The griffin's body heaved unevenly as it tried to breathe, its chest cage visibly shattered. Clearly it was about to die. The rider had a dirty spot on his helmet where he'd hit the ground. Other than that, he didn't have any obvious injuries. But he made no effort to clear out of the saddle like I was expecting him to do.

I swore. Then I turned to the man on my left, "Keep this wagon moving forward!" And then I ran backwards, staying close to our wagons at first, then dashing across to the griffin rider. A pair of supply boys from the third wagon were already on the way. We came at him from the west side, so the body of the griffin was partially between us and the crossbowmen. Though most of them were no longer firing at us anymore. They'd marched close enough to the center of the valley that they could shoot at 4th Battalion, who was in the fight of their lives.

We got to the rider. His legs were strapped in, but he wasn't trying to cut himself free. He'd lost his very long sword in the tumble down or impact on the dirt, but he had a dagger at his side and could have cut himself free as much as we could.

He wasn't doing that. We could hear his voice through the helmet that covered most of his face, which looked an elegant version of an upside down bucket with eye slits, a bucket with a dirty spot and a dent in the back where he'd hit the ground.

His voice moaned. I didn't know why. "Are you injured?" I shouted at him as we cut him down and pulled him beside the body of his still-dying griffin, on the west side with us, so the body oriented north-south would offer us some protection from enemy fire, still dying oxen bellowing in the background somewhere.

"Oh my dear friend," his voice said. And other things I didn't quite catch. I realized he was weeping for his griffin. What kind of bond is there between griffins and their riders? I had no idea.

"What should we do with him?" asked one of the supply boys, his voice raising anxiously. "Don't you suppose the dragon will come after him?"

"Take off his helmet," I ordered.

They fumbled a bit with the buckles used to secure it in place. But only a bit. Soon enough the helmet came off.

Then I saw the face of the griffin rider, the one who had been flying overhead, attacking the dragons who'd attacked us. With a shock I realized I recognized this face. It was Prince Rory-Galstaff.

⊣⊦ Chapter 10 ⊨

n the ring canyon, the bolt guided by Dario found its mark and killed one of the mages. When the few Shos Hillcountry militia still alive made it up the mountain, they found Alfredo's dead body, higher up than the mages. He had circled around somehow and with an Eastern crossbow he carried with him from the First Dragon War, shot and killed one of the Rysshurian mages.

The other one had cooked his brain, of course. They found Alfredo's horse around the side of the mountain and brought it down to the medical company, which had other horses (the Andreans there were in bad shape at that point, all either dead or wounded).

Arta went into hard labor, but she insisted that Dario send a magical message to the Iron Mountains hospital, which was near the Bond headquarters camp, so they could send over a runner to the headquarters—so somebody could send griffin riders. The griffins that came to our rescue.

If it hadn't been for her insisting on that, insisting on saving and bringing Dario, insisting that she needed to be there with her medical company before that—well, maybe we all would have been dead by the time the griffins arrived in that high mountain valley, because the Andrean message riders didn't arrive at headquarters for hours after our medics had already warned the Bond commanders.

I do wonder sometimes if maybe someone else might have sent the message if she hadn't. But she insists that nobody else cared, everyone else was too preoccupied with their own wounded and wounded Shos militia and wounded Andreans. But I don't know. The God works in unknowable ways.

Arta treated the wounded, too, with her company. For a while she did, until the labor came too fast and hard.

She wanted to come up to help with the wounded up in the high valley too, especially after she heard dragons were attacking us. But she could not. Her body had another appointment for her, one she could not resist.

The thing I said about every man having a limit applies to women, too, as tough and as stubborn as they can be. Sometimes they do things no man can do—like birthing a baby on a battlefield. But even women have their limits. Just like men. Just like Rory-Galstaff and I.

The prince's eyes were filled with tears. He looked back at me vacantly. Obviously not recognizing me. But I hadn't had as full a beard when he saw me last.

"Should we leave him?" asked a nervous supply boy. "The dragon saw him fall. It's bound to come back for him!"

The prince wasn't doing anything for himself at the moment. Whether it was because of head injury or his loss or whatever other reason, at that instant, leaving him behind while saving ourselves would have been simple and natural.

Something that perhaps no else would even know we did. Something no one would have blamed me for doing.

"Take him with us," I ordered. "And let's get outta here!"

The two supply boys took either side of his chest and I took his legs, and we scurried back to the supply wagons. I scanned the sky for dragon. The golden dragon was quite high up, but apparently headed our way.

"Dear the God, dear the God, dear the God," I said under my breath and "Shit!" said one of the supply boys who saw the same thing. Both reactions are natural under the circumstances, but since it's clear to me the God is real and at least at times hears prayers and has a plan—though one with aspects mere mortals will never understand—I'd say my reaction was the better way to respond. Though in reality, my own mouth had both cursed and prayed with shameful inconsistency.

"Hide him, hide him!" I shouted as we ran up to the trail vehicle, not having the slightest idea how to do that.

Fortunately for me, the supply corporal in the driver's seat was clearer-headed than I was. "Throw'im under the wagon!" He pulled his oxen team to a halt as he said it.

We stuffed him under. He wasn't limp like a dead man, but he didn't move for himself or resist us in any way either. I crouched by the side of the wagon and craned my neck around its edge in time to see a fireball flying down from on high. "Incoming!" I shouted. And *everybody*, all five of us in the area, scrambled to get under the wagon.

The fireball's heat made us sweat and the light brightened the wagon's undercarriage. The blast struck the dying griffin, not us.

"I think I just pissed myself," said one of the supply boys that had been out with me.

"You don't have to announce it to the world, Rorin!" said the other one, who'd been with me at the griffin's side.

I looked at Rorin's face and saw him flushing red, his eyes turned down in shame. "That's all right, Rorin," I told him. "I did myself, so much I ran out of piss a long time ago."

I realized I needed to know where the dragon was. I could have ordered someone else to look, but I was the one who needed to know. It was my job; I was bound by my duty, so I peeked my head out from under the cart.

"The dragon's gone back to chasing Andreans."

"Thank the God!" said the corporal. But I didn't feel thankful at all about that. Poor them.

"We still need to get these arrows forward. And I don't want the dragon or its rider to see who we've decided to rescue. How do we do that?"

He rubbed his black-stubbled chin for a moment. "If we had armor we could put him in that. Make him look like one of us."

I answered, "But none of these wagons carry armor. Though we could have one of our guys strip down."

"Naw," said the corporal. "But we got chain netting up above. We could make a…chain net or something to fasten him underneath, and keep 'em under the wagon, even when we move."

"That might be the dumbest idea I've ever heard of." He flushed red.

"But it's a lot better than any idea I've got. So you do that. Make sure he isn't draggin' on the ground. He's a bit out of his mind, I think, so strap him in. I'm gonna get the other wagons moving forward."

"Got it, sir!"

I crawled out from underneath that wagon and ran up to the next. The second already began moving forward. Its oxen were unsteadily pushing the first cart, their heads to its back, as were some of the men in the spaces left by the oxen, as I had done. Its forward movement was slow. At a literal crawl, because I got on my hands and knees, I passed the second wagon and got behind the first (staying low of course because crossbow bolts were still flying our way). A supply boy had crawled underneath the first wagon and from there had a shield covering his face. At intervals, he'd glance past incoming crossbow bolts and keeping guiding the wagon forward.

By that kind of hard effort, inch by inch led to yard by yard, and we covered the remaining fifty yards or so to the rear of our brethren fighting in the depression that cut across the valley. I heard many shouts and screams in front of us, but there was so much noise on the battlefield, it was like the mind could only hear part of it at once.

When we actually arrived at the back of our formation, we showed up there, by the mercy of the God, just as the arrows on hand were running out. Warriors first shocked by our arrival helped move the wagons down on the south side of the rock I'd known so well. Valinin's rock.

In my absence, the orange dragon, the one we'd hoped was dead, but which had returned to attack on foot, had hit our formation. It did so while Eastern crossbowmen were finally in range of our troops. The survivors say this was the very worst moment of the battle, dealing with both a roaring, angry dragon, and the blur of the enemy crossbow attack. I missed that entire part of the battle. Which bothers me at times—at times an inner voice tells me I should have been there and rises up to condemn me as a coward for not having been. Though I try to ignore that voice. I did what I could at the time. Even if it wasn't entirely the best thing.

Koto and Alfrin and Fernesto led men on the attack at various moments against the thrashing but fireless beast. Koto had been hit with crossbow bolts four times, but either by the strangeness of what no one can explain or by the plan of the God—though the two things may in fact be one and the same—his wounds had been through and through injuries to his limbs like the one that wound up killing Garin. A healer from the medic wagon had used cutters to remove the front and backs of Koto's bolts. Fernesto had taken plenty of hits in his armor, bolts somehow missing his head. His Andrean long sword had in fact delivered the blow that finished off that dragon.

Alfrin died in this engagement with the orange dragon. That's why I never got to ask him what he was thinking when I ran off to fetch arrows.

After the dragon died, killing who knows how many men before it did, the Eastern troops had the perfect opportunity to charge into our ranks. But I don't know—maybe because there were bodies of two dead dragons in that depression and innumerable beastmen (whose bodies had been stacked up into protected firing positions for our archers), they chose not to. Instead, they kept up the assault of crossbowmen, firing in ranks but not simultaneously, each crossbowman picking a target and firing within what must have been a time limit, then kneeling in turn as each rank fired, a deep formation some eight ranks back, which as a whole managed to keep firing continuously.

In the meantime some of their formations began to flank our battalion on both the North and South. I suppose they may have intended to surround us from all sides before attacking, as

Valinin had anticipated. (It was a tactic they'd used before in the First Dragon War, and was obvious enough, anyway.)

Our troops, in the act of returning the crossbow attacks, each bowman shooting on his own, nearly ran out of arrows by the time our wagons arrived. Though many were firing bolts back. Though the bolts being shorter than the arrows meant the bows could not be fully drawn, so they could only be launched back with partial force.

I like to try to think about what happened from a strategic point of view. "Try" because I don't have all the information. And "try" because it's hard for me to be objective about things. But the enemy had already shown a willingness to blow past us to get wherever they were going. Clearly killing all of us that held the pass was not one of their strategic goals. Getting past us was good enough. They in fact tried multiple times to run right around us. Clearly the beastmen were intended to break our ranks and open up the route for everybody else. It seems then the *longma* were to streak through the Eagle's Pass and make some kind of lightning attack on Bond forces on the other side, one perhaps designed to draw men away from the main pass, to open it up. Or perhaps to attack our supply chain. The dragons were called forth to facilitate the breakthrough and probably to do some more hard, fast attacking out west of the pass to crumple our lines and prepare the way for the Eastern regulars who would follow up afterward.

Their problem was, we kept screwing up their plan.

The Andrean Reserve Cavalry, old men mostly, the youngest of them in their late 40s up to the oldest in their 70s, had done a lot of the work in killing beastmen and the *longma*. Their efficiency was the reason the golden dragon was hunting them down, the dragon that it was said was ridden by Kung Tzu himself. But by the time I got the supply wagons to our troops, the Andrean Reserve Cavalry had ceased to exist as a fighting unit. Which did not mean all of them were dead—but most of them were. Though some had been thrown from horses and some had found corners in the valley to hide themselves in. But only a few still lived, because the golden dragon did its work well.

Perhaps if the remnants of the 4th Battalion had run out of arrows, the Eastern regulars would have simply continued to bypass us. Focusing on their strategic goals, still hoping to get past the Shos Militia and make some kind of important strategic strike on Western Bond forces on the other side of the pass.

But it so happened that a lull in crossbow shooting took place—their own supply apparently began to run low—at about the same time the supply carts I brought hit the depression. "Arrows!" I shouted, not able to think of better, clearer orders at the moment. The supply boys unbolted the wooden sides of the carts, which fell outward, revealing bundle after bundle of hollow-shaft steel arrows, the ones Valinin and I had designed together to go with the steel bows we invented.

And running around mangled and moaning, crushed and screaming bodies, over ground made wet with blood, the supply boys, some of the bowmen who responded on their own, and I, managed to get arrows out to our still-shooting bowmen. There were around 50 of them left. Elin included. Somebody, I don't to this day know who it was, shouted orders, and our archers took turns lobbing long shots at eastern forces crossing to our north and ones crossing to our south. They were passing us by in such large numbers, in such a rush as to not be sure to be out of our bow range, that our shooting, which really was more of a harassment than something truly able to stop them (because there were so many of them), happened to kill a fair number of Eastern troops. That particular battlefield reality came with a consequence.

"Dragon's coming—dragon's coming!" somebody shouted.

I looked out to the west, where I'd last seen the dragon. It was far off, but yes, coming our way. At the moment my arms were full of bundles of arrows we keep bound in leather straps. I dropped off half the stack of bound arrows at the archer closest to me and the other half at the archer next to him, who was caked with cooked mud and who fired his bow in spite of red and blistered fingers.

"What do we do, sir?" asked one of the supply boys, looking directly at me, at the verge of panic. That's the first moment it occurred to me that I might be the only officer still alive.

I paused for a moment, wondering. Then, dread or no dread, I scrambled up to the top of that rocky hillock, in hopes Valinin would have an answer for me. *He'll know what to do. He always does,* I thought.

And in the piece of rock where his body had been wedged, Valinin was there, his head tipped backwards so the back of his head finally rested on ground. His skin had a bluish tint and eyes were closed and his jaw was open wide. He was no longer flailing or struggling and with his mouth opened, his face almost looked like he was grinning. As if the last thing he'd seen was the welcoming arms of the God.

I would have liked to have had the time to say goodbye to him, to pray over his body. Or even to stand there in shock. But there was no time for any of that. I had a duty I was bound to.

"Get more water from the well!" I bellowed down. "Make yourselves wet and muddy!" As I looked down from the rock at exhausted men, sluggishly responding to my order, I realized what I was saying wasn't enough. "Fourth battalion! You've killed two dragons today! Looks like we'll have to kill another before bedtime!"

I don't know what I was expecting to hear when I said that. Cheers maybe. Or enthusiasm. I got complete silence and a few angry glares. But one of the senior sergeants began shouting after I did (maybe he was the same person giving orders before). "You heard the man! Get your butts moving! We are still alive and might just stay alive if we fight with all we've got. But if we lay around, if we don't even try, we are as good as dead! We have families; we have wives and children— let's come back alive for them. MOVE! MOVE! MOVE!"

He got more out of them than I did. But it was actually the remaining Southlanders that responded quickest after Koto (at that very moment a healer was cutting the ends off the bolts that passed through his body) shouted orders in the Southlander language, just after the Sergeant did. Then the Southlanders jumped up from the places they'd been under cover (to avoid incoming crossbow bolts) and they ran towards the well and began fetching water, shouting in rhythm one of their battle cries, which repeated just a few words, none of which I understood.

When that happened, then the Mountaineers really started moving. Long spears were pulled up from the dirt, archers sought better positions, men checked their dagger blades, while others sought spots to wallow in mud—even if the mud was made wet by the dark red of the dead and still dying.

I glanced back. The dragon was moving quite slow, much slower and making much more noise than the others had done. It would be perhaps as much as ten minutes before it hit us. Clearly the loss of wings affected it more and more over time. Even if it could breathe flames forever, it might not be able to fly forever. This thought inspired another one in me.

I cupped my hands to my mouth before shouting. "Supply section! Grab the shield chains and any ropes from the wagons. Get them up here—move it!"

Perhaps because I'd worked closely with them before, they were more responsive to my commands. Five of the supply boys moved up to my position in about two minutes with the chains that had been used to hide Prince Rory-Galstaff and a number of other chains, along with a single fifty-foot section of rope. (At the time I had no idea where the prince had gone since, but I found out later somebody moved him near Elin.) When they got to me, I said, "We need to anchor the chains to the rock!" Me saying that provoked a couple of confused looks, but they didn't ask why. But they did wonder how.

"We don' got any pins to drive into the rock to secure a chain," said one. While others gave puzzled looks.

"Here," I said, picking up one end of the chain and wrapping it around my waist. "We've got clip pins, right? To link different sections of chain together?"

"Yes, sir; that's right," several voices replied.

"I'll hold this end of the chain taut and you wrap it around the rock in big loops. At least three times around, wedged in good so it's anchored. Then you clip the loops together, tight as you can get them. That'll anchor the chain. And we'll need more than one length to throw up on the dragon, because I bet it can break one loop of chain easy enough."

When the supply boys heard that from me, I saw more than one pair of eyes grow wide with surprise, but they scrambled forward to execute my will. They looped chain around rock while I held it tight. They laid out three loops of chain linked to anchored chain, each about fifty yards long, while I freed myself from the chain. They moved fast, but the first blazing fireball slammed into our ranks before they'd finished. Lucky for us, it was aimed at archers to our left and not at our position.

I looked over my shoulder and saw that the dragon, still several hundred yards off but closing the distance, was having a hard time maintaining altitude. The wings it had lost were towards the back of its body, and while its head was quite high in the air, its tail drooped. *Oh the God, oh the God,* I prayed. *May this work.*

"Koto!" I shouted down. "I need some help up here! Three of your men with the best throwing arms." The dragon's first breath had done very little damage to the unit as a whole, since most of the men had the cover of dead bodies around them (far too many of whom were not beastmen) and had made themselves wet. I suppose the archer's bows or their strings would have burned up if they were not made of steel. Some did break when exposed to heat on the first draw afterwards. But most of the bows continued to shoot the entire battle.

Koto shouted in response and four of his men scrambled upward, followed shortly afterward by Koto himself. I suppose he believed in supplying more than the minimum. I didn't object.

Several bowmen now took shots at the dragon, since it had closed to 50 yards. I shouted down to them, "Shoot at the rider if you get a shot! Don't waste arrows on the dragon!"

It took longer than it had before for the dragon to throw fire down on us. Longer between attacks, I mean. The fireballs themselves streaked downward with the same speed and destructive force when they came. So the dragon had only fired one more time, to the right of the rock, when it stumbled into our trap.

I've wondered how it could have failed to see us and have concluded it must have. But while the dragon had to have seen us, the rider was mounted on a beast flying in a nearly vertical position, head over tail, the dragon's exposed belly shielding him from our archers. The rider could lean to his left or right and see in either of those directions. But he could not see directly in front of himself, due to the dragon's body being in the way. And it so happened where he flew in lined up with the great rock I stood on.

Thinking about it, trying to imagine what the rider saw and thought, it made sense for him to line up with the rock. The last time the rider may have had a clear view of it, probably only one person, me, was standing on it. While the bulk of potential enemies were on either side, on the ground. Hovering over the rock would provide a pivot point from which to rain down death from above. The plan, if that's what he really had in mind, made sense. We just happened to change things before the plan could be executed.

The tail flew right over our heads, only some five yards or so above us. The dragon held it in an upward curve, forming a loop, a natural place for the chains to go. I felt a sudden horrible fear that the beast would merely straighten the tip of its tail, making the chains slide off with no effect. Fire flew down from the dragon's mouth, in the general direction of Elin and those around him, to the left of the rock.

Even if it was an empty-headed plan, a good-idea-fairy concept gone wild, there was no other choice. Without bringing the dragon down, it could simply hover and throw down fire until all of us were cooked to death. I pantomimed throwing something up into the air and three Southlanders hurled chains, all of which passed over the target area of the loop in the dragon tail. The same Southlanders reached out for the chains as they came down the other side, joined by the surviving members of the Supply Section of the 4th Battalion, Iron Mountains Province Volunteers.

They pulled and the beast overhead, clearly still struggling with its own weight, lurched noticeably downward. A voice shouted, "Secure the chain!" and I don't even know if it was me shouting because of how fast everything happened. It might have been the supply corporal. Before anyone could react to the voice, the enemy moved.

I suppose it was the dragon, not the rider, whose first impulse was to lunge higher in the air by sudden greater flapping of wings, whose thundering hum grew deeper and louder at that moment, the wind it blew down on us flowing harder. The dragon lunged up, hauling six or seven men holding chains into the air, dangling, their feet off the ground, holding on to chains with all that was in them.

The dragon lunged upward with enough force to lift the men, but not enough to pull its still curved tail through the hasty loop, nor enough to break the chains. It seemed to be straining at the limit of what it could lift. My only thought was to try to help by adding to the weight. I grabbed the fifty-foot rope and tied off a hasty loop around my waist, securing it in a square knot my uncle had taught me as a boy. I tried to throw the rest of the rope over the loop but the rope impacted the side of the bobbing-up-and-down dragon tail.

Koto snatched it from the ground and threw it, making it over. I grabbed the other end of the rope and so did he. Our added weight caused the dragon to droop in the air. But it still lifted us off the ground.

"Need help!" I bellowed, meaning to bring the dragon all the way down. Koto shouted in Southlander at the same moment.

At around that same time, the supply corporal, hanging on to the loop closest to the tip of the tail, jammed a clip pin through a loop of chain as the dragon jerked. I realized I had a pin I'd tucked into my belt. While holding on to the other end of the rope wrapped around me with my left hand, I pulled the pin from my belt and jammed it into one end of a chain loop (the one closest to the head), the pin making a "click" as it locked in place. I twisted and jammed the clip into another loop of chain. In the twisting, shaking motion, my finger got caught in a loop of chain, which suddenly jerked upward, shearing the end of my right index finger off at the second joint.

I pulled the hand back in surprise. I barely felt any pain. I looked in astonishment for a moment at the blood spurting out, then squeezed a tight fist, my thumb applying pressure to my finger stub to stop the bleeding.

Meanwhile, without me being aware of exactly when it happened, other men, mostly Southlanders, grabbed the rope and chains, yanking the dragon downward.

As my feet touched down again on the rock, I craned my neck upward. Some hundred or so yards above me the rider twisted in his seat. Twisted in the dragon saddle, his head, fully covered in an ornate golden Eastern helmet that was unlike anything I'd seen Kung Tzu wear, was pointed downward. Right at me.

The dragon twisted backwards. Even though thicker than the other dragons, it was still supple as a snake. "Forward, forward!" I shouted, but Koto and the supply corporal were shouting too and already running. My body, which felt sick to the stomach at the moment and weak, somehow propelled me forward, eastward, towards the front edge of our rocky hillock. Heat erupted towards my back but I didn't look back until I reached the point where any further running would send me flying down the rock.

Our intuition was right. The dragon twisted and hurled fire, but by running towards its head, towards the middle of its body, we put the bulk of its body between us and its fiery breath. But not everyone reacted in time. Three flaming bodies in mountaineer chainmail tumbled down the rock. Two screamed and one did not scream, but maintained control, landing into the nearest patch of mud and rolled. I don't know why, but having seen that disturbs my memories nearly as much as remembering the two who screamed.

"Here it comes again!" shouted the supply corporal. I didn't bother to look up to verify it was twisting in the air our way once more. We ran back where we came from. This time though the dragon rider dropped his beast down, a head lunging towards its trapped tail, its body forming a giant loop in the air, moving like a snake. Though the face of this golden dragon, like all the others, wasn't like a snake's. It had that wide mouth, with its lips pulled apart, like a grinning cat with golden scales.

I backpedaled while Koto pulled the sword my uncle had given him from a leather scabbard he held at his waist with a rope belt. The dragon made a loop that anticipated where I and the cluster of others would go. That grinning cat head was flying towards me…and I tumbled backwards down the side of the rock, losing my footing and direction in my haste. As I fell backward, before I hit ground, my mind captured an image, like a painting in full color, but with only the center clear—the outside was blurry, like when you've got water in your eyes. Koto had crouched down and to the right, sword in hand. As the dragon zoomed past him, his body had already leapt into the air, the sword in his right hand chopping down at a side wing that moved up and down something like a regular bird wing. My mind's picture was Koto in mid-air, falling downward, as his sword blade fell somewhat faster than him. Slowly. I remember realizing the wing wasn't a blur anymore and also feeling puzzled that this scene was pulling away from me. An instant later I realized it was me falling away from the scene rather than the other way around. The moment ended when my upper back hit the ground below. At the same moment time sped up and the sword blade flashed through the wing, leaving a spurt of dragon blood flying upwards. My impact on the ground knocked the breath out of me. I rolled over to all fours, trying to suck in air.

The dragon caught a Mountaineer in its mouth as it pulled its loop upward. The beast roared between its teeth, nearly drowning out the sound of a human scream coming from the same location. Nearly.

The long dragon's body faltered downward to the left, since it had just lost another wing on that side. As I still tried to recover, it looped its body low in a left-hand circle, its tail still trapped, apparently trying to get its head back to what anchored it to set itself free. It wasn't far overhead. In spite of my previous order, several bowmen fired at the dragon's body without effect. But several of our spearmen and Southlander spearmen jabbed upwards, trying to move their weapons up against the downward overlap of the scales. Some of their spearheads came back black with dragon blood. I was up to one knee by the time the dragon's head was back around. Its teeth bit at the chains, which were ironically too small for them to bite. The beast touched down on the ground, right over me. I fell to my left side as it set its relatively tiny legs to the ground, four of them out of the eight. The second leg from the front was right next to me. Up close, the dragon leg was nearly as large as mine, though even thicker. The dragon body had a hollow spot that the leg could collapse partway into as the beast flew.

The dragon lunged forward. Its leg would have stepped on me and probably crushed me to death, but the foot slipped as it hit the bloody mess of a gray-faced dead mountaineer, giving me time to roll away. My memories sometimes fixate on that instant, the dragon's foot slipping in blood and gore. As I rolled away I shifted my gaze to the dragon's head. It had two of the chains securing its tail caught between its teeth and it yanked, snapping them with such force that when the broken end of one of the chains caught the supply corporal in the face (somehow he was nearby, perhaps linking the third chain, which still held the dragon). The end of the broken chain snapped back with such force that it passed clear through the back of the corporal's skull, obliterating his head. Another memory.

I had no time at the moment; the dragon shifted its bulk towards the rock. Since I was between it and our rocky outcropping, I scrambled backward, up the rock, to avoid being crushed, gaining some height.

I saw on the other side of the beast the senior sergeant (from 4th company) shouting, "Attack! Attack!" and men ran in with spears from tail towards the head, jamming their blades deep inside scales. The dragon roared and flexed the middle section of its body at them, hitting them hard, audibly snapping bones and leaving broken men on the ground, some screaming, some too broken to scream. Others backpedaled fast enough and other men ran in to attack again, spears piecing dragon hide, though not deeply.

Fernesto slashed off a wing facing him with his very long Andrean sword and vaulted over top the dragon when it thrashed at him, as did several southlanders. It turned its head back our way and hurled a fireball from its gaping grinning mouth. A Mountaineer on his knees in front of me on the side of the rock held up his shield and absorbed most of the blow, while I jumped downward, moving where the dragon had been. My face was down in bloody mud, but as I raised it, I saw the metal of the shield glowed red for a moment. And as the shield man cooked alive, he didn't make a sound. Another memory.

My face felt the heat, while men on both sides of the dragon shouted and screamed. The dragon itself roared, its head having moved so it was no more than ten yards in front of me as it turned back on itself, roaring with enormous force as its mouth came straight for me, so that the rest of the world around me was rendered silent.

In my silent world, the only sound being a lingering ringing from what had been my hearing, with smells of cooking blood and the seared flesh of men, I stood up, reached for my sword, and fumbled, forgetting I'd lost a finger. I expected to die, facing a dragon up close for the third time.

The dragon moved towards me, the world turned once again very slow. I breathed hard and managed to get my sword free and up in the air in my left hand. And then I realized something was moving above the dragon's head. I glanced up, and running along the length of the dragon's body was Koto, running from the direction of the tail towards the head. The sword my uncle gave him was naked in his hands and the glint of its blade reflected from the sun now descending in the west. His mouth was open in a shout I could not hear as he slowly plunged the blade into the dragon rider's back.

The rider arched backwards and the dragon rolled to the right, away from me. If that was because of a signal from the rider or the beast reacting by instinct, I don't know. As it rolled, Koto leapt off the dragon onto the rock. The twist in the dragon's body crushed a number of men standing or moving in too close, I don't know how many, because as the beast twisted, its tail twisted, too. And the rope still tied around my waist tugged forward. I nearly dropped my sword as it pulled me. I quickly reached out with my injured right hand and moved the leather strap my uncle had taught me to keep around a sword handle, pulling it onto my left wrist. The dragon, shining with iridescent hints of rainbow glinting off the edges of its scales, beyond the glory of ordinary gold, was once again upright, its strapped-in rider now a bloody mess in his saddle. The beast roared again while at the same time, launched itself into the air.

I don't know if the twist freed it from the third and last chain, or if the berserk launch into the air with the force of its legs and remaining wings broke the chain. But the chain for certain was broken, because the dragon flew. And the rope around my waist yanked me after it.

My mind perhaps should have been full of fear of falling and panic, but as the dragon launched itself westward, my airborne position allowed me to see the valley filling up with

Andrean Cavalry, the King's Special Regiment. They were engaging the Eastern regulars who had begun to cross into that side of the Valley of Death. The Easterners were now in full retreat, back towards us.

So I felt elation and joy an instant after my upward arc began. But that feeling altered as I realized the dragon began to arc downward. It did not fall like a rock, though. Its remaining wings flapped furiously in a blur—my hearing had begun to return enough to tell they made sound. So some part of me thought if only I could land in the right way, I would not be hurt too bad once I hit ground.

I wanted to land on my feet to try to absorb some of the shock of landing; I pulled back on the rope to right myself and prepared to crash into the ground feet first. But just before I impacted, the dragon shifted to the south, yanking the rope from my hands, and gained a bit of speed and altitude. Not enough to clear me from finishing my fall.

I hit hard, on my left side, my hip hitting ground first. I yelped like a kicked dog. The force of my landing caused my right leg to fly upward with unexpected force, then come slamming back down, making me feel like I'd been punched in the groin. The dragon, still moving, was dragging me across the dusty valley floor, small rocks pounding me. I slashed at the rope dragging me with the sword in my left hand. It took two swipes, but I cut through the rope I'd instinctively held onto with my right hand, while fresh blood pumped from my finger stump.

Once I cut myself free, my forward motion soon ended. Some hundred yards away from me, the dragon finally hit ground. I rolled over on all fours and crawled away as fast as I could. Something felt very wrong with me. I came to my feet and felt gushing warmth flowing down around my groin, like I had wet myself again. I touched myself with my left hand and realized I felt no wetness on the outside. The gushing feeling was coming from *inside* my body.

I perhaps would have been terrified by that, but nothing was on my mind more than moving away from the dragon. I moved my right leg forward to run away, but it, trembling, would move forward no more than a finger's breadth. I tried the left leg and it, too, trembled, while refusing to move more than a fraction.

I began moving as fast as I could, a single tiny step at a time, like a wingless duck waddling away from a charging wolf—though a duck could actually take longer strides than I could manage. My injury made no sense to me—how could I stand but not walk? My body shook and gushed inside, but I felt very little real pain. I wonder to this day why I didn't go back to crawling—except I suppose I feared I would not be able to stand up again.

I didn't look behind me, though my battered hearing reported roars which must have been very loud. A tremendous dust cloud and clods of dirt flew from dragonward, from behind me, so I knew it had to be thrashing around back there and possibly coming my way. As I looked towards the depression, to my surprise I'd only flown a bit more than a hundred yards from the place where the 4th battalion fought. Two Southlanders were sprinting back towards me. When they got where I was, they each took a side and put a shoulder under each armpit (after I sheathed my sword). I grasped their shoulders as they lifted. They trotted me back to the remnants of 4th battalion, holding up admirably under my weight. I said to them, "Thank the God for you!" They didn't answer, perhaps because they didn't speak Western.

Or perhaps because of lot of people find it hard to say much after what we'd gone through.

Our archers were still shooting. Maybe a dozen or so, but as Eastern troops passed back within range, our men were still drawing bow. I was struck again by the glory of war; that men who had endured so much could still function. It was like a miracle. But a terrible one; a horrific glory that was not worth what it took to provide it.

This particular moment meant more to me after the fact, when I had time to reflect on it, then it did then. During the battle, more than anything I wanted to turn around. To see where the dragon was. Back at the depression, I got my chance.

The beast still hurled fireballs and thrashed, but it did not move with any plan. It just lashed out at whatever was near it. Southlander and mountaineer spears still were stuck in its right side, even if partly broken. Andrean cavalrymen were dealing with the dragon—some dodging and drawing its attention, some attacking from behind, slashing with their impossibly long swords.

It kept spinning and hurling fire and it actually did catch some of them. But like a chained bear set upon by a pack of dogs, because it could not fly away, because no rider directed its attacks, its fate was sealed.

I had resented the Andreans for a lot of reasons. Their arrogance, their quest for glory at all times, their disdain for infantry, and most importantly, for their Tournament of Swords, which was not at all what we Mountaineers had thought it would be, which had cost us such a high price. But I've got to admit—I felt a lot better about them when they were saving our lives. Or dying for us, as Duke Reynaldo had done.

I wondered who was directing our men to shoot. To my surprise, the only voice of authority I heard was Elin's. He was still alive. His voice was faint though as he called out: "Battalion archers, alternate attacks to the north and south, on my mark: Shoot. Shoot. Shoot." Though I wondered for a moment if that was my battered hearing.

All the archers firing were relatively close to him, a lot of them like him, wounded. A louder voice was needed. So I took over. I cupped my hands, "Andrean cavalry are finishing the golden dragon as we speak! Eastern forces are in retreat! But it is not over yet. BATTALION ARCHERS, prepare to attack, alternating volleys north and south, ON MY MARK!" (I have always been able to bellow very loud.) "SHOOT." I paused, waiting longer than normal, so injured men could pull steel bowstrings, before I issued the command again.

The number of arrows flying in the air may have doubled. I stood on the north side of the rock, the well side, where the dragon had last been. I was surprised that anyone was still alive here, but plenty were. Most of the additional arrows came from the other side of the rock, where I had left Alfrin in command, where he had died in battle with the orange dragon.

I don't know how many volleys we fired, but the situation of us firing while the enemy retreated, while Andrean cavalry pressed on them, lasted a while. Eventually the men around me began to run low on arrows, even though the supply section, including Udin, were bringing new ones.

But as that time went on, while the sun inched closer to the western side of the valley, I saw a second sun rising in the east, smaller, moving fast. I blinked twice before realizing what it was my eyes beheld—another golden dragon. Another one!

Another!

I spent I don't know how long staring, mouth open, eyes glued to certain death revisiting us. But since my command to shoot had ceased, Mountaineer arrows no longer made their long arcs into the sky. In truth, the Eastern troops had mostly moved out of range anyway, having crossed back to the eastern side of the valley.

It was Koto who actually shouted, "Prepare water! Dragon incoming!" (Most of my hearing had returned by then, though my ears still rang as if they had their own internal bell.) And then Koto repeated himself in Southlander. Some men, especially the remaining Southlanders, immediately scrambled into action.

"Here it comes! Here it comes!" somebody shouted. Words finally returned to my mouth.

"Battalion archers, prepare to shoot! ON MY MARK!" Bows were pulled backward. I noticed one archer on his back, quite near me actually, who could not keep the bow pulled. It took me a moment to realize that was Elin. "That's fine, Elin," I said in a low voice, "You can pull and shoot after you hear the order."

The dragon first hurled batches of fire on the Andrean cavalry. They immediately broke when fired upon—the King's Special Regiment—and ran back at a full gallop westward. I was so angry when that happened. But in retrospect, that's what they were trained to do.

Heavy armored horses and riders can and did charge crossbowmen (their armor really was that good, better than any other horsemen in the entire Western Bond, and not made in our province). They could bait and cut up a dragon trapped on the ground, but what could they do against an airborne dragon? Literally nothing. Running was in fact their only option. Not that any of us has ever forgotten that's what they did…just as their regiment had done when faced by the dragon in my uncle's day.

When the Andreans broke and ran, a cheer rose up among the Eastern army several hundred yards in front of us, from infantrymen who had retreated in discipline and good order while being run down by western cavalry and harassed by western archers. Somehow, I felt surprise that them cheering sounded not much different from a group of men of the West cheering. And as they cheered, they surged back our direction.

The dragon led the way for them, this one even bigger than the last one. And the design on the rider's helmet I recognized as Kung Tzu's, the emblem I'd seen when he had come to arrange a truce. *This* was not just a golden dragon, but *the great golden dragon*, I realized, *this* was the beast ridden by the emperor himself, while the other dragon we'd killed was one like it.

The thought crossed my mind as the dragon flew in, burning some Andreans who could not gallop away fast enough, that the emperor was going to eliminate all opposition to the advance of the army this time—he hadn't come all this way with the Great Golden Dragon to fail—surely his next targets would be us. He would burn all of us to death—it was the only thing that made sense for him to do, to save his attack, to advance his troops. Once the Andrean regiment ran, we were the only obstacles in his way —unless the Shos Militia still held the pass behind us. If so, he'd deal with them in turn.

He would not land. He would rain down fire and death from above. Our only hope would be if he flew in within range of our bows. And there wasn't a single reason why he should do that.

"Aim for the rider!" I shouted. And somebody released his bow even though the range was too far. About half of the archers followed suit. "No, no, AS A BATTALION, aim for the rider, prepare to shoot!" Men drew back their bows.

The rider. Killing him was our only hope, of course. The dragons had shown without the rider directing them, they fall to the ground and prefer to fight with claw and tooth. Which was horrible, terrible, but it at least would give us a fighting chance. We didn't really have enough men to face a dragon on the ground anymore, but still. We had to kill the rider.

But of course, with his armor, it was very unlikely we could hurt him. Even if he closed within our range. But we had to try.

"Here it comes! Here it comes!" someone shouted.

"BATTALION!" I roared.

Kung Tzu flew towards us with the neck of the dragon down, right into the range of our arrows, exposing himself completely. I couldn't believe he would be so foolish, but I couldn't pass up the one chance, our one blow. "SHOOT!"

Arrows flew upward, well aimed, some thirty or so. Not many out of what had been a battalion, but enough to kill a dragon rider, if by chance an arrow could hit the right spot. But the emperor pulled back on his dragon right after we shot, raising its neck, as if he easily read what we were doing and easily countered it. Our arrows deflected harmlessly off the dragon's belly. The dragon tipped its head down again and a ball of fire erupted from its mouth, impacting by the well, near enough not to burn me, close enough my cheeks felt the heat. Mostly it was Southlanders, obeying their chief's call to fetch water, who died there that time. Good men dying because they were being good.

But then Elin, who had been too badly burned to hold his bow flexed, too wounded to follow my command as I gave it, at that moment he shot his arrow, after the rest of us. That single arrow, almost unnoticed by most of us, made its arc into the air. And impacted in a seam in Kung Tzu's armor, between his body and legs. As if the most unusual of chance events. Or as if the God himself directed it.

I did not in fact see the arrow land—I think I was looking over my left shoulder at the well. What I saw as I turned my head back was the emperor reach down and pull out an arrow from between his upper leg and groin. If he hadn't pulled it out, he might have lived.

Kung Tzu must have realized what he'd done to himself, because once he pulled the arrow—he was not even one hundred yards away from me in the air and I could see him well enough—he looked at it in his hand for a moment, it dripping with bright red arterial blood. Then he dropped it and he immediately turned his dragon back, eastward.

After the dragon turned in the sky, men who had been so battered I would not think they were capable of cheering, cheered. Eastern forces kept coming forward for a little while after that, but the King's Special Regiment returned, charging at them again and the Eastern retreat started up again. And did not stop.

The Battle of Eagle Pass was over. The Valley of Death extracted its gruesome toll. The sun set towards the west, the direction of home.

⊣⊢ Chapter 11 ⊨

Not long after the sun set, Elin died of his wounds. As did many others.

I didn't hear until months afterward, but the rumor among our forces was that Kung Tzu rode his dragon back to a place where his dragon handlers could keep the golden beast safe, rather than go to one of his wizard healers, who probably would have been able to save him. He loved the dragon more than his own life. The dragon handlers cut his dead body from the saddle and they buried him in a tomb of his ancestors. That's what the story says.

You might think the death of Kung Tzu ended the war, but it didn't. Kung Po, his son, ruled in his place. The war drug on for another *two years* and both First and Second Battalion of the Iron Mountains Province Volunteers fought in many battles. In the end, the war ended exactly where it had begun, with the Heavensfoot peaks being the border between East and West. Nothing changed, except tens of thousands of men on each side died. As well as numerous griffins, horses, and *longma*. And some dragons.

In the Valley of Death, the Shos militiamen who were not injured found a section of the depression in the middle of the valley to begin to stack the dead in. They covered them with dirt they scooped down from above in one mass grave. Our troops in the back made sure the metal tags we used to identify the Mountaineer dead were taken off the corpses. Many bodies were so burned, though, they fell apart when moved. For those, dirt was hastily heaped on charred ashes where they'd fallen. Our engineering supplies provided the shovels, but the work had barely begun when it got too dark to continue.

Mercifully, healers moved among us in the aftermath of our battle. Someone brought wood all the way from the ring canyon we'd gone past what seemed so long ago, and burned fires for warmth. Some of them doing so must have moved right past Arta, but I didn't know that at the time. Those of us that could move out of the depression in the middle of the valley went to the flat land just west of it, where our supply wagons had faced the crossbow attack (I crawled there).

Healers, most of them ours, but also some Andreans, with some help from Andrean cavalry, moved us wounded by torchlight several hundred yards west of there, because there were so many crossbow bolts on the ground, we could not safely lay down nearby. They labored all night over us. They provided water from the well and food rations for those that could eat. They bound wounds in dressings with oil and prayed over those who wanted prayer. They brought forward the blankets from the camp and covered those who could not stay warm. Someone made crutches out of thick branches of wood for me.

But in spite of the skilled ministrations of the healers, for many of us, the injuries went too far. In the light of a new day, some twenty who had been alive when moved by torchlight (Elin had died long before then) were gone in the morning. The healers covered their heads with blankets—they were buried the next day.

We took roll call in the morning. Eight-seven men were able to answer, out of the over eight hundred some that had been in 4th battalion. Or actually I should say 87 out of around 1600, since 3rd battalion had been in the valley as well. Only one of their men, a Sergeant Lugin, made it through that night.

But something very important happened before the morning. At a point after the sun had set, after someone gave me crutches formed out of thick, nearly straight branches (the bark still on them, with cloth wrapped around with leather on one end as padding for under the arms), a number of us were gathered around a large campfire. Koto was there, so was Fernesto, Danl, and a number of our men, including a couple of the supply boys. I had hobbled around with my newfound mobility, checking on our wounded. I still couldn't move either leg more than an inch at a time, but I could put both armpits firm into the crutches and swing both legs at once. My right hand throbbed when I did that from the missing finger, but that pain was so minor compared to everything else, I found myself ignoring it. At least for the first day I did.

As I was moving around, I saw a man under a blanket, staring in the general direction of the campfire with empty eyes, eyes unfocused as if staring out to a vast distance, a look many of our men had. "Can I get anything for you, soldier?" I called out.

But then I realized I was speaking to Prince Rory-Galstaff.

"I don't suppose you have a spare griffin?" he said softly.

"I'm sorry, Your Majesty. I'm fresh out of those."

"You saved my life back there."

I paused before answering. "I suppose the God allowed me to."

For a moment or two, his eyes actually focused on me before resuming that distant stare. "I think I know you. From before this."

Of course I knew what he meant. But I said, "From before this, when?"

"You and your friend came to kill me," he said with perfect calmness, his eyes still staring out into the distance. "But I killed him instead. And you two had come because I had killed your…uncle? Or…or other relative, years before that. In the Tournament of Swords."

I didn't answer. Perhaps it's funny, but even after all the death I'd seen that day, my uncle's death still moved me. Even though time had allowed that pain to fade.

"It was you, wasn't it?" his eyes fixed on me again.

I blinked and found my voice. "I am not that same person who came to kill you. Not anymore."

"Clearly not," he said, as his eyes left me again, his voice still very calm. "Or else you wouldn't have saved me."

I nodded my head. There didn't seem to be anything else to say.

"I will reward you for what you've done for me," said the prince. "Name what you will have of me and I will give it. Up to half of all I own."

I nearly laughed before answering. How little he knew me. It was because of what my uncle had taught me, what I'd finally understood, that's why I'd saved him. Not for the hope of a reward. "No thank you, Your Majesty," I said, as I turned and swung both feet back towards the fire.

"I will find you," he called out after me, "I will send men to your province—and I will reward you!" At the last his voice lost its cool detachment. Clearly, he really did want to repay me somehow. I'm honestly not entirely sure why. Perhaps guilt. Perhaps something else.

I moved back to the fire, seeing no reason to comment. I stood normally, but my legs still trembled in a strange way I'd never experienced before—or since. In the dark, the Andrean horsemen had built their own camp at the west end of the valley. Actually, they took over the spot where the Southlanders had been, whose losses in battle had been as great as ours. Though in fact the unit that suffered the most in the Battle of Eagle Pass, other than 3rd Battalion, was the Andrean Reserve Cavalry. Fernesto was one of a half-dozen of them still alive. Interestingly, he made his camp with us, and not with the other Andreans.

As I warmed myself by the fire, I saw the unmistakable sight of a large body of horsemen moving by torchlight (something that happened on the road outside of Tsillis from time to time). They were coming our way. I wondered what the Andreans wanted. I swung my body between the crutches their direction, moving pretty quickly that night, actually (the next day was much harder to move).

When I had moved maybe twenty yards their way their (of course the horsemen had done more to close the distance than me), they were within fifty yards or so. "Careful!" I shouted out. "There are wounded men on the ground here!"

They ignored me until they pulled up alongside me. A voice called out "Halt!" from among them, so they stopped. There were nine men on horseback, eight King's Special Regiment men in their polished armor forming a rough square, holding torches, and a civilian official of some kind in the middle, who I couldn't see very well because he wasn't holding a torch and because the riders each held their torch in their outside hand. But I realized it was him who had stopped the formation.

The civilian swung his leg out of his saddle and strode towards me. He had an overcoat with a hood that effectively hid his face in the dim light. "Who is in command here?" he demanded angrily.

The voice sounded familiar. While I tried to place it, I answered, "Um, I suppose I am, as much as anybody else."

"What kind of answer is that?" the figure's breath showed in the nighttime cold, but he pulled the hood back, to see me better, I guess. And I realized why I knew that voice. *Guffey.* I also realized why I didn't recognize it at first. I'd never heard him angry—even when dealing with life and death before, he'd barely raised his voice.

At that moment, even though some part of me told me I should care who he was, I didn't really care. I'd faced four dragons in battle that day and was still alive.

I rubbed my chin. "Well, I'm technically not in command of the Southlanders and there are some of them over here. And we've got an Andrean—"

"Where? Where are you keeping him?"

The urgency of Guffey's question gave me a hint about what his issue was. I had meant Fernesto when I'd said "an Andrean," but I offered something else: "Would you be looking for the missing prince?"

"Yes! I heard a rumor he was alive. And your men had taken him in chains!"

I nearly laughed, but then realized the rumor was in fact, nearly true. "Ah, well…just to save his life."

He glared at me.

"It's a long story. But…um, yeah, I can take you to him."

So I swung forward on my crutches and Guffey walked beside me. The eight horsemen followed us, their torches at least partially lighting the way.

I glanced over at the man who had once been a Tournament of Swords official. He looked down, eyebrows together, as if concentrating. Clearly, he was not as angry as he'd been a moment before.

His eyes moved up and over my way as he looked across at me. "Excuse me, Mountaineer, but don' I know you from somewhere?" His Midlander drawl stretched out the words as he spoke them, while in the evening chill, the steam of his breath erupted from his mouth. Not wholly unlike dragon fire.

I paused for a moment. "I was with the delegation of Iron Mountain troops that met with Kung Tzu. You were there, too."

He gave me a hard, piercing look. "Perhaps that was it."

I walked past our campfire. The Andreans on horseback stopped just before it.

Guffey and I went straight up to the prince, but whether because he'd passed out, perhaps from a lack of food and drink, or from the stresses of combat, or because he'd simply fallen asleep, he was out cold by the time we got to him. Eyes closed, head back, chest rising and falling. I prodded him a bit with my right crutch. "Wake up!" He didn't budge.

Guffey fell to his knees next to the prince. He slapped his face and shook his shoulders. The prince didn't respond at all. Guffey turned to me in vengeful rage, "What have you done to him?"

"I haven't done anything to him. You can see he's breathing, right?"

He stood when I said that and took two steps my way. Realization crossed his face and he took another step, so his nose was just below my own. He shoved me hard and I fell backward to the ground, my armor rattling. Instinctively I'd reached backwards with my hands to try to catch myself, dropping the crutches. Guffey snatched one up and kicked the second away from me as I reached for it. "I know your face!" he hissed, while waving an accusing finger at me while I was flat on the ground. "I know who you are and I remember what you did! How did you escape the punishment due you? How did you get out of jail?"

"Hey!" I replied back to him as I sat partway up. "My freedom was *paid for.*"

"Really? So you say. Well, you can say what you like, but I can see what you're up to here. You didn't get what you wanted then, so you're plannin' to do it now, while he's sleeping, when no one can see you!" He turned to the Andrean horsemen, "Arrest this man! He's a dangerous criminal."

"Oh for all the God-forsaken notions—" I said, but Koto, who'd already moved without me noticing, interrupted by grabbing the front of Guffey's coat with both hands. "Is this man bothering you, Therin?"

From there things got a little loud for some confused moments. Horses and riders pressed forward and Danl suddenly stood up and yanked one of the horsemen clean out of his saddle and threw him to the ground. Men who had been staring off into some imaginary distance around the fire suddenly came to their feet, swords in their hands. Even Fernesto stood as he pulled his very long Andrean blade free, the orange and reds of the campfire light glinting off it. Koto shoved Guffey back towards the horsemen, and even though he stumbled, he managed to keep his feet.

Andreans started pulling their swords as well. All of which happened almost at the same moment.

"STOP!" I bellowed. "Right there! Everyone!"

To my surprise, everyone actually stopped. "This is just a misunderstanding. The gentlemen here are just gonna collect the griffin rider back there. The one that dropped down on us from the middle of the sky. The one me and some supply boys saved from dragon attack. Then they are gonna go their way, while we stay here. They'll leave us alone—and we'll leave them alone."

My ears still rang. But not so loud I couldn't hear Danl huffing like an angry bear. At some point after throwing a man in armor to the ground, he'd pulled the sword my uncle gave him, with the giant shield I'd given him still strapped to his arm. I found myself very worried about that man on the ground for a bit. But he rolled over on all fours and stood to his feet. And Danl stood at that same piece of ground. Stopped, as ordered.

Before the Andrean rider was all the way up, Guffey said, "That man can say what he wants!" he pointed at me. "He's still a criminal and an attempted assassin! We are going to take him prisoner. If you give us any trouble, we'll come back here with the King's whole regiment."

I rolled to my own fours as the Andrean stood up. Koto pulled his sword from its dragonfire-singed leather scabbard on his rope belt and held it in his hands, as if inspecting the edge. Without looking up from the blade, he said, "Today, the men of the mountains and the men of the South killed *three* dragons. Do you really think we are afraid of the King's Special Regiment?"

The eyes of the Andreans whose visors were up, widened, showing plenty of white. I stood to my feet, without the crutches. "Just because I use crutches, doesn't mean I can't move without them." I pulled my own sword free from its scabbard. "Don't make me come over there, Guffey."

The official's eyes studied us, men who must have looked broken only moments before, swords in our hands and determination in our eyes. "We'll be getting the prince now," Guffey said, his voice much softer. He turned back to the cavalrymen and spoke in a voice quieter than I could hear. Two troops dismounted and moved towards the limp body of the prince. Guffey stepped forward as if to help them. Which put him close to me.

"This isn't over," he said in a near-whisper as he walked up next to me, looking forward in the direction of the prince, as if I didn't matter at all, as if pretending he wasn't speaking to me. "I will find you. No matter where you are. And I will see you get what you deserve."

I ignored subtlety. "Guffey, give me my crutch back!" It was still in his hands. He gave it. One of the supply boys gave me the other—though I should stop calling him that. He was no longer a boy, just like I no longer was.

The Andrean cavalrymen hauled Prince Rory-Galstaff over to the horses, still limp. Like a sack of provisions, he rode away from our camp hanging across the back of an Andrean cavalry horse. I saw it myself.

It's strange, son, as I think back on things. That was also the last time I saw the prince—unless I see him again someday. That's the funny thing about seeing someone for the last time. Lots of times it happens long before you realize it really was the last time. Cherish people, son, because some will go away and you will never see them walking this earth again.

Yes, some we'll see walking the paths of eternity, that's what the Book says. But I don't think anybody knows with complete certainty who will be there. Maybe about yourself somebody can know. But that's all. So…you just never know.

The next day the dawn brought a soreness to my body like none I'd ever experienced before. I could barely move. I got worse over the next several days. My lower abdomen, groin, and especially my privates turned nearly black with bruising. I still don't know what I did to myself, clearly I broke something inside me; I don't know what.

Of course, what happened to me was nothing compared to many others. Of the 87 alive the first morning, another twenty-three died over the next week, in spite of treatment from Arta's medical company. Some of whom didn't seem to be hurt all that bad. That's part of what I mean about never knowing when the last goodbye will come.

None of us digging that well had any idea what was going to happen next that day, that by the end of the day, most of us would be dead. It can happen that way in battle with great drama, but the same thing is true of the rest of life. No one knows in advance which day will be the last.

I rode home in the back of a supply wagon that had been cleared out to make room for men like me. We filled several wagons quite full.

Koto and the Southlanders split from us as soon as we cleared Eagle's Pass. I still think about him, wondering how he is. Danl and the Shos boys walked with us for about a month. Till it was their time to part as well. (By the way, I'm sure you'll want to know—Koto actually lost to the prince in the final bout of the tournament, but it was an honorable match, winning by points, nobody trying to kill anyone. I suppose killing my uncle had an effect on the prince, too.)

I skipped past something very important here in talking about riding back and parting with our dear allies. That is, me seeing your mother the first day, when I was too sore to move, when we passed down from the Valley of Death to the ring canyon. When I saw your mother. And you, as a newborn baby.

As we passed down into the ring canyon for the night, Arta had already heard how bad things were for us. How many were burnt. How many died. She'd asked several people to find me, but for whatever reason, nobody before the wagons rolled into the canyon had given her a clear answer.

After we arrived, somebody told her I was in the second wagon. Your mother, perhaps because she was a trained healer and seen horrible injuries, including on old wounded veterans when she was in training, was immediately seized by a fear of a fate other than me being dead. Which is what she'd feared at first.

Yes, some part of her rejoiced to hear I was alive, but she was terrified to find out what kind of mangled mess I'd become (many of the men carried horrific disfigurements, including missing limbs, even among those who could march).

Arta didn't know which wagon was the second one. She came to the one nearest her and called out, "Therin!" A man with his legs missing below the knees answered, "Not in this wagon!"

She went onto the next wagon and called out, "Therin!" She'd forgotten all about using my adopted name. In fact, I'd given up using it, too. (Later, on the way back I would explain to those who knew it, why I'd used it.)

I crawled in the cart over to Arta, painfully. She's let her red hair grow out since I'd last seen her, so it cascaded over her shoulders. And she had a tiny baby in her arms. I don't know if I've ever seen a more beautiful sight. But my first reaction was astonishment. "Arta! What are you doing here!"

"Saving your life! And having our baby."

"Why, what? I thought you were staying home with the baby, to keep him safe!" I said this with a touch of rage.

"I thought I lost him at first, Therin. That's why I came. Only to find out later I was still pregnant. Please don't be angry with me. Please."

"Wh…why," looking into her pleading eyes, my mood changed completely, "Uh, I um am just shocked to see you. You could have been killed!"

She wrapped her arms around me at that moment, holding our son next to me, and wept. "And so could you! And so could you!" We cried together for a good while, sorrow and joy mixed in a powerful outpour of emotion.

And I looked at baby you, admiring what a handsome son I had, even though smaller and earlier than expected. Eventually Arta asked me, "Are you…whole, Therin?"

The God knows why, but the question made me chuckle. "You mean, do I have all of my *parts*? Is that what you wanna know?"

Arta flushed red and mockingly slapped me. "Well?" she asked in a quiet voice. "Do you?"

I stopped laughing. "Well, yes, I do have everything. I'm not sure it all *works*, but I've got it."

"Well, after you heal a while—after I heal, too—we'll just have to find out, won't we?" she smiled mischievously.

I laughed. Then I kissed her.

Greda allowed Arta to join our unit as we traveled back.

While I was recovering, saying goodbye to Koto and other men I served with as brothers, bonded together by the sword, she traveled with me.

My mother had heard I was still alive, something she hadn't known for years about me. Arta had sent her a letter

THE BOND OF THE SWORD

about us as she left the Iron Mountains province, in case neither of us made it back. So my mother knew I had left with the Fourth Battalion.

When we finally got back into the province, some schoolboys ran up to our formation in some excitement. One of their first questions was, "Where are the rest of you?"

So, because of the garbled answers they got, rumors flew back to all the towns which had contributed men to our two battalions. My mother, your grandmother, heard, incorrectly of course, that only one man had survived in the 4th Battalion. She wept and prayed it was me. Then felt guilty for all the *other* families wanting their son back that she had prayed it would be me. So, she wept and told the God she was sorry, but that's still what she wanted.

Our formation, such as it was, consisted of forty-two men who could march and twenty-two who got a ride back in the remaining supply wagons. A couple of the men suggested we split up as soon as we returned to Iron Mountains province, but most wanted to return to High Crossing and disband there, where the unit had first formed up. I enforced the will of the majority on those who had other ideas. But I made an exception for those whose families came to collect them along the way.

So the rumor went out that families needed to come get the men, which was not actually true, I was going to release everyone anyway, but not until we got back to High Crossing.

By the time we passed into Rogin, the town was packed full of people who had not yet heard what had happened to their specific family members. Including my mother.

She pressed through the crowd, approaching our unit. Someone had taken the metal tags we wore, the ones that had been developed after so many men had been impossible to recognize after death in the First Dragon War and strung them on long wooden poles that went between the wagons, so families could collect them. Not seeing me among the standing men, she searched through the hanging metal nameplates, many of them nearly illegible because they'd been blackened by dragonfire.

She searched through name after name after name, for what she says seemed like forever. She saw Elin's name there, whom she had known for many years. Many other women were searching, like her, but she says the worst of it was seeing the old veterans of the First War, wondering what happened to their sons, most of whom could not even bring themselves to search.

Valinin's widow, who had joined our formation even before we entered our province, put her arm on my mother's shoulder and comforted her. She had already heard about the death of her husband.

My mother eventually found me and Arta both, and we had a wonderful, tearful reunion, but I insisted on traveling back with the men and not getting off in Rogin. I left her with a promise to return, but what happened with your grandmother isn't what this part of the story is about.

When we finally arrived back in our home, after passing through High Crossing and having our final formation, where the unit disbanded formally, Arta asked me, "Do you remember what I asked about you being whole?"

"Do you remember my answer?" I smiled.

"Well, we'll just have to find out, won't we?" she said, kissing me in an entirely different mood than on the way back. We did other things first, including putting our baby to bed, but that night we discovered that the God really had been merciful to me, in spite of my pain.

⊣⊢ Chapter 12 ⊨

What I've written you has exceeded by many pages what I thought this would be when I started. It took a long time to write most of it, even though I worked on it steadily, every night (or nearly every night) for a long time. Something like six months.

But now it has laid on a shelf for several months now, unfinished. Your original question, son, about the Dragon War and my wounds and all of that had long ago faded by the time I actually reached the point of writing about the Battle of Eagle Pass, the only real battle I ever fought in, which took place not even in one whole day. It lasted just a single long afternoon that faded into an evening.

I stopped working on what I wrote you after I finished writing about that battle. Writing it was something I didn't really want to do, but which seemed necessary for you to understand, because I want you to really know what war is. Because you'll be so much better off if you don't seek it out yourself. You don't need it.

Though in fact war is more than one thing. I had a conversation once with a member of First Battalion, who maintained that his three years of day in, day out battle after the Battle of Eagle Pass *was over, made him a veteran of war in a way I would never be. I almost angrily replied that at least most of First came home alive, which wasn't true for Fourth. But I stopped before I spoke. I realized he was right. Not that what he did was really any harder than my experience—but it was different. And I don't really know what his experiences were like, not completely. I never fought a way that lasted years. Except that I know it was still war—and that war is awful.*

Talking with members of my own battalion, when they bring up their experience of coming under fire from the Eastern troops, while being attacked by the orange dragon on the ground. They say it was the worst—but I wasn't there. But what I saw while I wasn't there, that crossbow bolt being pulled back through a young man's body… that is one of my worst memories of the war. One of many that comes back to me at times to wake me in the middle of the night.

I don't have as many of those nightmares as I used to. But I still have them.

I walk much better than I did when I first got back. But I still have pain in my hips; my joints pop. And ache when the weather changes.

I hear ringing in my ears every minute of every day, even though I can hear around it and still have ordinary conversations and something close to an ordinary life. But sometimes it isn't the nightmares that awaken me. It's the tune of my own ears, endlessly sounding a distant echo of a dragon's roar.

And of course, while my stub of a finger on my right hand no longer throbs with pain when I touch things and is grown over with healed skin, the finger itself isn't ever going to come back. Never.

As I look back at what I wrote you, the amount of words and letters it took to describe that one afternoon in the Valley of Death are as thick as year's worth of memories of more ordinary life—a life not without its dangers and adventures, mind you. And that somehow is exactly right. Moments where life and death are in the balances weigh heavier than ordinary times. They burn into the soul of people and change us forever.

I must say for the record that I also gained some things from fighting. Yes, I actually did benefit in some ways. I returned to my own name. I saw my mother again. I stopped being afraid of Guffey. (It's interesting to note, though, that neither the promises of the prince to reward me, nor the threats of his high government official —neither thing has come true.)

I grew up in some ways. But I'm convinced I didn't need war to do that. There are other ways to mature, to be responsible, even to take risk in a helpful way. Other than war.

Working as a healer is a very noble profession, as your mother did. Saving lives is not easy many times—it challenges a person, without doing all the things required by war. As do other types of leadership, business ventures, exploration, many other things. It's interesting to me that the war song composed about the Battle of Eagle Pass mentions a number of things I was involved with, but mentions me by name only once—when I saved Elin's life by stopping some beastmen headed his way (because he is the hero of the song—as he should be). And I am entirely satisfied with that. Saving another man's life is one of the greatest things that happens in a war —my uncle was right. Right that saving a life is a greater thing than killing a dragon. But saving lives is even better and sweeter when there is no war chewing up lives faster than they can be saved.

As for the war songs themselves, I have strong contradictory feeling towards them. I do not see them the same way I did as a boy, with a fully enthusiastic patriotism. I see the songs as full of exaggerations and very short of how much the courage they praise cost real men and women. Yet they make my eyes flow with tears sometimes nevertheless.

I meet at times with other veterans of our battalion, usually on the last Fiveday of the month. We don't talk very much about the *past—too many of us find it too hard. But on occasion we do. Some of us drink too much. And as I mentioned, it has happened among us that some of us have taken our own lives. I think that temptation is especially strong for those who look back on what they've done and feel they failed, either in performance of their job, or by surrendering to cruelty. Yet another thing about war I don't like.*

We do routinely drink a toast to each of the companies of the 4th Battalion—there are survivors from each one. Then we offer a toast to 3rd Battalion, from which only Sergeant Lugin survived. When we offer that toast, we pour out whatever remains of our cups onto the ground—or the floor if we are inside. As a memorial to their sacrifice.

Your mother has her own type of memorial, her horse, Alfredo. Which as I'm sure you now realize, did once in fact belong to an Andrean lesser knight who died trying to save your mother's medical company.

Sometimes, when I'm talking with my fellow veterans, the subject of the Andrean Special Regiment running from the golden dragon comes up. More than once I've laughed and said about our Mountaineer troops (like my uncle did), "We were too stupid to run!" Some of my fellow veterans laugh with me, though some don't think it's funny. Even after the fact, our views of war are not all the same.

You know, maybe "tribute" would be a better word than the one I used above, "memorial." I don't think any of us needs anything to remind us of what happened to us and the Third Battalion. The memories surge back on their own.

Without ever intending to, I find myself at times scanning the skies for dragon. Every now and then, when I do that, I see a dragonbird. And my heart pounds in my chest, because for a moment, my entire body feels like it is back in the Valley of Death again. I can hear again the deep hum of dragon wings. I find myself, like my uncle did, tossing a rock at the harmless thing to send it flying away. As I breathe deeply to calm myself.

It was a mystery to me when I was a boy why my uncle did not like to eat seared meat. Of course, it's no mystery now. Seared meat reminded him of the seared flesh of men burned by dragonfire.

I did not know that's what it would remind me of on the first Spring Festival after I came home. I was walking again, though not as well as I would later. You were a baby in your mother's arms still, growing and healthy. The passes cleared from winter snow and the first shipments out of iron goods had brought in the first food and other supplies from other provinces. We cooked outside over a fire as is our Mountaineer tradition. That particular day was warm for Spring Festival, sunny, as if the very sky was full of happiness that the winter had ended. Your mother and I celebrated at Rogin that year instead of High Crossing, with your grandmother. I remember Arta bringing by a plate of seared meat for me, meat my mother had cooked, which was salted just the way I always liked it.

I took one bite and froze, realizing what I'd done, understanding why the smell of my mother cooking had made me feel sick instead of hungry. I refused to let the nausea I felt overpower me. I forced myself to chew, blinking back the tears, each movement of my jaw as difficult as moving supply wagons forward under attack.

Arta noticed and whispered in my ear, "If you feel that way about it, for the God's sake, don't eat it! I can bring you something else."

She did. My uncle would have eaten boiled meat instead, but because of a particular moment by a well I helped dig, I'm not very fond of that either. Perhaps you've noticed that I will eat meat at times but I really prefer vegetables. That wasn't true of me before the war. The first time I had the lentil stew your mother makes for me was on that particular Spring Festival Day.

By the way, I can eat seared meat. But like my uncle, I doubt I will ever enjoy it again.

Similar to my uncle, who worked in a sword factory, I work with weapons. The steel bows that Valinin and I invented are now standard for all the battalions of Iron Mountains Province. I supervise them being built, even though I sincerely hope they are never used in combat, which is exactly how my uncle felt about the swords he helped make. To be ready for war does not force a man into eagerness to go to war. As my uncle understood.

I see how very much like him I have become. As a boy I barely understood him at times, but now I see him very differently. The Andrean prince killed my uncle, but it was no accident. My uncle, faced with an unexpected requirement of a law without mercy, saw only one way out, because the dishonorable way offered to him by Guffey was no option for him at all. Only one way to save our team. Only one way to save me.

So he did it, sacrificing himself outside the context of war, one of the greatest things that ever happens in a war. He laid down his life to save mine. And others.

I've learned so much from my uncle's example. I'm so glad to have become more like him over time. So, as much as my dear relative, my uncle, saved me by his death, in a much more important way, he saved me by his life.

There is so much more I could say, son, but I see I'm rambling now. I hope you learn from what I've written.

I believe I will save this for you until you are older. This is far too awful for you to see now. I hope you will eventually see that I have gone through the pain of writing it because I want you to understand—because I love you, the way my uncle loved me.

There are many things I hope you comprehend after reading this, but one of the least important has sparked my efforts to finish this work, getting me to write past the last of the dragon combat. Your friend Sorbin told you about the Tournament of Swords—how he knew I'd competed in the tournament, I don't know.

So when you came to me last week, breathless, excited about the chance to go sword fighting and hoping I would coach you, now I hope you realize why I said, "Why don't we have a nice local tournament instead?"

(Yes, I hope that made you smile, now that you see and understand.)

For you, my dear son Haelin, with all my love.

Your father, Therin.

About the Author

Travis Perry comes from a low-population mountain state in the United States that inspired the Iron Mountains Province of this book, though he deliberately obscured any direct references to Montana. He enlisted into the Army Reserve in his early twenties and first was mobilized for Operation Desert Storm in 1991 as a medical specialist. Eventually he became an Army Reserve officer and saw war in Iraq and Afghanistan, but also served in peacetime deployments to East Africa, Central America, and Europe. He never served as a "front line" soldier but did come under indirect attacks and knew people killed and wounded and helped in the aftermath of enemy action on a few occasions. He, like the principal character of this story, sees that warfare has glorious moments, but war is far worse than what the glory of war itself can justify. The term "devout Evangelical Christian" is probably a fair description of Travis's personal beliefs. He never believed he could get divorced, but it happened anyway, though he is happily remarried. He is a father of five living children, adults now, and three others. He's a student of the Bible, world history, and foreign languages. And he still serves in the US Army Reserve, well into his fifties, at the time of the publication of this book.

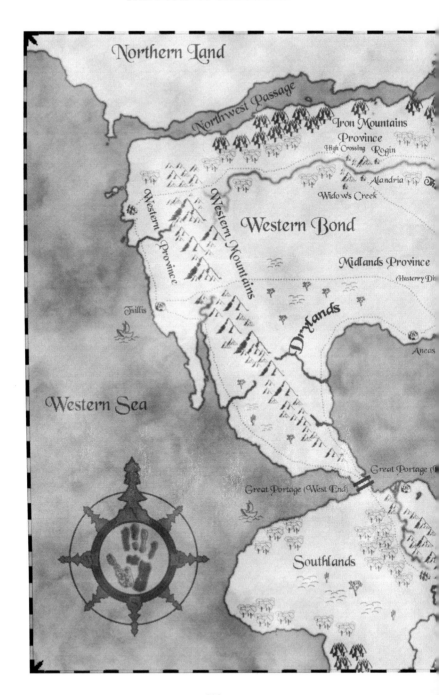

Made in the USA
Columbia, SC
05 July 2024

0700c716-b88f-4244-b9ee-e43baeb21915R01